Reviews fo  T0061861

THE TALES OF THE
LAWLESS LAND SERIES

'Complete with mysteries, secrets, and adventure, rich in detail,
delivering exactly what a reader craves.'
Steve Berry

'A mesmerizing sequel to the hugely entertaining
The Lawless Land... There is action galore. What a ride!'
Elizabeth George

'Any lover of historical mysteries or great tales
of adventure will find much delight in this novel.'
James Rollins

'A triumphant follow-up to *The Lawless Land*, with a puzzle
that will dazzle fans of *The Da Vinci Code*.'
Lee Goldberg

'A rollicking adventure.'
New York Times

'Gerard Fox could be Jack Reacher's ancestor, 700 years ago.'
Lee Child

'A novel full of both authenticity and thrills.'
Mark Greaney

ALSO BY BOYD AND BETH MORRISON

THE TALES OF THE LAWLESS LAND SERIES

The Lawless Land

THE
LAST TRUE
TEMPLAR

TALES OF THE LAWLESS LAND: BOOK II

BOYD ✠ BETH
MORRISON

An Aries Book

First published in the UK in 2023 by Head of Zeus
This paperback edition first published in 2024 by Head of Zeus,
part of Bloomsbury Publishing Plc

9 7 5 3 1 2 4 6 8

A catalogue record for this book is available from the British Library.

ISBN (PB): 9781801108706
ISBN (E): 9781801108713

Cover design: Ben Prior/Head of Zeus

Printed and bound in Great Britain by
CPI Group (UK) Ltd, Croydon CR0 4YY

Head of Zeus
5–8 Hardwick Street
London ECIR 4RG

WWW.HEADOFZEUS.COM

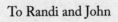
To Randi and John

The Eastern Mediterranean, 1351

Prologue

It seemed as if the entire city had come for the execution. Massive crowds lined both banks of the Seine, straining to view the stake set into a pile of logs on the tiny island of Île aux Juifs. A man holding a flaming torch waited for the command to do his duty.

In the fading light of dusk, the four men tied back to back around the tall post looked unafraid, even serene. They knew the horror that was to come and that insufficient fuel was deliberately used to ensure a slow and agonizing death. But they seemed at peace with their decision to recant the false confessions that had been tortured out of them. For this reversal, they'd been branded lapsed heretics, the most heinous crime imaginable.

Domenico Ramberti stood on the southern bank of the river, forcing himself to control the shivering and coughing that had racked his body on and off for the last six months of his long journey. Although he had occasional bursts of energy, today he felt older than his forty-eight years. But if Jacques de Molay, Grand Master of the Order of the Knights Templar, could maintain his noble bearing while he met his fate, Ramberti could keep his composure as well.

Many of his fellow knights had been tortured over the past seven years, ever since that dark Friday the 13th in 1307 when King Philip had ordered the simultaneous arrest of all Templars across France. Ramberti had escaped only because he had been in Italy at the time. Since then, he'd done everything he could to preserve his beloved order, but now he was here to witness the *coup de grâce*.

After this day, Ramberti would be the last true Knight Templar.

Molay, in his seventies, balding with a rim of white hair and a long flowing beard, stood straight atop the pyre, maintaining the dignity for which he was renowned. The marshal's cry to carry out the sentence was loud enough for all to hear. Molay didn't debase himself to watch as the executioner dipped his torch to the kindling, setting the logs ablaze.

Above the growing flames, Molay shouted something. The crowd grew still, eager to hear his final words. His voice carried across the water, strong and clear.

"God knows that the hearts of the Templars are pure. He knows who is in the wrong and has sinned. God will avenge our deaths. Make no mistake, all who have borne false witness against us will suffer because of what has been done to us."

The curse caused many of the spectators to gasp and whisper, but they kept listening. The flames grew, and black smoke belched forth. By now, Ramberti could feel the heat of the fire himself. To Molay the inferno must have been unbearable, and yet he continued to speak.

"I call for His Holiness Pope Clement to join me within a year and a day before God, where he will have to answer for his vile betrayal. I not only summon His Highness King Philip to the same fate, but his descendants likewise to fall and his family line to come to an inglorious end. At the last, the world will know the truth about our innocence. The brotherhood will be reborn, and no one will doubt the nobility and virtue of the Knights Templar."

As his final words rang out, the thick smoke obscured the men who so bravely endured their torture, sparing Ramberti from watching his beloved grand master being burned alive.

He could only hope that Molay's curse would come to pass. The king, who owed a fortune to the Templars, had concocted the false accusations that brought down the order so that he could wipe his debt clean and seize the vast holdings of the Templars for his own. The pope, a weakling and a fool, had succumbed to Philip's threats and joined him in condemning the Templars, disbanding them completely two years ago and handing over what remained of their holdings to the rival Knights Hospitaller.

But Ramberti knew something they did not, the real reason that Molay had finally recanted his confessions to fabricated crimes such as denying Christ and desecrating the cross. Just days ago, he had informed Molay that the resources to restore the Templars to their past glory were now well hidden from the French king, waiting only for the right time and worthy champions to restore the order's rightful place in the world.

Ramberti's determination to safeguard the remaining Templar wealth had grown into an obsession that consumed his every waking minute. Despite the danger, he had braved terrible hardship and illness, and had even forsaken his own family to come back to Paris to deliver the news to the grand master that the treasure was safe, giving Molay and his men the peace of mind to at last deny their false admissions of guilt so that they could face death as faithful Knights Templar.

Ramberti stayed long enough to pay his respects. He turned to melt into the throngs who had already grown tired of the spectacle and were receding from the shore.

He stopped abruptly at the sight of a face he thought he'd never see again. It was Riccardo Corosi, the young man who had betrayed everything the Templars stood for and doomed the order. Three stout men-at-arms stood to either side of him.

"You shouldn't have come back here," Corosi said. "I was hoping you had given up on your deluded quest to save the Templars, but I suspected you'd remain loyal to Molay until the bitter end. Now you leave me no choice."

"No matter what you do to me, the Templars will rise again. Loyalty is one of our sacred creeds, but you've betrayed every oath you've ever taken. You're nothing but a petulant child."

"And you're an old fool living in a dream world. The Templars have been extinguished forever."

"I know what you really want, Riccardo." Ramberti drew his sword. "I won't let you take me alive."

By now some of the gathered crowd had stopped to watch the unusual confrontation.

"Despite how you've wronged me," Corosi said, "I'll grant you a quick death if you tell me what I want to know."

"After I raised you and taught you the importance of a knight's honor, the best you can offer me is a quick death?"

Corosi barked a derisive laugh. "All I ever wanted was to be your knightly ideal, until the moment *you* betrayed *me* and I realized that every word from your mouth was a two-faced lie. But let's not talk in front of all these people. We should have some privacy." He nodded at his men. "Remember, I need him breathing."

The men-at-arms advanced on Ramberti. Even if there was a shred of devotion left buried in Corosi for his former mentor, he'd order his men to batter Ramberti into submission with the flats of their swords and haul him off to some dungeon for questioning under torture.

At his best, Ramberti might have successfully fought off six men, but in this weakened state, his defeat was inevitable. He couldn't let himself be captured, not with the secret he held. He didn't trust himself to withstand the brutality that he knew was in store for him.

He charged at the men, screaming and swinging his sword wildly. He hoped one of them would lose his restraint and strike him down in one deadly blow.

But the men were disciplined. They spread themselves out, blocking his thrusts but not going on the offensive, obviously planning to wear him out. Corosi watched from afar, keeping a careful eye on the proceedings.

Ramberti coughed from the exertion, which gave him an idea. He played up the spasms, hacking violently before pausing to seemingly catch his breath.

"You must have fallen ill on your long journey, old man," Corosi said, casually edging toward the circle of men surrounding Ramberti.

"I don't know what you mean," Ramberti said, spitting a gob of blood on the ground.

"You didn't hide the treasure in France. You'd want to get it as far away from King Philip as you could."

"I would be less worried about the treasure than about the king's letter to the pope that I took from you."

Corosi couldn't hide his fury and came even closer. "I will find out what you know. You will be begging to tell me."

Ramberti stood straight, as if gathering the last of his strength, and launched another flurry of strikes against the men-at-arms. He then feinted in the direction away from Corosi. While the men were adjusting to his move, he dived past their feet in the opposite direction, rolling and jumping up toward the shocked Corosi, whose drawn sword had been languishing by his side.

Ramberti brought his sword down with all his might. Corosi was able to counter the blow but fell backward, dropping his weapon. Ramberti leaped upon him, putting his knee on Corosi's chest. They wrestled with the hilt of his sword as Ramberti forced the edge of the blade to within an inch of Corosi's throat, the weight of his body overcoming the strength in Corosi's sinewy arms. Abject terror flared in the traitor's eyes.

"Kill him!" Corosi shrieked. "Kill him now!"

Ramberti went rigid as he felt something slam into his back like a hammer. His arms went limp, and he looked down to see the point of a sword protruding from his chest.

The blade was withdrawn, and Ramberti fell on top of Corosi, who pushed him off. Corosi scrambled to his feet, his tunic covered in Ramberti's blood. Corosi looked horrified at what he had done.

Surprisingly, Ramberti felt no pain, just a coldness enveloping his body. But he knew he had accomplished his goal. His life was ebbing away. No torture could touch him now.

Corosi, apparently realizing his mistake, bent down and shook Ramberti by the shoulders.

"Where is the treasure?"

Ramberti shook his head in disappointment. "I loved you like a son."

A fleeting expression of regret on Corosi's face showed that the words wounded him.

"And you were the one who cast me away in favor of Matteo. Now tell me where you've hidden it!"

"You'll never find it. You're not worthy." Ramberti was getting light-headed and dizzy. "Only Luciana and Matteo are."

"Matteo is dead. I killed him myself."

"No," Ramberti lamented. "They were to be married."

Corosi shook his head. "I destroyed all of your plans. Your beloved daughter didn't marry your favored pupil. I convinced her that Matteo betrayed you. After that, it was easy to persuade her to marry me. The generous dowry you left her before becoming a Templar is now mine. I have already used it to begin building my banking empire. I suppose I should thank you, *Father*."

Ramberti closed his eyes, with Corosi's jeering face as his final horrid vision. Despite Molay's dying pronouncement that they would someday rise victorious, the Templars would be doomed if no one were able to vindicate them by finding what Ramberti had hidden. As he took his last breath, he clung to hope that what Corosi said was a lie.

Because if his words were the truth, the trail Ramberti had left for Matteo and Luciana would never be followed, and the treasure of the Templars was lost to eternity.

THE NOBLE INHERITANCE

Tuscany

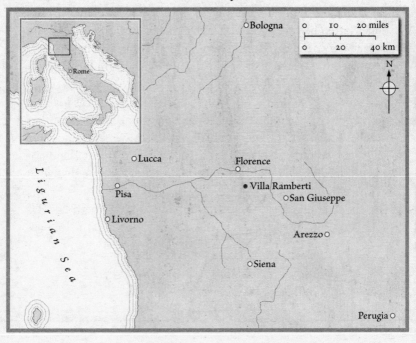

October, 1351

SAN GIUSEPPE, TUSCANY

Luciana Corosi's heart beat a little faster with every step her horse took as her Florentine entourage entered the small village. She hadn't been here in years because it was so remote from the main road between Florence and Siena, the exact reason she had chosen it for this morning's secret rendezvous.

On her left rode the captain of her guard, Umberto. He was dressed in a bright blue tunic and wore a hat with a white feather signifying that he was the leader of his six men-at-arms. All of them carried swords that Luciana hoped they would not have to use.

"Signora," Umberto said, his bushy black eyebrows knotted with concern, "I would prefer if you would ride into town behind us."

"Absolutely not," Luciana replied. "I know you are here to protect me, Umberto, but I cannot come into this meeting cowering behind you. Besides, the Sienese wouldn't dare try anything so bold as to attack us. The last thing Siena would want is a war with Florence."

"As you wish, signora."

On her right was her lady's maid Sofia, whose eyes darted to the foreboding forest surrounding the fields of wheat ready for harvest and pastures thick with sheep. Luciana couldn't fault the girl's apprehension. The large wooden chest on the wagon behind them would be a tempting target if any highwaymen knew of the riches it held.

"Calm yourself, Sofia."

"I'm sorry, signora," Sofia replied. "My eyes continue to deceive me. I see robbers in every gap in the trees."

Sofia turned to her and gave a half-hearted smile. Her maid was a true beauty, with ebony curls, unblemished olive skin, and wide brown eyes. Ever since Luciana had lost her longtime lady's maid in the Great Mortality three years ago, Sofia had been her most trusted companion. Now that Luciana was well into her fifties, the maidservant—more than three decades her junior—brought vitality and spirit into her life.

"If robbers were bold enough to take on Umberto and his men," Luciana said, "they would have done it long before we reached a settled village. We'll be rid of that chest soon enough, if that's what worries you."

"I admire your courage, signora. I will take strength from it."

Luciana was glad she was projecting an air of confidence, despite her nervousness. However, it wasn't fear that gripped her, but anticipation. If she was right, this transaction could be the means to solve a mystery that had gnawed at her for nearly forty years.

The village of San Giuseppe was nestled in a valley, split by a single road through the cluster of buildings that included homes, a tavern, and a stone church with stand-alone bell tower. The air smelled of freshly baked bread and brewing ale as they passed the residents going about their business. Most of them glanced up briefly at their unusual visitors before going back to their daily tasks. The only people who looked out of place were a man and woman putting their saddlebags onto two fine horses, one mottled silver and the other pure white. The couple was so deep into a tense discussion that they didn't even turn their heads to look at the strangers.

Up ahead in the center of town, Luciana could see that her counterparts had already arrived. As agreed, Piero Barbieri had only a commander of arms and six swordsmen in addition to the driver of the wagon that accompanied them. Piero, younger than her by two decades, was the cousin of Jacopo Barbieri, the owner of the most prominent bank in Siena. He was dressed in an elegant crimson surcoat and a jaunty bycoket with a peaked brim.

Luciana came to a stop. He took in her entourage before nodding at her, a look of disdain on his face.

"Signora Corosi, it's my pleasure to see you again."

"No, it isn't. I know you were against this bargain."

"Selling our bank's branch in Florence to your husband is a bad idea, but Jacopo insisted."

"Your cousin got sloppy. There's a reason we didn't loan money to the king of France for his war with England. Jacopo should have known it's dragged on so long that the king would eventually default on his debts."

He tilted his head at her. "So the rumors are true. You are well acquainted with Signore Corosi's financial dealings. I know sometimes merchant's wives learn their husband's trades, but I've never heard of a lady being so involved in her husband's business."

"Riccardo trusts no one else."

"According to the talk, you have a head for numbers. Is that the reason he trusts you?"

"I'm simply here to do my husband's bidding. Now, shall we complete our business?"

As they dismounted, Luciana saw the driver of her wagon jump down and go over to Umberto, dancing from toe to toe as he spoke in hushed tones. Her captain seemed annoyed and waved off the man, who scurried toward a group of people standing near the church.

"What was that about?" Luciana asked him.

"Elio needed to relieve himself, so I told him go away and find the latrine."

"Just as long as he's back by the time we're done."

With Umberto at her side, she walked up to Piero. "You have the contract?"

Piero nodded. "Signed by Jacopo."

"And the letter?"

He patted his scrip. "In here as well. You have the money?"

Luciana turned to Umberto and nodded. He called back to his men to bring the chest.

Four of her soldiers strained to carry the massive strongbox to them and set it at their feet. Luciana took the key from her pouch and unlocked it. Umberto raised the lid, revealing stacks of gold coins that filled the chest.

"Ten thousand gold florins," Luciana said.

Piero stared in wonder at the fortune, an amount rarely seen in one place, even for a banker. Usually, they would have used a bill of exchange for such a large transaction, but secrecy demanded coinage in this case.

"Do you want to count it?" she asked.

The question brought him out of his reverie. "Of course." He nodded at his captain, who kneeled beside it and began inspecting the one hundred linen sleeves each containing one hundred coins.

"You'll find them all there."

"I'm sure." He took the parchment contract from his leather scrip and unrolled it. The top and bottom halves of the scroll were inscribed with identical agreements. He showed her Jacopo Barbieri's signature on both sides next to where Riccardo Corosi had already placed his mark.

When Luciana indicated her assent that the contract was complete, Piero took out a dagger and cut the document in half in a jagged line. He handed her one part and kept the other for himself. Now neither side could forge a replacement, for it wouldn't match the pattern of the cut on its twin.

As Luciana rolled it up, she said, "And the letter?"

Piero drew out a much smaller folded piece of parchment. "I don't understand why this is so important to you."

"That's none of your concern," Luciana said as she took it from him more eagerly than she should have.

It was addressed to Matteo Dazzo. Jacopo had told her of a letter that had been delivered to Matteo's cousin, Jacopo's wife, after his death. His wife had always been fond of Matteo and had kept the letter for decades without mentioning it to her husband, who'd disliked her cousin. Jacopo had only learned of it after she'd died within the last year. He'd tantalized Luciana with the opening lines of the letter, telling her he would only hand it over after she persuaded her husband to negotiate a favorable deal that would provide him with funds for his struggling bank.

Piero shrugged. "Frankly, the letter doesn't even make sense, but your influence was necessary to get this bargain done. And now, if he ever needs a favor from you, he knows something that you're not telling your husband."

Luciana glared at him but said nothing as she slipped the letter and contract into her pouch.

Piero's captain was only halfway done with his counting when the church bell began to ring, far too soon to signal the midday hour of sext. The only reason to sound the bell other than the tolling of the time was to warn of danger.

They all looked around for some sign of smoke, the most common reason for an alarm.

Luciana asked Umberto, "Do you see a fire?"

He shook his head. "Nothing."

The bell didn't stop ringing.

"What's going on?" Piero said, finally looking up from the hoard of gold.

They all gazed up at the tower. Luciana was shocked to see that it was the driver of her wagon pulling on the rope.

"What the devil is he doing up there?" Umberto said.

Then Luciana heard something else. A low rumble.

She turned to the source of the sound. Only a few hundred yards up the northern road were eight horses charging toward the town. Every rider was wearing some form of armor and a helmet, and their swords were drawn for battle. They were led by a man in full mail and a great helm with brass fittings that gave the impression of sharp fangs on a hideous skull.

Luciana wheeled around to berate Piero for his treachery, but he made the accusation first in a terrified shrill voice.

"You harlot! You dare attack us now that the deal is done?"

"They're not with us, you idiot!"

"Signora!" Umberto shouted. "We need to leave now!"

Piero slammed the lid shut on the chest and didn't bother to ask for the key to lock it. He had his men hoist it toward their wagon.

Luciana remounted her horse, and she was about to flee down the road with Umberto, Sofia, and the rest of the men when she was horrified to see another eight armored riders coming up the road from the south.

That's why her driver had rung the bell. He had betrayed them all by letting the marauders know it was time for the assault.

"Stay behind us, signora!" Umberto yelled and formed his men into a line to face the approaching attackers from the north while Piero's men did the same to meet the southern riders. She didn't know how long they would be able to hold out. Though the numbers were nearly even, neither her guards nor Piero's were clad in armor.

She looked at Sofia, who seemed frozen with fright.

"Sofia! We'll make it through this!"

Sofia was jolted out of her paralyzed state by her name. She turned to her mistress and nodded, then focused again on the riders bearing down on them.

The villagers were scrambling like mad to get to some sort of safety. The noblewoman that Luciana had seen earlier was now on her white horse riding around calling for the villagers to go to the church for sanctuary. The nobleman she'd been with was nowhere to be seen.

Luciana looked for a way out of the town for her and Sofia if the battle went badly. They could go around the houses and back up the road, but any pursuers would soon catch them. The only other choice would be to try venturing into the forest.

Piero's men panicked while carrying the chest and fumbled as they were trying to shove it onto their wagon. The box tumbled off and slammed into the hard ground, spilling golden coins in all directions. The lid of the chest banged into its wooden frame like a thunderclap.

The sharp noise caused Luciana's already-unnerved horse to rear back. She wasn't yet settled into her stirrups, and the sudden movement caught her by surprise. She was launched from her saddle, floating in the air for a sickening moment before striking her head on something hard.

She was dazed for a few moments before her vision came back into focus. Her ears buzzed and she suddenly felt nauseated.

Her horse was nowhere to be seen. It must have run off. Sofia. Where was her lady's maid? She would help. Luciana raised her head and with dismay saw Sofia clinging to the reins of her own horse as it tore off through the wheat fields, probably frightened by the loud report that had alarmed Luciana's mount.

As her hearing came back, Luciana could make out the clash of swords. She struggled to her knees and saw that Umberto and his men were now locked in a vicious battle with the armored marauders. They fought ferociously, but she could tell that they were outmatched. It was only a matter of time before they were all cut down.

With her horse gone, Luciana called out to Umberto, but he was so focused on leading his men in the fight that he didn't hear her.

She tried to stand, and her dizziness forced her back down again. She blinked and there were hooves in front of her. Luciana looked up expecting to see one of the attackers, but it was the noblewoman on the white horse. With an expression of concern, she was speaking, but in her haze Luciana couldn't understand the words.

Something caught the noblewoman's attention, and Luciana followed her gaze. One of the marauders had broken off and was heading toward them, his bloody sword raised for more victims.

To Luciana's amazement, the noblewoman didn't flee. Instead, she plucked a bow from her saddle and reached into an arrow bag beside her.

With cool concentration, the noblewoman pulled the bowstring back and nocked an arrow while holding two more in her draw hand, a technique Luciana had never seen in her life.

The noblewoman loosed the first arrow, and it flew past the charging attacker. The miss just seemed to enrage him, for he yelled a piercing battle cry. The noblewoman launched the next two arrows in a blur, far faster than Luciana could have imagined.

The second arrow hit the marauder squarely in the torso. It simply bounced off the coat plates under his tabard.

The third arrow, however, found its mark. It plunged deep into the vulnerable spot between the top of his breastplate and the lower edge of his helmet.

The marauder dropped his sword and fell from his horse, landing less than a body length away from Luciana as his horse raced past them.

With her bow hand holding the reins, the noblewoman leaned down and reached her free hand out to Luciana.

This time, Luciana could understand her words. In English-accented Italian, the noblewoman said, "My name is Willa. Take my hand, signora, or we're both going to die."

2

Willa tried to steady her hand as she held it out for the woman to take. It was only the second time she had killed a man, and she could feel herself starting to tremble after the instinctive decision to defend herself and the helpless woman.

The age of the elegant lady she had rescued was difficult to tell, although her hair was the color of silver. There were thin lines around her alert brown eyes, but her smooth skin and soft hands indicated a life of luxury out of the weathering sun. Surely she was old enough to be Willa's mother, which made it all the more despicable that a marauder would intend to run her down. Her kirtle and surcoat were torn and dusty after her fall, but of fine material that indicated wealth.

Seeing the woman's servant gallop away for her life ignited a protective impulse within Willa. Her own lady had been killed in a similar attack by armed men earlier in the year, and she was still grieving the loss. She couldn't imagine ever abandoning her beloved mistress in a time of need, no matter the danger, and she was determined that this lady would not suffer the same fate.

For a moment, Willa didn't think the woman would take her help. Certainly the chaos of the situation made it difficult to trust a stranger, but after a slight hesitation she grabbed Willa's hand, put her foot in the offered stirrup, and expertly mounted the horse to take a position behind the saddle.

"Thank you," the lady said. "I'm Luciana. Where did you learn…"

"Let's get to safety first," Willa replied in Italian. "Then we can talk."

Though Willa had been in Italy for a relatively short time, her facility with languages allowed her to pick up the local tongue quickly, adding it to her repertoire of French, English, Breton, and Latin.

The fighting continued unabated, and the attackers were winning, felling the unarmored defenders one by one. Willa didn't know what was happening except that it must involve the gold that had tumbled to the ground. In the next instant, the nobleman dressed in crimson cried out when he took a sword to the gut.

"Piero," Luciana gasped as he toppled to the ground.

They couldn't go to the church. That would only put the villagers in danger since they didn't appear to be the target of the assault.

She was about to take off for the sheep pasture when a boy no older than eight scrambled out of one of the closest houses. The foolish youngster began scooping up gold coins and cradling them in his tunic.

"Stop that!" Willa shouted, but he paid her no heed. One of the marauders from the southern group spotted the boy gathering up the money and charged at him with his sword at the ready.

Willa drew three more arrows and loosed them in rapid succession at the rider. However, this man was more fully covered with armor, from his helmet all the way down to his gauntlets. The missiles simply glanced off the mail's riveted iron rings.

She could do nothing more and felt sick at the idea of the young boy dying senselessly. The man was only a few yards from completing his murderous mission when a horse came shooting out from between two houses at an astonishing speed.

It was Zephyr, the mottled silver stallion of Gerard Fox, the English knight who had changed Willa's life so profoundly. Gerard had one foot in a stirrup and his other foot hooked around the saddle so he could bend down close to the ground. He scooped up the boy a moment before the marauder's sword would have split him in half.

The boy's mouth hung open in amazement at being held aloft by a man clinging to a galloping horse. When Gerard was clear of the attacker, he slowed to let go of the boy and yelled, "Run!" The boy, who had dropped all the coins in his hands, didn't need to be told twice and sprinted for the safety of the church.

While Zephyr was still moving, Gerard grabbed his mane and the reins and released his foot from the saddle. Although Willa had seen him perform such impressive feats before, Luciana sucked in an astonished gasp as he swung his legs to the ground and kicked himself back into the saddle before drawing his sword Legend in one continuous motion. The swirled pattern on the Damascus-steel blade flashed in the morning sun. Gerard looked at his adversary with contempt as the rider swung back around to face him. The Englishman spoke to the marauder in Italian.

"I recently learned the word for coward, but this is the first chance I've had to use it. Are you afraid to fight someone who can defend himself instead of a harmless child?"

The man kicked his horse to charge. Gerard did the same, shouting, "*Oppugna*, Zephyr!" Latin for "attack."

Willa held her breath as they approached each other. The marauder took a mighty swing, but Gerard expertly parried the blow. He then swung Legend in an upward arc, knocking the helmet from his enemy's head. It dangled at his side, the chain connecting it to his breastplate draped awkwardly across his sword arm that he was desperately trying to free.

In a lightning-fast maneuver Gerard sliced the flailing man across his exposed face. The impact twisted the man's head so brutally that Willa didn't see the catastrophic damage the obsidian-sharp blade surely did, but the results were obvious. He was wrenched out of his saddle and landed face down on the road, unmoving.

With Legend still in his grip, Gerard rode over to her. Sweat dampened his shoulder-length brown hair and trimmed beard. His intelligent green eyes took in Luciana for a moment before settling on Willa.

"I thought I told you to get to the church," he said in English. The only time they'd used the language in the past month was with each other.

When the attack had begun, Fox had given her his bow and arrows just in case, before riding out to the fields to tell the farmers to lie down where they were rather than seek protection in the church as they normally would when the bell rang of danger. He worried they might be caught in the middle of the battle and be harmed as innocent bystanders.

"I couldn't go into hiding when the villagers were at risk," Willa explained. "As I was herding them to the church, this woman fell from her horse. She needed my help."

Gerard looked down at the attacker with the arrow sticking out of his neck.

"I gave you that weapon to defend yourself. This isn't our fight." His tone was more exasperated than scolding.

"And it was quite useful for defending this lady, thank you," she said, nodding back toward Luciana.

"Well, we can't go to the church now, not when we've killed two of their men."

"Where should we go?"

"They'll catch us on the road," Gerard said. "We'll use the forest path. Is she coming with us?"

Willa switched to Italian and looked back at Luciana. "Do you want to come with us?"

"*Sì, grazie*," Luciana said, looking somewhat dazed by all that she'd just witnessed. Then she turned toward the continuing battle and shouted, "Umberto, *andiamo!*"

Gerard spurred Zephyr into a gallop, and Willa followed him on her own horse Comis, with Luciana clutching her tightly around the waist. Zephyr was the fastest horse Willa had ever encountered, and Comis had difficulty keeping up, especially because she was carrying two people instead of only one.

Willa looked back and saw a knight in a blue tunic and feathered hat racing after them across the pasture, herds of bleating sheep parting before him like the water cleaved by a ship at sea.

When Fox reached the opening into the forest, he turned and stopped. It was the only path through the woods where the brush wasn't too thick for horses to traverse.

"Get behind me," he said to Willa, brandishing his sword at the oncoming knight.

"*Vi prego di parlare italiano*," Luciana said. *Please speak Italian.*

Gerard switched to her language and pointed at the man. "Do you know him?"

"That's Umberto, the captain of my guard."

Umberto rode up, his face and clothes splattered with blood, and said, "Are you all right, signora? Who are these people?"

"They're friends. They saved my life and killed two of the robbers."

"We don't have time for introductions," Gerard said, pointing at four horsemen galloping across the pasture toward them, the man in the fanged helmet at the front.

Umberto turned to Gerard and said, "Take Signora Corosi to safety. I'll hold them off as long as I can to give you a head start."

"No, Umberto," Luciana said. "Come with us."

"You must go. You're all that matters now."

Willa heard a sob catch in Luciana's throat. "I won't leave you."

"Your only hope is to lose them in the forest," Umberto said. "I will do my best to make you proud, signora."

"You're a good captain and friend, Umberto."

He gave his mistress a melancholy nod that told her he knew that he was giving his life for hers. "Now go."

"We'll do everything we can to protect her," Gerard said before prodding Zephyr to take the forest path. "*Vade*, Zephyr."

Zephyr took off at a canter, the fastest they dared go on the twisting narrow path, and Willa followed. Her last view of Umberto was him turning his horse to face the four mailed riders bearing down on him.

Gerard called back to Willa as they rode. "I hope he can give us enough time to reach the crossing."

Willa suddenly realized the destination he had in mind. If this didn't work, the three of them would be left with little possibility of escape.

"The river?" she replied.

"It's our best chance."

"What are you talking about?" Luciana said into Willa's ear.

Over her shoulder, Willa said, "The Arno River. We have to catch a boat."

3

Gerard Fox had known something strange was happening in San Giuseppe when he saw the two nobles with their retinues of guards enter the sleepy village, but he'd been so caught up in his discussion with Willa and their preparations to leave that morning that he'd paid the newcomers scant attention. Fortunately, their horses had already been saddled when the attack started.

Their first priority had been to make sure the residents didn't become inadvertent victims of an ambush that didn't involve them. He and Willa would have retreated to the church as well, but the woman riding behind her on Comis had changed everything. Fox wasn't happy about running from a fight, even one that was as good as lost, but he had two others to protect.

The day before, Fox had gone on a long ride to clear his head after a painful conversation with Willa. He'd taken the path all the way through the woods and came upon the ferry that the two of them had used to cross the river the week before.

Now that he had guided them out the other side of the forest, the wide expanse of the Arno was visible. Fox galloped down the open road toward its swollen banks, with Willa and Luciana close behind. After the torrential storm that had lashed the region two days ago, it didn't surprise him to see the river near its highest level. In fact, he'd been counting on it.

It would be impossible to cross on horseback at this flood stage. The ferry ahead of them was the only way to traverse the river for miles in either direction. By the time the robbers made it to the nearest bridge and back along the other side of the river, the three of them would be long gone.

If they made it across.

Fox glanced over his shoulder back down the road. The commander of the attackers in his fanged helmet was only a few furlongs behind them.

As they got closer to the river, Fox was relieved to see that the ferry was on their side. That had been the biggest risk with this plan. With the marauders so close behind, they couldn't wait for it to come across for them.

The ferry was simply a raft big enough for four horses and their riders. A rope was strung over the river and secured at either end by tying it to a stout tree. The rope was threaded through two pulleys attached to posts on the raft, which was pulled in either direction by the ferryman through brute strength.

With Zephyr's speed and endurance, Fox could have outrun the commander, but Comis was already tiring with two riders on her, and she was slowing by the moment. If they didn't make it onto the ferry and out into the river before their pursuers arrived, they'd never be able to escape along the riverbank.

When their two horses clattered onto the wooden boat, the ferryman was startled awake from a nap. With bleary eyes, he looked them over, taking note of their fine clothes.

"Thirty denari for the lot of you."

"That's outrageous!" Luciana protested.

Fox jerked a thumb toward the commander bearing down on them. "Do you really want to bargain right now?" He jumped down from Zephyr and lifted the man from his reclined position. "We're leaving."

The ferryman looked out at the rider racing toward them.

"Not with another fare coming, we're not."

"That's not a fare, you dullard," Willa said. "He'll kill us all if he makes it here before we go."

As if to prove her point, the commander drew his sword, which was still stained with blood.

"Maybe you're right," the ferryman said. He pulled on the rope, but the ferry didn't budge. He strained even harder, but nothing happened. They were still pinned to the riverbank.

"What's the matter?" Fox asked.

"I think we're stuck in the mud."

Fox joined him on the rope, and the two of them pulled with all their might. Still no movement.

The operator picked up a pole. "I'll have to lever us free."

Though the ferryman's upper body looked strong from pulling the raft day after day, he was also half a head shorter than Fox, who had to outweigh him by five stone.

Knowing his greater weight would give him more leverage, Fox grabbed the pole. "I'll do it. Willa, you and the lady help him pull."

Willa and Luciana dismounted and joined him at the rope, with no complaint about the manual labor.

Fox jumped off and rammed the pole under the raft to pry it loose. He could see that with the weight of two horses and three riders the wooden bottom had sunk into the mud just as the ferryman had said. He heaved down on the pole, careful not to snap it in two.

Despite his effort, the mud kept the raft in its grip. As he repositioned the pole, Fox stole a look at the road. The commander was getting close. He had only a few more tries left before the marauder was on them, and they didn't have time to float the raft free by getting everyone off.

He had to risk breaking the pole. He shoved it as far as it would go under the raft, then he used all his weight in a rocking motion to set the boat moving up and down. Finally, with a great sucking sound, the raft floated free of the muddy bank.

"Gerard!" Willa shouted.

Fox turned and saw the rider hurtling down the road. If the commander chose to jump the short distance across the water and onto the raft, a couple of swings of his sword would slay everyone on board.

Fox cried out, "Go! Go!"

He was partially hidden by the bushes and steep embankment, so the commander didn't notice until the last moment that Fox was swinging the long pole at him just as he was readying for his horse's leap.

The pole smacked the soldier in his midsection, and he went

flying off his horse, landing in the mud as his riderless steed plunged into the river. The horse splashed around and then ran back out of the water and up the road.

The ferry was now twenty feet out into the river. Willa looked at Fox with fear as she helped the ferryman pull the rope, but she said nothing.

Fox had to make sure that they wouldn't be followed. He ran up the embankment to get to the rope tied to the tree above him. He nearly reached it when a hand grabbed his ankle and tripped him.

He rolled as he dropped and saw that the commander had regained his footing surprisingly quickly. In one hand was his sword, and with his other he drew a wicked-looking bollock dagger half the length of his sword. The brass fittings on his distinctive helmet gave it an evil leer, likely designed to intimidate his enemies.

"Let us go and I won't kill you," Fox said in Italian, drawing Legend.

The helmet tilted slightly as if the man were entertained by the taunt, but he remained silent.

Fox edged backward. "You've got the gold. Why do you want her?"

Still no response.

Fox continued moving toward the rope. "Are you mute? No tongue? Or are you simply dazzled into silence by my wit?"

This time the helmet shook back and forth. Then the soldier charged him.

With a flurry of swings, the commander drove Fox up the embankment. Fox was barely able to parry the strikes. One slice from either blade would rip Fox open and end his life quickly. Meanwhile, the soldier was able to ward off several of Fox's counterstrikes with his mailed arms. Although the Damascus-steel blade was sharper than a dagger, it couldn't cut through armor.

They kept the dance going up the road and around to the top of the steep embankment that bordered the river. Now Fox could see why the commander had let him talk so much. Three more of his men had been following behind him. They were only a furlong away, and when they arrived, they would easily overwhelm Fox.

The commander thrust his dagger at Fox, who grabbed the man's wrist and pulled his opponent in close, their swords crossed and Fox's face only inches from that ominous helmet. They were the same height, and in their clinch, Fox could finally see the eyes through the slit. They regarded Fox with an unsettling amusement.

The soldier spoke in a gravelly rasp. "*Ti conosco.*" *I know you.*

The voice was unfamiliar, but the tone was sure. Fox didn't know what to make of the assertion, and he didn't have time to ponder. At least the commander hadn't realized the position Fox had maneuvered him into.

Fox dug his feet into the soil and, using the same kind of leverage he'd employed with the raft, drove the commander backward until he tipped over the edge of the embankment. Fox kept pushing forward, and together they plunged six feet onto the tangle of roots below.

Fox used his opponent's body to cushion his fall. The commander landed with a pained grunt, his helmet smacking into a stump. With the remaining raiders coming, Fox didn't have time to finish him off, but he was motionless, so he wasn't a threat at the moment.

Fox ran back up the slope and reached the rope when the other men were just thirty yards away. He slashed it free from the tree, sheathed his sword, and leaped down to the muddy bank. Without letting go of the rope, he dived into the river, the sound of the approaching horses at his back. If they'd had any crossbows, he'd already be dead.

He used the rope to pull himself hand over hand toward the raft, which was now halfway across the river. Willa left her place on the tow line to haul in Fox's end of the rope.

By the time Fox reached the raft and dragged himself aboard, he was spent.

As he lay there heaving from the exertion, Willa kneeled beside him.

"What were you thinking?" she asked.

He smiled at her. "You know I try not to do that too much."

He got to his feet, water dripping from his clothes. He didn't relish the idea of continuing their ride soaking wet, but there was nothing for it.

The ferryman was furious. "Why did you cut the rope?"

"They can't follow us now, can they?" Luciana said, who was breathing hard but still pulling on the rope.

"Now I've got to spend the rest of my day getting another boat, towing the rope across, retying it…"

"Stop your whining." She took a gold florin from her own purse. "That should not only pay for your lost fares but also for your closed mouth." The ferryman seemed both pleased by the payment and annoyed that he couldn't complain anymore.

Fox relieved the lady at the rope, and he and the ferryman took them the rest of the way to the opposite shore.

As soon as they reached the riverbank, they remounted the horses, this time with Luciana riding behind Fox on Zephyr to give Comis a rest. He was starting to admire this unknown woman, who had remained composed even in the face of all that had just happened.

He looked back at the commander on the other side of the river, who was being helped to his feet by his men. He shrugged them off and simply stood there motionless watching the three of them ride out of sight at a fast walk.

"Now that we are no longer in imminent danger of dying," Fox said, "perhaps we should introduce ourselves more formally. I'm Gerard Fox of Oakhurst and this is my wife, Willa." He glanced at Willa, who seemed to flinch at his words but remained studiously tight-lipped. Their personal situation was going to have to be put aside for the moment while they tried to figure out what to do next.

"Obviously, I'm pleased to make your acquaintance. My name is Luciana Corosi. Thank you both for saving my life."

"I'd love to know why we're now on the run from men-at-arms who seem intent on killing you," Willa said.

"So would I," Luciana replied. "Nobody was supposed to know

about that meeting, especially not my wagon driver. I didn't think he even knew where we were going today, let alone why."

"Is he the one who rang the bell for the ambush to begin?" Fox asked, looking back at Luciana.

She nodded, her fierce eyes glittering with outrage. "Someone betrayed me."

FLORENCE

From a window on the second story of the Palazzo della Signoria, Riccardo Corosi looked down on the shrinking shadow cast by the city's seat of government. As it neared the midday hour, the main piazza below teemed with vendors hawking their wares and travelers in town to trade their goods from around Italy and beyond. All Corosi saw was money.

As Florence's preeminent banker, he was the beneficiary of every one of these transactions. A portion of each florin that passed through the city's gates flowed in one way or another to Corosi's coffers. He'd learned from his time with Domenico Ramberti how to build real wealth.

He admired the Templars' simple method. The order had pledged to protect pilgrims to the Holy Land, and they found that the pilgrims' money and valuables were often stolen during the journey. So the Templars let the pilgrims deposit funds at their place of origin in return for a letter of credit that would let them withdraw money from the Templar coffers once they reached Jerusalem. In return for this service, the Templars would charge a fee. They also would often keep the deposits if the pilgrims died before they reached their destination or failed to return safely home.

Corosi modeled his own business on this version of international banking established by the Knights Templar, by which they had become the richest organization on earth. In addition, like the Templars, he'd extended himself into lending. Since charging interest for loans was forbidden by the Church, he called himself an investor. He provided funds to anyone who promised collateral and a percentage of their income to him, from merchants and ships to farms and castles. Even the Church borrowed money from him.

Taking a profit from exchanging currencies also provided him with a tidy sum. With traders using florins from Florence, ducats from Venice, livres tournois from France, and nobles from England, all he had to do was charge a fee every time someone wanted to use a currency that wasn't native to the region. Then he would simply collect the coins and ship them back to his bank branches wherever they originated.

History seemed to be on his side to help him build his wealth. A number of Florence's great banks became insolvent in the 1340s as the debts incurred by northern European monarchs during more than a decade of war between France and England continued to mount without being repaid. And the combination of the famine of 1347 and the depredations of the Great Mortality made Florence ripe for a sharp businessman who could take advantage of the situation.

Watching the masses from his lofty position gave Corosi a flush of dominion over his realm. There was nothing better than having all of his exquisitely laid plans come together so perfectly. He loved playing this chess game, of which he was the undisputed master. The pieces were all where he wanted them, and now he was making his final, carefully considered moves toward checkmate. In myriad ways, today was going to be a great step in his ascendancy to dominating Florentine rule.

In theory, the Signoria, a council of nine members drawn from the guilds of Florence, controlled the politics of the city-state. But as each member served a term of only two months, Corosi had realized that the power behind the council was even more important. Over the course of decades, Corosi had parlayed his banking acumen and wealth into influence over whichever guild members currently served in the Signoria.

Corosi turned away from the window and glided down the ornate corridor, his velvet robes flowing behind him. He'd kept his guest waiting long enough.

He passed a panel painting of himself kneeling in prayer to Saint Matthew, the patron saint of bankers and accountants. He'd commissioned it and had it hung in a place of honor near the great hall to remind anyone conducting business here that he was ever present in their lives and always would be. He felt that the silver temples, strong nose, and dark brows of the image not only were a remarkable likeness, but also represented him as a strong leader. He'd make sure that the marble statue of Saint Matthew he was going to have carved for the building's entrance would bear his commanding image.

He swept into the meeting chamber where Count Ettore Russo waited for him. The count's whispers hushed when one of his aides noticed Corosi's entrance.

Russo unsuccessfully tried to cover a pained expression with a half-hearted smile.

"Signore Corosi," Russo said deferentially as he approached. "It's a pleasure to see you as always."

"Is it?" Corosi replied. "I'd think you wouldn't be so happy to see me today."

"I know my debts are now due, but I'm sure we can come to an appropriate arrangement."

Corosi looked pointedly at the two underlings by Russo's side. "Are you certain you want to have this potentially embarrassing discussion with your attendants here?"

Russo's mask of confidence faltered, and he hissed at the two men to leave. When they were alone, he dropped the pretense completely and snarled, "I've seen what you've become over the years, corrupted by your own power. I know you've plotted to send me into bankruptcy, Signore Corosi."

"Of course I did," Corosi said. "I started planning it the moment you came crawling to me for money. But it wasn't easy. Do you know how much it cost me to drive the price of wool down for the past year?"

"Then you admit to a scheme to defraud me?"

"I call it smart planning. It's not my fault that you were too dense to compensate."

"And it wasn't my fault that I needed the loan in the first place. I simply had a run of bad fortune, and I needed funds to support my estate until providence smiled on me once more."

"As we all did when the Great Mortality descended upon us."

"Then you understand. Losing your son to that scourge should make you commiserate with my poor luck."

The mention of his dead heir hit Corosi like a hammer blow. Tommaso had been his pride and joy. He had shown such promise, even as a child. As he bloomed into a strong and clever adult under his father's tutelage, Corosi knew that it was his family's destiny to rule over Florence as a dynasty. All of that had been stolen from him when Tommaso was killed by the Pestilence. He would never stop lamenting his son's loss, but he had to ensure his own legacy. The subjugation of Russo was key to the launch of that plan.

Controlling his outward reaction, Corosi said smoothly, "You see, that's where you and I differ. If you had studied Greek philosophers as I have, you would realize what a foolish path you've trodden. You equate modesty with virtue, and pride with sin. But I have come to understand that ambition and the pursuit of glory are the most valuable traits, and fear and deception are the most effective means to those ends."

"You didn't used to be so ruthless as to plan the downfall of a man whom you'd once called a friend. It's clear now what a despicable rogue you've turned into. To use the kind of grandiose language you love to speak, I must remind you that I am a noble with a proud lineage that dates back hundreds of years."

"And yet your wealth is forfeit to me."

"Now that I know what you did to me, I refuse to simply hand over my estate."

"Then I will seize it under arms, with the full backing of the Gonfaloniere of Justice, who happens right now to be a member of the Guild of Bankers. The Signoria doesn't look kindly on a noble who defaults on his debts."

Russo seemed about to protest further, but Corosi's correct assessment stopped him. In a resigned voice, he said, "What can I do for you to forgive my liability?"

The entreaty sent a thrill down Corosi's spine. This was true power.

He waited for a long time, pretending to study the marble relief of a Roman battle of the gods that had decorated the fountain in the piazza outside, before it was removed to make way for the paving of the square twenty years ago. In reality, he was soaking in the moment that a man of such high status was bending to him.

"Do you know why the Titans lost in their war with the Olympian gods?" Corosi mused.

"I know nothing of that pagan religion," Russo replied.

"Pity. There are many lessons to be learned. One of which is that the Titans feared change. The Olympians embraced it, just as we have here in Florence. They created a dynasty that ruled the cosmos. We need to think of our own legacy if we are to make this city the most powerful one in Europe."

"What are you saying?"

"You have a daughter. Quite a fetching one. She is of marrying age, isn't she, with a fine dowry to be given for her wedding?"

Russo seemed confused by the abrupt change of subject. "You want me to sign over Veronica's dowry to you?"

Corosi smiled at him. "No, I want you to agree to marry her off without question to the man of my choosing. If you do, I will allow you to keep half your estate. Do we have a bargain?"

"And whom would she marry?"

"It doesn't matter for the moment. But I promise you it will be a match worthy of your name."

Russo hesitated so long that Corosi thought he might reject the offer. At last, he said through clenched teeth, "Signore Corosi, I'm forced to agree to your terms."

"Good." He held out his hand for the count, his social superior, to kiss as a final sign of capitulation. After a moment of struggle showing plainly on his face, Russo did it.

Without another word, Corosi strode away, leaving Russo to fume behind him.

As Corosi walked down the long stairway toward the palazzo's main entrance, he could feel the anticipation rising in him. As he exited the doors, he snapped his fingers for his attendant to bring his horse.

He mounted the black steed, and his mind turned to the most important event of the day. When Luciana had brought him an offer from his nemesis Jacopo Barbieri to buy his Sienese bank's Florentine branch, Corosi had rejected it out of hand. But her detailed financial evaluation of the proposed deal eventually convinced him it was too good an opportunity to resist. Just as with Russo, another man's misfortune would be his gain, in more ways than one. He would end the day with a contract proving that he was the owner of Barbieri's Florentine bank branch, setting Corosi on the path to become the most powerful banker on the Italian peninsula.

With a kick to his horse, he led his retinue of guards toward the Ponte Vecchio and the city's southern gate. He was eager to get news about San Giuseppe. He wouldn't be able to rest easy until he heard that everything had gone according to plan.

THE TUSCAN COUNTRYSIDE

During their ride away from the ferry, each time Fox turned his head to look back he caught a whiff of lavender from his passenger that took him back to his childhood. It was a flower his mother Emmeline often used to decorate the house. Although Luciana had silver hair and was darker in complexion, she carried herself with the same self-assured and elegant bearing.

Willa rode beside them on Comis, who was regaining her strength carrying only a single rider. Now that they were traveling at a pace suitable for conversation, Fox felt it was time to find out why they were fleeing for their lives. He and Willa would have to put aside their own problems for the moment, as the more urgent priority was understanding the current situation. Luciana had at first seemed hesitant about sharing details, but she told them about the deal to buy Jacopo Barbieri's bank branch in Florence.

"Do you think he's the one who planned the attack?" Fox asked.

"I doubt it, but I suppose he could have planned to take the gold and tear up the sales contract. He does need money. Siena was even more devastated by the Great Mortality than Florence was. Before the Pestilence, it was the banking center of Italy. The Sienese were the primary bankers for the Church, helping them to move large sums for the pope, as well as funding wars for monarchs across Europe. But everyone there has been in difficult financial straits ever since the Pestilence struck, with many businesses struggling, including Jacopo's."

"It's possible that Signore Barbieri didn't care for his cousin," Willa said.

"Piero was a thorn in his side, but I know Jacopo. He's incredibly loyal to his family, even the ones he doesn't care for."

That explanation wouldn't make sense anyway, Fox thought. Barbieri already had the signed contract, and it would have been easier for the highwaymen to attack Luciana and her men on the way into the town when they'd been the most vulnerable.

"Who else knew that you were traveling with so much money?" he asked.

"My husband Riccardo is very secretive. Only he, I, and the captain of my personal guard Umberto knew where we were going and how many coins we were carrying."

"Your captain was quite adamant about sacrificing himself so we could get away," Willa said.

"He was always very loyal to me. His father served under my father."

"Unfortunately, he's the likeliest culprit," Fox said. "And we didn't actually see him die."

Luciana's voice grew angry. "Not Umberto. I can't believe you would even suggest such a thing."

"Pardon me, signora. I didn't mean to offend you. But money can be a powerful…" Fox paused since he didn't know the Italian word for *incentive* "…a powerful reason."

"If Umberto was truly behind the morning's attack, then why did he help us escape?"

Fox raised an eyebrow at that. "I don't have an answer for you. I'm sure your assumption of loyalty is correct."

She softened again. "I am grateful Lady Fox was there to save me. You've both done more than I could expect. May I ask what brings you to the Italian peninsula?"

"We're on a pilgrimage," Fox said. It was the easiest explanation for why they were traveling together alone.

"To the Holy Land?"

He glanced at Willa, who looked pained by the question.

"Our current destination is La Sacra di San Michele near Turin," Fox said.

"Then I'm glad you were guided to San Giuseppe. I owe my

life to both of you. Not many would have gone to such lengths to defend a stranger. I'm certain my husband will reward you handsomely."

"I hope you don't think we saved you in exchange for a reward," Willa said.

"Not at all. I didn't mean to offend. I merely want to demonstrate my gratitude."

Up ahead, Fox spotted a small hamlet. They had taken a few turns to conceal their path and put some miles between them and the ferry, so he felt they could take a short amount of time to stretch their legs, relieve themselves, and water the horses. Although his braies were still a bit damp, he decided against setting his clothes out to dry in the sun. When Luciana took her turn to seek some privacy, Fox found himself alone with Willa.

Their heart-wrenching discussion in San Giuseppe still hung heavily over both of them, and Fox didn't know what to say. It seemed impossible that it was only yesterday their plans to wed had collapsed and they had decided to part ways.

"I'm sorry that today didn't go as planned," he said finally.

"It's a short diversion," Willa said without looking him in the eye. "We only need to pretend we're married for a little while longer."

"Perhaps we've made the right decision. I was a fool to think that we could marry, and I would just bring you along on my venture."

She flinched, as if hearing the words aloud made the situation real.

"And I should have been there to protect you today against that rider," he continued. "It's not right that you were the one to kill him."

"It was your training that allowed me to defend myself and Signora Corosi."

"But it's *my* responsibility to defend you."

Willa was starting to get irritated. "As if I am helpless?"

"Not at all," Fox said a little too strongly. "I simply want what's best for you. When we left the monastery at San Michele together, I promised to take you under my care as I sought a life worthy of a knight. Then the first time we have to do battle, you are made to draw blood before me."

Willa shook her head and sighed as if she were placating a child, which annoyed Fox in turn. "Perhaps you think you failed me. You didn't. You've made me stronger than I ever could have been on my own."

"It's my duty to protect you. This morning that responsibility was tested, and I was too late to answer the call."

"Because you were off fulfilling your vow as a knight. You were making sure that the villagers were safe. When I agreed to come with you on this journey to explore the world and help people, did you think I was simply going to sit by and watch you perform feats of gallantry while I cheered you on?"

"Not sit by, certainly. You are so clever and resourceful that you contribute in other ways. But not as a fighter. That's my role."

"Would you rather I was dead right now? Because that's what would have happened if you hadn't taught me to use your bow as a mounted archer."

"But I didn't think you'd use that skill to battle murderers."

"I'd use it to hunt rabbits?"

"Exactly."

Disappointment flashed across her face. "I thought you understood me better than that. Perhaps it's for the best that you're taking me back to San Michele."

The statement crushed Fox's heart. "I will regret to my dying day that I have to do that." As he looked at her now, he was trying to imprint her beauty on his memory so that it would be with him always.

An Italian voice interrupted them.

"Is that English you've been speaking?" Luciana asked as she appeared from behind the horses.

Fox broke his gaze from Willa and said, "We're both from Kent in southern England."

"You speak Italian very well for visitors, though your accents can be hard to understand sometimes. You must be blessed with an ability for languages."

"It has aided us in our travels," Willa said, "but we haven't had much time in Italy."

"Well, you are most welcome at my home."

"Is that our destination?" Fox asked.

Luciana nodded. "Villa Ramberti. We should arrive there well before nightfall. Do you mind if I ride on my own for a while?"

"Please, take my horse," Willa said. "I can ride with Gerard."

"Very kind."

As Luciana got onto Comis, Fox mounted Zephyr's saddle. Before he could help Willa up, she stepped into the stirrup and took a seat behind him, her arms clasped around his midsection.

The warmth of her body pressed against him and the smell of her freshly washed hair in his nose were almost too much to bear. He was very sure that she knew the effect her close proximity would have on him.

Fox couldn't help thinking how different things would now be if they had wedded the first time they had attempted it. It made him sad now to think how happy Willa had been that day.

6

TURIN

As she walked beside Gerard in this strange new city, Willa couldn't stop smiling. She had the strong urge to skip along the road from the tavern where they had stayed the night, but it would be unseemly. The sight of the local parish church they were approaching made her stomach flutter.

"Are you all right?" Gerard asked her. "You look like you want to jump out of your skin."

"Nervous, I suppose. I can't believe this is happening. It's all so sudden."

"We can't sleep in the common room at taverns for the rest of our lives. At least, I don't want to."

"Nor do I."

They'd agreed that sleeping in a private room together now that they were intending to wed would present too much of a temptation to break their chastity. Until their union was official, they would sleep with all of the inn's other patrons in the common room.

"I thought you wanted to get married," Gerard said. "Isn't that why you came with me?"

"Please don't tell me that your calm exterior is exactly what you're feeling."

"You mean, are my innards a roiling cauldron threatening to make me sick right here from nervousness?" he said with a smile. "I'll deny it to my last breath."

"I'm glad to know I'm not alone."

They had met in southern England and traveled the length of Europe together in a quest to save a precious relic from falling into the wrong hands. During the journey Willa had come to prize Gerard's kindness, innate nobility, and determination. It was only when they'd agreed that she should stay behind to become a nun at the abbey of San Michele that she'd realized she had fallen in love with him. Nonetheless, she'd turned down his proposal, convinced that she would become a burden to him. But after he left, she felt a hollowness inside her. The idea of living without him was intolerable, and she had changed her mind, riding to join him after all. She'd given up the peace and safety of the abbey to be with the man she loved and to share his adventures wherever he went.

They had departed from San Michele just the day before, and Willa was still afloat on the cloud of euphoria from her decision, but it didn't mean she had no apprehension.

"Do you ever wonder at how we arrived at this day?" she asked. "If you hadn't been on that lonely road in England that morning I rode by, we'd both likely be dead by now instead of getting wed in Italy." Only their chance meeting had kept each of them from falling into the hands of enemies who surely would have killed them.

"I certainly wasn't planning on falling in love."

"And with a lady's maid, at that."

Gerard looked around to make sure no one was within earshot. "And I'd wager that you wouldn't have thought you'd be betrothed to an excommunicated knight."

"We both know that's not the whole story. The Church may have banished you, but it was unjust. You said yourself that according to Church law, an unjust excommunication means you're not really a sinner in the eyes of God, even if you have to obey the law of the Church."

"Which is why I believe we can still be married by a priest. But that wouldn't carry much weight with a bishop, not unless we have proof that the excommunication was unreasonable."

"As far as I'm concerned, what Cardinal Molyneux did to you and your family was wrong and evil. He committed an unspeakable act against your mother and then blatantly lured you into attacking him in front of witnesses. No one who knew the crime he was guilty of would have blamed you for killing him, let alone laying a hand on him."

"Still, we have to stay quiet about it. With Molyneux gone, I don't know how to find anyone to testify to my innocence. I'll have to live out my days with this hanging over me."

Willa didn't like his downcast outlook, but she was sure this resignation was only temporary.

"Someday things will change," she said with determination. "I have faith. And I will be at your side as your wife when that happens."

He smiled at her. "And I will be your husband."

"It makes me giddy to think about actually being able to call myself Lady Fox. Just a few months ago, that idea would have been as ridiculous as the thought of sprouting wings."

Gerard opened the church's door for her. "Get ready to fly, my lady."

The priest was sweeping the floor around the altar as they walked up the narrow nave. Not much older than Gerard, with wavy hair and a round face, he looked up and regarded them with curiosity.

"*Posso aiutarvi?*" he said.

Having absorbed some of the local language since arriving in the region, Willa knew that meant, *Can I help you?* Both she and Gerard were learning Italian quickly, but as of now their use of it was too limited for this discussion.

Gerard asked if the priest spoke French or English. He shook his head. Then Gerard switched to Latin, a tongue the priest would surely know.

"*Inquirere volumus de matrimonio.*"

To Willa's ear, the pronunciation sounded quite like Italian.

"You want to ask about a marriage?" the priest repeated back. "Whose marriage?"

"Ours."

The priest broke into a smile. "Of course! That is one of my favorite tasks. That and baptism. It always thrills me to preside over such joyous occasions. My name is Father Aldo."

"I am Gerard and this is my betrothed Willa." They had decided that commoners would get far less scrutiny than members of the nobility, so he refrained from sharing his last name and title.

"A pleasure to meet you." Father Aldo frowned. "But where is Signorina Willa's father?"

"That's a sad tale," Gerard said. He went into the story they'd prepared. "Both of our parents died during pilgrimage to the Holy Land. We want to complete the journey that they started, but it would be unseemly for us to travel alone without being husband and wife. We were hoping to marry here."

"I would usually need permission from the maiden's guardian, but I understand your unusual circumstances, so I'll help you. Where are you from?"

"England."

Father Aldo looked at Willa. "And you are willing to marry this man of your own free will?"

"Very much so," Willa replied.

"Then it is a simple matter of posting the banns for the next three Sundays and performing the ceremony then."

The traditional posting of their names for all to see would invite scrutiny neither of them desired.

"Father, must we do the traditional posting of the banns?" Gerard asked. "We'd appreciate you performing our nuptials as soon as possible."

"We're eager to continue on our travels," Willa added. "I hope you understand."

The priest looked from Willa to Gerard with a disturbed expression.

"Even if I agreed to do such a thing, my bishop would find out what I'd done when I added your names to the diocese's marriage rolls."

"Perhaps you don't need to do that, either," Gerard said. "We'd be happy to make a substantial donation to your parish."

They still had a good sum of gold gifted to Gerard by the king of France for winning a duel during their travels from England.

Father Aldo gave Gerard a cold stare. "Are you attempting to bribe me, signore?"

"Not at all. I think my Latin is a bit out of practice."

"Is this lady with child?"

Willa gaped and raised her voice in outrage. "What are you implying, Father? I'm offended by your suggestion."

Father Aldo was rocked back on his heels. "My apologies, signorina. That was not my intent."

She regarded him for a moment before relenting. "Your apology is accepted."

"I suppose we will have to think about our options," Gerard said. "I thank you for your consideration."

Willa realized that they needed to get away as quickly as possible, but as they turned to leave, the priest seemed to soften.

"It's just as well," he said. "Why would you want to wed in a large city like Turin when a small village might be more suitable for your needs?"

"You make a good point," Gerard said.

"Thank you, Father," Willa said.

"Go with God, my children."

As soon as they were out the door, Gerard said, "I thought his eyes were going to pop out of his head when you shouted at him."

"What else could I do?"

"Oh, I enjoyed it. But now we have a problem. Word may spread amongst the city's clergy about two English people trying to get married quickly."

"True. I don't want to spend my honeymoon getting burned at the stake."

Gerard gave her a quizzical look. "You're not the one who is excommunicated."

"My dear betrothed, hasn't it occurred to you that the moment we are married, I will become just as much of a heretic as you?"

A dawning recognition tinged with horror crossed his face. "I confess it didn't. I can take you back to San Michele right now."

Willa shook her head. "Unlike you, I considered that thought before I left the abbey. We'll both be courting the same risk, but I go into it knowing the danger I'm agreeing to."

"Are you certain?"

She smiled at him. "How many times do I have to make you take yes for an answer? I want to face fate by your side, together."

They were alone on the street, so Gerard took her hand as they walked. "I only hope you know what you're getting into. But if you're sure, then we will have to put some distance between us and Turin to find the type of village that Father Aldo suggested. You know what that means."

Willa nodded. "More nights listening to the snores of strangers sleeping next to me in public houses."

"Or even worse, we'll have to listen to the grunting of those making babies in the dark around us. I dread waiting even longer until we are married."

"We spent two months on the road like that getting here," Willa said with a wink. "What's a few more days?"

"I tell you what it will be," Gerard said. "Torture."

7

October, 1351

TUSCANY

By the time Willa, Gerard, and Luciana arrived at Villa Ramberti, the sun was low over the western hills. The lush rolling terrain dotted with outcroppings of rock seemed so peaceful that it was hard for Willa to believe they'd been running for their lives just that morning.

Unlike the moated manors she was familiar with in England and France, the grand Ramberti estate consisted of two long buildings connected by stout walls, all made of fine Tuscan stone and topped with red tile roofs. A tower jutted from the larger of the two buildings to give watchers an expansive view of the valleys around it.

Willa had heard that during the Great Mortality, wealthy Italians had retreated to their country villas to escape the disease engulfing the cities. By the time the Pestilence had reached England, there had been a sense of dread at its coming, but at least they knew something about it by then. She couldn't imagine what it had been like here, where everyone was completely unprepared for its arrival. On their journey Luciana had told them of the death of her son, Tommaso, who hadn't been able to join his parents at the villa in time to escape the Pestilence, and Willa shared her own tale of grief in losing her parents at a young age.

Together they rode through the front gate into the courtyard that extended the length of the villa. They dismounted and were met by grooms who took the horses to the stable, past chickens and goats that mingled with the servants tending to the estate. Willa and Gerard collected their belongings before Zephyr and Comis were led away, although Gerard reluctantly left his sword and bow with Zephyr. Visitors didn't carry weapons into their host's home.

"Welcome to my humble villa," Luciana said. "You will be my guests as long as you care to."

"We don't want to impose on you," Willa said.

"Don't be ridiculous. You saved my life. You can stay here for the next year if you like."

She pointed at the two-story building without the tower and told them that was where the great hall was located, above the stable and kitchen. The building opposite had two external staircases, a wide one under the tower and a narrower one at the other end.

"Your quarters are up those stairs," Luciana said, indicating the narrow staircase. "My steward Diego will show you the way. Where is he?"

As she spoke, a man dressed in a well-made knee-length tunic came out of the residence in an agitated state, followed closely by an older man in a fine wool cotte, who stopped and stared at the three of them in shock.

He quickly collected himself and hurried down the stairs, all the while looking with suspicion at Willa and Gerard. He swept across to Luciana and took her hands.

"My dear, you look like something awful has happened. Are you all right? Where are Umberto and his men?"

Luciana had to gather herself before speaking, with tears pricking her eyes. "They're dead. All of them. Oh, Riccardo, it was horrid. Robbers attacked us in San Giuseppe just as we were concluding our business." She handed him the signed contract. "It was an ambush signaled by the wagon driver Elio. Soldiers in full armor were waiting for us to arrive."

"I knew I shouldn't have trusted Barbieri."

"Piero Barbieri is dead, as are all of his men. We think Umberto died, too."

"You think?"

"We didn't see it happen."

"Then he could be the one responsible," Corosi said.

"I don't want to believe that. It makes no sense."

"And the gold? They got away with it?"

Luciana nodded. "There was nothing we could do."

"Then there's your sense." Corosi's face clouded in anger before registering relief. "I'm just pleased that you're not counted among the dead as well." He turned to his visitors. "And who are these people?"

"Sir Gerard Fox and his wife Lady Willa Fox are the reason I stand before you now. They saved my life."

"Then my utmost gratitude is due to you both. I am Riccardo Corosi."

"A pleasure," Gerard said. "Your wife showed a great amount of courage today."

"As did Lady Fox," Luciana said. "I've never known a woman with such skill as an archer."

Corosi looked at Willa with curiosity. "Is that so?"

"I was fortunate to be able to help," Willa said, giving a quick glance to Gerard.

"I'm sure." Corosi turned back to Luciana. "And your lady's maid?"

"Sofia's horse panicked after I fell from mine. It took off and we haven't seen her since."

Willa had noticed Sofia's flight and thought that it had seemed more purposeful than panicked. But perhaps the maid was ashamed at her cowardice and was delaying her return, so Willa said nothing.

"I fear the worst," Luciana said. "I had hoped she would be here."

"I'm sure she was simply frightened by the battle. Not all women can be as fearless as Lady Fox seems to be. You must tell me everything."

Luciana looked down at her soiled clothes. "Not in this state. I need to change into clean clothes. I'll tell you the entire tale at supper. Diego, since Sofia is still missing, would you please send one of the other maidservants to help me dress?"

Since Willa used to be a lady's maid herself, she knew well that such a servant was more than just an aide. She would also have served as a confidante, friend, and even a confessor. For Sofia to abandon her mistress was unthinkable to Willa, who would never have left her lady's side in a time of need, no matter the danger.

"Signora Corosi, perhaps I can assist you," she said.

Luciana looked at her with surprise. "I couldn't ask a noble lady to help me with such a mundane task."

"Given the unusual situation, I would be happy to step in to help. Besides, you have a nasty injury to your head that needs tending." She told Diego the ingredients she'd need for a poultice.

"A healer as well?" Corosi said. "You're a woman of many talents."

"Thank you, Lady Fox," Luciana said. "Since you are offering so freely, I welcome your company. Sir Gerard, Diego will show you the way to your quarters."

"I didn't hear them mention your contributions to the rescue, Sir Gerard," Corosi prompted as Willa and Gerard handed their belongings to Diego.

"I didn't do much except take a nice swim."

"That's not true at all," Luciana said. "Sir Gerard enabled us to escape by successfully fighting off a man clad in full armor. It was quite impressive."

"It sounds like you two make a remarkable couple," Corosi said. Although his tone was gracious, Willa noted that the wariness never left his eyes. "I'm eager to hear more at our meal."

Corosi went off toward the main hall while Fox was led by Diego to the far staircase. Luciana took Willa's hand as they walked up the wide stairs under the tower.

When they reached her chambers, Luciana went to a large chest, took out a scarlet kirtle, and laid it on the bed's feather mattress. The curtains that would keep the heat in at night were drawn aside in their day position. Willa looked at the bed longingly, having never slept on a such a luxurious one herself. She'd gotten used to lying down for the night on the floor atop rushes or even on the bare ground as she and Gerard traveled. Having a bed would certainly be one advantage of living in a home instead of being constantly on the move.

"Before you change," Willa said, "let me look at your head."

"It's fine," Luciana said, waving her off.

"It's not. I can see blood on your veil."

Willa removed the covering from Luciana's hair and inspected the wound. It wasn't very deep, but the abrasion was atop a nasty bump.

A knock at the door announced a girl bringing the herbs, bowl, pestle, and cloth Willa had requested. Willa asked her to lay a fire as she saw the enormity of events settle in on Luciana now that she was safely home. Willa mixed the ingredients and soaked the cloth with it before pressing it against Luciana's injury.

"That smells of honey," Luciana said.

"Among other things. It's a recipe I learned in Avignon. It will ease your pain and heal your wound more quickly."

A brown and tan cat hopped onto the windowsill, startling Willa. Since cats were usually only allowed to roam the kitchen and other areas where rodents were a nuisance, it was a surprise to see the sleepy-looking animal jump down onto the floor and curl up next to the fireplace as if it had received an invitation.

"That old thing has been coming in here for so long that I can't remember when I first saw it," Luciana said. "Most people shoo it away, but I like the company."

"You have a beautiful home," Willa said as she untied the laces on Luciana's kirtle.

"Unfortunately, I don't get to see it very often. Most of my time is spent in Florence."

"Is that where you are from?"

"I'm originally from Siena. I still miss it." With laces loosed, Luciana removed the poultice from her head and pulled out a piece of paper that had been hidden in the breast of her kirtle. "Lady Fox, there's actually another reason that I accepted your offer to come to my chambers. Your husband said you are going to Turin. Will you be traveling through Florence on your way?"

Not wanting to reveal why she and Gerard were returning to Turin, Willa added to the fable about their travels. "It's one of the stops on our pilgrimage."

"Today I received a very important letter. I'm going to copy it and I want to give that duplicate to you. If you would be willing, when you are in Florence, I'd like you to give it to Count Ettore Russo. I was close friends with his late wife Francesca, so I believe he'll do me this favor. He is to send it on to a man named Giovanni in Venice."

"Why?"

"I can't tell you that. All I can say is that my life depends on it. You've saved me once today. Delivering this letter to Giovanni might save me again. I know it's much to ask from a stranger, but will you do this for me?"

"Does your husband…"

"My husband can't know about this," Luciana blurted. "Please. Umberto was going to carry it for me, but he's gone. Even if Sofia were here, she'd be coming with us to Siena in a few days, and I don't want to wait until we return to Florence. I need to send this letter right away. You're the only person I can trust with this task."

Willa saw her pleading look and nodded. "I'll take it to Count Russo. How will I find him?"

"Thank you, Lady Fox. I'll tell you everything you'll need to know when I give you the copy."

Willa turned to go and saw a beautiful young woman her own age standing in the doorway.

"Sofia," Luciana said in shock.

Sofia rushed to her lady and embraced her, sobbing, "Signora, I was so worried about you."

"I'm all right, child." Luciana held her at arm's length. "Are you well?"

Sofia cast her gaze at the floor and spoke so fast that Willa could barely make out her words. "I'm ashamed for failing you, signora. My horse went into a frenzy at the fighting and took off after yours. By the time I could stop and return, you were gone, so I fled south before those robbers could pursue me. That's why it took me so long to get back to the villa." She collapsed to her knees in tears. "Can you ever forgive me?"

Luciana pulled Sofia to her feet. "My girl, you did everything you could. Lady Fox came to my aid, and as you can see I'm fine except for a few bumps and bruises."

"I swear that I will never let you down again, signora."

"I'm sure you won't. You've been a faithful servant for these last three years through some of my most trying times. I'm glad you made it out of that ambush safely."

Sofia dried her tears with a kerchief. "Thank you, signora. You are too kind. Can I help you change?"

Luciana looked at Willa. "I'm in good hands now, Lady Fox. I appreciate everything you've done for me. I will find you after supper."

"Of course, Signora Corosi. It's been my pleasure."

Sofia took Willa's hands. "You can't know what it means to me that you saved my mistress."

"I only did what I'd want someone else to do for me."

That comment elicited a strained response from Sofia, whose lips tightened at the implication that she'd been derelict in her duty, causing Willa to wonder if she was being too harsh. Not every lady's maid had gone through the perils and ordeals that she herself had already survived. If Luciana could forgive Sofia, then Willa ought to be able to overlook her faults as well.

Willa left the two of them alone to find Gerard. She was directed to a sumptuous chamber with its very own feather bed. Gerard had taken off his tunic and was washing his face from a pewter basin.

"Don't worry," he said, nodding to the bed. "I'll sleep on the floor. How is Signora Corosi?"

Willa thought she detected more than simple concern for their hostess. His mother Emmeline had been cruelly taken from Gerard when he was only a child, and the loss weighed on him to this day. Emmeline would have been just about Luciana's age had she survived.

"She's better now that her maid has returned." Willa took a seat on the bed and nearly melted into its comforting softness.

"At least that's one bright spot of news for her today."

"I don't know what to make of her."

"The lady or the maid?"

"The lady. The maid seems a coward, but Signora Corosi is attached to her." Then she told him about Luciana's curious request.

"We can certainly take the letter with us, but this entire business has been odd. Something is off about Signore Corosi as well."

"Such as?"

"I can't put my finger on it. Something strange is happening in this household. Perhaps the signore and signora are keeping things from each other."

"I wonder if they suspect that we're keeping secrets from them as well," Willa said.

"My aunt Rosamund always said that everyone has secrets."

"That must be true, since this is the first I've heard you mention an aunt Rosamund."

"My father's sister. She helped raise me after my mother disappeared. She had a strong wit, a sharp tongue, and no respect for men who treated women poorly. You would have liked her."

"I'm sure I would have. She sounds like my own mother— always respectful to her lady, but with a fiery streak when she saw anyone in the household mistreated."

"I'm sure that got her in trouble sometimes."

"Now you know why I'm trouble sometimes."

Gerard nodded and chuckled. Willa wondered if this discovery about him helped explain why he wasn't like most men she'd come across, who simply wanted a quiet woman catering to his needs. He had always treated her more as a partner, while still wanting to protect her. Realizing how unusual Gerard was made their impending separation all the more heart-wrenching.

After coming so close to their dream of being wed, saying goodbye to him a second time would be even harder than the first.

 8

During the lavish dinner served in Villa Ramberti's great hall to celebrate Luciana's safe return, Corosi spent most of his time listening. Over pheasant, duck, and pasta with salted olive oil, his wife told the story of the attack, how the gold was spilled in Piero Barbieri's attempt to flee, and the details of their escape across the Arno. She interjected multiple times how grateful she was to her rescuers, and Corosi simply nodded along with a smile.

His guests, who added to the tale only when necessary, seemed curiously unperturbed by the ordeal. He could understand a capable man like Gerard Fox taking the assault in his stride, but he was surprised that Lady Fox was so composed. He would have expected a pretty young thing such as her to be a wreck after defying death so narrowly.

When the dinner was over, Luciana and Lady Fox excused themselves while Corosi adjourned to his solar and asked Fox to join him for a cup of wine. Now that he'd heard about the day's events, he wanted to find out as much as he could about this English knight.

They sat on richly embroidered chairs while Diego poured the wine. Corosi dismissed him with a wave of his hand, and when they were alone, he said, "You're a long way from home."

Fox shrugged. "I'm used to traveling." Although the Englishman was taciturn, Corosi noted that his eyes flashed with intelligence.

"Don't you have a manor to tend back in England?"

"My family had estates in both England and France. But they aren't mine. I'm my father's second son."

Corosi nodded. "A difficult position. Still, I suppose I should be thankful that you inherited nothing. Otherwise, you might not have been here to save Luciana."

"Yes, very fortunate. Willa and I were both glad to be of service."

"Your wife seems quite… unconventional."

"As does yours. That's meant as a compliment."

"Mine as well. But Luciana doesn't have your wife's skill with a bow. Luciana's praise of her technique was rather generous."

"Willa is an accomplished hunter."

"And fighter, it would seem. I'm surprised you would put her in harm's way like that."

The observation seemed to annoy Fox. "I didn't intend for her to be in that position."

"Some of us are simply better at minding our women."

"And I'm surprised someone of your position would entrust Signora Corosi with such a large sum of money."

"I'm a busy man, and Luciana is one of the only people I can trust with that task. My banking operation is vast, and I can't be involved personally with every transaction. Besides, we wanted to keep that meeting secret."

"Someone found out about it. They paid off the wagon driver to signal them. Who do you think would have done such a thing?"

"For that amount of money? My first thought would go to Jacopo Barbieri. He would want to get the gold I paid him without turning over the signed contract."

"But his cousin died. I saw him killed myself. And the attack happened after he handed over the contract. It could have been Umberto."

"True. Luciana said she didn't see him die. I plan to send some men to investigate. If Umberto survived the battle, I will know of it. Then I will spare no expense to hunt him down."

"It's good chance on your part that you received the signed contract. I suppose you expect Signore Barbieri to honor it."

"I had the gold delivered as promised. It's not my fault that Barbieri's men didn't protect it properly."

"That would have been difficult against the forces we were up against."

"We?" Corosi snickered. "Didn't you escape the scene of the battle with your wife and Luciana? Not that I'm impugning your character. From what I heard, you bravely fought their leader for a few moments before jumping into the river."

"I promised Umberto that I would get your wife to safety, and that's what I did."

"Of course. And you say you never got a look at the demon who led this barbaric attack?"

"Only his helmet."

"Can you tell me anything about him that would help me track him down?"

Fox hesitated. "He did say one thing to me."

"What's that?"

"*Ti conosco.*"

"Why would he say he knows you?"

"I don't know. Maybe I met him in Florence or somewhere else in this region without realizing it."

Diego entered and held up one finger, their prearranged signal. Corosi got to his feet, as did Fox.

"If you'll excuse me, Sir Gerard, I have another matter I need to attend to. Please stay as long as you'd like and enjoy the wine. I have it specially imported from one of the best wineries in France."

"It's a fine red indeed, but I will retire to my chambers. Again, I thank you for your hospitality."

"Anything for Luciana's savior. And her husband."

Fox smiled at the slight, but Corosi saw no humor in his eyes.

They parted, and Corosi went down to the stable. Twilight was settling over the courtyard, so he carried a lantern into the darkened stalls.

A single torch waved at the far end of the stable. It bobbed as it approached, and out of the gloom strode a beast that looked as if it emerged from Dante's *Inferno*. The hulking mail-clad figure with a sword hanging at his side carried a second sheathed sword in the hand without the torch. There was no face, just the gleaming silver helmet with brass fangs giving the appearance of a skeletal wolf stalking its prey, only he seemed to be limping, favoring his right leg.

Corosi stepped into his path and looked up at the man who came to a stop and towered over him.

"Where do you think you're going?" Corosi said without fear.

"To kill the owner of this sword. I want him to be holding it when I cut him down."

Corosi guessed it to be Fox's unusual sword that Luciana had described.

"You'll do no such thing in my home. Now take off that helmet."

The man hesitated as if he might defy the order to halt, but Corosi knew the soldier would never disobey him. He had too much at stake.

He threw the sword to the ground in anger and tossed the helmet back so that it hung behind him by the chain linked to his breastplate. Even in the dim light, Corosi could see the clean-shaven face that showed off his strong chin, prominent nose, and angular cheekbones.

His name was Sir Randolf Armstrong, a knight who had left England to make his fortune as a mercenary, and what better place to go than where the money was? Florence, Venice, and Genoa counted as three of the richest cities in Europe, and the antagonism amongst them meant there was a never-ending supply of funds to fight each other over resources.

"Is Umberto dead?" Corosi asked.

Armstrong nodded. "And the wagon driver Elio, just as you ordered."

"And the gold?"

"All accounted for and waiting on the wagon to be brought back here. I thought it better to come by myself first."

"Why didn't you kill my wife?"

"I tried but she got away across the river, and we couldn't follow."

"Because the ferry was disabled?"

"Because I can't swim," Armstrong said. "But I'm not letting someone defeat me and get away with it, especially not a heretic like Gerard Fox."

"So you *do* know Sir Gerard."

"He doesn't own that title anymore. It was stripped from him when he was excommunicated."

Corosi went cold with shock at the knowledge that he had just supped with an excommunicant. After a moment's thought, however, he recognized an opportunity.

"How do you know that?" he asked.

"I think every noble in London at the time went to the trial for him and his father."

"What was he accused of?"

"They attacked a cardinal. Both were found guilty, and their lands and titles were taken. This was right before the Great Mortality. He's the reason I failed to complete my mission today, and now I find him here as a guest in your home. Doesn't it bother you that an excommunicant is staying here?"

"Actually, I find it useful."

"How do you mean?"

"An Englishman conducted the raid on San Giuseppe. After we kill Fox, we'll just blame it on the wrong Englishman. Which means you need to put that sword back."

Armstrong glared at him, then bent down to pick up the weapon. He grimaced in pain as he rose.

"Where are you injured?" Corosi asked.

Armstrong turned and showed him the back of his right leg. His hose had been torn open, and there was a long gash in his calf. Blood still trickled from the wound.

"You're no good to me if that festers. Fox's wife is a healer. We'll have her look at it."

Armstrong grunted. "*Then* can I kill him?"

"My reputation would be in tatters if it were known that I let you murder the man who saved my wife while he was a guest in my villa."

"So you'd rob me of my honor? I have to live with being defied by an enemy of the Church?"

"Your men are nearby?"

Armstrong nodded. "In a local tavern spending their pay on drink and whores."

"Fox and his wife will leave tomorrow. I'll make sure of that. Then you and your men are free to do what you want with them as soon as they cross your path."

"You'll turn your guests out so quickly? What about your wife? Won't she object?"

"She won't be able to," Corosi said. "The poor dear hit her head when she fell off her horse this morning. I'll explain to anyone who asks that her injury was far worse than it first appeared. My beloved wife will go to sleep tonight and never wake up."

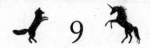 9

Every time Luciana looked at the letter from her father to Matteo, she had to fight back tears. Nearly forty years after she last saw him, it felt like her father was communicating with her across the decades, bringing a swell of emotion to her breast. The seal above his name at the bottom, Domenico Ramberti, as well as the date—February 3, 1314—confirmed Matteo's version of events. Riccardo told her the false story about Matteo two years *before* her father had written this letter. Now she wondered whether she would ever find out what had happened to her father, and why he had never returned to her.

She ran her fingers over Matteo Dazzo's name, and the words brought his image to mind—the excited flush in his face after a successful hunt, that boisterous laugh when he was amused by his own jests, the way he had comforted her after her mother's death. All the love was still there, as fresh as it had been when she was a young woman, tempered now by regret for being a foolish girl back then, gullible enough to fall for Riccardo's deceit. The fact that her entire adult life had been spent with the man who had killed her true love disgusted her.

After they'd wed, her husband had treated her with kindness, almost deference. He grew to trust her with the finances of his bank, leaving all the accounting to her. But over the years, she had seen him become a selfish, greedy man. And then after the death of their son Tommaso, he hardened into a man she could no longer respect. Before she learned of Matteo's letter, she never suspected that Riccardo might have tricked her into marrying him. Now she might be able to rectify the injustice done to Matteo and to her all those years ago.

Her first move had to be to contact Giovanni. Luciana couldn't believe her good luck at finding two such capable and trustworthy people who would be able to deliver her letter. Giovanni would know what to do when he received it. Still, she couldn't give Fox and Willa the original letter. Accidents happened. Things got lost. Robbers could attack the couple on the road and steal their belongings. And she didn't have time to memorize every line. So she sat at her personal desk, transcribing the letter onto a fresh piece of paper.

A similar letter had been delivered to her not long after her marriage when she had just come of age. It even bore the same date. At the time, she had considered it a sacred relic from her father, and she didn't want to share it, even with her husband. Eventually though, she had revealed it to Riccardo when she still trusted him, thinking he might be able to help her discern its clues.

Over decades they had tried to decipher its meaning, but without success. It was only a year ago that Jacopo Barbieri had told her he possessed a letter that Papà had sent to Matteo. Jacopo had quoted the first couplet to her, and she realized it wasn't a duplicate of hers, but a companion. She couldn't solve the puzzles in her letter because her father meant for Luciana and her first love to unravel the clues together.

Reading the first two lines of Matteo's letter sent a chill down her spine.

> *I bequeath to you this challenge that can be solved together with*
> *   faith and ingenuity.*
> *Begin the quest in the city that was nurtured by ferocity and avoids*
> *   shades of gray.*

Luciana's own letter was stored with other important family papers in the solar's lockbox, but she knew every word, having read it over and over. As she thought about the first two lines of her message, it seemed that they were related to the lines in Matteo's clue.

The Templars' noble inheritance will be found only by those worthy of its legacy.

The building that bends to the will of the people provides the starting point.

They both indicated the start of a quest, which led her to believe her father had created clues to find the Templar treasure that could only be solved by the two of them working together. She understood that the separate letters had been a safety measure in case someone had intercepted one of them, and Barbieri's possession of Matteo's letter had proved her father right. If Barbieri had known what the clues could lead to, he never would have turned it over to her. Desperate to have the other half of the puzzle, she had negotiated the business deal between her husband and his despised rival in Siena—Barbieri. Unbeknownst to her husband, she made the letter part of the transaction.

The cat that had been slumbering by the fire jumped onto her desk and sniffed at her cup, and Luciana worried that the animal would knock it over and spill wine across the page. She shooed the cat away, and it left through the window to look for its next meal among the pests in the kitchen.

She wrote quickly but clearly. Giovanni already had a copy of her own letter. Maybe he would be able to decipher this one once he had both in his hands.

She had just finished transcribing the message when there was a knock on her door. She folded up the original parchment and stuck it into the breast of her kirtle to keep it close to her heart. She placed the reproduction under her clothes at the bottom of the chest. She would stamp the copy with her seal so that Giovanni would be sure it came from her.

As she closed the chest, she said, "Come." Sofia entered holding a cup.

"I brought you some warm bone broth, signora," she said. "I think it will calm you for the rest you need."

"That's kind of you, Sofia. Just put it on my table."

Sofia walked over to the table and put it down before opening the chest.

"Would you like to get changed for bed?"

"Not just yet. I have one more thing to do before I lie down."

"Perhaps I can do it for you."

Luciana didn't want to bring Sofia into her plot and endanger her any more than she had already done that morning.

"I can take care of it myself."

"How are you feeling? I heard that you had a nasty injury when you fell."

"Lady Fox treated it with a poultice. My head still aches a bit, but I'm sure it will be gone in a day or two."

"She's done everything I should have done for you." Sofia cast her eyes to the floor. "Signora, I know I let you down today. I can't tell you how sorry I am."

"Nonsense. I couldn't have expected you to face down armored men."

"I just wish I could do something to make it up to you and show you I'm still worthy of your confidence."

Luciana lifted Sofia's chin and looked her in the eye. "I couldn't have gotten through the last few years without you. From supporting me through my sorrow over the Pestilence taking my son to helping me with the accounting, you've always been there for me. Today's events won't change that."

"Thank you, signora. It means so much to me to hear that. I couldn't have asked more from you, even educating me in reading and arithmetic."

For a moment, Luciana considered sharing her plans about freeing herself from Corosi, but then thought better of it. She didn't want to burden the poor girl any further.

"While you're gone," Sofia said, "I'll warm your bed with a pan, and then I'll fetch a fresh shift from the laundry."

"Thank you, Sofia. I hope today wasn't too hard on you."

"It was frightening, but I'll manage."

Luciana left Sofia shoveling hot embers from the fire and went in search of Willa to give her some instructions for tomorrow.

When she arrived at the guest chambers, she found Gerard Fox exiting the room.

"Is Lady Fox in there?"

Fox shook his head. "The steward came by and said that there was an injured man who needed tending in the solar."

"Are you going there now?"

"No, I was just heading to the stable to retrieve something."

"Then I won't keep you."

Luciana made her way down the corridor to the solar and looked through the door to see Willa holding a damp rag and bending over the calf of a knight she knew named Randolf Armstrong, who was sitting on a bench. Riccardo watched from the side with interest.

"I'm sorry," Willa said, "but this will hurt."

"Not as much as it did when I fell from my horse after it was spooked by a snake," Armstrong said. "Landed on my back, right on a root sticking up from the ground."

He grimaced as Willa cleaned the tear in his leg, packed it with the herbal remedy she had made, and bandaged it, but he didn't utter a sound.

When Willa was finished and her patient sat up, Luciana stepped next to Riccardo. "I'm surprised to see Sir Randolf here."

Armstrong had competed wearing the Corosi colors in Siena's Palio horse race for the last three years and won each time. Luciana knew that the Palio was a high point of her husband's calendar, along with the rest of Siena. Virtually every citizen joined in the festivities, as well as the wagering. Riccardo loved lording his wins over the other prominent families of the city, especially Jacopo Barbieri.

"Sir Randolf came to plan our strategy for the Palio this week," Riccardo said. "It looks like you weren't the only one to have a tumble from a saddle today. Sir Randolf, you remember my wife, Luciana."

"A pleasure to see you, signora," Armstrong said.

"I didn't hear your retinue announced, Sir Randolf," Luciana said. "Are you here alone?"

"Once my squires knew I was safely taken in, they went to the nearest town for supplies that they couldn't find here. They'll stay at the tavern there tonight, and I'll meet with them in the morning."

Luciana couldn't imagine what kind of supplies they could need from San Polino that they couldn't find at the villa, but she didn't ask.

"It's fortunate Lady Fox is here," Riccardo said. "His wound was almost as worrisome as the injury to your head. Is Sofia taking care of you?"

"Yes, she brought me some broth and is readying my room for a good night's sleep."

Riccardo studied her so intently that Luciana found it unsettling. Finally, he said, "I wish you would go back to your chambers and rest."

"I will soon. But I have something I would like to say in private to Lady Fox before I do."

"I won't be much longer," Willa said. "I just need to prepare an additional poultice for Sir Randolf to apply tomorrow."

"Then I want you to follow Lady Fox's advice and lie down for the evening," Riccardo said. "You've had a traumatic day. Let Sofia pamper you as she should."

She caught a brief glance between Armstrong and her husband. She didn't understand what it meant, but she suddenly wondered if he knew about the letter nestled in her kirtle. Then she dismissed the thought. If he had so much as an inkling about the danger it contained for him, he would have ripped it away from her already.

10

Willa handed over the cloth holding the poultice and said, "Sir Randolf, fasten this against your leg when you change your bandage tomorrow."

"You've done a fine job," he replied, standing to test his leg. He nodded in appreciation. "You would be a great asset on the battlefield."

"Apparently, she already has been," Corosi said.

"Yes, you mentioned her skill with a bow."

"I saw it myself," Luciana said. "Her accuracy was uncanny."

The praise was making Willa uncomfortable. "I simply did the best I could under the circumstances."

"Your best seems to be quite good indeed," Armstrong said. "I wish the men in my employ were as competent as you are."

"My dear," Luciana said, "may I have that word with Lady Fox?"

"Certainly," Corosi said. "I don't think we need her services any longer, do we, Sir Randolf?"

"I'm sure I'll be back in the saddle tomorrow as good as new."

"I'm only too glad to help," Willa said.

"You've done more than enough today," Luciana said, taking her hand. "Come, I have something for you."

"If it's one of the jewels I gave you," Corosi said, "I don't want to hear of it."

"Don't worry, my darling. This is something just between women."

Before Willa could say anything more, Luciana led her out into the corridor. When they reached the guest quarters, Luciana took her inside and closed the door.

"Lady Fox, I will give you the letter tomorrow as we are saying our goodbyes, but I won't be able to explain everything to you then in front of Riccardo. Do you still feel able to take it to Florence for me?"

"Of course. The one I will be delivering to Count Russo for Giovanni?"

"Yes. It's meant only for Count Russo," Luciana said. "No one else. If you cannot contact him, I want you to burn it."

"Burn it? Are you certain?"

"No one else can even know of its existence. I wish I could tell you more, but it's better for you if you don't know what's contained in the message. I confess that I don't even know if Giovanni will be in Venice when the letter arrives. You'll have to tell the count to have his messenger deliver it to Giovanni's ship."

"Is he a sailor?"

"He's the captain. If it's not at the docks, they might know when it's set to return."

"And what's the ship called?"

Luciana took a breath. "It's the *Cara Signora*. Giovanni will recognize my seal on the letter."

Willa waited for more explanation about Giovanni and his ship called the *Dear Lady*, but none was forthcoming. However, if Luciana had a lover in another city, it was none of her business, though it seemed like a lot of intrigue in service of sending a love note.

Luciana must have sensed a hesitation. "I know I'm asking too much of you, but I wouldn't bother you if I had any other choice."

"Not at all, signora. I will keep it safe and deliver it to Count Russo. I promise you."

"Giovanni may be at sea for months, but I feel hope now that he'll eventually receive it. Thank you, Lady Fox. I will give you the letter when I see you off in the morning. Good evening."

Luciana exited, leaving Willa to ponder what the letter could possibly say. Although she wouldn't dare tamper with the seal to find out, she could at least write down her conjectures. She'd been keeping a journal of her experiences, and this certainly seemed important enough to add.

She took out her quill and ink, then suddenly realized that her journal was still in the solar. She had been referring to it for the poultice recipe while she'd been tending to Armstrong.

Eager to write down her thoughts, she padded back to the room. The door was ajar, and she was about to enter when she heard Armstrong and Corosi speaking Italian in fierce tones. Not wanting to intrude on their business, she decided to wait outside for a lull in the conversation.

"I don't like this," Armstrong said.

"Why not?" Corosi replied.

"Do you think this will really work? She looked fine to me."

It didn't sound like they were speaking of the Palio or banking affairs. Were they talking about her or Luciana?

"Everyone saw what a mess she was when she arrived. That's why I talked so loudly this afternoon about her injury."

"And people will believe she died from it?"

"We've all known people who've succumbed to a head wound. Nobody will know it was Veleno."

"And if this doesn't work?"

"Then I'll send her to Siena ahead of me tomorrow, and she'll have another unfortunate encounter with robbers. This one fatal."

Willa put a hand to her mouth to stifle a gasp. She backed away slowly. She'd be dead for sure if they caught her eavesdropping.

She had to find Gerard and tell him what she'd heard so that they could formulate a plan to protect Luciana from Veleno, whoever he was.

Fox entered the stable with only a rushlight in his hand, the meager illumination casting an eerie glow through the cavernous space. He wouldn't be long. He'd come down to make sure the groom had taken care of Zephyr and Comis properly and dried their saddle blankets. He wanted to be ready to go first thing in the morning.

The stables were empty of people but not quiet. One horse at the back of the stalls whinnied, and that brought a chorus of neighs in answer. The call and response was repeated after a few moments of silence.

He was glad he'd come because he found both of their blankets balled up, which would leave them damp for the next day's ride. Despite Luciana's offer, Fox didn't intend for him and Willa to stay any longer than they had to.

As he put the blankets over the stall walls, he noticed something amiss with Zephyr's saddle, which was on the ground next to him. Fox bent down and saw that Legend was in the wrong place. Before supper, Fox had come in and slid his sword under the saddle to keep it away from prying eyes. But now it lay next to the saddle.

As another back and forth of whinnies echoed through the stable, he picked up his sword and pulled it from its sheath. The blade shimmered in the flickering light. Nothing else seemed out of place, so he put Legend into its scabbard and placed it back underneath his saddle. An over-interested groom, no doubt. If he found it moved again in the morning, he would have words with Corosi about the discipline of his servants.

He rubbed Zephyr's neck and said, "Don't let anyone else touch this." The horse chuffed in response, but he didn't expect Zephyr to cause trouble unless someone besides Fox or Willa tried to saddle him.

Fox inspected Comis as well, and everything here seemed in order. He was about to leave when the horse at the back whinnied again. It sounded as if it were in pain.

Fox walked all the way to the back of the stable and saw a black horse stamping around. It was still wet from a ride, so he guessed it was Armstrong's. The horse was carelessly tied, and the rope had gotten caught on an exposed nail in the wood, so the hemp was cutting into its muzzle uncomfortably.

Fox freed the rope from the nail and the horse instantly went quiet. To keep the nail from causing the same problem after he left, Fox looked around the stall to see if there were something he could use to hammer it back in.

A glint of steel on the floor caught his eye, so he bent down to see if the metal was usable as a tool. It was sticking out from under a cloak. When he got the rushlight closer, he saw that it wasn't a tool at all. The metal was riveted iron rings.

Mail armor. He nudged the cloak aside to see that the rings formed the edge of an entire mail shirt. As he lifted it further, he could see gauntlets and leg greaves as well. It was the suit of a soldier.

He tore the cloak fully away, his heart racing when he saw the final piece of armor.

It was the same helmet he'd faced just inches away at the river, the brass fangs of the polished metal even more grotesque in the dim lighting.

Corosi's guest for the evening was the commander of the marauders. Either the man had concealed his identity or Corosi knew it.

Fox took off at a run to find Willa. No matter the answer, he, Willa, and Luciana were all in grave danger.

11

Willa paced in her room, wondering what to do about the conversation she'd overheard. She didn't know how receptive Luciana would be to learning that her husband was plotting to have someone murder her. If a stranger came to her and told her that Gerard was going to have her killed, she didn't know whether she'd laugh in their face or slap them, but she certainly wouldn't believe them. Even worse, Luciana might take the accusation straight to Corosi, which meant they might not make it out of the villa alive.

The only places Gerard would have gone without telling her were the latrine and the stable. She checked the privy first and didn't find him there, so she hurried outside and down the stairs. Gerard was easing the stable door closed. Willa dashed over to him and spoke barely above a whisper.

"Gerard, I've overheard something awful about Signora Corosi. I think her husband is planning to kill her."

"I was just beginning to think the same thing myself."

Willa was taken aback. She thought she'd have to do at least a little convincing. "You were?"

"After what I've just discovered, it seems fairly clear. That man whose wound you just treated is the commander of the men who attacked us today. He must have been injured in the battle."

"His name is Sir Randolf Armstrong. He claimed to have fallen off his horse."

"He's English?"

Willa nodded.

"Then that explains how he knows me. It also likely means he's aware that I've been excommunicated. Did it seem like he and Corosi know each other?"

Willa nodded. "Very well, apparently. Armstrong seems to have represented Corosi in some kind of race in Siena. But when I overheard them talking privately, they said that someone named Veleno is going to murder Signora Corosi tonight. Why would he kill his own wife?"

"I don't know, but they're obviously trying to complete the job that Armstrong was supposed to do this morning."

"So it wasn't merely a robbery."

Gerard took her elbow and ushered her back up the stairs. "We need to pack up our things and leave right now, before they realize we know of their scheme."

"We can't abandon Signora Corosi."

"We're not going to. You tell her what we've discovered. Convince her that her life is in danger and that she and Sofia need to come with us immediately. While you do that, I'll get our belongings and saddle the horses."

"What if she won't believe me?"

"She has to. If she needs proof, bring her down to the stable and I'll show her the kind of friends her husband makes. But do it quietly. If the alarm is raised, we'll be fighting our way out."

"You don't have your sword."

"I can't risk being seen carrying it around. Corosi has too many guards, and we don't know where Armstrong's men are. Now go. I'll meet you in the stable."

They separated inside, and Willa went directly to Luciana's chambers. She rapped softly on the door as she thought about how to broach such a delicate subject.

When the door opened, Willa went inside quickly without an invitation and closed it behind her.

Luciana looked at her with concern. "Are you all right, my child? You're flushed."

"Signora Corosi, I know I'm a stranger to you, but I have something important to tell you. Perhaps you should sit down."

Luciana hesitated, then took a seat next to her desk, shooing away the cat licking from a wooden cup with a silver rim.

Willa nodded at it. "You might need some wine for what I'm about to tell you."

"It's not wine, it's broth," Luciana said rather impatiently. "Now please tell me why you're here. You look anxious."

"When I went back to get my book, I overheard your husband and Sir Randolf talking. This may be difficult to believe, but they're planning to kill you."

Luciana's face remained impassive, not the shock Willa was expecting.

"Are you certain you heard correctly?" she asked. "Even though your Italian is very good, you're not a native speaker."

"They plan to do it tonight in your own home, and failing that, Signore Corosi will have Sir Randolf and his men kill you when he sends you on your way to Siena tomorrow."

"Sir Randolf is his henchman?"

"You remember the fanged helmet we saw on the commander of the raiders this morning? Gerard just found it in the stable. It belongs to Sir Randolf."

"If what you're saying is true, then it wasn't Umberto who betrayed me this morning, but my own husband?"

"I'm very sorry, Signora Corosi, but we must all flee the villa as soon as possible."

Luciana shook her head and picked up the cup of broth. "I've had my own concerns about Riccardo for some time now, but it's difficult to believe he would actually kill me. You said he plans to do it inside the villa tonight?"

"It sounded like they intend to make it look like you died of the wound you suffered today. Signore Corosi hired someone named Veleno to carry out the murder."

The cup of broth was nearly to Luciana's lips when she froze. Then she slowly lowered the drink and put it back on the table, never taking her eyes off it.

"Are you sure that's the word Riccardo used? Veleno?"

Willa nodded.

"Veleno is not a person," Luciana said.

"Then it must be a word I don't know in Italian," Willa said. "What does it mean?"

"I don't know the word in English or French. It is something put into your food that causes you to die."

Suddenly Willa's stomach went cold. She immediately looked at Luciana's cup.

"Or in your drink. The word in English is 'poison.' Did you drink any of that?"

Willa held her breath as she waited for an answer. Finally, Luciana shook her head. "Not a sip."

"Thank goodness. Who brought it to you?"

"Sofia. Riccardo must have given it to her."

"Are you sure he did?"

Luciana's head whipped around. "Are you saying my own lady's maid put poison in my drink?"

"You believed Sofia fled this morning out of fear. Could she have abandoned you on purpose?"

"You have overstepped your bounds. I may suspect my husband of treachery, but Sofia has been my faithful companion for three years."

"Did you or Signore Corosi bring her into the household?"

"I did. She was the lady's maid of one of my oldest and dearest friends who was taken by the Pestilence. Now I'll hear no more of this."

"My apologies, Signora Corosi. You know her better than I do."

Luciana continued to stare at the cup of broth. "How can we be sure it really does have poison in it?"

Of course, neither of them could taste it for themselves. Then Willa remembered the cat licking at the salty broth.

She turned and saw the cat lying by the fire. Instead of curled up in a ball, it was on its side, its tongue lolling out. Willa went over to it and felt the animal's stomach. It wasn't moving.

"This is how we know," she said. "It's dead."

12

Luciana was holding the cup of broth awaiting Sofia's return with her nightclothes. She didn't believe for a moment that her lady's maid was a willing accomplice to her deceitful husband, but she had to prove Willa's suspicions wrong. The Englishwoman had collected the dead cat and was waiting in the adjacent room, listening at the door.

When Sofia entered, she was so fixated on the clothes she was carrying that she didn't notice Luciana's feigned ill expression until she placed them on the bed.

"Are you feeling well, signora?" Sofia asked with concern. "You look ashen."

Luciana's deception was aided by the shocking recognition that her husband had tried twice to murder her in a single day. If her lady's maid were also involved, the betrayal would be even more devastating.

"I think the fall today may have affected me more than I realized," Luciana said.

"Even more reason for you to have a good night's sleep. When you've changed and finished your broth, I'll leave you to rest."

"Before I undress, would you taste this?" Luciana held out the cup.

Sofia looked puzzled. "Taste the broth?"

"Yes. It has an odd flavor. I don't know if it's only my addled mind or not. I'm curious what new spice they may have been using in the kitchen."

"I can go ask the cook if you like."

"No need to do that if it's just my head injury that's altered my senses."

"Perhaps you need more treatment from Lady Fox," Sofia suggested.

"I don't want to bother her if it's nothing. I need to know if I'm right. Please. Try a sip and tell me the truth."

Sofia frowned at the cup, but Luciana couldn't tell if that was because she feared what was inside or simply because it was a strange request.

Luciana held it out, and Sofia slowly reached for it. As Luciana passed it to her, the wooden cup slipped out of Sofia's hand and dropped to the floor. The broth spilled out across the rug.

"Oh my goodness," Sofia cried out, bending down to mop up the liquid with her apron. "I'm so clumsy, signora. I will have this cleaned up immediately and bring you another cup of broth for us both to try."

The fumbled cup seemed like a genuine accident, but for the first time a seed of doubt was planted in Luciana's mind. Although she desperately wanted her good opinion of Sofia to be proven correct, she had to be sure.

"Did you do that on purpose?" she asked.

Sofia looked up with shock at the accusation. "Of course not, signora. Why would I do such a thing?"

"I'm not certain."

"I swear I will get you a replacement and drink the whole thing if that will convince you that I tell the truth."

Luciana gazed at her for a moment, until Sofia rose with the cup and soiled apron. The girl seemed genuinely aggrieved that her mistress would think her so deceitful.

Normally, she would have had to take Sofia at her word. However, Willa had anticipated this tactic.

"No need for that," Luciana said. "I poured half of the cup into that goblet when I thought I might share it with Lady Fox." She pointed to a pewter chalice on the table. "Drink that. Please."

Sofia cocked her head at Luciana and hesitated before saying, "Of course, signora."

She walked over to the table and picked up the goblet, looking at the broth inside, then at Luciana. She lifted the edge to her mouth and tilted it up slightly. She lowered it again and smacked her lips as if she were savoring it.

"It tastes good to me."

Sofia could have pretended to take in some of the broth. By now Luciana's heart was hammering in her chest.

"Then drink all of it," she said.

Sofia raised the goblet again. But she stopped just before it reached her mouth, and she lowered it. The mask of confusion dropped away. Suddenly her eyes were brimming with tears.

"I'm so sorry, signora," Sofia sobbed, the words coming out in a torrent. "I didn't know what to do. Signore Corosi made me put poison in your drink. He said he'd kill me if I told you about it. I had no choice."

Luciana knew how frightening her husband could be to those in his employ. She opened her arms and beckoned Sofia to her. The maid melted into her embrace and wept uncontrollably.

"My child, you've been through so much today," Luciana cooed in her most comforting voice. "I don't blame you for your weakness."

"You don't know how much I wanted to warn you. I'm so glad you discovered it." She looked up, a sheen of tears on her face. "You didn't drink any of it, did you?"

"No, it's all right. I didn't drink it."

"Thank goodness. How did you know?"

"The cat was lapping at the broth before I could take a sip. The poor thing died as I was about to drink it."

"How fortunate for you. I know you can't forgive me twice in the same day, but please let me go before Signore Corosi punishes me for not carrying out his plan. I will leave the villa at once."

"Where would you go?"

"I don't know, but I can't stay here now."

Luciana held on to her hands. "We'll go together. I can't stay either. Riccardo and Sir Randolf will kill me as soon as they learn I haven't taken the poison."

"You're right, but I have a cousin in Florence. She can hide us until we work out what to do. I'll go get some food for our journey."

Luciana didn't let go of her hands. She simply stared at Sofia. A sickening sensation overtook her at what her pointed comment had revealed.

"What's wrong, signora?" Sofia asked.

"When I said that Sir Randolf would kill me," Luciana said, "you weren't surprised at all. You knew he was the same man who led the attack this morning."

Sofia opened her mouth to protest, but she seemed to know the game was over. She closed it again and shook her head at being caught in her lie. Instead of tears, her eyes were now full of devious intensity.

"That mangy cat. If I'd known how much trouble it would cause, I would have strangled it years ago."

Luciana tightened her grip. "Lady Fox was right not to trust you. You're the one who betrayed me at San Giuseppe."

"The wagon driver was easy to buy. And now he'll never talk."

"If you had any capacity for love, you would never have deceived me."

Sofia sneered at Luciana. "If you only knew the circles of Hell I've journeyed through to be here."

"So you know Dante. Another surprise."

"You have no idea what I'm capable of." Sofia twisted her wrists out of Luciana's hold and stepped back. Luciana advanced on her, but froze when Sofia whipped a small dagger from her sleeve.

"I could kill you now, but that might make it harder for the next Signora Corosi to trust me."

"The next Signora Corosi?"

"He's already got one picked out. I'm leaving now."

"You're not going anywhere."

Sofia continued backing away. "Don't try to stop me."

"I won't. She will."

Luciana looked over the shoulder of her maid, who turned just as Willa swung the fire shovel at her head. The impact made a satisfying thump, and Sofia collapsed to the floor unconscious.

Willa picked up the knife and handed it to Luciana, who seethed with a swirl of emotions ranging from embarrassment and chagrin to rage and hatred at losing the last person in the household she thought she could count on. The dagger weaved back and forth in her fist.

"She would kill me in this situation, wouldn't she?" Luciana said.

"Maybe," Willa replied. "But you're not the same as her."

Luciana paused, then shook her head. "No. I'm not. We'll tie her up."

She took some linens from her clothing chest and gave them to Willa, who began to secure Sofia's wrists and ankles.

"Make sure to put one over her mouth," Luciana said. "We don't want her warning the others until we're long gone."

While Willa tied the knots, Luciana rummaged through the chest looking for the unsealed copy of the letter her father had sent to Matteo.

It wasn't there. She searched twice over, but it was gone.

She stalked over to Sofia, the dagger still in hand. She had a good mind to use it.

"Sofia took the copy of my letter. She must have noticed it when I got it from Piero today and went through my things while I was gone." She searched Sofia but didn't find the letter. "I'm sure Riccardo has it now."

"The letter intended for Giovanni?"

"Yes, but no matter." Luciana patted her breast, and breathed a sigh of relief that she'd kept the original with her. "We have no time for explanations." She started to throw several pieces of clothing into a satchel.

"No," Willa said. "Gerard and I might have an excuse for leaving, but if anyone spots you carrying a traveling bag, it might invite unwanted questions."

"You're right. I can get new clothes." She withdrew a purse from under her mattress. It held twenty gold florins.

When Sofia was fully trussed, Luciana took one last look at her traitorous maid and realized the price of her own gullibility. Now she was about to flee with two strangers from everything she'd known for the last thirty-nine years. Although it should have been a hollow sensation, she felt a new lightness. She now had nothing more to lose.

"Thank you again, Lady Fox."

"Don't do so too early. The safety of the road will be a better place for thanks."

They left her chambers as Sofia began to moan and stir. The two of them were only halfway to the stairs when Luciana heard a voice behind them that caused her and Willa to stop abruptly.

"I'm glad I caught you," Corosi said as they turned around. His hands were behind his back, and even though he was smiling, his words were chilling. "I have something for you."

 13

Willa knew that any suspicion about their plan to escape would cause Corosi to call out his guards immediately. By now, Luciana was supposed to have drunk some of the broth that her husband had sent to kill her.

"Signore Corosi," Willa said, putting her arm around Luciana, "I was just coming to your wife's aid. She told me she isn't feeling well, so it seems my ministrations aren't quite over for the evening."

Corosi seemed worried, though Willa knew it was false. "My dear, is your head wound bothering you?" If Willa hadn't overheard him plotting his wife's death, she would have thought he was genuinely concerned.

She squeezed Luciana's shoulder, prodding her to play along. The Italian noblewoman slumped her shoulders and rubbed her head as she nodded, but not so obviously that it seemed forced.

"It's been hurting more since dinner," Luciana said. "And now my stomach is aching. I appealed to Lady Fox's skills as a healer once again. She was taking me to her room so that she could prepare a remedy for me."

Willa could see that Corosi was so busy struggling to cover his glee at the poison's apparent success that he didn't even question why she wasn't tending to Luciana in her own room.

"Shall I send someone for medicinal herbs?" he asked her.

"Thank you, no," Willa replied. "I have everything I need."

"Except this." Corosi drew her book from behind his back, handing it to her.

"Ah, yes. Of course, I'll require my recipe for the mixture. Thank you for bringing this to me."

"Not at all. After all you've done for my wife and Sir Randolf, I'd like to pay you compensation. Name your price."

Willa bristled at his nonchalant offer, as if money were her sole motivation for assisting them, not to mention insulting someone he thought was a noblewoman by treating her like a worker. No doubt if his wife never woke the next morning, Corosi would blame her medicine for the death and accuse her of murder. In his eyes, she must be playing right into his scheme.

"No payment is necessary," Willa demurred. "Their health is reward enough for me."

"How generous of you. But I wouldn't hear of it. When we meet again in the morning, I'll see that you get everything you deserve."

Corosi was clearly reveling in his cleverness. Thankfully he and his wife slept in separate rooms. Willa enjoyed the thought of him waking to a household missing three of its occupants.

"Riccardo, I really am feeling poorly," Luciana said. "Perhaps you can excuse us. I will see you in the morning."

"Then good night to both of you. Please take care of my wife, Lady Fox."

"I certainly will," she answered.

After Corosi casually strolled away, Willa whispered, "We should go to my room and wait for a short time, just in case he checks on us."

Luciana nodded, and they proceeded arm in arm toward Willa's quarters.

As they walked, the tense encounter reminded Willa of the last time she'd attempted to help a lady flee from a brutal spouse. Isabel had died because Willa had failed to protect her. She would never get over that failure, but now she had a chance to make amends.

Willa vowed to do everything in her power to save Luciana.

Fox had the horses ready, but there was still no sign of Willa and Luciana. He couldn't wait any longer for them. If anyone came into the stable and saw the saddled horses, word would get back to Corosi and Armstrong. Successfully getting through the guarded gate would present its own problems, but first he had to make sure they were set to leave.

He extinguished his rushlight and peered out of the stable door to make sure no one was watching him. The guards at the gate and walls would be looking outward for threats, not inward, but still he had to be careful.

Satisfied that it was clear, he crept out and headed directly across the courtyard to the stairs up to the guest quarters. At the top of the steps he turned the corner, only to be surprised by a man of his height with a clean-shaven face.

The man gave him a polite smile and spoke in English. "You must be Sir Gerard Fox."

Fox kept his limbs loose but prepared for a fight. He maintained an impassive face at seeing this apparent stranger, attempting to avoid a confrontation that would endanger their escape.

"I must be. And you must be Sir Randolf Armstrong whom my wife told me of. I can't imagine that there are too many other Englishmen in this part of Italy, let alone in this one household."

"Your wife did a fine job treating my leg. Please share my thanks with her once again."

"I heard about your fall," Fox said. "That sounded quite painful."

Armstrong narrowed his eyes. "Just a nuisance to be taken care of. It'll be a distant memory in no time."

"Still, it's the kind of thorny problem that could linger if you're not careful."

"I don't let such inconsequential things bother me. Signore Corosi told me that you had your own trouble today. Being forced to run and dive into a river sounds a bit humiliating, but I suppose you had no choice."

"I always have a choice. In this case I chose to protect life rather than take it."

Armstrong nodded. "I know Signore Corosi is grateful for your intervention. It's lucky that two such able people were there to rescue Signora Corosi. Where are you off to next on your pilgrimage?"

"We're not sure. Our destination may be changing."

"I applaud your devotion to God and the Church. Only a true believer would be willing to make such a journey."

It was clear that Armstrong had indeed heard of Fox's past and was trying to goad him. He might have dismissed it as innocent conversation if he had not seen the helmet in the stable.

"Will you be staying here long?" Fox asked. "Perhaps we could share an ale tomorrow before we leave and talk about England. For the last month I've spoken nothing but Italian except with Willa."

"I'm afraid my visit is short," Armstrong said. "I leave in the morning. But if we are headed in the same direction, I would be happy to delay my departure so that we could ride together and trade stories on the road."

"What a splendid idea. I'm intrigued to learn what has brought you here. I'm sure it's quite the tale."

"As yours must be. It's not often I come across a husband and wife traveling alone. You are quite the unusual couple."

"I'll take that as a compliment. But given the recent attack on Signora Corosi, I couldn't ask for better added protection than your presence on the road. Until tomorrow."

Armstrong locked eyes with Fox. "I am genuinely looking forward to it."

Fox turned and walked as casually as he could toward his chamber, fully aware that Armstrong had not moved and was staring at his back. The sensation was unnerving, but Fox could do nothing about it.

Thankfully he found Willa and Luciana already in the room when he arrived.

"We have to go now," he said without fanfare. "I just met Armstrong in the corridor, and he's waiting for any excuse to expose us."

"We had our own fraught conversation with Signore Corosi," Willa said.

"How are we to get out safely?" Luciana asked.

"You're going to order the guards to open the gate for us."

"Don't you think it will be strange for them to see me leave after darkness has already fallen?"

"We can't worry about that," Fox said. "I have the horses ready to go."

"But surely Riccardo and Sir Randolf will come after us. I'm not the rider you both are. They'll run us down."

Willa gave a knowing look at Fox. She understood what he meant about the horses.

"No," she said. "They won't."

14

Before he prepared for bed, Corosi thought he'd check in on Luciana one more time. It had been a difficult decision to get rid of her. Although no longer the infatuated boy he was when they married, he still felt some fondness for Luciana and their shared history. She'd been a loyal wife and mother and was instrumental in his business dealings, but it was more important for him to secure his legacy, and her death would make that possible.

She hadn't looked particularly ill when he saw her in the corridor, so he wanted to see how much of the poison she had drunk. The worst outcome would be that she simply became sick and later recovered, but Sofia had assured him that the monkshood she had added to the broth was sufficiently lethal even if his wife took only a few sips.

Sofia should have stopped by with a report by now, but she had not made an appearance. Since their dalliance had begun, they'd been very careful to hide it from Luciana, lest she lose faith in her confidante.

In fact, if Sofia had been of better birth, she would have made the perfect second wife for him. She was young, beautiful, and could have borne him an heir. In fact, he was surprised she hadn't become heavy with child already, but she claimed to have a method to prevent it, which he didn't ask about.

Nonetheless, a servant was completely unsuitable as a wife, which was why he had tricked Russo into promising his daughter's hand to the man of Corosi's choosing, unaware it would be Corosi himself. Corosi didn't know her, but he assumed she would suit him admirably—young, pretty, and obedient. The important thing was that she came from noble stock, and any son she gave him would be of the highest breeding.

However, he would certainly keep Sofia around. Not only was she surprisingly skilled in bed, she was also as adept with the financial aspects of his business as Luciana was. He was loath to admit it to anyone, but Luciana was one reason his fortunes had prospered so abundantly, and he hoped Sofia would be as useful. Although Corosi was an expert in the machinations of deals, he had no patience for the more mundane functions of the business, and he didn't trust anyone else to manage his funds. And when Luciana had told her of the letter from Matteo a month ago, and she'd passed the information on to him, Sofia had also become his spy.

He would install her as his new wife's maid to keep her close. The only concern now was the trouble he was having in disposing of his current wife.

It pained him more than he thought it would to do away with her, especially now that her death would be within the walls of their home instead of in a far-away village. Still, he had no choice. A man without an heir might as well never have existed.

If Tommaso hadn't died in the Pestilence, things would have been different. His birth decades into their marriage had seemed a godsend. But over the succeeding years, his wife had grown distant from him. And her most recent actions had caused a chasm to open between them.

He knocked on her door. The only answer was loud groaning. Perhaps the poison was doing its work. He steeled himself for whatever state she was in and opened the door.

In the dim light of the fading fire, he couldn't make out her body under the covers. He crept over and realized that the bed was empty.

Then he heard that muffled sound again, as if someone were straining mightily, not the sound he'd expect from a poison victim's death rattle. The noise was coming from the far side of the bed. Did she fall off in her agony?

He circled around and jerked to a stop when he saw Sofia

trussed up, her ankles and wrists bound behind her, strips of linen wrapped around her mouth.

For a moment Corosi was too shocked to move. Sofia's thrashing at seeing him prodded him out of his frozen state. He took out his dagger and slit the linen apart.

"What happened?" he barked as he sawed at the wrist binding. "Where is Luciana?"

"She knows about the poison. She and that witch Willa knocked me down and tied me up."

"Did she drink it?"

"No."

"You didn't tell her about us, did you?"

"Of course not. Don't be foolish."

Sofia often overstepped her place, and he accepted it, but no one called him a fool.

"Watch your tongue."

"I'm sorry, signore. I'll make it up to you later."

"So Fox must know as well by now." His stomach went cold when he remembered the knight's wife accompanying Luciana. "The gate."

He dropped the knife for Sofia to finish cutting her bonds, leaped to his feet, and ran for the door.

"Armstrong!" he yelled as he dashed down the hallway. "Guards!"

There was commotion as his men-at-arms roused. Armstrong charged into the corridor in front of him.

"What's going on?"

"They know!" Corosi shouted without stopping. He exited onto the terrace at the top of the stairs, only to see that the gate was wide open. Luciana was astride her horse at the entrance. She was pointing at the opposite side of the courtyard. The two guards who had been manning the gate were running away from it at her instruction.

"No!" Corosi screamed. "Stop, you idiots!"

The guards were already halfway across the courtyard, but they halted when they heard their master's voice.

"Close that gate! Now!"

They looked at him in confusion. She'd obviously told them that she was conveying commands from Corosi himself, who was now countermanding them.

Armstrong came to a stop next to him, followed by Sofia. Luciana looked up at them, but she said nothing, only fixing her husband with a deadly glare of fury and hurt. All his earlier regret had been replaced by anger.

The guards finally took his orders and sprinted back toward the open gate. By now, the other guards were spilling out onto the battlements as they'd been trained, not into the courtyard.

"You men get down there now!" Corosi yelled, but the utter chaos was masking his voice.

"Where is Fox?" Armstrong asked. "His chamber is empty."

The stable doors burst open as if in response. Willa galloped out on her horse, a rope in her hand, leading a trail of all of the other stabled horses behind her. The guards who'd been running back to the gate dived out of the way.

Willa led the herd rushing through the gate, and Luciana kicked her horse to follow them.

Fox was last out of the stable, a sword in his hand to fight off any would-be pursuers. He stopped in the courtyard momentarily when he saw Armstrong at the top of the steps. He raised his sword and shouted, "Goodbye, Sir Randolf." Then he tossed Armstrong's helmet onto the ground and charged through the gate.

The guards from the wall finally reached the courtyard, but it was too late. Luciana, Fox, and Willa were gone.

"I assume that was all of the horses," Armstrong said.

"Yes, it was all the horses!" Corosi shrieked, stalking around the terrace and pulling at his hair. This day was supposed to be the beginning of his new life, but it had turned into a complete debacle.

And it was all because Fox and his wife happened to be in San Giuseppe that morning.

"I swear to God and everything holy that I will kill those two!"

"I'll help you," Armstrong said, his voice low and burning.

"My love," Sofia said, caressing Corosi's shoulder to calm him. "All is not lost."

He whirled on her. "How can you say that? All of our plans are for naught. Months of planning undone by a chance encounter."

"Because they didn't find where I kept this." Sofia held up a piece of folded paper. "It holds the clues to finding the treasure you've been searching for all these years."

He snatched the page out of her hand and opened it. He felt his temper cool as he read it and recognized that it was similar in structure to the letter from Ramberti to Luciana that he'd safely locked up long ago. No wonder she had risked everything to get this new one by proposing the San Giuseppe deal. He had always known Ramberti had succeeded in hiding the treasure—that much was evident from Luciana's letter. But decades had passed without him being able to solve the clues. With this letter from Ramberti to Matteo, he finally had the way to find the Templar treasure and secure his future.

But none of it meant anything if he couldn't remarry legally and sire a rightful heir. Now he had all the more reason to track down Luciana and kill her, even if he had to do it himself.

 15

Luciana had them release the horses a few miles south of the villa, sending them into a meadow where they would be free to graze until they were found. She felt she would be safer in her hometown of Siena than in Florence, so they continued in that direction. They rode mostly in silence. Luciana noticed the tension between her travel companions, but they said nothing. The day's events had been exhausting for all of them, especially Luciana. Despite her protestations that she could go on, Willa finally convinced Gerard to stop at an isolated forest glade so they could rest for the remainder of the night.

Luciana had never slept outdoors in her life, but she lay down without complaint by the fire. She was tired enough to go to sleep the moment her head came to rest.

When the dawning sun peeked through the leaves the next day, Luciana stirred to find Willa already awake and stoking the fire. The horses were still tied to their trees, but Gerard was gone, along with his bow.

"Are you feeling well, Signora Corosi?" Willa asked.

"Considering that I found out my husband wants me dead," Luciana replied, "I feel somewhat overwhelmed."

"As you have every right to."

Luciana sat up and fought back the tears in her eyes. "Pardon me, Lady Fox. If it weren't for you and Sir Gerard, I would be a victim of Riccardo's scheme to kill me. I suppose I should be grateful just to be alive."

Willa took a seat beside her and put her arm around Luciana's shoulder. "If you want to scream and cry and shout at the sky, I don't think the horses will mind."

Luciana cleared her throat and collected herself. "I lost a son to the Pestilence. My days of crying are over. Besides, Riccardo hasn't defeated me yet. I still have something to fight for."

"Where can we take you?"

"Lady Fox, you and Sir Gerard have done more than enough. I can't ask you to continue to put your lives at risk for me."

"Nonsense," Fox said as he emerged from the trees, two slain ducks in hand. "We're not going to abandon you to a dishonorable and cowardly man who would poison his own wife."

Luciana shook her head. "I just met you yesterday. Why are you protecting me like this?"

"Was it only yesterday?" He sat down and began plucking feathers from one of the ducks. "You remind me of someone. And it's only right to help you."

"We both feel that way," Willa added as she took the other duck from him. "And I think you should call us Gerard and Willa. Formality under these circumstances seems absurd."

"I agree, and you shall call me Luciana. I don't want to hear myself referred to by that man's name anymore. I ought to tell you what this is all about. Why I'm at war with my husband."

She drew the letter from her kirtle and opened it.

"This is the original copy of the letter that I was hoping you would take to Florence. It was sent by my father to my first love, Matteo Dazzo, nearly forty years ago. Matteo was the cousin of Jacopo Barbieri's wife, who died recently. Jacopo found the letter amongst her things. He may act like my friend, but he is a businessman first. He would only give it to me after I agreed to facilitate the deal I had been in San Giuseppe to complete. Riccardo wouldn't have anything to do with Matteo's family and he absolutely hates Jacopo, so it took a fair amount of convincing him that it would be to his advantage to buy Jacopo's branch in Florence. Only his greed finally made me able to overcome his qualms."

Willa eyed the letter curiously. "Why didn't Signore Barbieri's wife give it to you before then?"

"She always held a grudge against me for what happened to

Matteo." Luciana sighed. "For what I did to Matteo. But the whole story started even before that. The first thing you should know is that my father was a Knight Templar."

Fox's jaw dropped open at that. "I didn't think I'd ever meet someone who knew a Templar, and now I'm in the presence of the daughter of one. But wait, how can that be? Templars are celibate."

"He only took the vows after my mother died. Before joining, he assured my dowry and then was never supposed to see me again, but he broke the rules and visited me when he was in Italy. He was so valuable to the Templars that they turned a blind eye."

"What did he do for the Templars?"

"Do you know their story?"

"I do. I'm not sure Willa does."

"I know they were heretics who were burned at the stake and disbanded on the pope's orders," Willa said.

"That's what everyone has been told, but that's not the real story. The Templars were one of the wealthiest organizations in history. I don't know if even the Church itself was as rich as they were. My father rose quickly in the order's ranks, eventually being put in charge of the Paris Temple, which also doubled as the royal treasury where the Kings of France put their funds for safekeeping. The Templars' downfall came when Philip IV borrowed an extravagant loan from the Templars and either couldn't or didn't want to pay it back, so he concocted all sorts of false charges against them, things I know my father would never do."

"Such as what?" Willa asked.

"As I recall," Fox said, "the accusations included spitting on the cross during the initiation, worshiping idols, and denying the sacraments."

"All of which were ridiculous lies," Luciana said. "It was said that the final grand master of the Templars cursed the French king and Pope Clement while he was burned at the stake. The king and the pope both died within a year of that curse, but by then, it was far too late for my poor father and his brothers in the order."

"Was your father taken during the mass arrest?"

She shook her head. "Thankfully, Papà escaped King Philip's soldiers. He was in Italy at the time, so he was able to flee with his two squires. One of them was Riccardo. The other was Matteo."

Willa saw the implication straight away. "And both of them were in love with you, I'm sure."

"You know men well. The fact is that I found each of them charming and handsome, but it was Matteo who truly had my heart. I believe Papà favored him as well. Matteo told me that my father's preference drove Riccardo to a fit of jealousy. He came to hate my father and eventually betrayed the order."

"When did you learn of all this?" Fox asked.

"Thirty-nine years ago, Matteo returned to Siena without Papà or Riccardo. He told me that Riccardo had made a deal with the king of France to provide evidence against the Templars."

"Did you believe him?" Willa said.

"Of course, but then Riccardo arrived soon after. He had a letter from my father himself saying that it was Matteo who had betrayed the order. The news crushed me. Not only because my father had been deceived, but also because it had been done by the man I loved."

"What happened to Matteo?"

"Riccardo killed him in a duel that very day. I was devastated to lose Matteo, but at the same time I was glad that my father's betrayer had received justice. I was very young, and I believed the note that Riccardo had brought from my father saying that we should wed. It seemed that God had sided with Riccardo during the duel, so I married him. It was only when I saw the date on my father's letter to Matteo that I realized the note implicating Matteo must have been forged. And I never saw my dear papà again."

"What does the letter from your father to Matteo have to do with all this?" Fox asked.

Luciana took a deep breath. "About two years after I had married, I received a cryptic letter from my father. It had nothing personal in it, just five couplets. It seemed to be a series of clues, but I couldn't decipher them."

"Clues to what?"

"I suspected that it was a guide to find the riches accumulated by the Templars. Because of my father's position at the French treasury and the fact that he was the grand master's favorite disciple, I know that he would have been tasked with the mission to hide their wealth from the king when they were being persecuted."

Fox and Willa looked at each other, unsuccessfully trying to conceal their skepticism of her tale.

"Are you claiming you have a way to find the Templar treasure?" Willa asked. "Even I have heard of that legend."

"It's not a legend. The letter my father sent shows me it's real. I just couldn't solve his clues, and neither could Riccardo. Riccardo keeps the original locked up in his solar, but I read it so many times that I've memorized the words."

"Then what is the significance of the one to Matteo?" Fox asked.

"It has a similar structure but completely different clues from mine. I believe both are necessary to solve the puzzle. It was only yesterday when we got back to the villa and I read it that I was sure Riccardo had been lying to me all of these years. My father intended for me and Matteo to find it, not me and Riccardo."

"But if your father thought you would be with Matteo, why would he send two different letters to two places?"

"I think my father was afraid a single letter might be intercepted and used to find the treasure. Two different but complementary letters would reduce that possibility. When he sent them, my father had no way of knowing that Matteo was dead."

Willa gave her a sorrowful look. "That's so sad that you were never able to go on that quest with him."

"I regret it with all my heart," Luciana said heavily. "Riccardo didn't just rob me of my father's last wish, he stole my true love from me."

16

Thirty-nine years ago—March, 1312

VILLA RAMBERTI, TUSCANY

Luciana fidgeted with the buttons on the sleeves of her kirtle while she waited in the villa's courtyard next to her infirm uncle Silvio, who served as her guardian. He leaned on a cane and wheezed at regular intervals.

"Stop fussing, girl," he said.

"Do I look presentable?"

"He's seen you before."

Luciana could feel her cheeks flush red at that, but Silvio didn't seem to notice. Her mother's much older brother had looked after her ever since her father became a Knight Templar and left the estate to her as a dowry. His vows required him to give up all earthly ties with women, but the Templars looked the other way during his frequent visits back to Siena and her occasional travels with her father and his two squires.

"This isn't any typical day, Uncle Silvio. My betrothed is about to leave so he can post the banns for our wedding."

Silvio shook his head in exasperation. "Are you worried he won't post them if you have a spot on your kirtle?"

"A girl wants to look her best."

"Matteo is a fine man. He wouldn't take back the proposal even if you were covered in mud."

Her breath caught when the stable door opened. Matteo led his horse out with a confident strut and a broad smile. The sight of his long strides and luxurious black hair caused her to flush anew. She had already been attracted to him when he'd been a boyish squire under her father's tutelage. Now that he was a man, the beauty of his dark brows, slate-gray eyes, and cleft chin was absolutely dazzling in the morning sun, but it was the memory of his soft lips on hers that she couldn't forget. Thankfully, that was one part of her relationship her elderly uncle didn't know about. These past weeks since Matteo had returned from France felt like a lovely dream.

He didn't take his eyes off her as he came to a stop in front of them. He took her hand in his and kissed it lightly.

"You look ravishing today, signorina."

Luciana thought her knees would buckle.

"That's enough of that," Silvio admonished when Matteo's hand lingered too long on hers. "You're not married yet."

"We will be in three weeks," Matteo said as he let go. "Once I have the priest post the banns."

"A long time to wait," Luciana said.

"I don't think either of us likes waiting."

He winked at her and laughed, causing Luciana to blush again.

"What is so funny?" Silvio asked.

Matteo gave a lighthearted shrug. "Me."

That made Luciana laugh.

"The only thing that could make this day better is if my father were here," she said with a melancholy smile.

"I promise that once we are married, I will make it my mission to bring Sir Domenico back to you."

Matteo's loyalty to her father made Luciana love him all the more. She longed to give him a kiss, but Silvio's stern gaze kept her feet firmly in place.

With a fluid grace, Matteo swept onto his horse. After a bow and flourish of his hand, he raced through the open villa gate.

Luciana sighed heavily. "I wonder where my father is."

"It sounds as if he may not return for a long time," Silvio said.

She was glad he didn't add: "...if ever."

"Even if he can't be at my wedding in person, I know he'll be there in spirit."

"I'm sure that's true."

A call came from the guard atop the wall.

"Rider approaching!"

Silvio frowned at Luciana. People went in and out of the villa all day long, all of them known to the guards. It had to be a stranger.

Luciana followed Silvio to the gate as the guards stepped into the breach and wielded their halberds to stop the man. He dismounted and walked toward them with his hood drawn over his face.

"Stop there!" one of the guards commanded.

The stranger halted and threw back his hood. Luciana gasped when she saw who it was.

"Riccardo," she said in disbelief.

A year older than Matteo, he didn't strut, but rather glided toward them. Riccardo had also grown into a handsome man, but not dashing like his former friend. He had a more noble bearing, with an aquiline nose, sharp cheekbones, and a pointed chin.

"I thought Matteo said he was dead," Silvio said.

"Even if he was mistaken in that, given all the other things Matteo told me about him, I can't believe he dares to appear at the Ramberti gate." She called out to him, "Slither back into the hole you came from, you snake!"

Riccardo spread his arms in a gesture of peace. "I know that Matteo has been staying here. That's why I've come. To expose his lies. To save you from him."

"He told me you betrayed everything my father stood for. He told me who you really are."

"All said in bad faith. I'm here to reveal the truth and recover my good name."

"How can I believe you?"

"How can you believe *him*?"

"He delivered the words of my father. Things only my father would say to me."

"A clever ruse," Riccardo said. "I have proof of Matteo's deception."

"What proof?" Silvio asked.

"A personal note from Sir Domenico Ramberti to Luciana. He asked me to bring it to her."

"This is a trick," Luciana said to Silvio.

"Perhaps, but we should hear him out," Silvio replied. "After all, Matteo claimed he was dead, and yet here he is." He waved for Riccardo to approach. "Disarm yourself, then show us your letter."

Riccardo unhooked his sword belt and secured it to his saddle. He handed the reins to a guard and walked slowly toward them as he extracted a letter from his tunic.

None of this made sense to Luciana, whose heartbeat was throbbing in her ears. Matteo had been so sure that Riccardo was dead, punished for his betrayal. Clearly he was wrong. It was impossible that he had lied to her. There must be some other explanation.

Riccardo handed the folded note to Silvio. "You'll recognize Sir Domenico's seal." When Riccardo looked at Luciana, she saw only concern in his eyes. He seemed troubled to be giving them this news.

Silvio showed the letter to her. It was her father's seal from his signet ring, an eagle with its wings spread and talons bared surrounded by the words *SIGILLUM FRATRIS RAMBERTI*— Seal of Brother Ramberti. The wax was unbroken.

"May I?" she asked her uncle, whose sight was so bad he could barely read anymore.

He nodded and gave her the letter. With trembling fingers, Luciana cracked the seal. She read the carefully written words aloud.

"To my dearest Luciana, I hope this letter finds you well and healthy. I am sad not to be with you, but I have important duties to perform that must keep me from you. Alas, I have sent this letter to deliver grave tidings. It saddens me to tell you that I have been betrayed by Matteo Dazzo."

Luciana, her stomach churning with hurt, looked up to see Riccardo nod grimly, confirming the news. She continued reading.

"He has sullied his good name by falsely testifying against me and my loyal squire Riccardo Corosi. Riccardo will give further details on delivery of this letter. I have denounced Matteo and am sending this missive to you as quickly as possible so that you are not taken in by whatever cunning lies or deceitful behavior he might employ. I only hope Riccardo reaches you before he does. In recognition of Riccardo's selfless service and sterling character, I have pledged your troth to Riccardo with my fervent blessing in hopes for your wedded happiness and protection against all evils. I know he will make a fine husband and will take care of you always. I hope one day to return to you. Go with God, my faithful daughter."

Silvio shook his head and clucked his tongue. "I never thought Matteo could be guilty of such monstrous behavior."

"It's not true," Luciana said.

"My dear, that's Sir Domenico's seal, is it not?"

"It is, but…"

"What further proof do you need?"

"I wish my father were here. I want to hear it from him."

"With the Templars being hunted throughout France," Riccardo said, "I fear you may never see him again. It brings me no joy to give you this news. Matteo was like a brother to me. If you'll let me, I'll explain to you what he has done."

Silvio nodded. "Tell us in the great hall."

They retired to the hall, where Luciana was too stunned to speak as Riccardo told his tale, interrupted frequently by Silvio's probing questions.

Matteo had revealed the location of the Templar treasure to the French king, along with her father's whereabouts so that he could steal away to marry Luciana and receive her dowry. Riccardo had confronted Matteo about his heinous act and was injured in the subsequent fight, barely escaping with his life. As soon as he was able to ride again, he trailed Matteo all the way to the villa. Luciana's father had raced to hide the remnants of the Templar treasure from the king and hadn't been heard from since.

Luciana reeled from the revelations as if she'd been struck. She couldn't reconcile this story with the completely different one she'd heard from Matteo. She hadn't had time to absorb or even try to sort out truth from fiction when there was a commotion in the courtyard. The door of the great hall flew open, and Matteo stalked inside. He stopped when he saw Riccardo rise to his feet. His face was crimson. Luciana didn't know if it was from the exertion of his sunny gallop back from the church or because of overwhelming rage.

"So it's true!" Matteo shouted.

"I'm not dead," Riccardo said, "despite your best efforts."

"What lies has this devil told you?" Matteo demanded.

"How you betrayed Luciana's father," Silvio said flatly.

"He is the traitorous one!" He looked at Luciana. "I told you what he has done. What he is."

"Then what is this?" Silvio said, holding up the letter. "We have a letter sent from Sir Domenico with his own seal."

"More lies. Riccardo stole that seal."

"The seal on my father's ring?" Luciana said, her doubts growing. "He would never have removed it."

Matteo hesitated before speaking. "One night your father heard news that drove him to despair over the fate of the Templars, and Riccardo used the opportunity to get him drunk and steal his ring."

"And you accuse *me* of lying?" Riccardo spat. "I won't stand for your treachery any longer."

He slowly and deliberately drew a glove from his belt and threw it at Matteo's feet. Luciana held her breath as Matteo grinned and picked it up, tucking it in his own belt. Riccardo's challenge to a duel had been accepted.

Things were moving so fast, Luciana didn't know what to think. If Riccardo was willing to put his fate into the hands of God, could everything he had been saying be true? Could she really have fallen for a series of carefully conceived lies that revealed her beloved to be the opposite of what she believed?

"I thought it was clear to you who was the better swordsman," Matteo said. "No matter. I'm happy to fight so I can protect Luciana from you."

"So am I. The Lord will show us who is telling the truth and who is lying."

"Yes, He will," Matteo said. "Let's have it out in the courtyard. Then I can be rid of you forever."

Luciana screamed, "No!" She turned to her uncle and grabbed his hand. "You can't allow this! Please!"

Silvio regarded her with pity. "I'm sorry, my child. I don't see any other way to settle the matter. One of them is lying. Without your father here to reveal what really happened, only God can show us. I wouldn't be able to stop them anyway. The gauntlet has been thrown down and accepted. Honor as well as bloodlust now compel them to fight to the death."

Despite her protestations, they all went outside, and Riccardo retrieved his sword. The word about the duel had spread rapidly throughout the villa, and every servant and guard was gathered in the courtyard, on the stairs, and atop the walls to watch the fight.

Riccardo and Matteo faced each other, hands tight on their swords, hatred in their eyes. Luciana felt like an afterthought, a prize to be won. She didn't want to watch, but she couldn't look away. She had to know which man was honest about the crimes against her family.

"You can still leave," Matteo said, wiping sweat from his brow. "Run away like the coward that you are."

Riccardo shook his head. "Why would I do that when I'm the one in the right?"

"I'm glad to hear you say that. I'd rather kill you here and now."

The ashen sheen on Matteo's face and his clenched jaw seemed to belie his brave words. He shook his head as if attempting to focus on his mortal enemy.

They raised their swords and nodded to each other. Then they crouched into fighting stances. The duel had begun. Luciana could only hug herself with crossed arms to keep from shuddering.

Matteo went on the attack immediately. He strode toward Riccardo and whipped his sword down in a series of rapid strikes that Riccardo barely managed to block. It seemed that Matteo was correct. Riccardo looked overmatched from the start.

He circled around cautiously, staying out of reach of Matteo's slashes.

"Fight me, you dog!" Matteo yelled. He advanced again but suddenly stopped and briefly doubled over to grip his stomach. Luciana wondered at this sign of infirmity and worried that her worst nightmare was about to come true.

Riccardo charged in and let loose with a flurry of slashes. This time it was Matteo who was pushed back on his heels. He parried the strikes expertly, but he was flagging, retreating to catch his breath.

Matteo glanced at Luciana. She saw love and determination, but for the first time, she also sensed fear.

Her eyes turned to Riccardo, who regarded her with caring as well. But his look was also triumphant, as if his victory was already complete. His certainty fueled her own doubts.

"Now is *your* chance to leave," he said to Matteo. "Go and never return. I'll spare your life, but not your shame."

Matteo didn't reply. He seemed to draw from a reserve of strength and ran forward, his sword raised high. Riccardo crouched low as he readied himself.

Without warning or reason, Matteo stumbled, and Luciana cried out. Riccardo took advantage of the opening and thrust his sword into Matteo's belly before he could regain his footing. Matteo froze, a look of shock on his face as Riccardo withdrew the sword. Matteo's own weapon dropped from his hand, and he sank to the ground face down.

Luciana wrested herself from Silvio's hands and dashed to Matteo, kneeling to turn him over.

Blood dribbled from his mouth. He desperately tried to form words, but coughed instead. Luciana ignored the droplets of blood on her face as she caressed Matteo's cheek. She wanted to hear a final confession from his own lips, but he rasped one last breath and went still.

Luciana began to sob uncontrollably. Her world had completely turned upside down in the course of a single afternoon. She was only vaguely aware of Riccardo lifting her up before retrieving his blood-soaked glove from Matteo's belt using a kerchief.

"I'm so sorry, Luciana," he said tenderly. His own eyes welled with tears at what he had done. "I wish it hadn't come to this."

Silvio stopped next to them. "Signore Corosi, I apologize for doubting you. God has spoken. You obviously were telling the truth." Luciana turned tear-stained eyes on him, her mind still coming to terms with the inevitable conclusion.

"Thank you, signore. I hope you will honor Sir Domenico's wishes."

"Of course. You have my blessing. Signorina Luciana will become your wife."

Riccardo wiped a tear from her cheek. "I hope you can find it in yourself to love me now that God has spoken in my favor. I promise that I will give you the life you deserve, Luciana. Will you have me?"

She tore her eyes from Matteo's lifeless body. She could never look at him again, knowing what he had done. He had lied to her and betrayed her father. She couldn't fathom a more heinous crime.

She sniffed and straightened herself with resolve, forcing back the shame that threatened to overcome her. "I will marry you, Riccardo. Thank you for saving me."

October, 1351

As Luciana finished her story, Fox felt a sting in his chest at her anguish. He knew what it was like to have someone you loved taken from you. Though his heart was telling him to help rid her of the man who had caused her such misery, he didn't quite believe that the mythical Templar treasure could ever be found.

"It's been nearly forty years, Luciana," he began gently. "I think it's possible that the treasure has been discovered and looted in that time." He silently added to himself: "…if it ever existed."

Luciana shook her head. "My father was a clever man. If he hid the treasure, the only ones who'd have a chance to find it are the ones who have his clues."

"And what happens if you *don't* find it?" Willa asked.

A look of despair crossed Luciana's face. "Riccardo will hunt me down wherever I go so he can remarry and father an heir. He's already tried to kill me twice. He won't stop until I'm dead, and he has the resources to make that happen."

There was a long silence. Fox knew that helping Luciana on her quest could be a fool's errand. It would also delay escorting Willa back to La Sacra di San Michele so that she could make a life there, but the alternative was to abandon Luciana to her fate. How could he do that?

He looked at Willa, and her concerned expression told him that she was thinking the same. He imagined she shared a similar affinity for Luciana even though they'd known her for only a day.

He had lost his mother, Willa had lost her lady, and now they each had a chance to redeem those losses in some small way.

Willa nodded at Fox.

"Luciana," he said, "we would like to help you find the treasure if it will free you from your husband."

"If you'll let us," Willa said. "We've only known you for a short time. You may not be comfortable sharing your letters with strangers."

Luciana paused for only a moment. "My dear, the fact that you are saying that makes me trust you even more. You've saved my life twice now at great risk to yourselves. Although I may not be a great judge of character given my recent betrayals, I have to believe that there are some good people in this world. Not to mention, if I don't accept your help, I have nowhere else to turn."

Fox admired her decisiveness and practicality. "Then let's figure out what we need to do."

"I suppose it's time that I share the letters with you. My father wrote them in Latin."

"Latin is one of the languages I learned as a child." Willa took out her quill, ink, and journal. "You said you have the first one in your memory. Tell me."

He watched Luciana close her eyes and slowly begin to recite five couplets. Willa wrote as Luciana spoke, and when she finished copying the Latin, she translated the words into English for her and Fox to read more easily.

The Templars' noble inheritance will be found only by those worthy
of its legacy.
The building that bends to the will of the people provides the
starting point.

The most sinister beam points to the dwelling of God you seek.
Move four circles from that noble face and you will know the next
step.

> *The deity's element leads you to life everlasting in the temple of the Romans.*
> *His enemy flies above the square, the symbol of your next destination.*
>
> *Find the figure in white who resists all but the command of Christ.*
> *Beneath, next to the source of the seed of life, is inscribed the isle of your destiny.*
>
> *Follow the cast line to the word that begins the name of the sought-after stronghold.*
> *Disturbing its peace will lead to proof of the king's duplicity and fortune's fate.*

When she was done, Fox said, "It does seem purposely mysterious."

"I spent months trying to discern what building he meant," Luciana said. "I thought it had to be that he was speaking of the Palazzo della Signoria in Florence because it is the seat of the government. '*The building that bends to the will of the people.*' But after that I was lost. His puzzle was completely impenetrable. Then Jacopo Barbieri told me he had a letter to Matteo that my father sent him. As soon as he told me the first line, I finally understood why I couldn't solve the puzzle in my letter."

"Can you show Matteo's letter to us?" Willa asked. Luciana opened it so that Willa could translate it into English as well.

> *I bequeath to you this challenge that can be solved together with faith and ingenuity.*
> *Begin the quest in the city that was nurtured by ferocity and avoids shades of gray.*
>
> *Strive for the heavens to gain perspective and reveal the rays of Christ's halo.*
> *Find there the symbol of purity and sacrifice, loved by a virgin.*

In the civic heart, the font displays the pointed weapon of the god.
Above the Holy of Holies, this indicates God's prophet saved from
  certain death.

Where the patron saint is revered, study the embellishments of the
  golden veil.
Among his four gilded cousins, the chosen one is closest to the basin
  of the city.

At the palace gate the sun's shadow will point to the knight's hour.
There, circle west from the stairway to a faithful rock in the
  Templars' true colors.

"The letters talk of cities and destinations," Fox said. "Do you have any idea of the region where the treasure was hidden?"

Luciana shook her head. "Since it was the French king who condemned them, I'd think Papà would want to get it as far away from France as possible. My letter talks of an island, but there is no way to determine which unless we solve all the clues in order."

"The island could be virtually anywhere in the world," Willa said.

"But now I know where to start. We're supposed to begin in '*the city that was nurtured by ferocity and avoids shades of gray.*' That has to be my hometown of Siena. My father would have expected me to be living there."

"Why do you think it's Siena?" Fox asked.

"According to legend, the city was established by Senius and Aschius, the sons of Remus and nephews of Romulus, the twins who founded Rome. After their uncle murdered their father, they fled Rome with a bronze statue honoring the wolf that suckled Remus and Romulus, and that became the symbol of Siena. A city '*nurtured by ferocity.*'"

"And the shades of gray?" Willa asked.

"As they escaped, Aschius rode a white horse and Senius a black horse, which is why the Balzana, Siena's coat of arms, is a white band over a black band. It '*avoids shades of gray.*'"

"So we must go to Siena."

"Corosi might do the same," Fox said. "He has both letters as well."

"He likely will go there," Luciana said. "But I'm confident that Jacopo will provide us a measure of protection once I tell him how Riccardo double-crossed his cousin in San Giuseppe and got him killed."

"Then instead of the Palazzo della Signoria in Florence, we have to find the same type of building in Siena."

"There's no challenge in that," Luciana said. "The Palazzo Pubblico in Siena is even older. And its façade is curved inward to mirror the outward curve of the palazzo, so it is clearly '*the building that bends to the will of the people.*' But I still don't understand what we're to do then. The first line of couplet two in my letter says that '*The most sinister beam points to the dwelling of God you seek.*'"

"He wants us to go to a church," Willa said. "But it doesn't mention which one."

"And we have many churches in Siena."

"'*Strive for the heavens*' could mean a tower. And '*the most sinister beam*' has several possible interpretations."

"It seems as if we're to use the two sets of clues together," Luciana said, "but I don't know how."

"Perhaps we won't understand until we are there."

"Your father…" Fox said questioningly.

"Sir Domenico Ramberti."

"Since Sir Domenico meant for you and Matteo to join forces to find the treasure, he must have expected you to combine the letters. There are five sets of couplets in each letter. That seems intentional. Perhaps it's actually meant to be five sets of quatrains."

They tried different combinations of the two letters. Luciana's first and then Matteo's. The opposite way around. Putting each couplet before or after the other. Reversing the order. Nothing seemed to make any more sense than another.

Willa cocked her head as she studied the two letters.

"What if we interweaved them?"

"I don't get your meaning," Fox said.

"We combine each of the letters by alternating the lines in the couplets," Willa said. "Like the laces on a kirtle."

"That's a good idea."

"I never would have considered that," Luciana said with a measure of awe.

They tried starting with the first line of Luciana's letter, followed by the first line of Matteo's, and so on. That didn't seem to get them anywhere, so they switched and tried starting with the first line of Matteo's letter, followed by the first line of Luciana's, and so on. On this second try, Fox, who was watching Willa write over her shoulder, pointed at the result after the lines were interwoven and said, "Wait. Look at the first letter of each line."

"What do you mean?" Luciana asked.

"I have a book called the *Secretum philosophorum*, given to me by my mother. It is full of tricks, arcane practices, and other useful information. One section is about ciphers and secret codes. If you want to hide a message inside another message, you can do it in plain sight, and no one will see unless they know what to look for."

"Yes," Willa said excitedly. "I remember that now. It's like an *abecedarius* cipher, where the first letters of each line spell out the letters of the alphabet in order. But here, by using the first letter of each line in a message, you can spell out a whole new message."

"I remember my father mentioning that the Templars embedded their messages with secret codes," Luciana said. "It's very possible he used one in these letters."

"Do you recognize anything familiar in this order?" Fox said to Luciana.

She peered more closely to examine the Latin words. In English, it said:

> I bequeath to you this challenge that can be solved together with
>   faith and ingenuity.
> The Templars' noble inheritance will be found only by those worthy
>   of its legacy.

Begin the quest in the city that was nurtured by ferocity and avoids shades of gray.

The building that bends to the will of the people provides the starting point.

Strive for the heavens to gain perspective and reveal the rays of Christ's halo.

The most sinister beam points to the dwelling of God you seek.

Find there the symbol of purity and sacrifice, loved by a virgin.

Move four circles from that noble face and you will know the next step.

In the civic heart, the font displays the pointed weapon of the god.

The deity's element leads you to life everlasting in the temple of the Romans.

Above the Holy of Holies, this indicates God's prophet saved from certain death.

His enemy flies above the square, the symbol of your next destination.

Where the patron saint is revered, study the embellishments of the golden veil.

Find the figure in white who resists all but the command of Christ.

Among his four gilded cousins, the chosen one is closest to the basin of the city.

Beneath, next to the source of the seed of life, is inscribed the isle of your destiny.

At the palace gate the sun's shadow will point to the knight's hour.

Follow the cast line to the word that begins the name of the sought-after stronghold.

There, circle west from the stairway to a faithful rock in the Templars' true colors.

Disturbing its peace will lead to proof of the king's duplicity and fortune's fate.

Fox put the Latin texts side by side and covered everything but the first letters in each line. Luciana gasped when she finally saw a Latin phrase if she alternated between Matteo's letter and her own.

MATTHEUSLUCIANASIMUL
Mattheus Luciana simul.

Matteo Luciana together.

Now Luciana did cry. It was clear her father had wished for the two of them to be with each other. She buried her face in Willa's shoulder and heavy sobs racked her body. Fox took Willa's journal and gave them a moment together.

When Luciana was finally able to compose herself, she said, "Thank you. Now I know I have to find the treasure before Riccardo does. He took the life I should have had."

"You want the treasure so you can build a new life without him?" Fox said.

"I don't care about the riches," Luciana said. "The money doesn't matter."

"Then why are you so set on discovering it?" Willa asked.

"Because Matteo told me a story so improbable that I couldn't believe it. He said that my father had intercepted a written message from King Philip of France to Pope Clement. According to Matteo, Papà planned to hide the message with the treasure, to be used once we recovered it as proof to the succeeding pope and the rest of Christendom that the Templars were unfairly persecuted by the king and pope. He wholeheartedly believed the Templars could be resurrected, but I don't know if that was ever a real possibility."

"Certainly not anymore," Fox said. "Even in your father's time, the Templars were effectively wiped out, and the order would have taken an enormous effort to rebuild. But desperate people cling to hopes that can sometimes prove unrealistic." He exchanged a tense glance with Willa before turning back to Luciana. "What did the message say?"

"The king requested that the pope absolve Riccardo Corosi of the vows of poverty, chastity, and obedience he'd taken. At the time, I thought this was all part of Matteo's lies. But yesterday on reading the letter from my father to Matteo I realized everything he told me was the truth. If the king's message were turned over to the current pope in Avignon, Riccardo could be stripped of all his wealth, and our marriage would be annulled. I would get all the land back that had been bequeathed to him in my dowry. You see, the Church presently owes my husband an enormous amount of money. The current pope would be overjoyed to cancel those loans by declaring them forfeit due to Riccardo's religious vows. I'd finally be free of the man who betrayed me, my father, and Matteo."

"Why would Signore Corosi have taken such vows?" Willa asked. "What does that mean?"

"It means, Willa," Luciana said, "that my husband is a Knight Templar."

THE MOST SINISTER BEAM

Tuscany

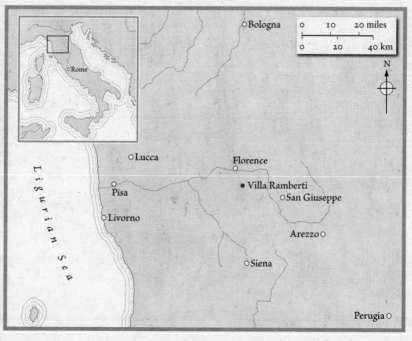

18

Tuscany

The horses were back at the villa by the afternoon following Luciana's escape. A local tradesman had recognized them as Corosi's and notified him. After Armstrong's men retrieved the herd, everyone, including Sofia, was now preparing to head south to Siena. She was standing to the side with Corosi and Armstrong as the horses were outfitted for the journey. It would be at least a full day's ride.

"She'll distract my men," Armstrong said to Corosi as if she weren't there.

"You need me," Sofia said, rubbing the back of her head. It still ached where Willa had hit her with the shovel.

"For what?"

"To help us find the treasure," Corosi said.

"Can she even read?"

Sofia's cheeks grew hot at the insult. Although her banter with Armstrong was amusing, he was in danger of going too far.

"If you'd ask me directly, you could find out."

"Why am I being spoken to by a servant?" Armstrong asked dismissively.

"Because she is critical to my business," Corosi said.

Armstrong shook his head and shrugged. "If you say so, signore."

Corosi seemed satisfied with that. Sofia was well used to men underestimating her. It was how she'd worked her way from her lowly position as a prostitute in the brothels of Venice to becoming the mistress and confidante of one of the most powerful men in Florence.

"Did you understand the clues that Ramberti left?" she asked Armstrong. "Or can't *you* read?"

"What use do I have for reading? That's for monks and clerks."

"Each of us has our place in this alliance," Corosi said impatiently. "I provide the funds and connections to pursue the treasure. Sofia, you've already shown your skills as a spy and can help us decipher the letter. Sir Randolf, you're a commander of soldiers and an expert horseman, as demonstrated by your ability to win the Siena Palio for me the last three years."

"I have the fastest horse in Italy," Armstrong boasted. "Why do you think I was able to catch up to Fox at the Arno?"

"And how did that end?" Sofia shot back.

Armstrong reared back with a hand as if to strike her, but he held off when he saw Corosi's withering gaze.

"I don't care what your feelings are toward Sofia, but if you ever hit her, I will find myself a new captain. Do you understand?"

Armstrong's nostrils flared in anger, but he nodded. Sofia smiled and put her arm through Corosi's.

Standing arm in arm with a rich noble banker might have been unimaginable to most street urchins growing up in the back alleys of Venice, but not Sofia. In fact, she began life as the daughter of a clerk, who taught her to read Latin and spoiled his clever little girl after her mother died until his own early death put her out on the street to fend for herself. Left penniless, she had survived long enough for her young body to mature. By then, she had encountered enough hardship to be willing to do anything to escape her precarious existence, including becoming a prostitute. She knew that her beauty was her one true asset, and she used it to work her way up in the trade, servicing sailors and merchants from the world over.

Unlike the other girls, who all eventually got pregnant, she never did. Although her barrenness would make her undesirable to any man who wanted a family, she was already damaged goods anyway. There weren't many options for her future. She would either be killed by one of her clients, contract some horrid disease, or become so old and undesirable that she would no longer be able to ply her trade.

It was around the time of the Pestilence that she had met Giovanni. He was attractive and charming, but also lonely and trusting. In a moment of drunken indiscretion, he had divulged the existence of a mysterious letter supposedly revealing the Templar treasure—a letter possessed by Riccardo Corosi, one of the most powerful figures in Florentine society. Sofia didn't really believe in the treasure, but at the mention of Corosi's wife Luciana, she had seen an opportunity to become something more than a prostitute.

Giovanni spoke frequently about Luciana. He hoped he might see her if she came to visit her dear friend who had married a nobleman in Venice. But when the woman died in the Great Mortality—as did Luciana's lady's maid—Sofia left Venice and presented herself to Luciana as the bereft former maid of her dead friend. The sad tale that Sofia concocted convinced Luciana to bring her into the household as a lady's maid.

Soon, though, Sofia chafed at this menial role and sought a greater station. With the knowledge she gained from Luciana about the banking business and by using her other talents as well, she had persuaded Corosi that she could replace Luciana's accounting skills if he found a younger wife. The discovery of Ramberti's letter to Matteo and the tantalizing prospect of finding the Templar treasure was the final spur that set her growing plan in motion.

With even a small part of what the treasure promised, she could return to Venice and dominate the prostitution industry, one of the few types of business where a woman could succeed on her own. She could even continue to work with Corosi, providing him with a ready supply of currency to exchange from customers around Europe.

The two letters were the key to finding the treasure. Sofia had been poring over them all morning while the men were gathering their arms and horses.

"So if your job is to tell us about the clues in those letters," Armstrong said, "don't make us wait any longer. Bestow your wisdom upon us."

"I can already tell that this will be a trying partnership," Sofia said, glaring at Armstrong. "It looks like the two messages are to be used together, so the first couplet of each message must be showing us where to begin." She read them out:

> *The Templars' noble inheritance will be found only by those worthy*
> *   of its legacy.*
> *The building that bends to the will of the people provides the*
> *   starting point.*
> *I bequeath to you this challenge that can be solved together with*
> *   faith and ingenuity.*
> *Begin the quest in the city that was nurtured by ferocity and avoids*
> *   shades of gray.*

"It must be the other way around," Corosi said. "We need to know what city it is first."

"These riddles are tedious," Armstrong said. "What does it mean?"

"The city that '*avoids shades of gray*' must mean black and white. That's the banner for Siena."

"Then we need to start our search there, in the building that '*bends to the will of the people*'?"

"The public building," Sofia said.

"You mean the Palazzo Pubblico?" Armstrong said. "The one with the tower in front of the Piazza del Campo?"

"You're brighter than you look. On the other hand, I suppose that isn't so difficult."

Armstrong gave her a tight smile. "And why is it that Signora Corosi got away? Oh yes. I believe it's because you were tied up at the time. How's your head?"

Corosi slapped his hand against the wall. "Enough! If Sir Gerard and Lady Fox hadn't come along, neither of you would have failed in your tasks. We were simply unfortunate, and they were lucky. Next time, we'll get the upper hand. Now stop arguing and let's find the treasure."

"Do you think Signora Corosi will be looking for it, too?" Armstrong asked.

"How could she?" Sofia said. "We have her letter from her father. Signore Corosi made sure of that."

"My Luciana has a fine memory," Corosi said. "She might remember enough to pursue it."

"Then it's a race."

"Maybe she's already deciphered the entire set of riddles," Armstrong said.

"Impossible," Sofia said. "These are sequential clues. It seems that they require a physical presence to understand them. Whatever we find at the Palazzo Pubblico will help us solve the next two couplets." She read them out:

The most sinister beam points to the dwelling of God you seek.
Move four circles from that noble face and you will know the next
*   step.*
Strive for the heavens to gain perspective and reveal the rays of
*   Christ's halo.*
Find there the symbol of purity and sacrifice, loved by a virgin.

"The tower on the Palazzo Pubblico," Sofia said. "That must be what it means to '*strive for the heavens.*' The rest I don't quite understand yet, but we will have time on our ride to Siena to consider it further."

Corosi nodded. "And the parts about Christ's halo and the symbol of purity and sacrifice, loved by a virgin? Those are about Jesus. But in what way?"

"We won't know until we climb the tower," Armstrong said. "I just hope Fox is continuing to help Signora Corosi. I'd very much like to see him again and give him a close look at the point of my sword."

"I would also like to see Willa again," Sofia said. "I have to repay her for the blow to my head."

Corosi smiled. "Finally, something you can both agree on."

"Vengeance?" Armstrong said to Sofia.

She nodded back. After all, they were working together toward a common goal.

"Vengeance it is."

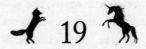

19

SIENA

On their approach to Siena through the lush surrounding hills of farms and pastures that fed into the city, Luciana's heart lifted when she could finally see the two most distinctive monuments of the hilltop city jutting into the sky. She pointed them out to Willa and Fox as they rode.

The first was the bell tower of the Siena Cathedral, built in layers of alternating black and white stone symbolizing the colors of the city's crest. The second was the Torre del Mangia, a watchtower made of ornate white stone atop a brick column. It was equal in height to the cathedral's campanile and rose from the not yet visible Palazzo Pubblico. Luciana explained that intentional parity of the two tall buildings was meant to reflect the equal powers of church and state in the city.

She recounted the stories her father had told her of a time a century before, when Siena had been the banking center of Europe, serving as the exclusive repository of the income of the Papal States. When the Pope moved to Avignon in France, however, Sienese bankers were excluded from the Church's financial activities. Luciana had grown up witnessing the city's steady decline in prestige and power. And after the Great Mortality had struck with such ferocity, she feared the city would never recover. Still, it was her beloved home, and the sight of its renowned buildings never failed to raise her spirits.

Like all travelers coming from the direction of Florence, they arrived at the north entrance to the city—a fortified outer gate, a courtyard surrounded by high walls with parapets for archers, and a second even larger inner gate—called the Porta Camollia.

She led them down the main route through the city, the horses' shoes clopping on the cobblestones. Siena had gained so much wealth as a banking center that its main thoroughfares were all paved, unlike many of the other cities she knew in Italy. Tall townhouses lined the street, rising to three or four stories and made of brick or stone, another sign of the city's former affluence. During their ride, Luciana had described what a bustling place Siena had been five years ago. Then the Pestilence had descended and wiped out a third of the population in just a few months.

"You cannot imagine how crowded this road used to be," Luciana said in a melancholy voice. "Our location as a crossroads of Italy means that the city is a trading center. You could barely walk without bumping into people from all over Italy. But at least it soon will be teeming like that again for the upcoming Palio."

The street wasn't empty, but there was plenty of room for them to stay mounted on their horses without causing trouble. Some of the doors had faded red Xs.

"What do those mean?" Willa asked.

"Those were homes where Pestilence victims lived. I suspect that some of them are still vacant."

The citizens who remained went about their business driving carts of sheep pelts, carrying loads of cloth, and hauling vegetables from late summer crops through the many alleys and back streets. Fountains were spaced at frequent intervals and fed by a vast series of underground tunnels called *bottini* that Luciana had explored as a child.

They passed a courtyard in front of a large palazzo, and Luciana glanced at it ruefully. It was three stories high, with gracefully arched windows, massive carved wooden doors, and crenellations along the top.

"Do you know that place?" Fox asked her.

She nodded. "It was my father's. He bestowed it to me as part of my dowry, along with the villa. Now it belongs to Riccardo."

They'd already agreed that they couldn't stay in her Siena home given the likelihood that her husband would be following them to the city.

"Are you sure Signore Barbieri will help us?"

"I can't be certain of anything. Jacopo Barbieri can be odd and capricious. Above all, he is a businessman."

"You mentioned that allegiances and rivalries can change with the wind in Siena," Willa said. "Couldn't Signore Barbieri align himself with your husband?"

"I can't imagine that," Luciana said. "I come down for the Palio every year, and I've known Jacopo since we were children. He's a member of the city's most powerful confraternity, one of those brotherhoods that men love to pretend are for charity, but are really just an excuse to spend time together away from their families. Many of the members are angry at a Florentine interloper—who is allowed to enter the race only thanks to his marriage—embarrassing the city's best families. Jacopo is consumed with envy for Riccardo's horse winning the race. And Riccardo was furious when Jacopo married Matteo's cousin."

"Then perhaps Corosi won't come here," Fox said. "He's probably aware that we'll let Signore Barbieri know who was responsible for his cousin's death."

"Riccardo will deny it, and we have no proof, do we? Besides, Riccardo has his allies here as well. Money and victory will do that. I think some of the Sienese who mourn how their home has been laid low by the Great Mortality want to team up with a representative of a city like Florence that is growing in wealth and influence."

"Greed is a great motivator."

"And it sounds like Signore Corosi knows how to feed it," Willa said.

They continued riding until they were close to the center of town. Although they were near the Palazzo Pubblico and Siena Cathedral, the tall townhouses kept them from spotting the two towers they'd seen easily from far outside the city.

The next square opened onto an even grander palazzo than the Ramberti home. Elegant marble and pristine white limestone made up the wide façade dotted with trefoil windows at all three levels. A single carved oak door twice Zephyr's height was set into the first story.

"Is this Barbieri's home or the Palazzo Pubblico?" Fox said in an impressed tone.

"Jacopo enjoys his luxuries," Luciana replied.

They rode up to the door and dismounted. Before they could knock, it swept open, and a steward dressed in blue and white livery stepped out.

"*Buongiorno*, Niccolò," Luciana said.

"A pleasure as always to welcome you to Palazzo Barbieri, Signora Corosi."

"Is Signore Barbieri in residence?"

"Yes, he is grieving the loss of his cousin."

"Then he's heard about what happened."

"I'm afraid so. The news just reached us this morning."

"May we call on him to convey our condolences?"

"Certainly, signora. I'm sure he will be glad to have your comfort. I'll take you to the solar."

Luciana introduced Willa and Fox so that Niccolò could properly announce them. He ushered them through the door and gestured for the waiting grooms to take the horses through the interior courtyard to the stable.

Up the stairs, past beautiful tapestries lining the halls, they entered a luxurious receiving chamber filled with carved furniture, a profusion of bright pewter plateware, and rich carpets imported from the Holy Land. Relaxing on a chaise next to a table overflowing with fruits, nuts, breads, and cakes, was Jacopo Barbieri. He didn't bother to rise from his reclined position and instead waved them in after Niccolò presented them by name.

The reason for his reluctance to get up was obvious, and Luciana was surprised anew as she always was when she saw his enormous girth. He was the fattest man she'd ever seen, and it looked like he was even larger than the last time she'd been in his presence.

He didn't seem to be mourning his cousin Piero too heavily because he beamed at the sight of Luciana. "My dear Luciana!

Come in and sit next to me. I was worried for you when I heard the news of that nasty business at San Giuseppe. I'm so happy to see that you escaped unscathed to reassure me in my time of grief."

She walked over and kissed his hand before sitting. "You hide your sadness well."

"You are a bright spot in an unpleasant time. Though I loved Piero dearly as family, of course," he said half-heartedly, "I have other reasons for grieving his loss that I won't bore you with."

Barbieri looked up and noticed his other two guests for the first time. "And I'm pleased to make your acquaintances, Sir Gerard and Lady Fox."

Both Willa and Fox were staring at their host with wide eyes. In a world recovering from the deprivations introduced by the Great Mortality, the sight of a man with any extra fat at all was astonishing.

"Please don't take offense at their stares," Luciana said, causing Willa and Fox to become beet red and avert their gazes. "Your plumpness is quite marvelous."

"Offense?" Barbieri said with a hearty guffaw. "Why, I welcome it! How better to show off my wealth? Please sit." When they were seated, he turned back to Luciana. "I do hope you'll stay for the week. Although your husband is likely to win the race yet again now that Piero can't ride for me, the parade before it always raises the city's spirits." He paused as if he were about to broach a delicate subject with Luciana. "About the gold that was due to me. Do you know what happened to it?"

"I think it would be better if you ask Riccardo about that."

"Oh, I most certainly will. You and I have always been friends, despite Riccardo's abhorrence of my wife and my distaste for him. It was only because of you that the deal between your husband and me ever came to pass, so I understand your reasons for keeping your silence."

"You do?"

"We all do what is necessary when we have to." He grinned at Fox and Willa. "You're English, yes? The Palio is quite the spectacle. You will be treated to a sight that people journey for days to see."

"I'm afraid we won't be able to enjoy it," Fox said. "We are in somewhat of a hurry."

"No?" Barbieri took a handful of grapes and popped them into his mouth one by one. He motioned that they were welcome to partake of the food, but none of them moved. "Then what brings you to my home?"

"We need a place to stay while we are in Siena," Luciana said. "May we trouble you for some rooms? We won't be here long."

"You're always perfectly welcome to stay here as long as Riccardo isn't joining you. But why? Has something unfortunate occurred at Palazzo Ramberti?"

"It might if I go there." She took a deep breath. "My husband wants to kill me."

That caused Barbieri to sit up for the first time. "Really? Tell me everything."

Luciana related the entire story, from the attack at the village to their night-time escape from the villa, only leaving out any mention of her father's letters. Barbieri gasped throughout the account and shook his head in bewilderment when she finished.

"That is a fantastic tale."

"I can vouch for its truth," Willa said. "I heard Sofia admit to her role in the plot."

"And I recognized Armstrong's helmet," added Fox. "He was definitely the man who killed your cousin."

Barbieri seemed amused. "You don't have to convince me. Perhaps you misunderstood my Italian. I mean that the story is wonderful. You understand? I love hearing that Corosi was foiled at every turn by you two. It must be causing him to boil inside."

"But Riccardo has the contract confirming that he now owns your branch in Florence," Luciana said.

Barbieri's expression turned dour at that. "That is a difficulty. I am in need of the ten thousand florins I would have gotten in exchange for it. Now Corosi has received my branch for nothing. I'm only sorry I didn't think of perpetrating the same trick first, but I suppose that's the price of being an honorable man. Now I have to think about how to get back at him and perhaps recoup my money."

"If I can bother you further," Luciana said, "we will also need to get into the Torre del Mangia." Luciana thought that would also be an appropriate name for Barbieri's home, given that Torre del Mangia literally meant "Tower of the Eater", so called because of the gluttonous tendencies of its first bell ringer.

"For what reason?" he asked.

"I'm afraid I can't tell you."

"You test my curiosity, Luciana. First that mysterious letter to Matteo you wanted so badly, and now this." Barbieri considered it for a moment, then said, "I just have one more question, my dear. If you are not safe here in Siena, then surely you won't be any safer in Florence. What do you intend to do once your business is concluded here? As much as I would like it to be otherwise, your testimony against him is worthless. His wife and two outsiders versus the word of a pillar of the Florentine community?"

"I can share something with you that will help," Luciana said.

Barbieri leaned forward, his eyes shimmering with interest. "I'm in complete suspense."

"If we find what we're looking for, it will ruin Riccardo. I will be free of him, and so will you."

He grinned at her. "Don't tease me."

"I'm not teasing. We have the chance to thoroughly devastate him."

"This all sounds quite extraordinary. But if there is any chance that what you say is true, my dear Luciana, I will give you the benefit of the doubt."

"Then you'll help us?" Fox asked.

Barbieri considered his question for a long while, to the point that Luciana wondered if he would show them the door.

"Until I have reason not to," he finally said. "I'll have Niccolò prepare chambers for you."

"We appreciate your kindness," Willa said.

"And the Torre del Mangia?" Luciana asked. "You'll arrange for us to climb it?"

"I'll get access for Sir Gerard, but the ladies will be too conspicuous to be worth the trouble. Give me tomorrow to make the arrangements."

"Thank you, signore," Fox said.

"Just promise me one thing."

"What's that?"

Barbieri took a giant bite of cake and spoke with his mouth full. "Come back here and describe for me in excruciating detail the look on Riccardo's face when he realizes he has been utterly defeated."

 20

Randolf Armstrong blended with the masses as he walked with them toward Siena Cathedral, called there by the bells signaling vespers. The iconic church faced with alternating stripes of black and white stone glowed in the setting sun. He hoped the evening service would be crowded enough that a surreptitious rendezvous wouldn't be noticed.

The cathedral was one place he wouldn't expect to see Fox. His heretical assault on a member of the clergy was shocking to Armstrong. He'd attended the trial and saw Fox and his father battle fiercely against the authority of the Church while trying to make excuses for their rebellious behavior. Armstrong found their accusations against the cardinal unconvincing, as did the court.

But what Armstrong really couldn't abide was the fact that Fox had wasted his chance to inherit his father's estate after his elder brother James died in the Battle of Crécy. Like Fox, Armstrong was the second son of a knight, so his brother Paul had inherited his family's land and fathered three boys of his own. As a younger son with no land, Armstrong had only two choices. He could join the Church, but quiet contemplation in a celibate life held no appeal for him. Or he could strike out on his own as a man-at-arms and make his fortune that way. Armstrong chose this life out of desperation, while Fox had squandered everything that had been given him.

The Pestilence had strangely been a boon for a man of Armstrong's fierce talents. Nobles were clamoring for mercenaries to collect taxes, provide protection against marauding bands, and put down peasant revolts, so Armstrong had no shortage of work. After earning a knighthood in England, he learned that the cities of Italy were the richest in Europe, so he made his way to Florence, where he would no longer have to contend with the harsh winters of the north.

He soon came to find that unlike the north, where the ruling families were nobles closely linked with royalty, in Italy it was just as often the successful guildsmen who owned the land, controlled the government, and reaped the riches, especially the bankers.

Armstrong sold his services to Corosi as a rider in the Siena Palio and used his fame as a knight to recruit a cadre of soldiers loyal to him. Corosi gained his unswerving fealty and quietly began using him to carry out tasks that he didn't want anyone to be aware of. Some knights subscribed to outdated notions of chivalry with its sentimental notions of courtesy and idealism. Armstrong, however, believed his only duty was to the Lord and to his lord, and any orders in either service were lawful and just, including killing the lord's wife.

But the thought of recovering the Templar treasure was also a powerful incentive. Corosi had only recently shared the news of its existence with him in order to convince him to take part in the attack at San Giuseppe. Armstrong hadn't believed it at first, but when Corosi revealed Luciana's letter and told him about the conversation between Matteo and Ramberti he had overheard long ago, Armstrong had become convinced it was true. If the king of France was sure it existed, who was he to doubt it? The potential payoff was too tantalizing to dismiss.

He entered the cathedral and took in its magnificence as he crossed himself. Massive columns of black and white supported the soaring nave. Frescos and statues lined the walls, while small alcoves and chapels allowed for more contemplative prayer. Even the floor of the cathedral was becoming a site for decoration, as the plain stone pavers were beginning to give way to intricate mosaics. The huge dome above the altar was the envy of Florentines, who were supposedly planning one even larger for their yet unfinished Duomo.

He headed for the small chapel dedicated to Saint Anthony of Padua, patron saint of lost things. Given their quest for the

Templar treasure, he thought it was quite appropriate for this rendezvous.

He made the sign of the cross again and kneeled at the tiny altar set in front of a painting depicting Saint Anthony preaching to the fish. The only other person inside the chapel was a woman wearing a hood.

She turned her head and smiled at him, her beauty apparent despite the dimness of the candlelight. Even though they were in a place of worship, Armstrong couldn't deny that her fragrance was alluring.

"You were certainly generous with your insults back at the villa," Sofia said in a hushed voice.

"I thought they were quite good at throwing Signore Corosi off," he replied. "We can't let anyone know of our secret, not even my own men. I trust them to be quiet when they are sober, but their tongues can loosen when they drink."

"If you want me to bed you again, perhaps you'll dull your barbs."

"I rather enjoyed our wordplay."

"I must admit you were a worthy adversary. It did provide a thrill."

Armstrong was loyal to his lord, but he was also a man with carnal needs. He hadn't known Sofia was also Corosi's mistress until after their torrid affair had already consumed him. Because of Sofia's background as a prostitute and her role as his lord's mistress, not wife, his conscience didn't bother him, although Corosi had to be kept from finding out.

This was the first chance he'd had to be alone with her since before San Giuseppe. If they only needed to exchange information, they usually rendezvoused at churches where it would be easy to explain their meeting if someone were to see them. A tumble at an out-of-the-way tavern was more desirable, but much harder to arrange.

Sofia reached out and stroked the back of Armstrong's hand. He drew it away. She played with him even though she knew he found it unseemly to indulge their urges in church.

"Where shall we go?" she asked.

"Not tonight, as much as I'd like. Signore Corosi is expecting both of us back at his palazzo to plan what we should do next."

"It seems a shame that we can't find the treasure ourselves."

Armstrong was taken aback. "What do you mean?"

"You know Signore Corosi will take most of the fortune for himself if we ever find it."

"We will all be rich if we find it."

"Not nearly as rich as he," Sofia said.

"His statement at the villa was true. We need him as much as he needs us."

"Perhaps not. I've deciphered the code that allows the letters to be used together as intended. You have to weave the couplets together by alternating lines from each letter. That sentimentalist Ramberti hid Matteo and Luciana's names in the verses to make sure they got the message."

Armstrong took a moment to consider this new information, then shook his head.

"We still need Signore Corosi to get us into the Torre del Mangia. Who knows how many more of his resources we'll need during the quest?"

Sofia put up her hands. "You're right—I was being too hasty. I'll tell Signore Corosi about the interweaved couplets as soon as we're back at his palazzo."

"Do you understand the other clues we need to solve?" Armstrong's strength was fighting and riding, not decoding puzzles.

Sofia took out the paper she had in her pouch and read it in the candlelight.

Strive for the heavens to gain perspective and reveal the rays of Christ's halo.
The most sinister beam points to the dwelling of God you seek.
Find there the symbol of purity and sacrifice, loved by a virgin.
Move four circles from that noble face and you will know the next step.

"Perhaps the '*rays of Christ's halo*' will be revealed when we climb the tower. The depictions of Christ's halo always show shafts of light radiating from it. There must be something visible from the top of the tower that looks similar. And '*the most sinister beam*' will point to a dwelling of God, meaning a church."

"How do you know such things?" Armstrong asked.

"Do you mean how does a lowly wench such as myself know these things?"

"Not in so many words, although I can save that insult for when we're in public."

"My father gave me my education at an early age. He thought I'd become a merchant's wife at the very least, perhaps even a nun if I were fortunate." She laughed at that. "Now I'm putting that education to better use." She peered down at the letter again. "What I don't know is why a ray of Christ's halo would be sinister."

To his surprise, Armstrong's mind flashed to a duel he once witnessed. "'Sinister' has another meaning. We use *le main sinistre* to make pacts during duels or challenges. The left hand."

Sofia grinned in appreciation of his insight. "The left-most ray will lead to the church where we will find the Christ figure with the four circles. That deserves a reward." She leaned toward him with a lascivious gaze. Her intention was obvious.

"I told you, not here."

She pouted. "You don't know what you're missing."

"That's my problem. I do."

"Then later?"

He was tempted, but he had to be mindful of his objective. Despite his desire for Sofia, the pull of the treasure was stronger.

"We'll find a time when it's safe." He put up a finger as he rose from the altar. "Remember. Discretion is our ally. If Signore Corosi discovers us, we're finished. So you better make it convincing when we return that you've just worked out the combination of the verses."

She stood up as well and looked unperturbed. "I deceived Signora Corosi for years, no?"

"You did. But now we need to be even more careful."

"Then we'll talk again about our situation concerning Signore Corosi when we're nearer to the treasure?"

Armstrong saw that she wouldn't relent and nodded unenthusiastically. He left the chapel after she did, all the while wondering how he had gotten himself into such a complicated position and how he was going to get out of it.

21

According to Barbieri, the guard manning the Torre del Mangia atop the Palazzo Pubblico during the midday posting could be easily bribed. All Fox had to do was hand over a gold coin once he reached the top of the tower, and he'd be given as much time as he needed to decipher the clue.

With Willa and Luciana beside him, he entered the bustling Piazza del Campo. The main square of Siena's civic district was actually shaped more like a tilted scallop shell than a square. Along the rounded border of the northern side of the piazza were homes and businesses, with a gentle slope down toward the palazzo where it abutted the piazza's southern edge.

The tower soared high above, casting a minimal shadow from the noon sun. When they'd remembered that the Church said those who sit at the left hand of Christ at the end of time will be damned to Hell, they'd realized that the Latin for "sinister" could also mean "left." They'd guessed he was supposed to look for the leftmost ray of Christ's halo, whatever that was. He hoped it would be apparent when he got up there so that he didn't have to stay long.

"I still don't know why Barbieri couldn't show me how to get to the Palazzo's roof instead of the tower." He turned to Luciana. "You said the Torre del Mangia was completed only a few years ago, so your father had to have written his clue in 1314 based on what he saw from the roof or one of the top-story windows."

"Except that you would look conspicuous roaming the upper halls of the palazzo unaccompanied," Willa said.

"We can't even be certain the clue he left still exists," Luciana said. "Much has changed in Siena since his time. The Piazza del Campo looks similar, but it was paved with brick only two summers ago, replacing the stone."

Fox squinted again at the campanile and imagined looking down from that vertiginous spot.

Willa put her hand on his shoulder. "I wish I could go with you."

"Barbieri thought it would be less noticeable if I went alone. Just stay out of sight. Hopefully when I get back down we can unravel the rest of the clue and be on our way."

"We'll wait in that side street," Luciana said, pointing to a shadowy alley up some stairs to her right, where they could still see the top of the tower but wouldn't be noticed.

"Be careful, Gerard," Willa said. "If there is any resistance to you going inside, come back out and we'll find another way."

Fox nodded and left them, walking down toward the palazzo. The front entrance was flanked by two guards holding poleaxes. Barbieri told him that they were there for show. Dressed like a noble as he was, Fox expected to easily pass them and go right inside.

As he approached the guards, the absence of a sword swinging from his hip felt like a missing appendage, but walking around with a weapon of war was not allowed in most large cities. He had nothing more than a dagger in his belt.

His apprehension was unwarranted. Barbieri was correct. The guards merely glanced at him as he walked by with the purposeful stride of someone who belonged there.

His eyes adjusted as he entered the darkened entry hall. The entrance to the tower was to his left, but he didn't head straight there. He took a turn around the hall leading to the interior courtyard first to make sure no one was observing him unduly.

When he was satisfied that he wasn't being watched, he went to the low arched doorway that led up toward the tower stairs. At every point, Fox braced himself for someone to call out asking why a stranger was accessing the city's watchtower, but he didn't encounter anyone. In a time of impending war, the door might have been secured, but with Siena currently at peace, it was completely unguarded. Fox ducked in and went up a series of steps until he reached the entrance to the tower itself.

The narrow stairs wound up and around a central open shaft, with a guard wall no taller than his waist that acted as a railing on the inside of the steps and tiny windows set at distant intervals on the outside to light the passage. The empty core of the stairwell was so narrow that he felt like he could almost touch the opposite side by stretching out his hand.

Before he began climbing, Fox leaned over the guard wall and peered directly up the tower interior. It gave him an unimpeded view to the top.

He took a breath and started up. He found himself breathing hard by the time he was halfway to the top. Only once did he venture over to a window slit and see the ground now far beneath him.

Near the top he looked over the guard wall. It was like peering down a well that disappeared into an infinite distance below. He couldn't imagine making this climb regularly, which seemed like rising from the depths of Hell.

Sunlight beckoned from a door at the top of the stairway. Just two sets of steps down from it was a heavy door opening into a small room with a stool and a bucket that stank of urine. Fox guessed that this was where the guard posted on the tower could retreat to in inclement weather. Given the weight of the door, it might also have been used as a prison cell when needed.

Fox kept going up and out into the sun, where a stiff wind buffeted his hair. The tower observation level consisted of a narrow walkway around a set of stairs leading up to the bell that could be rung in times of emergency, such as a fire or the approach of an army.

Fox saw the full breathtaking view of miles of the surrounding countryside far beyond Siena's city walls. Any foreign invaders would be seen half a day before they arrived, giving defenders plenty of time to reinforce the walls with soldiers and barricade the gates.

"*Buongiorno*," Fox said loudly as he circled the walkway.

"Gustavo?" He took out a gold coin from the pouch at his side. "Signore Barbieri told me you would be pleased to let me view your fair city from here." There was no answer.

Perhaps Gustavo was relaxing against one of the pillars holding up the massive belfry, but Fox went all the way around the tower and was surprised to find that he was completely alone.

Willa wished she could have gone with Fox up the tower. Just the thought of looking out from the heavens was exhilarating to her.

"Have you been up there?" she asked Luciana.

"No, but when I was a child, I did sneak in to climb the bell tower at the cathedral. My backside hurt for a week when my father found out, but it was worth it. The view was unlike anything I'd ever seen."

"Perhaps we can climb it again before we go."

"I think the priests at the cathedral would have some objections to two women going up there. Even as a child it was hard to get by them."

"Those same priests would blanch if they knew what I've been through already in my life. A venture into a campanile is nothing."

"You are an unusual lady," Luciana said. "When we are out on the road again, I should very much like you to regale me with your stories."

In their short time together, Willa had come to think of Luciana in the same way she thought of the lady she had grown up with. Isabel shared her defiant spirit, and Willa couldn't help but be reminded of all the time they had passed telling each other outlandish stories or reading to each other from tales of romance and chivalry. She couldn't bear to think that Luciana might suffer the same fate as her beloved English mistress.

Ever since Gerard had gone into the building, Willa had been watching the tower observation level to see if she could spot him.

A man leaned out over the battlements, and she thought she recognized Gerard's beard and flowing mane of dark hair.

"Is that Sir Gerard?" Luciana said, pointing up.

"It must be," Willa replied, although he was so far away that she couldn't clearly see his features.

"I wonder if he can see us."

"Maybe if we wave to him?"

Willa was about to step out of the shadows when she saw two familiar faces.

Sofia and Armstrong were walking along the front of the Palazzo Pubblico, trailed by three of his mercenaries.

Willa grabbed the arm of Luciana, who gasped when she saw who Willa was pointing to. The five of them disappeared into the front entrance of the Palazzo.

"What are they doing here?"

"They must have worked out the clue too," Willa said.

"And found a way to get all five of them into the tower."

"Gerard will be trapped. We have to warn him."

Willa dashed out into the piazza, waving her arms frantically to get his attention. But given how high up he was, she knew it might be in vain.

 22

The few streets leading away from the Piazza del Campo didn't look like rays of Christ's halo to Fox. He'd seen paintings showing beams of light radiating from the Lord's head, but as he focused on the roofs of the buildings below, nothing looked close to that. From his perch, he could see many churches, any of which could be the one they were supposed to go to. None of them had any decoration or structural design that looked like rays.

He looked down at the piazza below, and his attention was drawn to two women frantically waving their arms. He immediately recognized the blue and green kirtles that Willa and Luciana were wearing. He couldn't see the expression on their faces from this far away, but they certainly seemed upset.

He waved back, and they instantly reacted with a different gesture. Willa pointed at the entrance to the palazzo and then up to him. He leaned out over the parapet as far as he dared, but he couldn't see anything unusual below.

He followed the line of travertine marble back up to Willa at the far side of the square, and he suddenly realized that there were eight of them separating the nine triangular sections of brick. All of the lines originated from the same point just in front of the palazzo, like rays coming from the sun—or a halo. Although the bricks would have been paving stones in Ramberti's time, the array of radiating lines had to be the meaning of her father's clue.

He was so excited by the revelation that he ignored Willa's continued wild gesticulations and thought about the first part of the line—"*the most sinister beam*." The left-most line below him pointed straight at the black and white cathedral. Whatever the depiction of Jesus was that they were being steered to—"*the symbol of purity and sacrifice, loved by a virgin"*—it had to be found somewhere in that church.

With this clue solved, he looked triumphantly back down at Willa, but she seemed even more agitated than before. Now she was pointing to Luciana's—gown? Arm? Sleeve? Luciana held her arm high above her head, and Willa was now shaking it. Her motions seemed urgent, but this was one riddle he wouldn't be able to solve until he returned to the piazza.

With his newfound solution to the puzzle of the sinister beam, he went to the stairs. The dimness enveloped him again as he began descending the long stairwell.

One flight down, the noise from the wind at the platform level had abated enough for him to hear voices and footsteps from below. Perhaps Gustavo was finally returning, but it also sounded like he had at least one companion, maybe more.

Fox stopped and peered over the guard wall. There was a single high-pitched voice among the sounds of men. Strange that a woman would be coming up with the guards. He couldn't see them clearly in the gloom, but then he caught one word that made his blood freeze.

Corosi.

He couldn't be sure, but the timbre of the voice was reminiscent of Armstrong's. Then it suddenly hit him what Willa was trying to tell him by pointing at Luciana's arm. It was a good idea, but "Armstrong" would never have occurred to him.

As they climbed nearer to him, Fox could make out the sound of at least four men clomping up the stone steps. He had only a few moments to plan how to fend off four mercenaries with nothing but the dagger on his belt.

"How long do we have alone in the tower?" Sofia asked Armstrong as she climbed the steps of the Torre del Mangia with the knight and his three men.

"Signore Corosi said the guard was paid to stay out until an hour after sext," Armstrong said.

Given their conversation the evening before, Sofia thought this was a great opportunity to have a little fun with him in front of his soldiers.

"That should be plenty of time for you to polish your sword while I figure out the clue."

"Perhaps I'll be the one to solve it."

"Your brain isn't made for such things. Leave the thinking to me."

Armstrong's expression darkened. Apparently, he didn't like insults any better than she did, even pretend ones.

"Maybe I have no reason to be here then."

She slathered on the sarcasm. "What would I have done if Riccardo hadn't sent you with me? I'm so relieved that a virile man of your fighting skill and tactical wisdom agreed to come with me for my safety."

"Signore Corosi puts his trust in you, despite my misgivings, so I am bound to his command."

"Now that is the first intelligent thing I've heard you say today."

One level down from the observation platform, they came to an open door into an alcove with a stool and a bucket. Sofia wrinkled her nose at the smell.

"That's revolting," she said.

Armstrong's eyes glinted as he teased her in return. "Given where you come from, I'm sure you've smelled worse."

"I have. He's standing right in front of me."

That brought a snicker from one of his men. Armstrong slammed his elbow into the soldier's chest, causing him to reel back against the guard wall and catch himself to avoid going over.

"I may not be able to lay a hand on her, but I don't have to put up with it from you. Wait here out of my sight and let us know if anyone is coming up."

The man rubbed his chest and nodded. Sofia knew she wouldn't hear a peep from either of the other two men.

"If you're finished with this display of your manhood," she said, "shall we continue up?"

"After you," he said. "I wouldn't want you to follow my stench."

She flashed a smirk at him and went up the final flight of stairs. The wind was blowing fiercely, but it was clear that Corosi had done his job. The observation level was empty.

Sofia was already proceeding around the battlement to look through the crenellations. Armstrong joined her while the two soldiers stood on the other side gazing out at the view.

"What is it we're looking for?" he asked loudly over the noise of the wind.

"Remember, I'm the one who is looking," she shot back.

"For the rays of Christ's halo?"

"Yes, now leave me to think."

Armstrong slapped her on the behind, and she jumped, smiling at him when she saw that he had done so because his men were otherwise occupied. He winked at her and left her alone. Sofia shook her head and forced herself to focus on solving the puzzle as she looked down at the Piazza del Campo.

Fox remained as still as he could behind the open alcove door. He hadn't even breathed when he heard Armstrong outside talking to Sofia. He had been hoping all of the men would go up to the top of the tower so he could sneak down behind them, but he silently cursed when Armstrong cuffed one of his men and ordered him to stay behind.

They hadn't seen him in his hiding place on the way up, so his best chance was to simply wait until they all went back down. Of course, that would mean his group would be behind if Armstrong and Sofia solved the clue as he had. They'd go directly over to the cathedral, delaying Fox, Willa, and Luciana's opportunity to decipher the next part of the riddle. But that was a problem they'd tackle when he got out of here safely.

Fox couldn't see the mercenary outside, but that didn't mean he was gone. He could be lounging anywhere in the stairway out of his view, so Fox couldn't risk going out. Although the wind was noisy above, a loud yell by the soldier would alert Armstrong and the others to his presence, so he stayed motionless.

Footsteps stomped his way, and Fox tensed. Armstrong's soldier entered the alcove and went straight over to the piss bucket, lifting his tunic.

This was Fox's chance to steal away. But he hadn't moved more than an inch when the door creaked, causing the mercenary to turn his head. The moment he saw Fox, he dropped what he'd been holding and opened his mouth to shout. Fox rushed to clamp his hand over it before the man could let out a sound.

The soldier grabbed Fox's wrist with both hands and launched himself into him, knocking over the bucket and sending a flood of foul liquid through the alcove.

He pushed Fox through the door and against the low guard wall on the stairs, pressing all his weight against Fox until they were both hanging over it.

Fox felt himself slipping. He was about to go over, so he let go of the man's mouth. To keep him from screaming, Fox punched at his throat.

The impact simultaneously made the soldier release his grip and took Fox over the side.

As he tipped away from the guard wall, Fox drew his knees up and thrust his feet against the mercenary's chest so that he propelled himself across the narrow shaft, barely catching onto the opposite guard wall's top edge with one hand. As he dangled there, he saw the soldier staggering and holding his neck, but he made no sound above a squeak.

Fox scrabbled to grab hold of the top edge with his other hand. By this time the mercenary had recovered enough to draw his dagger and career down the steps. One stab at Fox's hands would loosen his hold, and he had no hope that he would catch himself a second time.

He finally was able to find purchase on the stone as the soldier rounded the turn, but he knew he wouldn't be able to pull himself over before the mercenary reached him. He would have to time his next move perfectly.

He waited until the soldier reared back with the dagger to stab his right hand. The moment it came down, Fox let go and the knife jabbed into the stone. At the same instant, he latched on to the mercenary's wrist.

Instinctually, the soldier pulled back, lifting Fox from his predicament. He looped a leg over the wall and flipped over. The mercenary freed his wrist, but now Fox had the advantageous position, a few steps below the soldier and close to the outside wall of the tower.

As the mercenary thrust the dagger at him, Fox ducked down under it and grabbed hold of the man's boots. With all the strength he could muster, he lifted the man by his ankles and dumped him over the wall.

The mercenary didn't utter a sound before he slammed into the bottom of the shaft.

Fox got to his feet and looked down to see the man sprawled on the stone floor with his head in an unnatural position.

He took a moment to catch his breath and then started down, taking the steps two at a time. Fox was halfway to the ground level when he heard shouts from above. They must have noticed the overturned bucket and the dead man at the bottom of the stairs.

When he reached the corpse, he heard Armstrong and his men not far behind. Fox sprinted down to the entry hall of the palazzo and ran up to the guards at the entrance.

"*Guardie!*" he shouted at them in a breathless and terrified voice. "There is a dead man in the tower. I think the men coming down killed him!"

The two guards took their poleaxes and dashed toward the tower, calling for assistance as they ran. Fox thought that would slow Armstrong down and give him time to get away.

Outside the Palazzo Pubblico, Willa and Luciana were waiting for him across the piazza. When he reached them, Willa took his hand and said, "Thank goodness you got my message."

"I don't know how long they'll be detained," Fox said as he sucked in air. "We need to try to solve the next clue before they can get free."

"Then you solved the first one?" Luciana asked. "Where are we going?"

"Siena Cathedral." As they headed uphill toward the stairs leading to the basilica, he indicated the line of travertine they were following in the piazza bricks. "The most sinister beam showed me the way."

23

Siena Cathedral was only a short distance uphill from the Torre del Mangia. Willa glanced behind her, but she saw no sign of Armstrong or Sofia.

"How many statues and paintings of Jesus Christ are in the cathedral?" she asked Luciana.

"Many. Too many. The cathedral is enormous. This may take some time."

"If we don't solve it right away and move on," Gerard said, "Armstrong will likely talk his way out of the Palazzo and place his men-at-arms around the cathedral to ambush us."

"We should separate and each look for something that fits the clue," Willa said.

"Exactly how did it go?"

Luciana recited the last two lines of the relevant quatrain. "*Find there the symbol of purity and sacrifice, loved by a virgin. Move four circles from that noble face and you will know the next step.*"

"So we're looking for any image of Christ that relates to circles," Willa said.

"You two take a quick look around the church and then meet back near the entrance," Gerard said. "I'll stay by the door to watch for them coming. If I see them, I'll shout a warning and we'll meet… where?"

"By the altar," Luciana said. "There's another door in the transept that leads outside. Jacopo's palazzo isn't far."

Luciana took the left side of the cathedral while Willa took the right, moving as fast as she could during her search. She quickly dismissed anything that didn't have an image of Christ. The first chapel she came to featured a fresco depicting the Lord, but he was a baby being cradled by the Virgin Mary surrounded by saints. Nothing looked circular in the painting except for the vaguely round heads. She tried counting four heads from the Christ child's face, but it didn't reveal anything but Saint Sabinus kneeling in adoration.

Willa continued on and found two different statues of Jesus on the cross. Again, there were no circles around the crucifix.

The stained-glass windows were a possibility, but she quickly decided they wouldn't work. They were too far above her to inspect them clearly. Luciana's father had made the clues obtuse, but Willa didn't think he would have made them that physically difficult to see.

Her eyes were drawn back occasionally to Gerard who stood guard at the cathedral door. By this time, he was tiny in her vision, but he hadn't moved, so she took that as a good sign.

Luciana was at the altar when she arrived there.

"Anything?" she asked.

Luciana shook her head. "The circles are the key. The image must be here somewhere."

Because they had stayed on the periphery of the church looking in the side chapels where most of the artworks were located, they hadn't yet looked at anything in the nave between the main pillars.

They marched down the central space, carefully checking for any possible picture or sculpture of Jesus.

When they neared the front, Gerard was impatiently waving at them to move faster.

Near the front entry, Willa looked down and saw a mosaic in the floor. She could barely keep herself from jumping up and down with excitement when she saw that it was filled with circles.

"Look!" she said.

Luciana shook her head. "I thought of this mosaic immediately. The She-Wolf of Siena welcomes worshippers as they enter the cathedral. But as you can see, there is no depiction of Christ. It's a series of animals representing the cities of Italy."

Willa's elation dissipated when she saw that Luciana was correct. There were eight circles surrounding an image of the

She-Wolf suckling Romulus and Remus that represented Siena. Each of the outer circles showed a different animal with a Latin city name beside it: a lion for Florence, a rabbit for Pisa, an elephant for Rome, a unicorn for Viterbo…

That animal stopped Willa short, and her heart started racing.

"The unicorn," she said, grabbing Luciana's arm before she could walk away.

Luciana looked at it, confused at what Willa meant.

"We were looking for the wrong symbol," Willa went on. "The unicorn is '*the symbol of sacrifice and purity*'."

Luciana's eyes went wide. "'*Loved by a virgin*.' Of course! One of my favorite stories is the legend of the unicorn, that it is a fierce woodland creature of such purity and nobility that it can only be lured into the arms of a loving virgin."

"All we need to do is count out the circles from the face of the unicorn, and that's where we are to go next."

Willa counted out four circles and came to a horse with "Aretium" below it.

"Arezzo," Luciana said. "That's east of Siena."

"Then that's our destination."

Gerard came upon them at a trot.

"Armstrong and Corosi are crossing the square outside with eight men. We need to leave now whether you've solved the clue or not."

He hurried them toward the altar.

"Actually, we have solved it," Willa said triumphantly. "We're going to Arezzo."

Luciana suddenly gasped. "No, we're not."

Willa looked at her in confusion. "But that was four circles from the face of the unicorn."

"A unicorn?" Gerard said. "I thought we were looking for an image of Christ."

"So did we. But Luciana remembered that the unicorn is a common symbol for Christ. Are you saying that Arezzo is not the correct city?" Willa asked Luciana.

"That's what I'm saying."

"Then what is the correct city?" Gerard asked.

Luciana looked dismayed as she steered them to the side door of the cathedral.

"I can't remember."

While the guards at the Palazzo Pubblico had detained Armstrong and his men to question them about the corpse at the bottom of the tower stairwell, Sofia was able to play the terrified damsel and escape their clutches. She made her way directly over to the cathedral. To minimize the chance of being seen by Luciana, Fox, or Willa, she entered a side door instead of the main one.

It took some time prowling around the vast nave, but she finally spotted Luciana inspecting every painting, statue, and stained-glass window that she came across. Willa was on the other side of the cathedral doing the same, and Fox stood at the main door as a lookout. Sofia observed Luciana from afar, carefully staying out of sight.

They hadn't seemed to linger on anything for very long until she and Willa reunited near the entrance. They grew excited about a mosaic on the floor, pointing down at it and obviously counting something out.

Then Fox whisked them out of the church through the same side door where she'd entered, and she soon saw why. Corosi and a furious Armstrong came charging in with a cadre of men. Hurrying from her hiding place to the entry, Sofia pointed Armstrong and his soldiers to the exit the three had taken, and they gave chase, though it seemed unlikely they'd catch their quarry.

Corosi walked over to her.

"The guards at the Palazzo Pubblico were ready to throw Armstrong into a dungeon for murder until they fetched me and I could explain that his man's death was just a tragic accident. On our way here, he told me how you solved the first part of the clue. What about the second?"

"It seems that your wife and her friends may have solved it for us."

Together they walked the short distance over to the mosaic. The circles indicating the surrounding cities must have been what they were looking for, but Sofia didn't know why. Corosi frowned at them.

"I don't understand. I thought we were looking for an image of Christ."

"From my view, they seemed to be looking at one of the circles at the bottom."

They looked for a good while before Sofia clapped her hands and pointed at the animal indicating Viterbo.

"The unicorn?" Corosi said.

Sofia nodded. "We might have searched for a long time before I realized we were looking for the wrong symbol of purity. The unicorn and the virgin represent the relationship between Christ and the Virgin Mary."

"I didn't know that."

Sofia counted four circles ahead of the unicorn. "Then it's Arezzo."

"Let's hope that's what they think the answer is."

Her face screwed up in confusion. "That's not correct? The clue said to '*Move four circles from that noble face.*'"

"Ramberti wrote his clues in 1314. He was probably expecting Luciana and Matteo to solve his puzzles immediately after receiving the letters. But now it's been thirty-seven years. Things have changed."

Sofia immediately understood what he meant. "Including the mosaics on the floor."

"The She-Wolf of Siena—the one Ramberti would have seen— was replaced just before the Great Mortality. The cities were in a different order in the previous version. I remember because I always loved the lion of Florence. It was not in that place."

"Do you remember what the original order was?"

"I only remember where Florence was, but I don't remember where the unicorn was."

"Then who would?"

"I don't know," Corosi said. "We have to find someone who has a strong memory of the original and wasn't killed by the Pestilence."

 24

Back in the security of Jacopo Barbieri's solar later that afternoon, Fox and Willa were trying to nudge Luciana's memory about the original version of the She-Wolf mosaic, but she couldn't be certain which city they were looking for. It was frustrating to be so tantalizingly close to solving the clue.

"When was the last time you saw it?" he asked her.

"I don't know. We used to play games on the circles when I was a little girl, which is why I remember it was different, but I haven't really looked at it in years."

"Can you close your eyes and imagine it in your mind?" Willa asked.

Luciana shut her eyes. After a few moments, she opened them again. "All I see is the new one."

Barbieri waddled in and settled his bulk onto the chaise. His steward Niccolò set a tray of candied fruits down on the table next to him.

"I just heard from some friends at the Palazzo Pubblico," he said. "It took a visit from Corosi to vouch for Armstrong and free him. I enjoy the thought of him having to explain away a dead body."

"Then you're not angry?" Fox said.

Barbieri grinned. "Not at all, young man. Anything that causes consternation for Corosi is welcome."

"Then maybe you can help us with another problem," Luciana said. "Do you remember the original mosaic of the She-Wolf of Siena?"

"On the cathedral floor? Of course."

Fox felt a flicker of hope.

"Do you recall the order of the circles listing the cities before it was redone?" Willa asked.

Barbieri laughed. "I didn't commit its design details to memory."

An incorrect guess would send them in the wrong direction. Given the travel time required, if Corosi somehow actually did know the correct city, he could be weeks ahead of them in the quest when they finally realized the error.

"Why on earth would you want to know such an obscure detail?" he asked.

"All I can tell you," Luciana said, "is that learning that information will help me rid myself of Riccardo."

"You have me intrigued, but I still don't know the answer. I could guess for you."

"We need to be certain," Fox said. "Do you know anyone who would have that knowledge?"

"As a matter of fact, I think I know how we can find out the answer."

"Jacopo, we would be in your debt if you would guide us to the solution," Luciana said.

"I'm sure you would, but it would require retrieving a diagram from the cathedral library. I believe the drawing of the original design resides there."

"We would very much appreciate seeing it," Willa said.

"The library is not a place that allows outsiders. My confraternity commissioned one of the chapels in the cathedral, and the library clerk is a member. I could use my connection to him to obtain it and bring it to you, but it would be at some cost to me. Therefore, it would have to come at some cost to you."

Fox carefully reminded Barbieri of his pledge to help them do anything to make his rival's life miserable.

"If we could see the drawing," he said, "it will further our cause to bring down Signore Corosi."

"And that is tempting, indeed. But this is a much touchier subject. If it were learned that I'd compromised the cathedral's library, I would be dismissed from the confraternity, which would deprive me of all sorts of business benefits. I'm afraid I can't think of anything you could give me that would make it worth that risk."

At that moment, Barbieri's steward Niccolò entered.

"Signore, you have a caller. Signore Corosi."

"Riccardo is here?" Barbieri said. "Is he alone?"

"No, signore. His Palio rider is with him. Shall I tell Signore Corosi that you are occupied?"

"By all means, bring him in. I'm sure we have much to discuss."

Niccolò nodded and left.

"We should go," Fox said. He made a move to leave with Willa and Luciana, but Barbieri put a hand up to stop them.

"Oh, no. Stay. This obviously has to do with all three of you."

"I don't want to see him," Luciana said.

"Don't worry, Luciana. You are safe here. But if Riccardo has risked coming see me in my own house, I'd like to hear what he has to say."

"He wants me turned over to him."

"You forget, my dear. This is my city. Riccardo has no power over me here."

Niccolò led Corosi into the solar, followed by Armstrong, who shot a sly grin at Fox.

Barbieri made the effort to get to his feet and exchanged the customary greetings with Corosi before returning to his chaise. He indicated for Corosi to sit while everyone else remained standing. After Niccolò poured him a goblet of wine, Barbieri toasted him.

"So good of you to come visit me, Riccardo. Much better than your palazzo, I imagine. Luciana was telling me of the rat infestation there. I was happy to let her stay here until it's taken care of. I suppose it's fortunate that it's my family's turn to host the celebration feast after the Palio this year."

Corosi didn't touch his wine. "She's lying to you, Jacopo, and you know it."

"Do I?"

"What other lies has she been telling you?"

"This is an awfully unpleasant way to start our conversation. Wouldn't you rather talk about the upcoming Palio?"

"I'm sorry, Jacopo, but you should know the kind of people you're harboring."

"I don't appreciate your tone, Riccardo. Luciana has asked for the protection of my home, and it's my duty to honor that request." Barbieri leaned forward, and his amiable demeanor vanished. "But since you are making accusations, I must tell you that there is doubt about who is responsible for that frightful attack in San Giuseppe. The one in which my cousin Piero was killed."

"Are you saying that I was involved?"

"I never received my gold, and yet you received the signed contract selling you my banking assets in Florence."

"Do you have evidence that I plotted the attack?"

"I have this man's claim that he discovered that the helmet of the man standing next to you was the same worn in the assault."

"Signore," Armstrong said, "you cannot believe a thing this man has told you."

"And why is that?"

"Because he is a heretic. You are hosting a man who has been excommunicated by the Church."

Fox felt all eyes turn to him in shock. Even Willa didn't have to feign her horror at Armstrong's accusation.

That got Barbieri to his feet.

"How do you know this?"

"Because I saw his trial when I was back in England, after he had assaulted a cardinal. He was excommunicated for his crime."

Barbieri turned to Fox with a look of disgust. "Is this true?"

If Fox admitted that he'd been excommunicated, they would all be turned out in an instant. He had to think quickly and speak carefully.

"I am just as appalled as you are by this accusation being laid at my feet," Fox said. "Perhaps Sir Randolf saw someone else in London. I swear that I would never commit a crime against the Church that would merit excommunication, and to accuse me of doing such a thing is false."

All of it was technically true. He considered the Church's

excommunication invalid because of the heinous events involving the Fox family that precipitated the charge.

"I can't trust my own eyes?" Armstrong said, advancing on Fox.

"I wouldn't trust anything about you."

"Says the heretic."

Barbieri put up his hands. "Gentlemen, there will be no fighting in my house. Luciana, were you aware that you were traveling with an accused excommunicant?"

Luciana edged away from Fox. "Absolutely not."

Barbieri turned to him. "These are serious charges, Sir Gerard."

"I suppose it's my word against his," Fox replied. "Only the records at the Papal Palace in Avignon would be able to decide the matter in my favor." Also in principle true, even if they would inevitably be decisive against him.

"And it would take weeks or months to get a reply to an inquiry such as this."

"Very likely."

"Don't tell me that you believe this stranger?" Corosi said.

"I don't know who is telling the truth," Barbieri said.

"My man is not only my Palio rider, but he has sworn an oath of loyalty to me. Do you want to take a chance that you are harboring a known excommunicant?"

Barbieri studied his guests. "Perhaps not."

Just fraternizing with an excommunicant was damaging, so Fox wasn't surprised that Barbieri was beginning to waver. He racked his brain for how to salvage the quickly deteriorating situation, but before he could come up with anything, Willa spoke.

"Piero was to be your rider in the Palio, wasn't he?"

Barbieri frowned at her. "What has that to do with anything?"

"You've said how important the Palio is. Let Gerard ride for you. He has the fastest horse in Christendom."

Fox gaped at her, as did Barbieri.

"Pardon me?" said the Sienese lord.

Luciana jumped in. "It's true. He's an excellent rider. I saw it during the fight in San Giuseppe. He did things on his horse that defy belief."

Fox thought the odds of him winning were long, but he realized this might be their best option.

"If I outrace Sir Randolf in the Palio," he said, "then we will know whom God has favored."

"You can't seriously be considering this, Jacopo," Corosi said.

"I thought you had confidence in your man," Barbieri said.

Armstrong smiled. "I'll be happy to race him."

"Then perhaps we should make it more interesting," Corosi said.

Barbieri raised an eyebrow. "A wager?"

"Exactly. If Sir Randolf beats him, you will turn Luciana over to me without delay for associating with an excommunicant. Sir Gerard and his wife will be revealed as heretics."

Fox knew what that meant. Because he had been excommunicated for more than a year without seeking absolution, he could be tried by the Church for heresy, and Willa with him for knowingly consorting with an excommunicant. Even if they could somehow escape being turned over to the Church, Armstrong and his men would be waiting for them outside the city gates.

"And if Sir Gerard is victorious," Barbieri said, "we will know that he was telling the truth, and you will pay me every single florin stolen at San Giuseppe before you leave Siena."

Corosi grumbled at the condition and looked to Armstrong, who nodded confidently.

"I accept your terms," Corosi said.

"Excellent," Barbieri said, pushing himself out of his chair. "Rest assured I will be telling my confraternity what you have promised me if you lose the wager."

"I wouldn't think of attempting to get past the city guards without paying my debts. Of course, I won't have to worry about that. In three days' time, Sir Randolf will win easily once more."

"These women seem to think otherwise."

Corosi regarded Luciana and let out a huge laugh. "What do women know about racing? Come, Sir Randolf. We need to prepare for our victory."

Corosi swept out of the room. Before he went out as well,

Armstrong turned to Fox and said, "I'll see you on the course. It should be entertaining."

When they were gone, the solar was silent. Barbieri was the first to speak. "I hope you are telling the truth."

"Armstrong doesn't know the full—" Fox started to reply, but Barbieri cut him off.

"I was talking to Lady Fox. If you are lying about Sir Gerard's skills as a rider, the three of you will be in grave trouble. I won't be able to protect you. Nor would I want to."

"If you doubt me, why did you agree to the wager?" Willa asked.

"Quite simply, I have nothing to lose and everything to gain."

"Gerard is a master horseman atop Zephyr."

Barbieri looked at Fox with amusement. "Your horse has a Greek name? Interesting. Is it fast?"

Zephyr had never raced before, but he wasn't named for the god of the west wind because he was slow. Fox nodded.

"It had better be. I've seen Armstrong best every rider put against him in the Palio, and with ease. At least you can't be worse than Piero. He was the most competent rider I had, and he still had little chance of victory."

"I have one request," Fox said. "If I win this wager for you, you will obtain the drawing of the She-Wolf mosaic so that we can see it."

Barbieri nodded. "It would be worth the risk to my reputation if it meant seeing Corosi on the losing side of the Palio and recouping my monetary losses. I'll show you the drawing after the celebration that evening. *If* you beat him."

Fox didn't like this one bit, but he was committed now.

"If I'm to race, I should know the rules."

"What rules there are. Interfering with other riders and their horses is not out of bounds. Although weapons aren't allowed, the riding sticks that the competitors carry can deliver an effective blow. The race is run through Siena from the Porta Camollia in the north to the Porta Romana in the south. The first horse to cross the finish line is the winner. That's it."

"What is the course?" Willa asked.

"There is no course," Luciana said. "Riders can take whatever route they want through the city."

"Although almost all riders take the main road through town," Barbieri said. "It's the shortest distance."

"And all Gerard has to do is beat Armstrong to the finish?" Willa said.

"I said the first horse to the gate is the victor. Not the rider. A riderless horse has won, though rarely. As you can imagine, the competition can be brutal. Something I hope you'll keep in mind as you race."

"Then I suppose I should ready my saddle."

Barbieri put up a finger. "That's the other rule. Competitors ride bareback. Reins only. You'll be wearing the colors of my family's standard, naturally."

"And all I have to do is beat Armstrong."

"Yes, but keep in mind that Corosi will have some allies in the race. You'll need to be wary of them. Which makes me realize that I need to inform my own allies that you'll be riding for my *contrada*. Oh, and you might want to practice racing on our stone streets. They can be slippery. You don't have much time to prepare, so I'll leave you to it."

Fox didn't like the idea of risking a broken leg for Zephyr on the paving, but he was committed to the race now.

As soon as Barbieri was out of the room, Luciana stalked over to Fox, her face livid with rage.

"You really are excommunicated, aren't you? That's why you and Willa travel around with no aim, without servants, in a foreign land."

Fox looked at Willa, who nodded.

"It's true," he said. "I'm sorry we didn't tell you. I didn't actually swear a false oath just now—every word I said was the literal truth. I had to make them think I'm not excommunicated. But we won't keep the truth from you."

"And in that spirit," Willa said, "we should also tell you that we are not married, even though that's what we led you to believe. I sincerely apologize, Luciana."

Luciana's eyes went wide, and she took a step back. "Do you realize what a terrible position you've put me in? I shouldn't even associate with you now that I know what you are, but doing so would confirm Jacopo's suspicions. He'd expel me from his house and seal my fate with Riccardo."

"It is an invalid excommunication because it was unjust," Willa said.

Luciana shook her head. "Invalid? In what way?"

Fox took a deep breath. "The cardinal who accused me of assaulting him abducted my mother, raped her, and held her captive. I never saw her again because she died in childbirth bearing him an illegitimate son."

Luciana softened at that. "Didn't you report this at the trial?"

"Of course, but I had no evidence, and nobody would believe a minor noble over a cardinal. My father died in the Pestilence because we had nowhere to turn."

"Then the cardinal—"

"Is dead. And I'm condemned for the rest of my life."

"Unless we can find proof that the cardinal committed his crimes," Willa added, glancing at Fox. "I believe that would allow for absolution by the pope."

Luciana pursed her lips. "I want to believe you, and if you win, I will. But if you lose…" She looked up at him. "Just don't lose."

"I have faith in Gerard, Luciana," Willa said.

Luciana nodded, but Fox could see that she was still appalled to be in his presence. She retreated from the room on her guard, as if he had been transformed into a demon.

Once she was gone, he shook his head at Willa. "That was a simultaneously foolish and clever thing to do."

"Volunteering you to be Signore Barbieri's rider? What other option did we have? He was about to shove all three of us out the door on the chance that he was consorting with an excommunicant." Willa paused for a moment and then said quietly, "You remember what happened in Sezino."

Fox nodded. It had been a difficult lesson for both of them.

25

Three weeks ago—September, 1351

LIGURIA, ITALY

In the fortnight since leaving Turin, Fox was starting to wonder if he and Willa would ever find a place to marry.

"I'd guess that Father Lorenzo has the entirety of the Church's canon law memorized," Willa said as they rode side by side, alone on the road between Genoa and Florence.

Fox nodded. "Word for word. I'm sure the parishioners in Sezino have nightmares where he won't stop reciting it to them."

"I'm glad you didn't get as far as proposing the idea of marrying us without posting the banns. He might have ridden to Genoa to report us to the archbishop himself."

"Shouting papal pronouncements all the way. If there were a prize for adhering to rules, he would be named champion."

The small town behind them was just the latest in a string of places where they'd had no luck locating a priest who would wed them. To avoid drawing too much attention to themselves, they'd made their inquiries more subtle than they had in Turin. If it didn't seem as if the priest would be amenable to their request for speed and privacy, they quietly moved on.

Fox found the delay maddening. If it went on much longer, he would be sorely tempted to challenge their premarital chastity vow. But they'd agreed to wait until they found a priest prepared to administer the sacrament on their terms, so he would simply have to bear the frustration.

"I'm hoping we'll come across someone near Florence who will be a bit more willing to bend the rules."

"I have faith it will happen," Willa said. "In the meantime, the journey is helping improve our Italian."

Fox and Willa had spent a good portion of their travel in the company of pilgrims and merchants who were happy to converse with foreigners in their native tongue. They already both spoke and read Latin, so the new language was coming to them more easily than they were expecting.

Since they were alone at the moment, they spent time testing each other on different words as they rode, pointing out various objects in the forest they were passing through, its leaves turning pleasing shades of red and gold. Fox was trying to recall the word for "root" when their game was interrupted by a loud crash accompanied by a man's scream from farther into the woods.

"That sounded like a tree falling," Fox said as he brought Zephyr to a halt.

"Foresters?" Willa asked.

Fox listened but heard no other voices. "Perhaps a single one by himself."

"He might be hurt."

They had decided when they left the Sacra di San Michele to help those in need. This was their first chance to do so.

He dismounted and guided Zephyr into the trees, followed by Willa and Comis. There was no more noise to direct them.

They wandered for some time without seeing anything unusual. Finally, Fox saw a brighter spot in the trees where a new opening in the leafy autumn canopy had been created. A splintered stump sat underneath it, the massive trunk lying on its side. He could see where an axe had cut into the wood, but now that it had fallen, the rot in its core was visible.

He gave Zephyr's reins to Willa and walked along the trunk, climbing over branches that impeded his progress. When he stepped on something hard, he looked down and found an axe head. The handle had been broken in two by the impact.

He kept walking until he suddenly saw a pair of feet sticking out of a clump of leaves.

"I've found him!" he called out.

Fox circled around, preparing himself for the gruesome sight of a man crushed by the thick tree. He pushed a leafy branch aside to see an unconscious man in tattered clothes. He was on his back next to the trunk, and the left side of his temple was scraped and bloody. He must have been hit as he'd run away from the tree after its rotten core unexpectedly shattered. Fox couldn't tell if he was still breathing.

Willa came over and kneeled beside the woodsman. She put her hand on his chest.

"He's not dead, but his head wound needs tending." She checked the rest of his body. "It seems to be his only injury."

"They must know him in Sezino," Fox said. "We'll take him back there."

"Let me bandage his head before we move him."

Willa retrieved a kerchief from her saddle and wrapped it around the woodsman's head to stanch the bleeding. When it was secure, Fox put two fingers up to his mouth and whistled for Zephyr. The horse trotted over while he lifted the motionless man onto his shoulder. Zephyr came to a stop beside Fox, who laid the woodsman as gently as he could face down over the saddle.

As they walked the horses back to Sezino, the woodsman didn't move. Fox grimly thought it likely that the man would never awaken.

It was midday by the time they reached the village. The townspeople gawked at the sight of the prone man draped over Zephyr.

Although they had only stayed in Sezino for a day, Willa had become acquainted with one of the local women named Felicita who shared an affinity for healing herbs and poultices, so they steered their horses to her home.

When she heard the commotion outside, Felicita, heavy with child and not much older than Willa, came out of the house and said, "Signorina, you've returned? What's happened?"

Willa dismounted and pointed at the man draped over Zephyr's back.

"We came across him in the forest. He's badly injured and needs your help."

"Of course. Please bring him inside."

Fox unslung him from the saddle and turned to carry him into the house when Felicita staggered backward in fright.

"No! He cannot come into my home."

"But he's hurt," Willa protested. "I don't understand."

Felicita just shook her head and dashed into her house, slamming the door behind her.

Fox glanced around him, and the other villagers seemed just as dismayed by the man's presence. From the church, Father Lorenzo, a small man with thin lips and thinner hair, marched toward them, waving frantically.

"You must put him down at once!"

"What are you talking about, Father? He needs help."

"He is unclean! If you continue to assist him, you will be condemned!"

The man seemed to be regaining consciousness and Fox felt him faintly stirring on his shoulder. He groaned and writhed, so Fox, not knowing what else to do, carefully slid him down and sat him against the town's stone well.

"Are you saying you won't help this man?" Fox demanded.

"We cannot. None of us. That means you as well. Alfonso is a heretic. He has been excommunicated."

Fox froze, his stomach ice cold. Other than his own father, he'd never met anyone else who had been excommunicated.

"For what crime?" Willa asked.

Alfonso, moaning and holding his head, croaked out an answer. "For baptizing my child."

Father Lorenzo practically spat at the injured woodsman. "That is a lie! He continues to blaspheme."

The injured man struggled to get the words out. "Giulia died. No midwife. Alessandro was so weak. I baptized him. He died before we got to Sezino."

Fox frowned at the priest. "He was excommunicated for that?

I thought Church law says that anyone can baptize a baby if necessary when a priest isn't available."

Father Lorenzo looked at Alfonso with disgust. "Alfonso told me the words he used. 'Alessandro, *ego te baptizo in nome Patris, et Filii, et Spiritus Sancti.*'"

Fox immediately understood the problem. "He said '*nome*' instead of '*nomine.*'"

"Exactly. The Italian word instead of Latin. It was not a legitimate baptism. His son is therefore unnamed and will spend eternity in limbo."

Alfonso rose for a brief moment in fury. "He is in Heaven with Giulia!" His energy sapped, he fell back against the well.

"*That* is why he was excommunicated," Father Lorenzo said. "Despite my warnings, he continued to make his blasphemous claim. The bishop knew it was a challenge to Church teachings and had to be punished. Alfonso refuses to recant and seek absolution."

"My son is in Heaven," Alfonso mumbled, then he groaned in pain.

Willa bent down to adjust the bandage that had come loose.

"Stop!" Father Lorenzo commanded.

"But his dressing needs tending," Willa protested.

"I will forgive your assistance to him up to this point, but now you are aware of his excommunication. The Church orders that he is to be shunned. If you continue to aid him, I will have no choice but to consider your actions heretical as well and report you to Church authorities."

Willa shot a pleading glance at Fox, but he shook his head at her. He knew how dangerous it could be for them if they were accused of consorting with an excommunicant. Crisis situations could be judged as exceptions by individual priests depending on their interpretation of Church law, but Father Lorenzo would not be one of them.

"We have no choice," Fox said.

"We can't just leave him here in the dirt," Willa protested.

"You must," Father Lorenzo said.

She looked down with pity at the woodsman.

"You've been kind enough," Alfonso said weakly. "Go. I want to join my family in Heaven."

Fox didn't know how close to death Alfonso was, but consorting with him further would make them targets of the Church.

"I'm sorry, Alfonso," he said.

"God be with you," Willa said.

Fox took her arm and led her away. The villagers didn't even glance at Alfonso lying on the ground. They were too afraid of the combined wrath of God and Father Lorenzo.

"I knew the decree would impact what we could do," Willa whispered to Fox, "but I didn't imagine it would be like this."

"Now you understand why we're being so careful in our attempt to get married. Does this change your mind?"

He thought Willa hesitated just a moment before she shook her head.

"My future is with you."

He nodded and smiled at her. "And mine is with you."

For the first time, Fox noted a band of traveling pilgrims who had stopped to watch the commotion as they were passing through the village. He asked them which way they were headed.

"To Florence," one of them replied.

Fox asked if he and Willa could join them. They enthusiastically agreed to have an armed nobleman and his lady accompany them.

After the spectacle they'd witnessed, Fox knew the pilgrims would be horrified if they realized they'd consented to travel with an outcast like the man lying in the dirt.

26

October, 1351

SIENA

On the morning of the Palio, Luciana sat in Barbieri's section of the temporary stands especially built for the nobles next to the finish line just inside the huge Porta Romana gate. Eager citizens lined the stretch of road leading up to the ribbon that would be pulled across the line for the winning horse to break. Virtually the entire city had turned out for the event, plus thousands of others who had come from miles away to share in the excitement.

Many of the spectators were wearing or carrying the colors of their *contrada*, or neighborhood, all seventeen of which would be represented in the race. Their riders were chosen by each *contrada*'s most prominent family. Amongst the sea of colors, plenty of people wore Barbieri's *contrada* colors of blue and white, but nearly as many wore Corosi's red and black.

Everyone was waiting for the pre-race procession. All of the horses would parade from the finish line to the starting point so that the viewers would get a good look at them before they went racing by in the other direction. The Porta Romana gate was draped with the traditional *drappellone*, a banner designed yearly that would be presented to the victorious *contrada*. This year it showed the Virgin Mary and Saint Roch, the patron saint invoked against the Pestilence, trampling a figure representing Death.

Barbieri was yet to arrive, but he had arranged for Luciana to sit with him. Two of his guards stood at the entrance to the stands nearby. She knew what was at stake, and she was so deep in thought that she was startled when her husband spoke from behind her.

"It's a glorious day for a competition, no?"

She turned to see Corosi, alone, smiling up at the blue sky then down at her. She felt her body stiffen at the sight of him, but she was confident he wouldn't do anything to her here in broad daylight.

"I know you're bitter, but you should also know that our disagreement isn't personal. Although I loved you once, I have to think about the legacy of the Corosi name. If you could bear me another son, I would gladly take you into my chambers this evening."

"That will never happen again."

"It hasn't happened for a long time. Besides, I wouldn't want to spoil my victory celebration with something so pedestrian. Luckily your maid has been far more accommodating, and more skilled, I might add."

Despite her disgust, Luciana dug her fingers into her hands and kept a measured tone. "I shouldn't be surprised that she is a whore as well as a traitor. Although she'll be a prime consolation prize to comfort you in your loss tonight, you'll probably be too drunk."

"Barbieri does serve some of the best wine in Tuscany."

"Isn't your seat at the opposite end of the stands?"

"The most favored position to watch my horse cross the line in the lead."

"The only way you'll win is by cheating."

"I don't cheat, but I do take advantage of a good opportunity. It worked for me in my duel with Matteo."

Finding out that Sofia was his mistress had been only a pinprick compared to this comment, delivered so casually. "What are you talking about?"

"Matteo was so confident in his skill as a swordsman that he didn't notice the special oil I had spread on the glove that I threw down. From the moment he touched it, he'd already lost."

"You poisoned him?"

"I took advantage of an opportunity, and I was victorious because of it. He was outwitted by his better."

In one moment, all she had based her life on crumbled before her eyes. That duel had decided her fate, and all these years she had thought that she must have made the right decision because God chose the victor. Now she knew it was all a lie. She mourned anew for Matteo's death and the life with him that she was never allowed to have. Her sense of loss was soon displaced by a growing rage, exactly what Riccardo wanted. But if she lashed out at him, it might be just the excuse he needed to haul her away.

She tamped down her fury and calmly said, "So you used a tool of the Devil and cheated. God didn't actually favor you in that duel."

"Of course He did. I won."

"You're a coward and a liar."

"Your taunts are pathetic. I simply came over to remind you that your time will come."

"As will yours."

"I know it will. Just not in the same way." He leaned down. "No one makes me look like a fool. Especially not my own wife."

"I think I already have," Luciana said through a taut smile. "Either kill me here and now or leave me be."

Corosi's hand rested on the bejeweled dagger in his belt. His fingers tensed as if he might really do it. But another voice caused him to drop his hand from his dagger.

"Riccardo!" Barbieri boomed as he lowered his bulk down into his seat next to Luciana. "Are you coming to join us on this end of the stands?"

Corosi straightened up and spoke loudly for the surrounding nobles to hear. "I'm here to wish you luck. You'll need it. I'll even let Signora Corosi stay here so that she can lend her ear when you're wailing after your loss."

"And who will console you when you lose?"

"I haven't even considered that possibility."

With a sweep of his cloak, he went down to his chair among the other nobles allied with his *contrada*.

"He's a confident one," Barbieri said. "I'll give him that."

"He thinks he's invincible."

"I hope your friend Sir Gerard can disabuse Riccardo of that notion. My money is riding on that horse of his."

"God will favor Sir Gerard," she said.

Now that Luciana realized Matteo's loss in the duel was not a true judgment by the Lord, she had renewed confidence that a Fox victory would be a fair indication that he was being truthful. If he did win, she could rest assured that his excommunication was, in fact, undeserved, just as he'd said.

Her eyes wandered to the staging area inside the Porta Romana, where she caught a glimpse of Willa affectionately rubbing Zephyr's nose. Then she saw Corosi regale his seatmates with his tiresome boasting, which made Luciana worry more than ever. If he would cheat in a duel to the death, she could only imagine what he and Armstrong had planned for the Palio.

Women were uncommon in the paddock before the race, but no one paid attention to Willa. There wasn't much activity for the squires since the horses were equipped with just the reins and a small wooden board between their ears, painted in the *contrada*'s colors.

Zephyr had been blessed the day before in an elaborate ceremony at Barbieri's parish church, the same kind of rite that took place in churches across the city. Among the solid brown, black, and white horses, Zephyr's mottled silver coloring stood out.

Willa saw Armstrong in a red and black tunic standing next to his sinewy black courser. It was so energetic that he was having to hold it tightly to keep it from bolting.

"That horse certainly is spirited," a voice said beside her.

It was Gerard, who was dressed in a short blue cotte with dagged sleeves over a white tunic. His parti-colored hose, with one leg blue and the other white, were meant to show off his physique, which she thought they did quite well. The same colors even embellished a fancy velvet cap with a feather that Barbieri insisted he wear. His only equipment was a blunt wooden stick the length of his forearm used to prod the horses since spurs were not allowed.

Willa suppressed an amused smile as she took in his outfit.

"I don't want to hear a word," Gerard said.

"I think you look dashing," Willa said.

"I look like a jester."

Willa grinned at him. "Stop fussing. All the other riders are dressed the same way. It makes you easier to pick out during the race."

"These hose will make it a challenge to stay on Zephyr. I should have practiced riding in the actual clothes."

Willa turned serious. "I heard that horses often slide and fall on the stones."

"Then that's my best strategy for knocking Armstrong out of the race."

She followed his eyes down to Armstrong, who looked back with a mixture of supreme assurance and disdain.

"Do you remember the route?"

Gerard nodded. He had spent the entire previous day walking the streets of Siena to familiarize himself with them.

"I can find my way back to the main road if I get steered off course."

"I know you'll win. The Lord is on your side."

"I'm glad you have such confidence."

"Still, I don't know if I'll be able to breathe after the bell rings."

The race was to start at the midday canonical hour of sext. By prior arrangement, the only bell in the city that would ring was the one atop the Torre del Mangia to signal the start of the race.

"When you win," Willa said, "I hope you'll take it as a sign that someday you'll be absolved of your excommunication."

They hadn't spoken of this for several days. She thought Gerard might respond with exasperation at her bringing up this issue again, but instead he seemed genuinely touched by her faith in him. It was the first glimmer she'd seen that he might be changing his mind about pursuing absolution.

"You won't give up on that, will you?" he said.

"No, and neither should you. I have confidence in you. I'll be cheering for you here beyond the finish line."

"Let's hope you see me at all."

Just then, the race marshal cried out, "Riders, mount your horses!"

"God be with you," Willa said and squeezed Gerard's hand.

He nodded and squeezed back. Then he gripped Zephyr's black mane and pulled himself onto the horse's bare back.

Willa stepped away as the riders began their procession and the throngs let out a hearty cheer at seeing the *drappellone* leading the way.

Gerard looked behind one last time at Willa and waved, then turned away. She knew he would now be focused on nothing but how to keep Armstrong from beating him.

Fox had participated in a tournament before, but that experience didn't prepare him for the sheer lunacy of the Sienese fans screaming for their favored horses as they rode by. There didn't seem to be an open space anywhere along the route. Not only did crowds jam the side roads, but hundreds of others leaned out of the windows of the buildings lining the course. All of them seemed to be shouting at the tops of their lungs, and the race hadn't even started yet.

First he passed the stands where the nobles would observe the final stretch of the race with an unobstructed view for three hundred yards up the road from the finish line. Corosi watched him with obvious contempt. Like the other riders who were soaking in the adoration, Fox waved, directing it at Corosi.

Luciana looked nervous and was one of the few not clapping as she watched the parade. Barbieri raised his hands and applauded Fox daintily. His demeanor didn't fool Fox, who knew the Sienese banker would likely be as ruthless as Corosi if he didn't get what he wanted.

The race marshal was leading them at a stately pace on his own horse, holding the *drappellone* before him for all to see. Vying for position wouldn't occur until they were at the rope across the Porta Camollia that would drop at the ring of the bell. Fox stayed in the middle of the pack as they walked, trying to get a sense of the other riders, all of whom took notice of the stranger in their midst.

Fox looked behind him to see Armstrong closing the gap, weaving his way through the pack. When he caught up, he matched Zephyr's gait.

"I have to say I'm surprised to see you here, Fox. I thought you would have turned tail long ago and fled with that supposed wife of yours."

Armstrong's omission of Fox's title had to be an intended slight, so Fox shot it right back.

"But then I wouldn't have the pleasure of seeing you again, Armstrong. It must have stung after our encounter at the river to know that you were bested by someone like me."

"Bested is a strong word. Lucky is more appropriate."

"Perhaps I'll be lucky again today."

Armstrong laughed. "The race will be long over by the time you cross the finish line."

"Are you certain about that? My horse is quick."

"You've never even seen the Palio. You'll soon learn that speed is not the most important factor in this race."

"And what is?"

"Something that you sorely lack. A willingness to do whatever it takes to win."

"I might surprise you again."

"No, you won't. You lost your land and your title. I know you were a second son, just like I was. But unlike me, you inherited your father's estate anyway. You had everything and then you just pissed it away because you couldn't control yourself. It sickens me."

Fox had no quick comeback to that. He'd never heard it quite put that way. The worst part was that, from a certain perspective, Armstrong was right. But Fox knew the truth that his excommunication was a sham.

He sat up straighter. "If you really do get sick, try not to get any of it on me."

Fox didn't wait for a response and kicked Zephyr into a trot, leaving Armstrong behind.

27

The crowd at the Porta Camollia on Siena's north end was nearly as large as the one at the finish. The seventeen horses and riders were cordoned off from everyone else while the race marshal conducted a final inspection of each rider and horse to ensure that no one was carrying a weapon. Anyone caught with so much as a needle would be immediately disqualified.

As they waited, Armstrong surveyed his competition. Five of the riders were allied with him. They knew a large payment would come to them and their sponsors if he won. Fox only had two riders who might protect him, and Armstrong had already identified them. They would be the first taken down when the race started.

Once the inspections were over, there was nothing to do but wait, the horses circling each other as the riders constantly nudged each other for a better position. The rope was stretched across the starting line waiting for the bell to ring, though no one knew exactly when that would be.

Fox remained isolated from the fray, carefully observing the other riders. Although Armstrong would savor this victory, he had to admit that someone who showed enough courage to wade into battle against overwhelming forces, as Fox had done at San Giuseppe, was worthy of some admiration. And fighting an armored opponent to a draw at the Arno River demonstrated skill and cunning. If the two of them weren't at odds with each other, he might have been a formidable ally.

Armstrong couldn't guess Fox's strategy for the Palio, but his accomplices already knew what to do as soon as the race began. The street was wide enough for just four horses abreast, so passing was a fraught endeavor. Armstrong knew that as long as he could get off to a fast start, he could hold the lead all the way to the end.

The sun looked to be directly overhead, so the bell could ring at any moment now. The spectators were buzzing like a hornet's nest from the tension. Watchers leaned out of every window overlooking the expected course, and at the cross streets every intersection was full of people on both sides. Few dared to stand against the buildings along the racecourse, knowing that the horses could easily trample anyone foolish enough to get in the way.

Armstrong edged his horse to the front and center, kicking at the riders on either side to clear a path. One tried to hit him with his riding stick. Armstrong leaned over and punched him in the face, knocking him from the horse.

Armstrong gripped the reins tightly in his hands, his eyes on the rope handlers.

The bell rang. An enormous cheer went up from the crowd, and the rope dropped to the cobbles.

Armstrong launched his horse forward. It took a moment for its shoes to find a foothold on the smooth stones, but he quickly accelerated. Once he was at top speed and in the lead, the road was fairly straight for another few hundred yards, so he stole a glance over his shoulder just in time to see his plan set into motion.

Three of his allies were close behind him, blocking anyone else from catching up, while the other two took aim at Fox.

One tried to grab hold of Fox's reins, but Fox was ready for that tactic. He jabbed his riding stick into the man's face and kept the reins in his hands.

But that attack was meant merely as a distraction. The man on the other side pushed himself from his horse to jump onto Fox.

Fox saw the assault just in time and elbowed the man so that he couldn't get a firm grip. The plan would have failed except that the man was able to latch on to Fox's leg as he slid down.

Without a saddle to hold on to, Fox was yanked from the horse's back.

Armstrong smiled as he turned back to focus on his path. He knew the race was as good as over. No matter what happened now, Fox had no chance of catching him.

The next few moments happened in a flash for Fox. He thought he'd been ready for anything, but he didn't anticipate someone essentially forfeiting the race by jumping off his horse. Now he understood Armstrong's point about doing anything to win.

The spectators actually cheered when he and the other man fell. It was probably far more exciting than simply watching the horses gallop by.

But Fox didn't fall all the way off Zephyr, snagging his mane as he dropped. The man was still holding on to his leg, so Fox put a boot into his head, finally freeing himself from the grasp.

Then instead of stopping Zephyr completely to get back on him, Fox used a trick that he and his brother had practiced when they were young.

He pulled his feet up so that they were no longer dragging behind, his entire weight hanging from his grip on Zephyr's mane. Then he slammed his feet into the stones ahead. The impact caused him to pop up, and he used the force to yank on Zephyr's mane and pull himself onto the horse's back.

The cheer that erupted was even bigger than the one when he'd fallen.

He could still see the main group of horses in the lead. Although they were nearly halfway to the city center, there was still time to make up the distance with Zephyr's otherworldly speed.

Fox bent low over Zephyr's neck, dug his heels into Zephyr's haunches, and shouted, "*Vade!*"

It was almost as if the horse had been waiting for the command to go faster. Zephyr seemed to find a reserve of energy hidden inside him. Fox had to concentrate to hang on as the wind whipped past him.

By the time they were nearing the Piazza del Campo, Fox and Zephyr were approaching the rear of the pack.

But it was clear that was as far as he could go. Every time he tried to pass, Armstrong's allies would knock against him. Fox was concerned that another one of them would leap over to Zephyr, and this time he would fall all the way to the ground.

The turn was coming up for the main road leading to the Porta Romana, and Fox had a decision to make. He could try to continue on the shortest route, fighting his way through the competitors to get to Armstrong, or he could take the longer, riskier path.

Armstrong looked back, and Fox read surprise and worry on his face at seeing Fox still in the race. He shouted something back that Fox couldn't make out clearly, but he was certain that it was instructions for his accomplices to stop Fox no matter the cost.

Fox needed to take a chance to catch up. As the pack of horses eased up on their speed so they could make the tight turn, Fox didn't slow down.

He knew why the main route took that turn. Straight ahead was a steep flight of stairs leading down underneath a low-hanging arch into the Piazza del Campo. Having committed to his new course, Fox just hoped Zephyr would be sure-footed. They plunged down the stairs as Fox ducked his head. He could feel the stone brush his cap. Another few inches and Fox's brains would have been dashed all over the pavement.

Then he was out into the sundrenched piazza and racing down the incline of the deserted square, where he could really let Zephyr reach his top speed.

Now Fox just had to make sure he didn't get lost. One wrong turn, and he'd be left behind for good.

28

Armstrong was leading by more than two horse lengths as he barreled down the shadowed street toward the last stretch. He took another look behind him and didn't see Fox's distinctive dappled silver horse. He assumed his accomplices had finally gotten rid of the heretic for good.

As he passed one of the cross streets, something caught his eye in the periphery. It was movement on the next street over. It went by so fast that he wasn't certain if his vision was deceiving him.

He made sure to look when he went by the next intersection. His stomach lurched at what he thought was impossible.

To his shock and dismay, he glimpsed the tail end of Fox's horse as it flashed by. Not only had he gained on Armstrong, but he seemed to be pulling ahead.

Armstrong prodded his horse even harder, racing as fast as he could, the slippery cobbles be damned.

At one point, the horse's shoes slid as they rounded a curve, but Armstrong was able to keep him on track without slamming into a wall. One of the horses behind him wasn't so fortunate, going down and crushing the screaming rider against the bricks of a townhouse.

At the next intersection, he saw an even worse sight than the tail end of Fox's horse. He saw nothing, which meant that Fox was ahead of him.

His only advantage now was that Fox would have to turn onto a side street to get back to the main road before the final stretch. There was only one likely point for that to occur.

Armstrong switched the riding stick to his right hand since that was the direction from which Fox would be coming. If he could get a good swipe at Fox's head as he rode through the intersection, he could end the comeback then and there.

Armstrong raised his hand, ready to strike.

Freed of interference, Zephyr had shot down the empty street like a crossbow bolt. Fox could see that he was now in the lead, but he still had to make it back onto the main road.

He recalled the street layout in his mind. There were no gaps or alleys between the houses he could use as shortcuts. His last opportunity to rejoin the pack was a very tight turn at the end of this street.

The problem was that the intersection would be jammed with spectators. An English stranger trampling citizens of Siena to win the race might not be looked on too kindly.

As he approached the turn, he began shouting at the top of his lungs. He wanted to cry out, "Watch out!" but in the frenzy of the ride, he couldn't think of the proper Italian word, so he yelled the closest thing he could think of.

"Alerto! Alerto!"

He knew that was wrong, but he hoped it would get the message across for the spectators to get out of the way.

He rounded the corner as fast as he dared on the slick cobbles, and Zephyr scrabbled for grip, nearly throwing Fox into the wall. Up ahead he could see people tightly packed together.

"Alerto! Alerto!" he shouted nonstop.

Finally, the people at the back turned at the unusual noise. Several of them shrieked at seeing him approaching at top speed. They scrambled to get out of his path, frantically pushing others around them to keep from being run down.

Fox had to tighten the reins slightly as he waited for a slim path to clear. To the left of center it looked like there would be just enough space for him to squeeze through, but he had to ease up even more at the last moment to keep from knocking down a screaming woman.

That slight hesitation allowed him to keep his head on his shoulders.

As he emerged onto the main road, Armstrong took a swing at his skull with his riding stick. Another foot forward and Fox would have taken the full brunt of the impact to his ear. Instead, the tip of the stick slashed across his temple. Blood coursed down his face, but Fox was able to twist around and give chase.

The attempted blow unbalanced Armstrong, who took time to regain his seat on the horse, enabling Fox to make up ground.

The final turn was only moments away. Armstrong would have to reduce his speed to make it, and that would give Fox his best opportunity to pass him.

He pulled forward so that Zephyr's shoulders were even with the haunches of Armstrong's horse. Armstrong lashed out with a foot at Zephyr's head.

Zephyr didn't like that at all. He dodged the blow and bit at Armstrong's boot. Fox knew how strong his horse's bite could be. If he'd gotten hold, Zephyr might have been able to tear Armstrong from his horse.

Suddenly, Zephyr whinnied and their pace began to slacken as they rounded the last curve. Fox was worried that Zephyr had stepped on a nail and was pulling up lame. But then he felt his horse buck and looked back to see he had a new problem.

When he and Armstrong had both reduced their speed, it had given one of Armstrong's trailing confederates time to catch up. He got just close enough to reach out and grab Zephyr's flailing tail. He had it firmly clenched in his fist and was yanking it back hard.

Fox tried to weave to the side, but the man's grip was too firm. He couldn't shake him, and now Armstrong was starting to pull ahead again.

The finish line was only a few hundred yards in front of them. Fox's senses sharpened in these final moments.

The crowds lining the street on either side were roaring with their hands in the air. Everyone in the stands was on their feet, even Barbieri. The ribbon signifying the finish line was ready to be breached by the winner.

And he could see Willa in her bright blue kirtle and her golden hair just beyond it.

He wasn't going to catch Armstrong, not with someone latched on to Zephyr's tail. He knew he had to take a drastic gamble when he suddenly had a crazy idea. He only hoped Willa remembered the strict rules of the race and would know what to do.

Without thinking it through further, Fox vaulted onto his feet so that he was crouching on Zephyr's back. Before he could lose his balance, he swiveled around, took two quick steps backward, and launched himself at the man clutching Zephyr's tail.

 29

Willa gasped when she saw Gerard throw himself off of Zephyr and wrestle the rider behind him off his horse. Gerard landed on the man, and then they both rolled for several feet.

Despite losing his rider, Zephyr, his teeth bared, pounded on in close pursuit of Armstrong.

But Willa knew Gerard wouldn't have thrown away his chance of winning. He must have had some other reason for sacrificing himself like that, letting Zephyr continue on without him…

He did have a reason. She remembered what Barbieri had told them about the rules. It wasn't the rider who crossed the finish line first that won. It was the first horse across the finish line.

And now Zephyr didn't have the weight of a man on his back. With Armstrong just over a hundred yards from the finish line, there was only one way to keep him from winning.

As Gerard had taught her, Willa put two fingers to her lips and blew a high-pitched whistle that cut through the cheers from the mass of spectators.

The call spurred Zephyr on better than any kick from a rider. His ears pricked up and he galloped as fast as she'd ever seen him run, the reins bouncing on his neck.

Although the men around her stared at this unusual sound coming from a woman, Willa didn't stop whistling.

Zephyr was now pulling even with Armstrong. The race would be over in moments. It was going to be close.

Armstrong realized too late that Zephyr was beside him and outrunning him. In desperation he leaned over and tried to grab the flying reins, but the action caused his own horse to falter for an instant.

That was the opening Zephyr needed. He dashed ahead out of Armstrong's reach and broke through the ribbon first by the length of his neck.

The crowd erupted in a massive roar. Willa ran to the gate where Zephyr came to a stop. He was mobbed by residents and fans of Barbieri's *contrada* who wanted to touch the miracle horse that had defeated the seemingly invincible Armstrong.

Gerard sprinted up and told the gathered crowd to give them room. He rubbed Zephyr's neck and took the reins from Willa as he embraced her.

"I knew you'd understand what I was doing," he said into her ear.

"That was a clever move jumping to your feet on Zephyr's back like that. It almost looked like you were putting on a show."

"I was. For you."

Fox smiled at her with pure glee, all tension swept aside in the flush of joint victory. He stepped back, and Willa saw blood running down the side of his face.

"Oh, my goodness! You're hurt." She touched the wound, and Gerard winced.

"It will be fine once you work your healing powers."

"But you're all right otherwise?"

"The bumps and bruises will pain me longer than this will. I'm just glad Zephyr made it through in one piece. He could have easily broken a leg on those streets."

Armstrong stomped past them, his horse nowhere to be seen.

"Sir Randolf," Gerard called out, "I suppose you were right."

Armstrong turned, his cheeks livid with anger. "And how's that?"

"You finished in front of me. But perhaps that's small consolation about being wrong when you said I wasn't willing to do whatever it takes to win."

Armstrong stalked up to Gerard and stopped when they were eye to eye. Willa instinctively moved to put herself between them, worried that he would try to attack Gerard right here and now.

Over her head, Armstrong said, "I think it's still clear who the better man is. You had to let your horse win for you."

"I believe the important word in that phrase is 'win.' But second place is nearly as good."

Willa decided to end their posturing. "Sir Randolf, you lost. Gerard won. If you're going to cry about it, please do your weeping elsewhere."

Gerard obviously wanted to maintain his tough composure, but his lips quivered as he tried to suppress a laugh.

Before Armstrong could respond, Barbieri, Luciana, and Corosi walked up to them.

With a broad smile on his face, Barbieri clapped Gerard on the back and said, "Sir Gerard, that was some excellent riding. Simply marvelous."

"I had some help," Gerard said, looking at Willa.

"Yes, that is a swift horse," Barbieri said. "I'll pay you a handsome sum to add it to my stable. I'll win so much that I'll become as hated as Signore Corosi here."

"He's not for sale."

"Well, if you change your mind, just name your price. And speaking of money…" He turned to Corosi, who stared at Armstrong as if he wanted to rip him in half.

"I know," Corosi said.

"You owe me ten thousand florins."

"I said I know! I'll send it as soon as I return to Florence."

Barbieri laughed. "You can't think I'm that stupid." He raised his hand and snapped his fingers twice. Eight burly guards surrounded Corosi and Armstrong. "These men will be happy to escort you to your palazzo. I know you have sufficient funds in Siena."

"And if I don't pay?"

For the first time, Willa saw Barbieri go cold. "Then you'll become a permanent resident of my city. There's a lovely graveyard just outside its walls."

Corosi sneered at him. "You'll have your money. Even though your rider cheated."

"An accusation of cheating," Barbieri snickered. "The last refuge of a loser."

Luciana regarded her husband with a satisfied grin. "My dear, Sir Gerard was merely taking advantage of the rules."

Corosi's lip curled into a snarl at that.

Barbieri gestured to his men. "Show Signore Corosi to his vault."

"Don't worry," Luciana said. "They shouldn't have any trouble finding it. I've told them exactly where it is."

"I won't forget this," Corosi said. He stalked away with Armstrong and the eight guards trailing behind.

"God has favored you, Sir Gerard," Luciana said. "It's clear you were telling the truth. I am very happy that you're on my side."

She nodded at Willa, who took her gesture to mean that Luciana believed his excommunication was unjust and would continue to accept their help.

"This has been a most successful contest," Barbieri said. He took Gerard by the shoulders. "I suppose I owe you an apology for doubting your word."

"None is needed, signore," Gerard replied.

Barbieri turned to Luciana. "I will be flying the *drappellone* over my palazzo for the next twelve months because of you."

"I have to admit, I didn't expect that I would enjoy my time here so much."

"And now you'll let us look at the diagram of the original She-Wolf?" Willa asked him.

Barbieri smiled at her. "My lovely lady, we have a gala celebration to revel in first. I have to show you off. You will all be my guests of honor. I'll dress you in the finest clothes…" He looked Gerard up and down, taking in how sweaty and dirty he was. "Once you are all clean, of course."

"But then we will see it?" Gerard persisted.

"Yes, yes, absolutely. Once the feast is over, you can inspect it to your heart's content. And then you can stay as long as you like. In fact, I wouldn't mind if Sir Gerard stays through next year and wins the race again for me."

"Thank you, Signore Barbieri," Gerard said. "We appreciate your hospitality, but I think it's safe to say that we'll be leaving at first light tomorrow morning."

"And where will you go?"

Willa, Luciana, and Gerard all looked at each other. Willa said, "That, Signore Barbieri, is exactly the right question."

Corosi marched back to his palazzo with Armstrong, their unwanted escort trailing behind.

"How could you be so blind as to let that horse pass you?" Corosi said.

"Fox is craftier than I allowed for."

"I should have you strung up for your incompetence, but I need you. Perhaps this loss will spur you to take him seriously."

Corosi looked back and saw that the guards were following at a respectful but careful distance. Even if he somehow eluded or defeated them, he had no doubt Barbieri would make sure he didn't get past the Siena gates. He would have to pay off the bet.

He lowered his voice. "I will take the loss of my wager out of your share of the treasure. That's all that matters now. I will invest everything I have to ensure that Luciana does not beat me to it."

Sofia scurried up to them and put a consoling hand on Corosi's arm.

"I'm sorry about the race, my love."

Corosi wasn't in the mood for her pity. "Where have you been?"

"Getting something that I believe will ease the pain of your defeat. Or some*one*, I really should say."

"Stop being so cryptic. I get enough of that from those ridiculous puzzles that Ramberti left us."

"I found an artisan. He expects to be paid."

"An artisan? What am I paying him for?"

"Actually, he *was* an artisan. Now he's a cripple I found in the hospital."

"And what am I supposed to do with a crippled artisan?"

"He used to specialize in mosaics."

Corosi was about to chastise her for wasting his time when he recognized the pleased look on her face. "You mean…"

Sofia nodded. "He is the last living man from the team that installed the original She-Wolf of Siena. For a price, he'll tell me the next step in our quest for the treasure."

30

Fox pulled at his collar, but the stiff material didn't give. Not only did he feel uncomfortable in the clothes Barbieri had given him, but he also felt ridiculous. He wore a newly fashionable tailored doublet in green and gold with rows of tiny buttons, closely fitted hose, and pointy-toed shoes. He'd even taken a real bath, rather than the quick dunks in a river that usually sufficed.

The doublet was so short that he felt he was in danger of exposing his backside every time he bent forward. It didn't help when Willa took note of his concern and purposely dropped her kerchief for him to pick up. He had to squat in a most undignified manner to retrieve it, much to her amusement. Every nobleman at the feast was dressed in a similar manner, so at least he didn't stand out.

The extravagant gala spilled out from the main hall into the enclosed courtyard in the middle of the palazzo. The victor's *drappellone* hung above festive blue-and-white banners. Torches specially made to look like horses with fiery tails ringed the tables set with a lavish array of food, much of which Fox had never seen before—platters heaped with noodles slathered in butter, steamed water creatures that looked like giant stingerless scorpions, cheese made from the milk of goats, and a creamy rice dish made with broth and cheese.

Fox tried a few of the more unusual items to be polite to his host sitting next to him, but he mainly dined on the delicious venison, chicken, and vegetables flavored with exotic spices imported from all over the world.

"Are you enjoying the meal?" Barbieri asked when he noticed Fox nibbling suspiciously at a piece of round flat bread topped with garlic, salt, and a hard cheese called parmesan imported from a region north of Siena.

When he chewed it, however, the flavor was surprisingly good, and he took a larger bite.

"This is excellent," he said through his mouthful. "What do you call it?"

"That is a pizza."

"We didn't have anything like it in England. Now I'm sorry I didn't visit Italy sooner."

"Wait until you try our custard tortes. They're made with real cane sugar from Cyprus."

"I look forward to it."

"Corosi hates them. He says they're too sweet, but he's always had terrible taste."

"Where is he?" Fox asked. "I haven't seen him yet."

"He's probably moping about his loss and plans to make a late appearance."

Fox was wondering where Willa had wandered off to when he spotted her speaking to an older woman who was covered in jewels. "Excuse me, signore. I will be back soon for that torte."

"Splendid. And to make good on my bargain, I'll have the drawing of the She-Wolf brought out at the same time. You and the two ladies may study it at leisure in my private chamber behind us."

"I appreciate that, Signore Barbieri. Pardon me."

Fox stood and went over to Willa. Like Fox, she had been gifted a set of elegant clothing by Barbieri. She was radiant in a shimmering magenta silk surcoat over a green kirtle, and her golden hair was braided and looped at her temples, covered by linen bosses woven with golden thread. She seemed to be in a deep conversation with the noblewoman, who was playing with the many rings on her fingers.

When he stopped next to them, he said, "I hope I'm not intruding."

"Oh, Signora Donato," Willa said, "please allow me to introduce my husband, Gerard Fox of Oakhurst. Gerard, this is Marcella Donato of Siena."

"My pleasure, Signora Donato."

"No, no!" she exclaimed. "The pleasure is all mine. I've watched dozens of Palios in my life, as you can imagine, and I've never seen one as exciting as your victory this morning. It's a true honor to meet you. I do hope you'll return for the race next year."

He didn't want to disappoint her, so Fox said, "I will do my best. May I borrow Lady Fox for a moment?"

"Perhaps we could conclude our trade first?" Willa asked.

"Trade?"

"I was telling Lady Fox earlier that I was in need of more rouge for my cheeks," Signora Donato said. "After all, a lady has to keep up appearances, especially at my age."

"As it happens, I have some ground angelica leaves from the far north that I use for medicinal purposes," Willa said, holding up a small cloth bag. "It's good for treating fever and rashes, but it can also be used as a red powder to enhance the cheeks."

"I am most appreciative. It is almost impossible to find angelica in Italy. I will be the envy of every lady in my *contrada*." She unclasped a golden brooch engraved with flowers from her gown and handed it to Willa in exchange for the bag. "I shouldn't tell you this, but I would have paid you with a jeweled piece."

Willa smiled at her. "That's all right. I would have accepted a silver one."

They both laughed at that, and Signora Donato thanked her and walked away clutching her prize.

"Now you're a tradeswoman?" Fox asked in amazement.

"And not a bad one at that," Willa said, showing off the brooch. It was simple, but glowed with a soft luster. "I actually would have taken a dozen silver soldi. We can trade this for at least two florins."

"You're an astute bargainer."

"How do you think I acquire the herbs I need for healing elixirs and poultices like the one I applied to your head wound?"

Fox realized yet again how much he'd come to rely on Willa

and her manifold skills. He would have lost the race without her, she had solved the clue about the unicorn, his head injury from the race was already on the mend because of her, and now she was providing funds for their continued travels. For a moment, he tried to envision what those travels would be like without her, and he knew they would be not only lonely, but would lack the vibrancy her presence added to all aspects of his life.

"It's good I'm skilled with a horse and a sword," he said, "or I might not know what I bring to this quest. You're a remarkable woman. Do you know that?"

She gave him a brilliant smile that threatened to melt him. "And you're a remarkable man for noting that."

Fox's heart ached that they couldn't be together. Despite all they'd gone through with each other over the past week, he still saw no path out of their predicament.

He pushed those troubling thoughts aside as a train of servants paraded out of the kitchen carrying trays brimming with all kinds of cakes, tortes, and mouth-watering candied and fresh fruits. He noticed Barbieri was now holding a large scroll.

"Come with me," Fox said. "Barbieri is going to let us look at the drawing of the original mosaic now, so we may be one step closer to discovering the location of the treasure."

On their way, they collected Luciana, who was talking to several ladies prying for the latest word about the important families of Florence.

"Signora Corosi," Willa said, "we have that matter we need to attend to."

"Oh, yes," Luciana said. "If you'll excuse me." When they were out of earshot, she said, "Thanks for rescuing me. I find gossip so tiresome."

At Barbieri's table, he handed the scroll to Fox as he gestured toward his personal chamber. "You may close the door to have some privacy, but return the scroll to me when you are done. It needs to be back in the library before morning. I hope you find what you're looking for."

"As do we," Fox replied.

Candles lit the small room, and Luciana took one of them from its sconce while Willa shut the door behind them. Fox spread the scroll on the table.

The ink had faded over the years, so the black lines were faint, but it was obvious that the design was similar to the mosaic that currently decorated the floor of Siena Cathedral—eight circles of animals around the central figure of the She-Wolf. Other than the fact that some of the animals were shown in mirror-reverse, the primary difference was that the eight circles designating the cities weren't in the same order.

Fox counted around from the unicorn designating Viterbo. One, a stork for Perugia. Two, a hare for Pisa. Three, an elephant for Rome.

"Oh, no," Luciana said with a measure of doom in her voice. "It's too dim for me to read those words, but I know what the lion means."

Four, a lion for Florence.

"We need to leave as soon as possible," she said. "We must get to Florence before Riccardo does."

"Why?" Willa asked.

"He has relatively little power here, but Florence is his home. He will have men looking for us everywhere."

"Then we'll leave first thing in the morning and ride as hard as we can," Fox said. "I think we can make it in two days."

He rolled the scroll back up and they exited the chamber.

When he handed it back to Barbieri, the Siena lord said, "That didn't take you long. Did you see what you needed?"

"Yes, thank you," Fox said. "And I'm afraid we will have to turn in early."

"And miss the rest of the party? Whatever for?"

"We appreciate your hospitality, Signore Barbieri," Willa said, "but we must leave Siena at sunrise tomorrow."

He looked at Luciana. "And you as well, Luciana?"

She nodded. "We have urgent business to attend to."

"It's just as well. You won't be able to rub Corosi's face in our victory anyway."

Luciana took a sharp breath at that.

"What do you mean?" Fox asked.

"While you were off perusing the drawing," Barbieri said, "I got word that the weasel didn't have the backbone to face me at the celebration at all. I understand that he left this afternoon almost immediately after settling our wager."

"Do you know where he was going?" Luciana asked through taut lips.

Barbieri shrugged. "Since he left out of the Porta Camollia to head north, I assume he was going home to Florence with his tail between his legs."

31

PANZANO, TUSCANY

The knight charged toward Fox, gleaming swords in both hands. He was wearing the steel helmet with the brass fangs, but it couldn't have been Armstrong. The figure was impossibly huge, riding on the back of a galloping lion. Blood dripped from the helmet's fangs, and the eyes behind the slit glowed a demonic crimson.

Fox was mired in mud and couldn't move. The only weapon he had was his bow and a single arrow. He tried to draw the bow, but the string was far too heavy to pull back. The knight bore down on him, the lion's paws hitting the ground so jarringly that the earth rippled.

But Fox realized he wasn't alone. Next to him was a woman attempting to yank him free from the mud. He couldn't see her face, but her silver hair waved as she moved.

"Get away!" Fox yelled, but she wouldn't listen. She kept pulling at his arm, which was the reason he couldn't draw his bow.

He grabbed her arm to stop the pulling so he could defend her. She paused and turned to him. Time seemed to stop.

It was the face of his mother Emmeline. Although her hair was silver, her features were just as young and beautiful as the last day he saw her when he was a boy. She cupped his face with her hand and smiled at him with tears in her eyes.

"I know you'll save me," she said.

The lion leaped the last few yards, and the hellish rider swung both his swords. The blades were descending on his mother and Fox seemed to move in slow motion, knowing he would never be able to interpose his body between them in time.

His eyes flew open. In the darkness it took him a moment to remember that he was sleeping on the floor of a tavern's common room. It was the night after the Siena gala, and they had stopped for the evening in Panzano on the way to Florence.

Then Fox realized why he'd been awakened. He was sleeping on his side facing Willa, with Luciana at his back. His leather scrip was beside him, its strap looped under his arm.

The strap was being slid out from beneath him.

He turned over suddenly and saw two men hovering over him and Luciana. He couldn't make out their faces in the gloom, but he could see that the second man already had Luciana's pouch in his hands.

They were being robbed.

Fox lashed out to grab the robber's wrist, but he spun away with the scrip in his hand.

"Thief!" Fox shouted.

That roused the eight other people in the room, but it was too late. The two robbers fled out the door.

Fox jumped up and gave chase in his bare feet, Willa and Luciana calling after him. He crashed through the tavern door after them.

Pouring rain soaked Fox to the skin within moments of stepping outside. The robbers ran in opposite directions down the muddy street. Fox didn't hesitate. He had to retrieve Luciana's scrip, difficult as it was to see his own belongings disappear around a corner with the second thief.

He sprinted as fast as he could to catch up with the wiry man, who had the scrip clutched in his hand. If Fox could wrestle him to the ground, he could make the robber tell him where to find his friend.

He was making up the distance despite the slippery road. The man looked back over his shoulder, a mistake. That hesitation allowed Fox to snatch the dangling strap of the pouch.

Fox pulled on it, but the robber's grip was firm, and he yanked it back. Fox's footing in the mud was precarious, and the sudden motion caused him to slide.

His feet went out from under him, but he didn't let go of the strap. He splashed into a puddle on his backside and pulled the scrip free from the robber, holding it close to his chest to keep it from getting submerged.

The robber, likely seeing the size discrepancy between them, didn't press his luck. He fled into the darkness and disappeared.

The other scrip was gone. There would be no way to find it without the thief to reveal his partner's whereabouts.

Fox stood and turned to make the hike back to the tavern. When he got there, he found Willa and Luciana waiting inside for him. The other patrons saw his bedraggled figure return alone and went back to sleep, leaving the three of them by themselves near the hearth.

"Are you all right?" Willa asked. She had a blanket ready for Fox and wrapped it around his shoulders. She placed a few more logs on the fire to warm him up.

"You're having to ask me that a lot these days. Other than feeling like a wallowing pig, I'm fine."

"Thank the Lord for that," Luciana said.

"During our travels from now on we should pay for a private room for the three of us."

"What did they get?" Willa asked.

He held up the recovered pouch of Luciana's. Glancing at Willa, he said, "They got my scrip. The two of them separated after they left the tavern and I had to make a choice. I went after the one who had Luciana's. I only barely got it back, and the other robber was long gone."

Luciana took the scrip and checked inside. It was waxed, so the contents were all clean and dry, including the precious letter from her father kept carefully hidden in the bottom under her other possessions.

"Thank you, my dear," Luciana said. "I don't know what would have happened without you. I didn't even wake up until you cried out. I'm sorry you lost your own belongings. Was it anything valuable?"

"Thankfully, Willa had been using the book my mother gave

me because she wanted to read about dyes and colorings, so it wasn't in my scrip. I lost some clothes and half of our money." Glancing at Willa, he added, "The ring, too."

Willa closed her eyes for a moment as if in pain, and then looked directly at him. "You made the right choice."

Luciana looked at them, confused. "A ring?"

"Willa's wedding ring," Fox said.

"But I thought you weren't married."

"We almost got married," Willa said.

"When did this near-marriage occur?"

"It was to be in San Giuseppe," Willa said.

"Oh, no," Luciana gasped. "I wasn't the reason you canceled the wedding, was I?"

"Not at all." Willa took a deep breath. "We made our decision the day before you arrived in San Giuseppe."

She looked at Fox, who nodded permission for Willa to tell their story.

32

Willa could tell that being inside the church made Gerard uncomfortable. It was the only time that he fidgeted with his hands. Father Antonio, San Giuseppe's genial parish priest, didn't seem to notice.

"I completely understand your situation," he said. "Of course you don't want to be tied here for three weeks while the banns are posted."

Willa finally felt a glimmer of hope that they had found the place they were searching for. The priest wasn't old enough to be inflexible and set in his ways, but not so young that he felt pressure to do everything dogmatically.

"Then you wouldn't mind refraining from reporting our names to the diocese?" Gerard asked.

When Father Antonio raised an eyebrow at the request, Willa said, "I'm sure that reporting our names to your bishop would invite all kind of awkward questions about the marriage of two English strangers in your town."

Before the priest could consider that, Gerard added, "And we would be happy to donate twenty gold florins to your parish, although you obviously don't need such a lavish sum. Perhaps I'm insulting you simply by bringing it up."

Father Antonio practically fell out of his seat when he heard the amount. Clearly the church needed costly repairs, as did the bell tower next to it.

"That would be very generous of you," he said. "I see no need to tell the diocese about the marriage. You'll likely be on your way soon after the wedding anyway."

"Yes, we plan to go on to Siena," Willa said.

"Where you can hire the servants you need and be able to continue on your pilgrimage."

"Shall we have the ceremony tomorrow?" Gerard asked.

"That should be fine. We'll conduct it on the church porch as is custom and then have the wedding service in here when the vows are completed. Will you be placing a ring on your bride's finger?"

Not everyone was wealthy enough to afford a ring.

Gerard nodded. "I purchased a gold band in Turin."

"Excellent. Then I think there is nothing else to do except be here at the midday bells tomorrow."

"Thank you, Father," Willa said. "You don't know what this means to us."

Father Antonio smiled at her. "I'm always happy to bless the happy sacrament of marriage in God's name."

He turned and walked off without seeing the sting in Gerard's expression.

"Let's go," he said.

When they were outside, he seemed to breathe easier.

"Are you all right?" Willa asked him.

"I get a sickly feeling in my stomach deceiving him like this."

"Your excommunication is unjustified. You've been denied the rites of the Church without good cause."

Gerard hushed her as two villagers walked nearby. "Let's find somewhere more private."

He looked around and fixed on the bell tower. He guided her to it and opened the door.

"No one will hear us up there."

He took her by the hand and led her up the four stories of the winding staircase.

When they reached the top, Willa was sorely tempted to pull on the rope of the bell, which wasn't supposed to ring again until the hour of sext. They edged around the bell and leaned against the parapet, looking out on the countryside. The tree leaves were turning a beautiful shade of orange, wooly sheep grazed in the pastures, and peasants toiled in the grain fields harvesting the crops. On the road that cleaved through the town, a lone wagon carrying straw rolled north.

"I love this view," Willa said.

"It reminds me of going up in the tower at Caldecott Mote during the fall."

He'd spoken several times of his home south of London, always in a wistful tone like this morning.

"I would like to see it someday."

"So would I, but we both know that is never going to happen."

"I think it may."

Gerard chuckled ruefully. "I love your faith, despite how unwarranted it may be."

Willa turned to him. "You don't think there is a chance you will regain your estate at some point?"

"I may never step foot in *England* again."

"Why not?"

"We'd live like outcasts the moment someone recognized me. I'd rather live on the road where we can be whatever we want."

"But you realize that will have to end."

"What do you mean?"

"I mean, we can't spend the rest of our lives traveling, living hand to mouth. I've loved seeing the world with you, and I want to continue to do so while we can, but one day don't you hope we'll have children? We can't provide a home for them on horseback."

Gerard looked stunned by her statement, and Willa was just as shocked that he had never considered that future.

"We'll manage that situation when it arises," he said. "We'll find a place to settle as soon as we need to."

"Don't you want to return home?"

"Of course I do!" he blurted. "But I don't dwell on the impossible."

"So you're giving up?"

"I have no evidence that could back my claim that Cardinal Molyneux plotted against me and my family. It's over."

"You could repent to get the excommunication absolved."

Gerard shook his head. "I refuse to repent for the sins of that evil cardinal, no matter how difficult the excommunication is to live with. And now that I've been excommunicated for more than a year without recanting, if the Church ever finds me, they would immediately try me for heresy. The only potential absolution would come from finding evidence that doesn't exist."

"That you know of."

"Please, stop it," Gerard said. "I thought we came up here to plan what happens after we wed. Instead, you're dwelling on things that can't happen. I thought that marrying you meant a new start, where I could leave all that behind."

Willa put her hand on his shoulder.

"I decided to join you instead of staying at the abbey because I love you. You are the most capable, intelligent, thoughtful man I've ever met. But I also need to believe I have a future with you."

"You do. But it may be one that you didn't intend. I'm sorry, but you'll have to resign yourself to be married to an excommunicant for the rest of your life."

"I can live with that if it's what God wills. What I won't live with is you giving up all hope."

Gerard's jaw set hard. "Wanting to reverse my excommunication isn't a hope. It's not even a dream. It's a fantasy."

Willa could feel a sharpness in her throat as she fought the tears welling in her eyes. "That's not the man I want to marry. There has to be hope. If not for you, then for our children. You do realize that unless we get the excommunication lifted, they will be considered bastards if anyone ever finds out. And I'm risking my future as well. We'll always be on the run, because if the Church ever finds you, then I would be branded a heretic just for consorting with you willfully."

Fox went silent and turned away from her. He gripped the side of the parapet for a long time.

Willa had had moments during the past weeks of travel together when she sensed that there was tension between them about their future, and now she regretted not bringing it out into the open sooner.

Finally, Gerard said, "I'm so sorry. You don't deserve that fate."

"Neither do you."

Another silence.

"Then what can we do?" he asked.

"You really don't see any hope of reversing your excommunication? Returning to your home and retaking your rightful title?"

Gerard swallowed hard. "Living with that false hope will grind and wear on me. It will crush the life out of me. You won't want to be tied to that."

"Maybe we can find witnesses to your mother's abduction. Or written records from where she was being kept. Something to show that Cardinal Molyneux had her with him all those years."

"Don't you think I tried to find that kind of evidence? I searched for two years. The future husband of your lady Isabel was my best chance for testimony on my behalf, and now he's gone, too. Don't you see? It's hopeless."

"As long as you're alive, there's hope."

"You're saying that you can't live without *me* having hope. But I can't live with futile hope eating away at me. What kind of future does that mean for us?"

Willa didn't know what to say to that.

When Gerard saw her hesitation, he asked, "I didn't know you felt this way, and I'm having a hard time seeing how my idea of the future can ever tally with yours. Do you see a solution where we can remain together? Is this the life you want?"

"I don't know."

"Perhaps you were right to reject me back at the abbey. You could live out your life among the nuns, reading and writing to your heart's desire."

"Are you giving up?"

"Not on you. I just want what's going to make you happy."

"What makes me sad is the thought of watching you lose hope at getting justice for yourself. You don't think that will change?"

Gerard looked into her eyes. She knew his answer even before he said, "No. I don't."

Willa's lips trembled as she said, "Then what do we do?"

Another long pause. "Perhaps I should just escort you back to La Sacra di San Michele."

"You mean… the wedding…?"

"What else is there to do? You'll live a better life without me."

At San Michele, she'd been the one arguing that they shouldn't stay together. Now Gerard was the one saying the same thing. The horrible truth was that no matter how desperately she wanted to be with him, she knew she couldn't settle for the life he was offering. And she couldn't take a chance on the wishful idea that she could get him to change his mind. That was something only he could do.

When she took too long to answer, he said, "Then we'll leave in the morning for San Michele." He looked down and opened his palm. He'd been holding the gold wedding band during the entire conversation. "I very much wanted to give this to you."

"And I wanted to wear it," Willa sobbed. She couldn't believe how quickly her dreams had turned to ashes.

"I'm sorry I couldn't give you the life you deserve." Gerard kissed her cheek. "I should tell Father Antonio that the wedding is off. I'll give him a few florins for his trouble. Then I might go for a ride to clear my head."

He started back down the stairs. Willa stayed at the top of the bell tower to cry alone.

WEAPON OF THE GOD

Tuscany

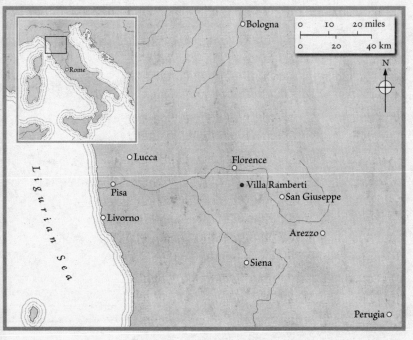

33

October, 1351

FLORENCE

Riccardo Corosi was happy to be back in his home city, even if it wouldn't be for more than a day or two. Knowing that guildsmen ran the cities in Italy, Corosi had never disclosed his knighthood. After his return from Paris all those years ago, he'd gradually risen to Florence's upper echelons, and he now considered the city his. Siena, however, left a bitter taste in his mouth. He'd loved lording his previous Palio victories over its citizens, but his unfair loss put him off staying there any longer than he had to. He felt a new vigor now that he was exiting the Palazzo della Signoria with part of the Florence clue deciphered.

He met Sofia and Armstrong outside. Wooly tufts of clouds dotted the morning sky.

"You're smiling," Sofia said. "Does that mean you solved it?"

"It wasn't easy. Once I inspected the carvings closely, however, I was able to infer the meaning of Ramberti's puzzle."

The solution actually was simple as soon as he could see the front of the marble font, but he wasn't going to tell them that.

He held out his hand. "Show me the message."

Sofia gave him the piece of paper combining the two letters to Luciana and Matteo. Corosi was fairly certain that he was right about their next destination, but he didn't want to make a fool of himself if he were wrong.

In the civic heart, the font displays the pointed weapon of the god.

*The deity's element leads you to life everlasting in the temple of the
    Romans.*

*Above the Holy of Holies, this indicates God's prophet saved from
    certain death.*

His enemy flies above the square, the symbol of your next destination.

They'd deduced the meaning of the first line on the trek from
Siena. The *civic heart* of Florence was the Palazzo della Signoria.
Well before wRamberti's time, a series of Roman marble
architectural fragments carved with the Olympian gods battling
the Titans had been reused to form part of the large fountain in the
piazza. When the piazza was paved with stone about fifteen years
ago, the fountain was removed, but the carved pieces showing the
warring gods were placed inside the palazzo as a decoration and a
reminder of the glory of the ancient empire.

Corosi read the second line of the clue twice and was now sure
he was right.

"Where are we going?" Armstrong asked.

"It's a short walk," Corosi said. For once he enjoyed being the
one with the mysterious information. "Come with me."

He headed north, occasionally nodding to nobles who passed by.

"Are we going to your palazzo first?" Sofia asked.

Corosi's city home lay in the same direction, an ideal location
overlooking one of the most important squares in the city. Like
other tower houses in the city, it was composed of living quarters
attached to a defensive tower via an internal passageway.

"We don't need to. We may solve this before nightfall."

"Then we still have a head start over your wife and Fox,"
Armstrong said.

"Perhaps a day at most. But now that we know where they will
have to go, we can end their quest right here."

"A trap?" Sofia said.

Corosi nodded and looked pointedly at Armstrong. "Hopefully
more successful than the one in San Giuseppe."

"Fox will be expecting it," Armstrong said.

"Then you will have to be more clever than he is. For once."

"Where will it take place?" Sofia asked excitedly. "Perhaps I'll watch."

"This will not be a spectator event, although I might be able to observe it myself. My tower overlooks the piazza where we can catch them."

Armstrong looked thoughtful about the revelation. "I'll have my men watching from all corners. When they show their faces, we will surround them."

"Just make sure they don't get away," Corosi said. "Even one of them surviving with the clues to the treasure would be trouble for us."

"What about the Palazzo della Signoria?" Sofia said. "They'll have to go there, too."

"I've already left word with the guards there. If they see Luciana enter the building, they are to detain her and send for me at once. I've also alerted the guards at the city gates to be on the lookout for three nobles fitting their descriptions so we'll know when they arrive."

"I don't think it will be that easy," Armstrong warned.

"Please," Corosi said. "My wife is one of the most recognizable women in Florence. If she comes here, I will know it within the hour."

"Maybe she *won't* come here," Sofia said. "What if she sends just Willa and Fox into the city?"

"There is no chance that Fox will be able to get into the private rooms of the palazzo by himself. Luciana will need to be with him. He doesn't know where the marble panels are."

They discussed the details of the ambush as they walked through the crowded streets until they emerged onto another bustling square.

If the Palazzo della Signoria was the civic center of Florence, then the Piazza del Duomo was its religious center. Corosi was proud that his tower looked down on it from the north side of the square.

Although the cathedral was named the Basilica of Santa Maria del Fiore, like the rest of Florence's citizens he simply called it the

Duomo. It didn't even have a completed nave yet, let alone the dome that would one day serve as its crowning glory. Construction had been halted during the Great Mortality, but Corosi had made a generous donation to ensure that it was restarted the next year, and now scaffolding covered the structure like a spider's web. He was assured that the apse would soon be finished, and he could already tell that the cathedral would be a masonry marvel.

The front of the church was adorned to match the chiaroscuro of white, green, and red marble that decorated the campanile—also called Giotto's Bell Tower after its designer—but it had only been completed to just above the main doorway, while the rest remained a blank façade of brick. At this time the campanile was three stories high, but it would outshine anything in Siena, Pisa, Venice, or Rome when it eventually reached its full height. Then the Sienese citizens who visited would wonder at it with more than a little envy.

The third element of the square was the Baptistery of Saint John. The huge octagonal building in the middle of the piazza was the oldest building in Florence, built centuries ago upon the site of an old Roman temple. It shared the same design pattern as Siena's cathedral and bell tower, which had always irked Corosi, as if they had copied the Sienese instead of the other way around.

The baptistery was famous for its elaborate twelve-foot-high bronze doors, with twenty-eight panels cast in bas-relief depicting the life of John the Baptist and the eight virtues. Corosi hadn't spent much time looking at them, but he loved that the great artist Andrea Pisano had been specifically coaxed to Florence to create a celebrated artwork that now resided in the very place where he lived.

The doors of the baptistery faced the Duomo, and today they were already open. Corosi was disheartened to see why.

Two lines of priests and monks streamed out of the Duomo toward the baptistery. It seemed that both buildings were in use for some kind of ceremony. Then he remembered that it was the feast day of Saint Luke the Evangelist, whose Gospel began with a long account of Christ's nativity and childhood, making the monks' use of the baptistery on this day logical, if infuriatingly inconvenient.

"What do we do now?" Sofia asked as she frowned at the horde of robed clergymen.

"This can't take all day," Corosi said. "We'll find out when they'll be gone."

"And while you do that," Armstrong said, "I'll go fetch my men. I've got an ambush to plan."

 34

Alone except for Zephyr, Comis, and Luciana's horse, Fox entered Florence through one of the east gates. The guards gave him a cursory glance as he paid his toll to the clerk and rode through. He rubbed his clean-shaven jaw yet again. The feeling was strange. He couldn't remember the last time he had been without a beard, but he no longer stood out as much from the majority of Italians who kept their faces bare.

At least the new look had so far successfully kept him unnoticed by anyone Corosi might have had looking for him. His next stop was the southern gate.

When he arrived, he didn't have to wait long. From a hundred feet away, he saw two women shuffle through the gate without being required to pay because of their obvious status as poor pilgrims. Each of them was dressed in a brown cloak, carrying a staff and scrip, with their hoods pulled up tightly over dirt-smeared faces.

They came directly toward him, losing their tired gait when they were no longer observed by the guards.

"It seems as though our plan worked," Willa said.

Luciana was smiling. "I've never been this filthy in my life, but the adventure was quite invigorating."

They had suspected that Corosi would put out word to watch for a nobleman and two women arriving on horseback. Their relative ages, Willa's golden hair and Luciana's silver locks, and Zephyr's distinctive coloring would combine to give them away.

So they had persuaded two of Barbieri's peasants to sell their clothing to Willa and Luciana, as well as staffs and scrips to create the appearance that they were coming into Florence on pilgrimage. When they reached the nearest town to Florence, the two women had dismounted, lightly daubed their faces with dirt to complete the image of lengthy travel, and walked the rest of the way to the city while Fox rode to a separate gate carrying their belongings.

"Where do we go now?" Fox asked.

"Luciana and I were talking about the supplies we would need as we walked together. She thinks we can find them on a bridge."

"The Ponte Vecchio," Luciana said. "I know that several vendors there sell spices."

"Spices?" Fox said as she began to lead the way.

"You'll see," Willa said. "We can't shave like you did to disguise ourselves."

Florence was much flatter than Siena, although the city was ringed by hills. It didn't take long to reach the Arno River, much wider here than where they'd crossed it on the ferry.

Luciana explained that the Ponte Vecchio had only recently been rebuilt, after a great flood had washed away the previous bridge a decade before. Now serving as a commercial street as well as part of the city's fortifications, crenellated buildings had been constructed on either side along much of its length. The middle had been left bare for a piazza that provided views up and down the river. Even with the buildings lining it, the main roadway was wide enough for the multitudes haggling with the merchants, butchers, and tanners, as well as the horses and carts crossing the main thoroughfare connecting the northern and southern halves of the city.

Luciana led the way to the bridge. Once there, she volunteered to hold the horses and stay far from anyone's attention while Fox and Willa went to get what they needed.

As Fox and Willa passed stalls selling a bewildering array of spices, from pepper and cinnamon to grains of paradise and spikenard, Willa told him how these rare products were traded overland by Saracens who sourced them from as far away as India. The wars waged by the Church to free Jerusalem from the infidels had resulted in a vast increase in the spice trade, with members of the nobility willing to pay high prices for perfumes and medicines, as well as flavorings for their food. Fox was impressed at her knowledge not just of their uses, but also their origins.

The merchant, who stood in front of a vast array of ceramic containers at the stall she selected, looked at the two of them in puzzlement as they approached. A nobleman accompanied by a pilgrim wasn't a typical pairing.

Nonetheless, Fox looked like he came from money, so the man addressed him with a supplicating grin.

"Signore, I have just the thing for you. Pepper and some ground fennel to give your manhood all the vigor you could desire."

Fox was confused by the words the man used for a moment until he realized he was being offered ingredients for a love potion.

Fox regarded him stoically. "What makes you think I need that?"

The man's smile faltered a bit. "Well, signore, we all need that once in a while, don't we?"

"I don't."

"Of course, you don't! It was a mistake to even say it. What can I get you?"

"Nothing. You should be speaking to her."

He indicated Willa, and the vendor's smile disappeared, probably surprised by this foreign nobleman having him talk to a pilgrim.

"Do you have licorice root?" Willa asked the dumbfounded merchant.

He collected himself quickly. "Why might you want that?"

"Why is it your business?"

The merchant looked to Fox, who remained impassive as he spoke. "Answer the question."

"Of course, it isn't. How much do you need?"

"Two handfuls."

"I have enough for you. Do you have enough for me?"

Willa took out the gold brooch she'd been given by the Sienese noblewoman in exchange for angelica.

The merchant's eyes sparkled when he saw it. "That will do."

He reached for it, and Willa snatched it away. "I know the value of this piece. It's worth more than what you're offering."

"What else do you want?"

"Saffron."

"Saffron is very expensive. What would you do with it?" Only the richest nobles used the pricey flavoring in their foods.

"If you'd rather I take my money elsewhere, I'm sure there are many more sellers with licorice root."

She looked at Fox and nodded. They turned to leave, and the merchant squawked at them to stay.

"No! I can sell you saffron."

She told him the amount she'd be willing to take, and he went back into his shop, presumably to where he kept his most precious items.

Fox leaned over to her and said, "What *are* we going to do with saffron?"

"It's highly sought-after and easily tradable," Willa replied. "And it's very light, so we can carry it in our saddlebags. It's as good as gold."

Fox nodded. She truly was a shrewd tradeswoman.

The vendor returned with two linen bags, the smaller one already filled. He opened one of the ceramic jars and emptied some of its contents into the larger bag. He set them both down on the table so that Willa could inspect them. She leaned down to sniff the herbs and reached in to rub them in her fingers. When she raised her head, she handed over the brooch.

The merchant bit into it and then weighed it. Satisfied with his acquisition, he handed over the bags.

To Fox, he said, "It was a pleasure doing business with you."

As they walked away, he said, "Do you think that was a fair bargain?"

"More than fair. Luciana told me that saffron merchants come to Florence first because it's such a big city for trade. That means I can likely sell it in another city where it's more scarce for twice what I paid."

"Clever. And the licorice root?"

Fox knew it had medicinal purposes, such as to numb pain or help one sleep, but he had no idea why Willa wanted it.

"You'll see," was all she would say.

When they reunited with Luciana, she directed them to a side of Florence teeming with taverns and far from the noble houses where she might be recognized. They rented two rooms at an inn. Willa and Luciana asked for water and a wash basin and retreated to one of the rooms while Fox went to stable the horses and refresh their supplies.

When he returned later in the morning, he knocked on their door and was told to enter. His jaw hung open at the sight that greeted him.

Instead of being dressed as two peasant women, Willa and Luciana were now in the elegant gowns they'd worn at Barbieri's feast, and their faces were clean and adorned with cosmetics. But even more surprising was their hair color.

Just a short time ago, Willa had been blonde and Luciana's hair was the color of light silver. Now both of them had dark brown hair. The effect had nearly caused him to close the door because he thought he'd barged into the wrong room.

"The licorice root?" he asked when he could finally speak.

Willa smiled and nodded. "Mixed with a few other ingredients."

"What do you think?" Luciana asked. "Doesn't she look incredible as an Italian woman?"

"You're both striking," Fox said without taking his gaze from Willa.

He could see that her fair skin and high cheekbones were accentuated by her brunette locks. Her eyebrows had always been several shades darker than her hair, so they didn't stand out. It was almost as if he were with another woman, though one who was just as alluring.

"If we are to get into the Palazzo della Signoria to decipher the first line of the clue," Willa said, "we wouldn't get very far if Signore Corosi is looking for us, which we know he is. Luciana would be instantly noticeable with her lovely silver hair."

"And as you've seen," Luciana added, "Willa's golden hair is just as notable in Italy."

"We're going there now?" Fox asked.

"Not yet," Luciana said. "We'd never get to the private areas of the palazzo without someone to escort us."

"And you know someone who will do that?"

She nodded. "His name is Count Russo. And he absolutely hates my husband."

35

Willa was amazed by the sheer number of private tower houses in Florence. She'd seen nothing like them in her travels. During their walk, she'd already counted twenty-three. Luciana told her that there were over one hundred and fifty scattered throughout the city.

Luciana pointed to the tallest one in view, stretching eight stories in height. "That is Count Ettore Russo's. His family is one of the oldest in Florence."

"That must explain the size of his tower," Gerard said.

"A hundred years ago, it reached twice as high, but the city government decreed that all towers must be lowered to a maximum of nine stories to reduce rivalries within the city."

"But it didn't stop the hostility between Count Russo and Signore Corosi," Willa pointed out.

"I think Riccardo wants to own all of Florence," Luciana said. "His ambitions have kept pace with his growing power. The more he gets, the more he wants. And if that means driving every noble into bankruptcy, he'll do so without hesitation. I'm ashamed to say that I was helping him succeed."

"It doesn't sound like you had a choice," Gerard said.

"We always have a choice."

"And do you think Count Russo will choose to help us?"

Willa was as dubious as he was. "Having him send a letter on for you is one thing. But we'll be asking him for a much bigger favor."

"That's why I come bearing a gift."

Gerard knocked on the door. It swung open, and a steward regarded the unexpected callers with interest. Their expensive clothes led him to treat them as esteemed guests.

"May I help you?"

Luciana spoke for them. "I am Signora Corosi. Please ask Count Russo if we may have an audience."

The steward stiffened at the mention of the Corosi name. He considered them for a moment, and then stood aside to let them in. They stepped into an arched corridor of fine stonework opening into an interior courtyard.

"Wait here," the steward said. "My master is in his private apartments upstairs, so it will take a moment for me to convey your inquiry to him."

While they waited for the steward to return, an attractive young woman entered the courtyard. She startled when she saw the three strangers in the house.

"Pardon me," she said. "I didn't know my father had company."

"Signorina Veronica," Luciana said. "Don't you remember me? I am Luciana Corosi."

The girl's eyes widened in recognition. "Signora Corosi, I'm so sorry. Your hair is so different from the last time I saw you."

"It's thanks to… my new lady's maid."

"I think you look beautiful. Are you here to see my father?"

"Yes, we are."

"Then please follow me," Veronica said. "I was just on my way to see him."

She led them up a winding series of stairs, chatting with Luciana about the latest happenings in Florentine society. She even mentioned that her father might have found an appropriate suitor for her.

The steward met them as he was coming back down.

"Count Russo has no interest in seeing you, Signora Corosi. You may convey your message through me."

"Nonsense, Mario," Veronica said. "Father can't be so rude to someone of such standing as Signora Corosi, especially when she was so close to my mother."

"I'm afraid he was quite clear."

"Well, I won't hear of it. Come with me, signora."

As they passed the enraged steward, Luciana laughed. "You

should be glad, Mario. She just saved you another journey up and down the stairs."

They entered a large room with a view looking out toward the Palazzo della Signoria. A man in his forties was poring over an accounting ledger laid out on a table. He looked up and scowled at seeing the four of them enter.

Veronica went to kiss him on the cheek. "Father, Signora Corosi has brought friends to visit us."

The steward must have informed Russo about her new look. He studied her brown hair with interest.

"I told Mario that I didn't want to see her."

"I don't know what kind of quarrel you would have with such a kind lady."

"It's her husband with whom I have a quarrel."

"Then you should be pleased he's not with them."

"Count Russo," Luciana said, "I think you will be quite interested in what I have to say."

Russo slammed the ledger closed and rose to his feet. "If you're here to change the terms of my bargain with your husband, he has sorely misjudged me. I have a mind to send you back with word that I've canceled it entirely."

"Signore, my name is Gerard Fox. I might be a stranger to your city, but I do know one thing. If Riccardo Corosi is your enemy, then Signora Corosi is most certainly your friend."

Russo still looked dubious.

"Perhaps it would be better if we spoke in private," Luciana said.

After a pause, Russo said, "In respect to my dear departed Francesca, I'll hear what you have to say. Veronica, can you excuse us?"

"Happily. I was just coming to ask permission to join Signorina Maria and her family at the market."

"All right. But be back by supper." Russo handed her a few coins. With an indulgent smile that he tried to hide from his visitors, he said, "Buy some cloth for that new gown you've been wanting."

Veronica squealed. "Thank you, Father!" She took her money and ran out of the room.

"You dote on her," Luciana said.

"Too much so," Russo said wistfully. "With her mother gone, I have no appetite for restraining her." He came out of his reverie. "Now why have you invaded my privacy?"

"We need a great favor."

Russo laughed. "And you think I would grant such a thing?"

"I'm hoping you will if you despise my husband as much as I do… ever since I discovered that he wants me dead."

Russo's mouth dropped open. "The Devil you say."

Willa spoke up. "It's true, signore. I was there when Signore Corosi tried to have her murdered."

"Twice," Gerard added.

"Who are these people?"

"Sir Gerard Fox and his wife Lady Willa Fox. I recently happened upon them by chance, and they've been my faithful companions ever since."

"Why should I believe you aren't an agent of Signore Corosi himself here to trap me in another one of his schemes?"

"Because I can prove he defrauded you."

That got Russo's attention. "How?"

"Those sheep of yours that supposedly died when they were swept away during the flooding last spring? They are grazing at my villa south of Florence as we speak. Their ears still bear your mark."

Russo pounded the table with his fist. "I knew that scoundrel couldn't have played fair. He made me promise to marry my daughter to the man of his choosing."

"And you agreed?" Luciana asked.

He swallowed hard. "I had to."

"I think I know the intended bridegroom," Gerard said.

"And who would that be?"

"Signore Corosi himself," Willa said. "With Signora Corosi gone, he would need a new wife. He badly wants an heir, and Veronica would give it to him. His son would be your grandson."

Russo's face turned bone-white.

"No! No! I won't allow it!"

"He will keep you to that bargain," Luciana said. "He would ruin you if you backed out of it."

"But if you help us," Gerard said, "and it leads us to exposing Corosi for what he really is, you will never have to pay that debt."

"What he really is?"

"A cheat and a liar," Willa said.

Russo looked across all three of them. Finally, he said, "What do you want me to do?"

"Nothing too difficult, we hope," Luciana said. "We want you to sneak us into the Palazzo della Signoria."

 36

Luciana might have been recognized going into the palazzo as a noblewoman, even with her newly dark hair, so this time she took the role of lady's maid. She borrowed a more humble wool kirtle and a white veil from a maid at Russo's home, and her assumed identity felt freeing to her. She was sure no one would be examining her.

"How do I look?" she said to Willa, who was beautifully aristocratic in her silk gown.

"You still stand out too much. Believe me, I know how lady's maids are supposed to move. They're generally meek and deferential, although I was never good at that. Try tilting your head down as you walk."

Luciana took a few steps around the chamber with Willa studying her.

"Is that better?"

Willa frowned. "I suppose it's difficult training a lifetime of command out of you in just an hour, but I think it will have to do. And remember to walk slightly behind me."

They left the room and met Fox and Russo in the front hall.

"Are we ready?" Fox asked.

"Yes," Willa said. "Luciana makes a wonderful lady's maid."

Russo shifted uncomfortably from foot to foot. "And what is our story if anyone asks?"

"You are showing Signore Moretti and his wife around the palazzo," Luciana said. "They are visiting from Pisa, and I am the lady's maidservant."

"But try not to draw anyone's attention," Fox said. "We go in, up the stairs to the room with the fountain carving, and then back out again. If we don't have to talk to a soul, we'll be the happier for it."

Russo nodded and girded himself as they stepped out into the afternoon sun. Luciana wondered if wandering directly into the lion's den was a bright idea, but it was endangering Fox and Willa on her behalf that worried her more.

She couldn't have gone into the palazzo alone with Russo. It would have begged too many questions from those who recognized Russo, and the same would be true for Willa. Fox could have accompanied Russo without them, but Russo didn't trust him. He insisted Luciana go with him or he wouldn't do it. So all four of them were going.

She grew more apprehensive as they crossed the piazza toward the government structure. She looked up at the multiple stories of rusticated stone, topped by a projecting crenellated battlement. The entire structure, including its off-center tower rising higher than all others in the city, struck her as ominous today. Two guards holding poleaxes were stationed at the main door. As they passed by the soldiers, she kept her head down as Willa had instructed her. To her relief, no alarm was raised.

Luciana had been in the building many times before, primarily for special events and functions. She had entered the room with the marble panels once, so she knew they existed, but on that visit she hadn't inspected them closely, which was why they had to take this chance now.

Russo nodded at several of the other nobles as he walked by them. They glanced at the newcomers, but nobody stopped him to talk or be introduced. As Luciana had hoped, her dress as a commoner made her virtually invisible to them.

They went up the stairs and then down the corridor toward the room holding the marble reliefs they needed to see.

Halfway down the hall, she heard the one voice she'd dreaded call out from behind them.

"*Buongiorno*, Count Russo," Corosi said. "It is good to see you again so soon."

The four of them stopped, but Russo was the only one of them to turn around. He barely covered his terrified expression.

"We'll keep walking while you dispense with him," Fox said under his breath.

The others continued slowly down the corridor while Russo went back to Corosi. Their conversation carried quite well through the halls.

"Signore Corosi, I'm pleased to see you again."

"Are you?"

"Always."

"And how is your lovely daughter Veronica?"

"She is very well. I hope to meet her suitor soon."

"You will," Corosi said. "I have to leave the city on an urgent matter, but I will introduce you upon my return."

Luciana could hear the strain in Russo's voice as he said, "I look forward to it."

"Then I will leave you to your business."

Russo quickly marched back to them. Luciana glanced behind her and saw that Corosi was gone.

"Before he decides to return," Russo said, "let's finish here." He nodded to the door on his left. "The carvings are in there. I'll wait out here and keep watch."

"Thank you for doing this, Count Russo," Luciana said.

"If Corosi is to be the one ruined this time, I am happy to help you. Now go."

They entered the chamber and found it empty. It was an impressive reception room, decorated on three sides with frescoes depicting the life of Saint George, famous for his military prowess. Mounted on the fourth wall opposite the main door were the bas-relief carvings from the old fountain that had once sat in the piazza outside before it was paved.

They walked toward it, and Fox said, "Now I see why you couldn't remember it in detail."

The intricate carving was one continuous scene taking place across four panels, each of which would have adorned one side of the font. Together, they depicted the battle between the Olympian gods and the titans that led to the latter's downfall. Dozens of them were locked in an epic struggle for control of the world, all at each other's throats, writhing in a confusion of limbs and tortured faces.

Luciana recited the relevant verse from the letter:

In the civic heart, the font displays the pointed weapon of the god.
The deity's element leads you to life everlasting in the temple of the
  Romans.

"So we're looking for a pointed weapon of some kind," Willa said. "Perhaps a lightning bolt like Jupiter would have wielded?"

"It looks like a lot of the weapons have broken off or been worn away, probably centuries before Ramberti saw it," Fox added. "Here is a god striking with a hammer, but it isn't pointed."

Willa indicated a figure ramming his weapon into the side of a horse. "Here's one with a spear."

"That's not a god," Luciana said. "That's a Cyclops, an ally of the Olympians. If you look closely, you can see that he has only one eye."

"Of course," Willa said. "How silly of me."

"Did you know that?" Fox asked in a low voice.

"Actually, no."

He shrugged. "Neither did I."

Luciana stopped when she came to a bearded god rearing back, ready to throw his weapon. She nodded to it excitedly.

"That's Neptune."

"And that's a trident," Fox said.

Willa quickly walked down the rest of the pieces and returned. "It's the only other pointed weapon left in the carving."

"Then that must be it," Luciana said.

"*The deity's element leads you to life everlasting,*" Fox recalled.

"Neptune's element is water," Willa said. "I know that."

Suddenly, Luciana understood. "Water leads to life everlasting when you are baptized."

"Then we're looking for a church," Fox said.

"Not a church. A baptistery. And I'm sure I know which one."

"How?" Willa asked.

"The Baptistery of Saint John is directly across from the Duomo not far from here. It's a building that dates from centuries ago. It is said to stand on the place that originally held a Roman temple dedicated to Mars."

"The god of war," Fox said. "That's not a comforting omen."

"Do you know what the rest of the clue means?" Willa said. She repeated it:

> *Above the Holy of Holies, this indicates God's prophet saved from certain death.*
> *His enemy flies above the square, the symbol of your next destination.*

"The Holy of Holies is the altar, of course," Luciana said. "I remember that there is an intricate mosaic above it, but I can't recall anything specific."

"Then we'll have to see it for ourselves," Fox said. "There's still enough light in the day."

"I'll be glad to be out of this building," Luciana said as they left the room.

Outside, Russo said, "Did you find what you needed?"

"Yes, Count Russo. You've been most helpful. I fully intend to repay your kindness."

"All you need to do is keep Corosi from marrying my daughter."

"If we're successful," Fox said, "not having an heir will be the least of his problems."

"May your quest be blessed."

They returned to the stairway, looking forward and backward for Corosi the whole way. It was only when they were outdoors again that Luciana was able to breathe easily. They thanked Russo once more and bid him farewell before setting off for the Duomo piazza.

Luciana felt that if she could get just a few moments inside the baptistery to remind herself of what the interior looked like, they would be able to solve the last part of the clue. Assuming they were directed to yet another city, they could quickly be on their way out of Florence. Every hour they stayed increased the danger that she would be recognized by someone who would report her to her husband.

When they reached the bustling square with the baptistery, Duomo, and campanile, she picked up her pace. She wanted to get this over with as quickly as possible.

They were only part of the way there when Fox grabbed both her and Willa's arms and steered them right, past the campanile and parallel to the nave of the Duomo.

"What are you doing?" Luciana protested.

"Quiet, signora," Fox said. "We're being watched."

Luciana turned her head. "By whom?"

"Don't look around. Keep your eyes straight. I've been watchful ever since we entered the city because I thought your husband would set a guard and I just recognized one of Armstrong's men observing the entrance to the baptistery."

"He isn't the only one," Willa said. "I'm fairly certain I just saw Armstrong on the far side of the piazza."

"There's only one entrance to the baptistery, and they'll likely be watching it day and night," Luciana said. "We'll never get in without them noticing us."

Fox cocked his head as if he had an idea. "At least, not without a distraction."

37

As Sofia and Corosi entered the Baptistery of Saint John, she paused to admire the exquisite doors cast in bronze. They were so tall that she had difficulty seeing the detail in the top panels, but the ones she could inspect closely were a testament to the skills of artist Andrea Pisano. The panels just above eye level depicted the temptress Salome dancing and then holding John's decapitated head on a platter. She'd always rather admired Salome. Maybe she'd commission the artist to create doors for her own estate when she got her share of the Templar treasure.

"What are you doing?" Corosi asked impatiently. "You've seen these doors a hundred times. Now that those infernal monks are gone we can finally solve this clue."

"If we can't enjoy the finer things in life, why are we pursuing the treasure?"

"We'll have years to enjoy the finer things once we find it. Now let's go."

She sighed and went with him into the baptistery. Obviously, wealth and power didn't buy culture or taste.

The interior of the building was dimming in the waning sun. They only had a short time to examine what they needed before it became too dark to see its details. The gold tiles of the mosaics covering every inch of the soaring vault flickered and gleamed as they caught the last of the light.

The alcove for the altar was at the far side of the room. The high chamber, now empty except for them, echoed with their footsteps on the marble floors. Both of them reflexively crossed themselves as they approached it.

When they stopped in front of the altar, Corosi took a deep breath and his face took on a serious cast.

"What is it?" Sofia asked.

"My son was baptized right here. If God blesses this quest, I will stand here again to witness another son of mine being baptized, and I will gaze up at the image above with thanks for making it possible."

Sofia wondered why God would give someone like Corosi His benevolence while letting her be thrown into poverty and prostitution as a child, but she didn't think that sentiment would be well received.

"I'm sure He has," she said half-heartedly as she took out the letter to make sure she had the clue correct. She read it aloud:

> *Above the Holy of Holies, this indicates God's prophet saved from certain death.*
> *His enemy flies above the square, the symbol of your next destination.*

"So we need to find the right prophet," Corosi said.

The mosaic above the altar was on the underside of a wide arch. It depicted a wheel supported by four men kneeling on columns. Between each spoke of the wheel was a different servant of the Lord, their names spelled out using hundreds of tiny tiles: Moses, Isaiah, Jeremiah, Ezekiel, Daniel, Jacob, Isaac, and Abraham.

Sofia knew about Moses, of course, but the others were only a vague memory, not that she would admit that to Corosi.

His finger tapped against his lip as he considered the mosaic.

"We can discount Abraham, Isaac, and Jacob immediately, of course," he said.

"Why is that?"

He threw a condescending glance at her. "Pardon me. I forgot that I grew up with a much more rigorous religious education than you. All of these men supported God's mission through the Lamb, Christ's redemption of our sins. But Abraham, Isaac, and Jacob are patriarchs, not prophets."

"That leaves Moses, Jeremiah, Ezekiel, Daniel, and Isaiah. Were they all saved from certain death by God?"

Corosi shook his head. "Ezekiel was an exile who received a message from God, and Isaiah prophesized the destruction of the Assyrian army that marched on Jerusalem. Neither of them was saved from death by the Lord."

"And the other three?"

"Surely you know that Moses and the Israelites were saved from the Egyptian pharaoh when He parted the Red Sea."

She frowned at him. She wasn't stupid. "Surely. Then the enemy we're looking for could be an Egyptian."

Corosi shrugged. "Possibly. But I don't understand. '*His enemy flies above the square.*' Does the clue mean a standard is flying? Above a square that is a symbol?"

"We need more information. What about Jeremiah?"

"He was saved from the sons of Aaron called the Antothites. He is known as the 'Weeping Prophet.'"

"Why?"

"Probably because he complained so much about his many plights. He foresaw the destruction of Jerusalem and was persecuted for it. God revealed the plot by the Antothites to kill him and spared his life."

"So who was his enemy?"

"He had many. Besides the Antothites, a priest had him beaten and false prophets attacked him."

"That doesn't help narrow it down much. And Daniel?"

"He was thrown into a den of lions by Darius, the king of Babylon. God saved Daniel for his unwavering piety."

"Do you know of any statues of Darius or Babylonians?"

"No. I will have to ask some of the more well-traveled guildsmen," Corosi said. "Perhaps they've seen one."

"There must be something we're missing that narrows down the clue to a single prophet."

"Let me see the letter again."

Sofia handed it to him and he read it to her.

"'*Above the Holy of Holies, this indicates God's prophet saved from certain death.*' That's not specific enough to point to any one of the three. Ramberti would have given us everything we need. We are not seeing something that we *should* be seeing."

Sofia looked up at the mosaic again, searching for anything revealing—in the columns, the men holding the wheel, the spokes, the clothing the men wore, the way their hands were held. There was only one more part of the image they hadn't considered.

In the middle of the wheel was a circular phrase written in Latin.

HIC DEUS EST MAGNUS MITIS QUEM DENOTAT AGNUS.

Sofia translated it as she read it aloud. "'This is the great gentle God, who is represented by the Lamb.'"

Corosi squinted at it. "As I mentioned, these men were the most faithful servants of the Lamb."

Sofia looked up at the mosaic again and realized she had the answer. It seemed so obvious now that she could see it.

She let out a jubilant shout that echoed jarringly in the vaulted space. "Aha! '*His enemy flies above the square, the symbol of your next destination.*' I know where we need to go next."

"I don't like it," Armstrong said.

"We need transport, don't we?" Sofia countered. "The next clue says that we'll be going to '*the isle of your destiny.*' So I should go ahead to secure a ship for our voyage. Then we'd be ready to leave as soon as the next clue was solved."

Armstrong had been standing at his post watching the entrance to the baptistery when she and Corosi had emerged and hurried toward him. At nearly the same time, a priest carrying a set of keys closed the door to the baptistery and locked it for the night.

After Sofia explained what she found, she suggested the idea of going ahead of them.

"You can wait for us," Armstrong said. "We might have Fox and the others in our hands tonight, and then we'll be able to set our own pace to the treasure."

"Do you want to take that risk?"

"She'll go ahead just in case we don't capture them," Corosi said. "Don't bother watching the baptistery again until morning. Even if Fox could somehow break into the building this evening, it would be far too dark for him to see the detail in a mosaic that high up on the ceiling."

"And I need to hurry," Sofia said. "The city gates close at the bells for vespers. No one goes in or out again until dawn."

"You want to ride alone all the way?" Armstrong asked. "It will take you a week to get there."

"Then the sooner I leave, the sooner I'll arrive to make our plans."

"You trust her enough for her to go on her own?" he asked Corosi.

"I trust her implicitly," Corosi replied, then he furrowed his brow. "But Armstrong has a point. I *don't* trust the people you'll be meeting on the road. A woman traveling alone? It's not safe. Too many highwaymen and marauders."

"I'll send two of my men with her," Armstrong said. "They can keep her... safe."

"No, you need your men in case we spot Fox," Corosi said. "I have guards who will do the job. I'll make sure they understand that she is not to be touched. In any way."

"As you wish."

Corosi nodded to Sofia. "Quick. Go and get the horses ready. You can just make it. I'll see you off."

Sofia squeezed Corosi's hand and sprinted away.

"Are you sure this is a good idea, signore? Should she not stay with us?"

"You're worried about the treasure?" Corosi said.

"Aren't you?"

"Why do you think I'm sending my own handpicked men with her? They're experts with a blade and experienced horsemen. I'll tell them to trade the watch every night so that she's never out of their sight." He smiled at her as she waved back toward them before disappearing into his house. "If she attempts to escape them, my guards will cut her down before she gets ten paces."

38

It took until late in the afternoon the next day for Fox to put his plan into motion to gain entrance into the baptistery unnoticed. The timing would be critical. Fortunately, Armstrong had made it easy for his men to be identified. They stayed out of the way at the edges of the piazza, but their watchful and alert stances made them stand out.

He hoped that he and Willa would only need a short time in the baptistery to decipher the clue. Luciana had told them she'd spent long afternoons taking in the mosaics that made the baptistery an artwork of surpassing beauty. She remembered the wheel depicted above the altar and a few of the men depicted in it, but she didn't recall it well enough to draw it accurately. At least she had given Fox and Willa an idea of what to look for.

With everything in place, the three of them walked into the piazza in front of the cathedral from the south end just as they had the day before. Each of them was wearing a hood to shadow their faces. Fox counted eight mercenaries watching the square, including Armstrong himself at the base of Corosi's tower on the north side.

Although none of the men wore swords, presumably so they wouldn't be so noticeable, they were all equipped with the same kind of long-bladed dagger that Armstrong had strapped to his belt. Fox expected that, once they were spotted, the orders would be to wait until all three of them were inside the baptistery so that they could be cut off at the single exit. It would then be a simple matter to capture them by those famous doors.

Fox didn't intend to let things get that far.

They were fifty feet in when Willa said, "I think he sees us."

Fox could see that Armstrong's stance had changed. A moment ago he'd been relaxed against the wall. Now he was standing straight with his hands ready at his sides.

"Now?" Luciana said quietly.

"Not yet," Fox said. "We have to make it look good."

They walked twenty feet more so that they were just even with the campanile. Fox put his hands out for them to stop and looked up as if he were seeing Armstrong for the first time. He swiveled his head around as if to suddenly notice the other men and realize that they were in trouble.

"Go, go!" he yelled.

He pushed them to run to their right behind the cover of the half-completed bell tower. One of the mercenaries stood in their way. He was frozen by their unanticipated movement toward him.

"Get them!" Armstrong shouted from across the piazza as he sprinted after them. All of the other soldiers left their posts and ran in their direction as well.

Fox let the riding stick he'd kept from the Palio slip out of his sleeve, and he swung it as the nearest mercenary was drawing his dagger. The solid wooden stick struck the man in the side of his head, dropping him like a sack of flour.

He wouldn't get another clean shot like that. They kept running into the street along the south side of the campanile. Their horses were just up ahead. Fox looked behind him, but none of the guards had appeared around the corner of the bell tower yet.

He reached out and grabbed Willa's hand.

Armstrong raced across the square between the cathedral and the baptistery, cursing his contingent for being spotted so easily. They should have been more careful, but his men were fighters, not spies. Still, he had a chance to catch the three of them. Fox might have been quick on his feet, but he was with two women, one of them practically in her dotage.

He passed the man who was knocked unconscious on the ground and rounded the corner of the campanile. Three of his men had been located near the campanile and were ahead of him, the rest behind him. He should have been elated at having this kind of manpower to capture them. But he was incensed at the sight in front of him halfway down to the next street.

That mottled silver horse that beat him at the Palio was there along with two others. Fox and Willa were already on their horses, and Luciana was climbing onto hers.

They took off as soon as she was seated. His men came to a stop when the horses bolted, but Armstrong kept running.

"Don't stop, you fools!" he yelled as he passed them.

He wouldn't give up until they were out of sight. Fox may have been a fine horseman, but he'd already seen Luciana bucked from her horse once in San Giuseppe. If he had any luck, it would happen again.

The three of them were galloping down the street, shouting for the few pedestrians on this side road to get out of their way. It seemed as though they would soon turn a corner and disappear from sight, but then something unexpected occurred.

Luciana stopped her horse as Fox and Willa rode ahead. She came about to face her pursuers and held out her palm at Armstrong as a signal for him to halt.

He stopped fifteen yards away. Fox and Willa finally halted as well at a spot near the end of the nave that was still being constructed. They didn't even have Luciana's courage to return and face him, their faces half-hidden by their hoods.

"Don't come any closer," Luciana ordered.

Armstrong put out his arms to signal his men, who gathered behind him. All of them were breathing hard from the chase. From this distance, there was no way to make a surprise attack on her. She would just spur her horse and outrace them.

"So you've returned to Florence just as we thought you would," Armstrong said.

"No, we're still in Siena," Luciana said, rolling her eyes. "Obviously, we're here."

Armstrong spat at her sarcasm. "The meaning is that we clearly expected you."

"And you did a poor job of capturing us."

"At least you won't get into the baptistery. We know you need to see inside."

"Oh, is that why you were all standing around as obvious as warts on a toad's back?"

"Do you tarry here simply to insult me?"

"No," Luciana said. "We know you must have solved the next clue. Therefore, I want you to deliver a message to my husband."

"If I must."

"Then listen carefully."

 39

Corosi woke with a start. He had nodded off in the top-floor loggia of his tower. The wait for Luciana, Fox, and Willa to appear had been maddening, and he'd gotten bored watching for them. He was certain he would hear the clamor when Armstrong caught them in the square.

He yawned and rose from his bench, took a swig of wine to wash out the stale taste in his mouth, and walked over to the parapet. The crowd on the street eight floors below was fairly sparse at this time of day.

He looked for Armstrong's men to make sure they were attentive in their observations. Strangely, he couldn't spot the man who'd been standing across from the baptistery door.

He searched for the others in his view, and they were gone, too. He leaned out as far as he dared to look straight down, and Armstrong was nowhere to be seen either.

By God's fingernails, what was going on?

Then he spotted two figures scurry out from between the cathedral and the campanile and run over to the baptistery. He couldn't see the man and woman clearly before they disappeared inside.

Corosi was still waking from his nap, so he wondered foggily why a couple would be in such a hurry to go into a building generally used only on Sundays.

The lightning bolt of realization finally jolted him fully awake, and he dropped the wine goblet.

No!

He ran for the stairs.

Willa and Gerard had waited until all of Armstrong's men had passed their hiding spot behind the bell tower before rushing into the baptistery. It had been Gerard's idea to convince Russo and Veronica to act as their impostors. The ruse had worked perfectly, leading all of the mercenaries away from their posts. The hardest part had been getting Zephyr to accept Russo as a rider.

Luciana's job was to delay them as long as possible. Willa knew that she could only hold Armstrong's attention for so long. They had to work fast. She repeated the clue as they approached the altar:

> *Above the Holy of Holies, this indicates God's prophet saved from*
> * certain death.*
> *His enemy flies above the square, the symbol of your next*
> * destination.*

She gazed up at the ceiling above and counted off the prophets that Luciana hadn't remembered. Fox dismissed Isaiah and Ezekiel because they weren't saved from certain death.

"So it must be Moses, Daniel, or Jeremiah," she said.

"But what indicates which prophet is the right one?"

"There has to be something else Luciana's father left in the clue."

She read the sentence inscribed inside the circle. "'This is the great gentle God, who is represented by the Lamb.'"

"Maybe it has to do with the lamb. Only I don't know any symbols with a lamb flying above a square. Perhaps it's referencing a stained-glass window high above in a church."

Willa squinted at the phrase. Something about it nagged at her. *This indicates…*

She took in a sharp breath when it suddenly occurred to her.

What indicates? *This* indicates.

"Look at the inscription," she said excitedly. "*Hic*, the Latin word for *this*. It's written directly over Daniel's head."

Gerard nodded. "You're right. That has to be what Ramberti meant. Now we just have to figure out which enemy."

She remembered the story of Daniel being condemned for praying to God after doing so had been outlawed in Babylon. Although his master King Darius had been distressed about the verdict, he was forced to throw Daniel into the lions' den. The Lord found Daniel blameless and spared his life by sending an angel to close the jaws of the lions.

"It's not Darius the king," she said. "He didn't want to kill Daniel. He was tricked into it by Daniel's rivals who envied his close relationship with the king."

"It can't be the jealous rivals. That's not specific enough."

"Then it must be the lion. God saved Daniel from his enemy."

"I don't know of any lion flying above a square. A banner or coat of arms, perhaps?"

Willa was aware that they'd already spent more time in the baptistery than was wise.

"Perhaps we should consider this question somewhere else."

"You're right," Gerard said. "I think we have everything we need from here."

Willa nodded. She took one last look at the mosaic above the altar and then turned with Gerard to leave.

Armstrong tapped his foot impatiently as Luciana continued to ramble on worse than a drunken knight at a tavern listing off his dubious accomplishments in battle.

"…and he should know that I will never give up fighting him. Riccardo has betrayed everything in his vows to me, to the Lord, to the Church, and I also feel…"

Finally, he interrupted her nonstop grievances. "Signora Corosi, does this have an end?"

She shot him a withering look. "Sir Randolf, I have just a few more points I would like you to deliver. Now you will stand there and hear them." She continued babbling away.

Not only was there no way Armstrong was going to remember all this, but he wouldn't tell Corosi if he could. His quarrel with his wife was of no concern to Armstrong except when it stood in the way of him getting a piece of the Templar treasure. Surely she couldn't expect him to repeat all of this nattering verbatim to…

His stomach went cold when he understood that she had no intention of him relating her speech. She was doing this to keep him here for some reason.

His eyes snapped to the riders in the distance. He couldn't make out the man, but the woman noticed his attention and gave him a furtive glance for just a moment before averting her gaze.

Armstrong didn't know who she was, but it wasn't Willa. This entire affair had been a trick.

"Come with me now!" he shouted to his men and sprinted back toward the baptistery.

The clatter of hooves behind him meant Luciana and the impostors were now fleeing.

He rounded the bell tower at full speed and took in two sights without stopping. One was Corosi stumbling out of his tower and screaming something at the top of his lungs with four of his personal guards behind him.

The second was a man and woman dashing out of the baptistery. The formerly bearded man was clean-shaven and the woman he had known as a blonde now had brunette hair, but Armstrong was close enough to identify both of them as Fox and Willa.

They halted for a breath as they saw Armstrong charging at them, but there was no safety in Corosi's direction, either.

They made a quick decision and kept going straight across the piazza and into the cathedral.

Armstrong knew the cathedral better than these two strangers, and he was sure of one thing. The extensive construction inside had blocked all of the other entrances.

He had them trapped.

 40

Fox led Willa deep into the partially completed nave of the cathedral.

"We need a door," Fox said as they ran. Several priests cried out as they dashed past showing no regard for the holiness of the space.

He could tell that someday this already grand edifice would be a monument that would rival the cathedral in Siena, but as of now it was a work in progress with the far end of the great nave a vast construction zone.

"Curse it, this whole end is blocked," Willa said, pointing to the latticework of scaffolding in front of them. With the waning light, the workers had shut down all work in anticipation of vespers. The cathedral was eerily quiet.

They kept going, looking for any exit to the exterior, but none was to be found. By now they could hear the sound of shouting and the pounding of boots echoing through the chamber from behind them. Fox stole a glance back and saw Armstrong and his men swarm into the nave, their wicked daggers already drawn. It didn't seem as if merely capturing Fox and Willa was foremost on their minds. Though the priests also shouted at their pursuers to respect the church's holy ground, perhaps Armstrong believed that the unfinished building didn't count as a sanctuary.

When Fox and Willa reached the construction zone, he was relieved to find a door. Fox pushed against it, but it wouldn't budge.

"Is it stuck or locked?" Willa asked as she helped him push.

The pile of building materials, tools, and supplies stacked beside the scaffolding gave the answer. It was a tempting target for thieves.

"Locked," he replied.

He looked around for another egress as Armstrong and his men drew closer. The transept had already been built up at least eighty feet high and was open to the sky. He guessed that this vast rotunda was the place where a dome would eventually cap the cathedral.

The scaffolding rose up the wall in a graceful complex framework, reminding him of the branches of the oak trees that he climbed back home in England when he was a boy. He followed the crisscrossing levels all the way up and was delighted to see the familiar shape of a huge windlass that towered high above the unfinished wall.

The wooden wheel was large enough to hold a man who would walk inside it to hoist and lower stones, mortar, and support beams that would be too heavy to carry up by hand. The crane featured a huge boom that could swing to and fro to bring its material-carrying platform from either the floor below or the ground outside of the cathedral to the top level of the scaffold. The winding motion of the windlass pulled a rope around the wheel to raise it or lower it.

"Come on."

He grabbed Willa's hand and ran to the lowest level of the scaffold.

She didn't resist, but asked, "Where are we going?"

"Up."

She looked at the open sky above. "There? Why?"

"No time to explain," Fox answered, and he didn't really want to. Willa was a courageous woman, but if she knew what he was planning, he wasn't sure how she'd react. Still, with Armstrong closing in with an overwhelming force, they had no other option.

"Trust me," Fox said, as he drew his dagger.

He slit Willa's skirt from top to bottom, and she tucked the ends into her girdle. He climbed up onto the scaffolding and pulled Willa up behind him. With the voluminous folds of her gown out of her way, she clambered up as nimbly as a cat.

They were only four levels high when Armstrong and his mercenaries reached the scaffold. Fox was afraid they'd try to pull the entire structure down, but they either didn't consider that option or feared that even Corosi's influence wouldn't protect them if they destroyed it.

They started scrambling up from below, like spiders on a web stalking their prey.

"Faster," Willa said.

"Happily."

Fox increased his speed, but at the cost of security. Once he almost lost his grip pulling himself to the next level, causing Willa to gasp. For a moment he dangled by his fingertips trying to swing his legs up, fully aware that a fall from this height would do the job for Armstrong.

With a push from Willa on his backside, he regained his footing and climbed up. A short time later they were standing on the wall next to the windlass, an expansive view of Florence spread out before them. The roof of the building across the street seemed close enough to touch, but that was just an illusion. It was at least four stories lower, and the gap was much too wide to jump.

Far down on the narrow street below were Luciana, Russo, and Veronica. They were still waiting for Fox and Willa to return from the baptistery on the route they'd prescribed around the north end of the cathedral.

Fox yelled down, "Up here!"

All three of them looked up. They were too far away to see the expressions on their faces, but he heard a tight yelp from Veronica.

"I know you brought us up to this spot for a reason," Willa said.

Fox again drew his own dagger and started to saw through the rope holding the platform that was now resting on the top of the wall.

"You may not like why."

"I think I can guess."

"Are you up for it?"

"Do I have a choice?"

Armstrong and his men were just two levels behind.

"We always have a choice," he said.

"Then I choose to go with you."

He smiled at her as he finished cutting through the rope. He wrapped the end around his wrist and guided Willa along the wall, playing out the rope as it slowly unwound the heavy windlass. He just hoped it would unspool slowly enough for this to work.

By the time Armstrong pulled himself onto the top level of the scaffold, Fox had enough length to try his plan.

Armstrong's gleeful expression at trapping them dissolved when he saw the rope in Fox's hand. "What are you doing?"

"Saying *arrivederci*," Fox replied.

Willa waved at Armstrong, looped her arms around Fox's waist, and kissed him for luck. When her grasp was firm, Fox leaped off the wall as Armstrong rushed toward them shouting, "No!"

Just like the rope swing Fox and his brother James had made to jump across the stream near their castle when they were boys, he felt the stomach-churning weightlessness as they soared high over the street. To the squeals of the onlookers below, they arced across the road. Fox could see the windlass beginning its slow turn, playing out the rope as they swung.

It gained speed, and they headed for the roof of the building across the way. For a moment Fox thought he'd misjudged and they would plummet all the way to the ground.

At the last moment, however, they were suspended above the roof, alighting upon it like snowflakes drifting down from the heavens. He immediately let go of the rope lest Armstrong try to yank him from their perch, but he needn't have worried.

The windlass was now rotating at great speed, and the rope continued to unspool until it was completely played out.

Armstrong could only watch with evident fury from not more than fifty feet distant.

"It's always a pleasure to see you, Sir Randolf," Fox yelled to him.

Armstrong didn't respond. He simply shook his head and turned away.

"You enjoy taunting him, don't you?" Willa said.

Fox grinned. "It has its delights."

"Well, now that you've had your fun, let's find a way off this roof before he can get his revenge."

 41

After Fox and Willa's daring rooftop swing, Fox had shouted down for Luciana to leave the Duomo, so she accompanied Russo and Veronica back to their palazzo. She trusted that her two English friends would be able to complete their escape from Armstrong and his mercenaries.

Her confidence was rewarded when they arrived breathless at Russo's home. Willa quickly changed into an undamaged kirtle. When she was ready, they all gathered in the palazzo's foyer.

"That was most exhilarating," Veronica said. "I've never experienced anything like it in my life."

"I appreciate you putting yourselves in harm's way," Luciana said. "You may never know how much that means to me."

"Your plan worked perfectly," Russo said. "If our participation helps to bring down Signore Corosi, it was well worth the risk."

"Do you think Sir Randolf recognized you?" Willa asked.

Russo shook his head. "I believe we were too far away for him to see us clearly. Besides, he doesn't know us."

"Still, we shouldn't dawdle," Luciana said and turned to Fox. "Did you get the information we need?"

He nodded. "Although we don't yet know where we are going."

"We'll need your guidance for that," Willa said.

Luciana understood. She smiled at Russo and Veronica. "Please excuse us. We must be leaving now."

The horses were already prepared for travel, and Fox and Willa donned cloaks.

"God bless you in your quest, Signora Corosi," Russo said. "I will pray for your success."

"As will I," Veronica added. She took Willa's hands. "I only hope that I may be as brave as you someday."

"I recognize much of myself in you, signorina," Willa said. "I wish you a happy and enjoyable life."

"Thank you for your help, Count Russo," Luciana said. "I hope to return with good news."

The bells for vespers would ring soon, signaling the closing of the city's gates.

Fox must have sensed Luciana's apprehension.

"We should go," he said. "Lady Fox and I give you our utmost thanks."

They left Russo's palazzo and mounted their horses.

"Which gate?" Luciana asked.

"The closest one," Fox said. "We don't want to be stuck here overnight. If we can't find a tavern outside the city, we'll have to sleep outside again."

Luciana waved off his concern. "I can endure any discomfort to be out of Riccardo's clutches."

They rode south as quickly as they could without drawing undue attention. Surely Riccardo wouldn't be able to organize a trap at every one of the city gates fast enough to intercept them.

As they trotted, Luciana said, "What did you discover in the baptistery?"

"The prophet we were seeking was Daniel," Willa said. "His enemy was a lion, but we don't know of any banner or coat of arms flying a lion over a square."

"Could it be another mosaic or a fresco?" Fox asked.

"Or maybe it represents a king in some way."

Luciana thought again about the last line of the verse.

His enemy flies above the square, the symbol of your next destination.

She considered all of the arms of noble families she knew throughout Italy, but she was aware of none that featured a lion and a square.

They rode past the Palazzo della Signoria toward the Ponte Vecchio, and when they passed the large gathering space in front of it, the answer revealed itself.

It wasn't a square *shape* they were looking for. It was a *piazza*.

"The lion is flying," she said, "but not on a banner. My father meant that literally. A lion with wings."

She looked at Willa and Fox, expecting them to blurt out the answer, which was so obvious to her, but they stared back blankly.

"Ah, I forgot that you're not familiar with our region," she continued. "Everyone in Italy knows that the statue of a winged lion sits atop a column overlooking the piazza of San Marco. It's the center of the city of Venice."

"How long will it take to get there?" Fox asked.

"I've only been there once with my husband," Luciana said, "but I recall that it took us at least a week."

"Then it's good we are starting now. That will give us plenty of time to work out the next clue."

"And you mentioned that perhaps we'll find an ally there as well," Willa said.

She meant Giovanni, to whom Luciana had originally asked her to deliver the letter. Luciana knew she had to reveal her relationship with him at some point before they arrived in Venice, but she wasn't ready just yet.

As they approached the city wall, the bells for vespers rang out. They were the last three people to exit the city before the gates closed behind them.

Corosi paced around the loggia of his tower, shaking his head at Armstrong, who stood with his arms crossed as he looked out.

"I hope you're not expecting them to return," Corosi said. "They were in there long enough to figure out that Venice is the next place we need to go."

"No, I'm thinking about who might have been helping them. Do you know who that could be?"

Corosi had been wondering about that himself. But he had enough enemies in Florence that it could be any one of a dozen people that Luciana knew.

"That doesn't matter now. The three of them are probably out of the city by this point. I want to be ready to go when the gates open in the morning."

"My men are preparing for the journey now," Armstrong said.

"What am I to do with you?"

Armstrong turned. "Signore?"

"You were incompetent and underestimated Fox yet again. I'm beginning to think that I've allied myself with the wrong English knight."

To Corosi's surprise, Armstrong nodded. "You're right about one thing. I should have anticipated that Fox would seek help from your enemies. Does that placate you, signore?"

"Why do I get the sense that your apology is, in fact, insolence?"

"Fox escaped today only with a decent amount of luck. His good fortune can't last forever. I have faith that things will change in Venice."

"And should I have faith in *you*?"

"Signore Corosi, I swore my allegiance and loyalty to you. And I don't think you'll find the treasure without me."

"These setbacks try my patience."

"And mine as well. I promise you, signore, the next time we meet Fox, we will have the upper hand."

Corosi stewed for a few moments, but Armstrong was right. They needed each other. As much as he wanted to punish the Englishman for his failures, Corosi was intelligent enough to know that would only cause him to fall further behind Luciana in the search.

"I hope your confidence is rewarded," he said. "For both our sakes. We do have one more advantage."

"What's that?"

"Sofia. Thanks to her, we'll be ready to sail the moment we decipher the Venice clue."

Corosi hoped what he told Armstrong was true. The closer they got to the treasure, the deeper the pit grew in his stomach. He had to find it first. If Luciana beat him to it, Corosi would lose everything, a threat that had been hanging over his head for nearly four decades.

42

Thirty-nine years ago—January, 1312

PARIS

Corosi breathed a sigh of relief as he walked out of Louvre Castle. Simply meeting the king of France was a nerve-jarring experience. Bartering with him was even more harrowing. But he had emerged with everything he wanted, including his head. Now to secure his freedom, he would ride to Vienne and another awe-inducing encounter, this time with the pope himself, who was leading a council of five hundred of the most powerful men in the Church to determine the fate of the Knights Templar.

He put the hood up on his chaperon and walked as fast as he could without running, keeping one hand at all times on the precious leather scrip hanging from his shoulder. The afternoon clouds were heavy with a coming storm. Given the cold, snow was a definite possibility, and he wanted to get on the road before it started to fall.

He rounded a corner into an alley for a shortcut to the bridge over the Seine and abruptly stopped when he saw a familiar figure standing before him.

"Hello, Riccardo," Domenico Ramberti said, his hand on the sword that was concealed by his mantle. Although he was old enough to be Corosi's father and had long acted as the only father figure in his life, Ramberti looked every bit the formidable Knight Templar that he was.

Corosi didn't have his own sword. One didn't enter the king's presence armed. He turned to make an escape, but he felt the blade of a dagger at his neck.

"We're very disappointed in you," Matteo Dazzo said into his ear.

"Why is that?"

"You were my best friend. I could never have imagined this kind of treachery. Did you think we wouldn't figure out that you'd be meeting with the king?"

"Obviously I didn't or I wouldn't have let you surprise me like this. You really are dense sometimes, Matteo."

Matteo had been like a younger brother to him ever since the fire that had killed both their parents and Ramberti's wife. The grief-stricken Ramberti had essentially adopted them both, and their relationship growing up, like many brothers, had been composed of equal parts camaraderie and rivalry. Recent events had tipped the balance toward the latter.

The blade pressed against Corosi's skin.

"And how smart is it to insult someone with a knife at your neck?" Matteo said. "Maybe I should just kill you right here for what you've done."

"But then Sir Domenico wouldn't be able to ask me any questions about what I've been doing, isn't that right?"

"Correct," Ramberti said. "We need to know exactly what you said to His Majesty." He stepped forward and drew the knife from Corosi's belt, tossing it aside. Then he carefully removed the scrip.

He opened the leather pouch and took the signet ring he found at the bottom. Ramberti put it on his finger.

"And I thought our bout of drinking last week was to help drown our mutual sorrows at the news of the suffering of our Templar brothers, while you saw it only as an opportunity to take this from me. Once I figured out that it was you who'd taken it, we had to follow you today. You certainly needed the seal for something, and you're going to tell us what that was."

He reached in and took out the only other object in the scrip. It was a parchment letter with the French king's seal holding it closed.

Ramberti raised an eyebrow. "This is what you wanted from the king?"

"What does it say?" Matteo asked, the knife still at Corosi's throat. "No, let me guess. It's a proclamation from the king naming a breed of pig after him." He let out a half-hearted laugh at his attempt at humor.

Ramberti broke the seal and unfolded the letter. He scanned it without reading aloud. When he was finished, he shook his head in disbelief and focused on Corosi.

"It seems that my loyal apprentice no longer wishes to be a Templar. The king is formally asking the pope to release him from his lifelong vows."

"Why would His Holiness do that?"

"Apparently the king is threatening to reveal damaging information about the pope if he doesn't absolve Riccardo of his vows and disband the Knights Templar."

Matteo growled into Corosi's ear. "His Majesty must be getting something valuable in return for making that kind of request for this scum."

"We will confirm it later," Ramberti said, "but I'd wager that Riccardo revealed the location of the Templar treasure to the king."

"What good is it to you now?" Corosi taunted. "The Templars will soon cease to exist."

"Because of you!" Matteo blurted.

"You really are too impulsive, Matteo. It'll be your undoing someday."

"If I were that impulsive, I would have slit your throat already. See how much restraint I have?"

"You needed my seal," Ramberti said, "because you've concocted false evidence that somehow seals the order's doom. Would you care to tell me what that is?"

The conclusions about the treasure and the evidence were correct. Corosi had forged a letter in Ramberti's name and given it to the king. It stated that the pope had long known about the Templars' secret initiation ceremony involving the worship of idols and dark, forbidden practices, yet the pope still refused to censure them. It was the Templars' power within the Church that stayed his hand—the reason he hadn't yet disbanded the order.

The trials against the Templars had largely been based on information obtained through torture. Corosi's false letter in Ramberti's name—one of the highest-ranking knights in the order and a close associate of the French king as the royal treasurer—provided independent corroboration of the vile accusations as well as implicating the pope in the sphere of blame. Such a revelation could shake the very foundations of the Church and necessarily erode its moral power.

The king would use the falsified letter to force the pope to condemn the Templars and suppress them forever, delivering their wealth in France to King Philip. Only then would His Majesty rip up the purported evidence of the pope's apostasy.

Corosi said none of that, though he might under torture if that's what it came to. Instead, he simply smiled and remained silent.

"Why, Riccardo?" Matteo asked in a hurt voice, revealing the boy he still was. "I was your brother. Sir Domenico was like a father to you."

"Then why did you betray me?"

Matteo barked out a laugh. "*I* betrayed *you*?"

Corosi felt the hurt well up inside him. It had been building up for months as he planned his retribution, and now he couldn't stop himself from responding.

"You both did! We had a pact. Matteo and I would secretly become Knights Templar and carry on the order under the tutelage of Sir Domenico. The risk would be great, but we were going to do it together. I happily took the vows knowing Matteo would be joining me in a year when he was old enough. But then you tossed our agreement away like it was nothing."

"Because I am to marry Luciana?"

Ramberti shook his head in disbelief. "That's what this is about?"

"How could you not see it? I gave up everything to become a Templar with Matteo." Corosi focused his rage on Ramberti.

"You knew that we were both in love with your daughter. The only fair thing to do was make it so that neither of us could marry her. We'd both devote our lives to the vows of chastity, poverty, and obedience as Templars. But then you changed your mind on a whim. You promised her to Matteo after I'd honored my part of the bargain. You always favored him!"

"I was doing what was right for Luciana," Ramberti said. "I couldn't leave her unprotected, and Matteo truly loves her. You and I would seize the adventurous life promised by the order, while Matteo would take care of Luciana. Now you've betrayed not just me, but all the Templars. For nothing."

"You've only reaped what you deserve. And you went behind my back, Matteo, sure of the prize of Luciana, never mentioning it before I took my vows."

"She's not a prize to be won," Matteo protested.

"You treat her like one. You waited until I was bound forever before asking Ramberti for her hand. You both speak of brotherhood and honor. But that's all it is. Talk. Now I'm the one taking action."

A pair of men came around the corner and saw Corosi being held at knife point.

"A thief," Ramberti said, nodding at Corosi. The two men decided to stay out of the dispute and kept walking.

"We can't stay out here," Matteo said.

"Let's take him back to the house."

Matteo held on to Corosi's arm and let him feel the prick of the dagger in his back. Ramberti took the other side, his sword at the ready under his mantle.

"Move," Matteo said, and yanked him forward.

They went back to the main street and turned onto the Pont aux Meuniers, the bridge from the right bank of the river to the Île de la Cité. The island where Notre Dame cathedral was built was in the center of Paris, so the bridge was heavily used.

The narrow wooden bridge was supposed to be limited to pedestrians, but a mule, two donkeys, and several other animals competed for space with the people. The cacophony of noise was augmented by the grinding sounds from the floating mills underneath that gave the bridge its name, their paddle wheels suspended from boat hulls to take advantage of the current.

A donkey bumped into Ramberti, causing him to jostle Corosi. It wasn't enough of an opening for Corosi to make an escape attempt, but it gave him an idea.

They were coming up behind the plodding mule, which was weighed down with a huge load of straw. The three of them would have to go around it. As they approached its hindquarters, Corosi pretended to stumble. He lunged forward and slapped the mule's behind, then ducked out of the way.

The sudden move made the mule kick backward at the offender. But instead of Corosi, it caught Matteo in the side, sending him reeling.

Corosi tried to run, but Ramberti was too quick. He grabbed at Corosi's cloak, clutching just enough of it to trip Corosi, who smacked into the bridge's parapet.

Ramberti advanced on him, pulling his sword partway out of its sheath. "Don't make me do this right here, Riccardo."

"In front of all these people?"

"If I have to."

Matteo staggered over, holding his ribs and grimacing.

"You swine! That hurt!"

The two of them had him cornered, and they wouldn't be fooled by the same trick twice.

So Corosi took a chance. Without any indication he would do it, he vaulted over the parapet.

Corosi heard Ramberti and Matteo shout above him as he plunged down, not knowing if he would hit water or one of the mills beneath the bridge.

Thankfully, he slammed into the water feet first, but the shock of the cold knocked the breath from him. He could feel the current pulling him beneath the bridge.

Corosi surfaced and flailed to find anything to hold on to. His hand snatched a rope, arresting his movement. It was a line tying one of the mills to the bridge. The churning paddle was mere yards away.

The boat had a covered hut where the millers could stay warm while they worked, so he hadn't yet been spotted. A plank was suspended between the mills so workers could pass from one to another. If Corosi could reach it, he'd be able to pull himself out of the freezing water.

He lifted his arm, but the motion caused his cloak to float loose. It threatened to get caught in the paddle mechanism and drag him to his death. With one hand on the line, he frantically raced to untie it from around his neck.

At the moment he got it unlaced, the cloak was wrenched away and swirled into the paddle wheel. The cloth wrapped around his foot, yanking it at a painfully awkward angle before tearing his boot away as it was drawn into the mechanism.

The paddle wheel stopped, and the millers inside came out to see what the matter was. Corosi was about to call for their help when he saw Ramberti and Matteo sprinting across the planks connecting all the mills.

"I think he went in over there!" Matteo yelled.

Corosi used the line to pull himself into concealment by the boat, his ankle screaming at him every time he kicked with it. He was shivering uncontrollably and his fingers were starting to go numb. If he didn't get out of the water soon, the cold would kill him instead of Ramberti and Matteo.

Footsteps pounded across the plank.

"That's his cloak," Ramberti said.

"And his boot," Matteo added.

A rough voice responded. "Whose cloak and boot are gumming up my machine?"

"A friend of ours," Ramberti said. "He fell off the bridge."

"Sorry to say it, but your friend is feeding the fish somewhere downriver by now. I've seen men crushed by these paddles."

Freed from the cloak, the mechanism started working again, and the men went back inside.

"We can't question the knave now," Matteo said.

"There's nothing we can do about any documents Riccardo forged in my name," Ramberti replied, "but we have to assume he told the king where the treasure is being held. It will take some time for him to assemble his men. If I ride fast, I can get there first and ship it out before the king's men arrive."

"We'll leave right now."

"Not you. Luciana needs you."

"But I want to go with you."

"No. This will be a long and dangerous journey, and I need to fulfill my oath to let the grand master know that it has been safely hidden. You'll take my place in safeguarding my daughter. I need you to tell Luciana that I love her very much, even if I never see her again. Marry her, be happy, cherish my grandchildren. Will you do this for me?"

The answer was reluctant. "Yes, signore."

"Good man. Now let's go make ready to travel."

The footsteps receded across the planks.

Corosi waited as long as he could before grabbing on to the plank and pulling himself out of the water using his last bit of strength.

He got to his knees and crawled to the door of the millers' shack. His ankle would take time to heal, meaning that Matteo would no doubt reach Luciana before he could, but he already had the inkling of an idea for how to best him in their inevitable confrontation.

First he had to survive the rest of the day. Corosi knocked on the door. It swept open, and one of the millers poked his head out. He looked down in astonishment at the sodden man at his feet.

Corosi said through chattering teeth, "Blanket. Now."

October, 1351

NORTH OF FLORENCE

Fearing that they might be followed despite their escape through Florence's closing gates, Willa, Gerard, and Luciana rode north until the moon set. They camped in a clearing and slept a few hours under a blanket of clouds.

At sunup they quietly saddled the horses and extinguished the fire. Since they were still near Florence, Fox was anxious to get on the road, but it was also the first time he'd been alone with Willa since the ride from Siena. While Luciana went into the woods to get water from a nearby creek, he edged closer to Willa and spoke in a low voice, finally ready for a conversation he'd had at the back of his mind for days.

He took her hands in his.

"Do you think that part of the reason we agreed to help Signora Corosi was because you and I weren't ready to part with each other?"

She nodded. "I've been thinking the same thing. We are a good pair, aren't we?"

"Perhaps we were too hasty about our decision in San Giuseppe."

Willa raised an eyebrow. "Are you saying there's hope?"

"I'm saying that my mind may be changing."

Willa squeezed his hand. "Then I have hope for us."

"In Siena I wasn't entirely convinced that these clues pointed to a real treasure, but after what we found at the baptistery, it seems like Luciana's father is truly leading us somewhere. She's nearing the end of a quest that began nearly forty years ago. She didn't give up. I was thinking that maybe I might not need to, either."

"Your excommunication?"

He nodded. "And my land and title. She's on the brink of changing her life for the better if we can help her gain her freedom. Why shouldn't that beacon of hope be out there for me as well?"

"For us," Willa said gently. "I won't give up if you don't."

Fox had thought that seeing his family estate Caldecott Mote in England ever again was out of the question, but if they actually found the legendary Templar treasure, anything was possible.

"Then one day, we may call Caldecott Mote *our* home."

Willa's eyes widened as she understood the implication. "Do you mean it? As husband and wife?"

"I do. I've realized over our time with Luciana that we truly belong together. It's not just that we make a great team, but I love the way that you help me to look at the world differently. I want that for always." He pulled her to him and kissed her softly. "After we have found the treasure, I promise we will find a way to marry."

"I hope so. I hunger for you every night."

"I wish my hunger was only limited to the evening hours," Fox replied.

Willa looked around with a red face to see if they'd been observed and stepped away.

"First, we need to make sure we find the treasure. Venice is still a week's ride away. Don't you think we need to know if this Giovanni fellow will really be able to help us?"

"I do." The same thing had been bothering him. "If her lover can be an aid in finding the treasure, it's hard to turn down an ally, but she seems reluctant to talk about him."

"And how do we know we can trust him? After all, her own husband tried to have her murdered. Twice."

"I feel the same way. It's more a matter of how we broach the subject."

"If she's been unfaithful," Willa said, "she's likely ill at ease about telling us."

"We need to know now so we can start thinking of alternatives."

"I'm sure it will be a sensitive topic for her."

"Also we must find a ship," Fox said. "Either Giovanni's or another one." Luciana had mentioned that he was a ship's captain.

"Right," Willa said, nodding. "The next clue says to travel to an island."

"Which could be anywhere. There are thousands of islands in the Mediterranean alone. I know the Templars were active on Cyprus and Sicily, but those islands are enormous. We'll never find the site of the treasure without solving the puzzle."

"Giovanni must be familiar with some of those islands."

"And he might be just as greedy as Corosi and try to get the treasure all for himself."

Willa grinned at him. "Are you going to accuse her lover of being a cheat and swindler before we even find out who he is? Even better, why don't you ask her if he's a pirate?"

"I think we're entitled to learn as much as we can about him. Given what we know about her husband, it's clear her judgment of people can be suspect."

"She trusted *us*, didn't she?"

"That's different," Gerard said, smiling. "We're very trustworthy."

"Except when we're lying about being married or excommunicated."

"That's… also different. But I see your point."

"I just mean that we need to approach this tactfully."

"I'll take your lead." Fox nodded at Luciana, who was just returning with a full waterskin. She was humming a ditty under her breath as she swung the waterskin in time to her tune. He was surprised at how spirited she seemed, but perhaps the imminent meeting in Venice was giving her renewed heart.

"Shall we keep going?" she said. "We want to stay ahead of Riccardo and Armstrong."

"Luciana," Willa said, "you know that we are committed to helping you on this quest, but we do have something important to ask you."

Luciana looked at them both. "This sounds serious."

"It might be a delicate issue," Fox said.

"We know you've been reluctant to speak about Giovanni," Willa said. "But now that we are going to Venice, if we're going to have to rely on him for help, Gerard and I feel that it's time to talk about how you came to be involved with him."

Fox quickly added, "We understand that Signore Corosi is not an honorable husband. It would drive any woman to another man's arms."

Willa grimaced at his clumsy statement. Fox felt himself flush.

Luciana regarded them both with confusion. "What are you saying?"

"You can tell us the truth about Giovanni," Willa said. "If he can aid us in our quest, we need to know that he won't betray you. And you know that Gerard and I aren't purists when it comes to relationships condoned by the Church."

"You think Giovanni is my lover?"

"You wanted us to get a secret note to him without your husband knowing," Fox said.

"There's no reason to be ashamed," Willa added.

Luciana chuckled and shook her head. "I don't have an illicit lover in Venice or anywhere else, although I now understand why you might have thought so. I haven't told you more about him because it is a tender subject for me."

Now it was Fox's turn to be confused. He exchanged a glance with Willa and said, "Then who is this man?"

"Someone who I'm absolutely certain would never betray me. Giovanni is my son."

THE GOLDEN VEIL

Northern Italy

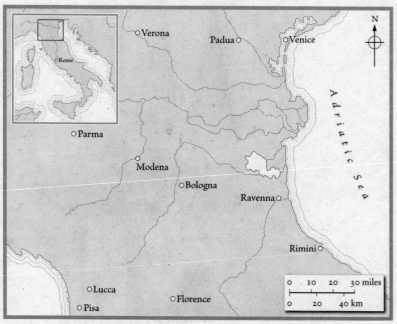

44

EAST OF PADUA

Sofia was close enough to Venice that she could smell the sea surrounding the city. Daybreak's salty breeze brought every kind of emotion swelling from the depths of her soul—memories of a pleasant childhood with a loving father, the gut-wrenching pain and misery of starving on the streets after he died, the years she had spent in degradation being passed from client to client, the pride and comfort when she rose out of the grime to become a businesswoman in her own right. Despite all of that—or perhaps because of it—the city still held a special place in her heart. There was nowhere else like it on earth, and she both loved and hated it. By the end of the day, she would be home.

She opened her eyes to see that Rocco was the one who'd gotten the second half of the night's watch. The other guard who Corosi had sent along, Cesare, was snoring on his bed of rushes in the abandoned farmhouse that they'd appropriated for the night.

Although they'd stayed in a few taverns when they'd come through larger cities like Bologna during their week-long trek, they'd frequently taken advantage of the many houses that had been emptied by the Pestilence and never reoccupied.

It was apparent that Corosi hadn't entirely trusted her not to slip away. The two guards had explained that they were instructed to keep her safe by splitting the evening watch duty between them. They'd been traveling with as few pauses as possible, stopping only for meals and to let the horses rest.

All three of their steeds stood inside the house that had likely been home to ten or more residents before they had succumbed to the Great Mortality. The occupants would have brought all

of their animals indoors each evening to safeguard them from
predators and the elements. It wasn't uncommon for farmers to
sleep among their goats, sheep, and chickens. Sofia thanked the
Lord that the only creatures stinking up the place now were the
guards and their horses, though the body odor of the sweaty men
was far the worse of the two.

"Good, you're up," Rocco said to her. "I'm starving."

The pair likely had never made a meal for themselves in their
lives, so she'd gotten in the habit of boiling a stew whenever they
couldn't find a town that could serve them hot pottage. The coarse
bread and salted meat they had in their saddlebags was strictly
for the road so that they could keep going during the day without
stopping to build a fire.

"We've got kindling and wood, but no more fresh meat or
vegetables."

Rocco kicked Cesare in the rear. "Wake up."

Cesare bolted upright. He looked around in surprise until he
realized what had happened and rubbed his backside. "What's
the idea?"

"We need food."

"Then get it yourself."

"I have to make the fire. Take her out and get whatever she
needs to make the stew."

"I saw the remains of a garden in the back," Sofia said. "I think
there are unharvested carrots and cabbage."

"I could go for some good mutton," Cesare said, staggering to
his feet.

"Did you see any sheep out there when we arrived, you
blockhead?" Rocco said. "See if you can find a duck or a rabbit or
something."

"A duck? What am I supposed to do, swat it out of the air with
my sword?"

"You're right. You couldn't hit it if it landed on your head."

Sofia rolled her eyes at them. Their constant sniping during the
entire journey had driven her to distraction.

"I can make a tasty stew with just the vegetables and some

flavoring I've brought," she said. "Now help me gather the ingredients."

She and Cesare rooted around in the untended garden until they had enough carrots and cabbage to load the pot that she filled with water from the nearby creek.

By the time they returned to the cottage, black smoke was already belching from the center of the roof. The simpleton had used some of the rushes to stoke the flames too high, which would give the stew a burnt flavor. No matter. They'd eat it just the same.

She set the pot into the middle of the fire, cut up the carrots, shredded the cabbage, and sprinkled in the herbs she'd retrieved from her travel bags. When the stew was ready, she served it up in the wooden bowls they carried with them.

She handed the bowls to Rocco and Cesare who blew on them until the food was cool enough to swallow. Then they slurped the stew down in the same disgusting way they always did, barely pausing to savor the taste.

They did seem hungry because Sofia gave them second helpings, and they both drained their bowls again.

Rocco belched voluminously. "That did its job."

Cesare scratched himself and nodded at her. "Aren't you eating?"

Sofia shook her head. "This meal wasn't very tempting. Besides, you ate it all."

"It went down well," Rocco said. "Your cooking has improved."

That was as close to a compliment as he ever gave her. Sofia didn't care. She watched him closely for the first signs.

"I suppose this makes up a little for us having to keep our hands off you," Cesare said.

"That's quite gentlemanly of you."

Rocco snorted. "Corosi would have our heads if he thought we'd touched you." He wiped his brow. "Is it hot in here?" Sweat was beading on his forehead.

"I was just thinking the opposite," Cesare said. "I suddenly have a chill."

Sofia suppressed a smile.

"Well, we should saddle the horses and go," Rocco said. "We can be to Venice before nightfall."

As he got to his feet, he swayed and fell back to the ground. He shook his head as if he were trying to clear his vision.

"What's wrong with you?" Cesare asked.

"I don't feel so good."

Now Cesare was going pale. He put a hand to his stomach. "Neither do I."

They both looked at the empty pot.

"Oh no," Sofia said innocently. "Do you think the carrots were bad?"

"Or the cabbage," Rocco said. With a sudden heave, he turned over and vomited. Sofia held her nose, but the acrid smell wasn't as bad as his sweat-stained clothing.

A moment later, Cesare did the same. They both continued until their stomachs were emptied, and even then they couldn't stop.

Sofia was disgusted but also fascinated by the effect. She'd stirred in her whole supply of monkshood and heavily salted the brew to mask any unusual taste. She'd never seen the potent poison act so fast, but then again she'd never administered such a large portion at one time. The amount she'd put into Luciana's cup had been a fraction of what Rocco and Cesare had consumed, and just a few sips would have led to her lady's certain death by morning.

"You both should lie down until this passes."

Neither of them was in a position to argue. They fell to the floor and moaned as they writhed in pain.

Sofia had put up with them for the bulk of the trip because they'd been useful to protect her from any ruffians they might meet along the way, but now they'd outlived their purpose. She could make the rest of the trip to Venice on her own, and they would have simply gotten in her way if they'd made it there with her.

Their breathing was becoming ragged. Rocco's moaning paused when he grabbed weakly at her skirt.

"This is you," he said. "You did this."

Cesare stared at them in confusion. The poison appeared to have varying effects on them.

Sofia snatched her skirt away from Rocco's grimy hands.

"I'm just grateful that it took you this long to figure that out."

Cesare cried out at her through a foaming mouth and tried to push himself up to attack her, but his trembling arms wouldn't cooperate. He slumped back down and went limp, air hissing from his dying lips.

"Why?" was the only word Rocco could get out.

"Because, you smelly clod, you two are more nuisance than you're worth."

He attempted to lunge at her once again, but he only succeeded in planting his face in the dirt. His body jerked with spasms and then he went quiet.

It took her longer than she thought it would to saddle the horses on her own, but she was pleased with herself when she was done.

She picked up one of the burning logs by its cool end and threw it into the rushes. The dry tinder caught fire instantly and spread rapidly to the wooden walls.

Sofia guided the three horses outside and got into the saddle of her own. She'd lead the other two to Venice and get a nice price for them before taking a boat over to the island city. Besides, she couldn't leave them in the house to burn up with Rocco and Cesare.

After all, she wasn't a monster.

45

VENICE

Sofia took a ferry across the wide lagoon separating the island city from the mainland, her first visit in more than three years. The bobbing of the boat was a familiar feeling in this place dominated by sea travel. As she saw the buildings get closer, the sense that the crowded port floated on the water was hard to dispel.

She hadn't realized how much she'd missed seeing this magical place rising out of the water like something out of a fairy tale. Although many of her memories were painful, she chose to think of the time that her father took her out on a gondola just to see a fiery sunset lighting up the buildings, making them look like an elegant stained-glass depiction of a floating town. On that day, she understood why Venice was also known as La Serenissima—The Most Serene.

When the ferry reached the northern docks, Sofia disembarked with her belongings and a purse full of Venetian ducats from the sale of the three horses and their saddles before departing the opposite shore. She knew Giovanni preferred the western docks, but since she was on the other side of the Grand Canal, she'd first need to head south to get there.

To strangers, Venice's maze of winding canals and narrow streets were as complicated to navigate as the minotaur's labyrinth of Greek legend. Most of the canals did not have streets bordering them, and there were no signs for guidance. Buildings were often constructed with a sheer face that went directly into the water.

Numerous bridges arced over the canals, imposing a challenge to carters who had to haul their loads up and over them without the aid of horses or donkeys, which were uncommon sights in the narrow alleyways and crowded paths. In many of the narrower canals, the bridges were simply long planks of wood that could be easily pushed aside to let a gondola through.

Every square featured a fountain with a well, the only sources of fresh water in the city. The distinctive look of each one provided a way for Sofia to orient herself. Without recognizing individual landmarks, it was easy to turn oneself around and go back in the opposite direction unintentionally. Although the map in Sofia's head was usually accurate, it wasn't fresh. Even she took a few wrong turns before reaching the Rialto Bridge.

The Rialto was the only bridge across the wide and teeming Grand Canal. The majority of the boat traffic through Venice flowed along this winding body of water that snaked through the center of the city. Doge Andrea Dandolo and his governing council had sometimes spoken of building a stone bridge to withstand the heavy daily pedestrian traffic across it, but Sofia noted that it remained a wooden structure. It had two ramps meeting at a movable central section that could be raised to allow the passage of tall ships.

After more than a week of riding, she decided that she deserved to take one of the many gondolas that transported people and goods throughout the city. With her newly acquired funds, she hired one of the smaller boats with a single gondolier. She eased into the seat of the slow but stable vessel that was used to haul cargo and passengers right up to the steps of many buildings whose doors opened directly onto the water.

While they were in the Grand Canal, the gondola bobbed up and down every time one of the four-rower caorlinas passed by. They were more than twice the size of their smaller brethren, cruising up and down the Grand Canal at high speeds for those in a hurry. Sofia had enough money to use one of those, but she preferred to travel at a slower pace so she could simply enjoy being back home.

They emerged out into the lagoon along the western docks, and she peered at the myriad ships that were tied up at the piers. It wasn't as crowded as before the Pestilence descended on the city, but it seemed like the economic recovery was well on its way. The hordes of seamen, merchants, and financiers who had once thronged the city's streets were returning, as La Serenissima was the acknowledged trading capital of the Western world. The city's reputation for international commerce also made prostitution a lucrative profession, as she herself had experienced.

Years ago Sofia started building a business with hopes of becoming a wealthy madam running her own house. Then in January of 1348, the first victims of the Pestilence staggered off their ships to spread the disease throughout the city. Those days had been terrifying, with bodies piling up in the streets and nowhere to bury them on the island.

Health officials had frantically tried to limit the plague's impact by forcing sailing ships to anchor at one of the nearby islands for forty days before offloading their cargos. This so-called quarantine from the word *quaranta*, meaning forty, had only limited success. The prostitutes of Venice, who were almost always the first to welcome sailors who had been long at sea, died by the hundreds.

So when she'd heard from Giovanni about his mother and her losses to the Pestilence, she took a chance and left for Florence to build a new life. Three years later, that gamble was finally about to pay off, but only if this last piece fell into place. She studied each of the vessels hoping for one in particular.

With a burst of excitement, she spotted the three-masted carrack she'd been searching for, glad that it wasn't out to sea. On the stern, bright white paint spelled out *Cara Signora*. Sofia shook her head. Giovanni always had shown a devotion to his mother that was both touching and a little pathetic. Sofia supposed that it had worked to her advantage.

She told the gondolier to let her off at the nearest dock. She'd rehearsed what she was going to say, but the prospect of seeing him again still made her nervous, the only man who made her feel butterflies in her stomach.

Long ago, she had come to the conclusion that trusting any man was dangerous. They were simply pawns to be moved about the chessboard of her life on her way to checkmate. But Giovanni had been different. Their dalliance started off like all the others, but she developed a fondness for his witty conversation and lively companionship, and he seemed to come to genuinely enjoy her company, with the commercial part of the transaction fading away. She eventually realized that his persona of a ne'er-do-well rogue actually hid a genuinely honest and caring man, one of the few she had ever encountered.

She walked over to the *Cara Signora* and stood at the gangplank. A sailor carrying a sack off the ship couldn't help but notice a woman alone on the docks. He stopped in front of her.

"Are you looking for some business?" he said, his eyes wandering up and down her figure.

"You couldn't afford me."

"You might be surprised."

"I would, but that's not why I'm here. Is Giovanni on board?"

"The captain? I think he's in his cabin. Is your business with him?"

"Yes, and it's none of yours."

She started up the gangplank, and the sailor called up after her.

"Where do you think you're going?"

"Believe me," she said without looking back, "he'll want to hear what I have to say."

She remembered that his quarters were in the aft part of the ship, which had a high forecastle separated from the stern by a broad deck where seamen were stitching up rips in the sails. They all paused in their work at the strange sight of a woman on board, but no one stopped her. They must have thought Giovanni was expecting some midday entertainment.

She went inside the main cabin and was met by the rank odor of men crammed into tight quarters for weeks on end. The door to the captain's compartment was closed, and the sound of clinking coins came from inside. She took a breath before knocking.

There was a shuffling noise before a familiar silky voice said, "What is it?"

"May I enter?"

The sound of a woman must have been the last thing he was

expecting. The door was flung open, revealing a rugged figure dressed in only a shirt and braies. The linen material clung to muscles honed by years at sea, and his obsidian black hair was unkempt but somehow attractive at the same time. His face was understandably a bit more weather-beaten than the last time she'd seen him, but his beard was as neatly trimmed as ever.

Giovanni stared at her in astonishment.

"Sofi? What are you doing here?"

"I expected a warmer welcome than that."

Sofia walked to him and kissed him lightly on both cheeks. He peered at her cautiously.

"It's been three years," he said. "When you disappeared and I couldn't find you, I assumed you had abandoned the city and me on purpose. I thought I'd never see you again."

"I didn't know if I'd ever return, but I've come with good reason."

"I think our time together ran its course."

"I suppose I deserve that."

"You ran away without so much as leaving a note for me. I thought the Pestilence might have gotten you."

Sofia had to do her best work now. Neither Armstrong nor Corosi knew she had intended to contact Giovanni—the entire reason for her early departure from Florence. She wanted to secure a ship, as she had told them, but it was to find the treasure for herself. Convincing Giovanni to take her there was her most attractive option. As an honest man, he would be more easily duped.

She put a hand up to caress his face. "I'm so sorry, my darling. The brothel had become a tomb, with my friends dying one by one. After my last friend died, I just had to escape the horrors of this city. I was worried that if I came to you to say goodbye, my parting gift to you might be the Pestilence. Since your stories of Siena were so glowing, I went there, determined to start a new life."

Since Luciana hadn't wanted Corosi to know about her correspondences with her son, she'd sent all of the letters after the Great Mortality through Sofia, who was able to destroy any that mentioned her. Giovanni would have no idea she was his mother's new lady's maid.

"After you left, I got out of the city myself," he said. "I suppose we all do what we have to."

"If you'll grant me another chance, I think you'll be glad I'm back. You'll be astounded to hear why."

"You have my attention."

He guided her to his chair and sat on the edge of his writing desk.

"You remember the letter you mentioned to me? The one that your grandfather sent to your mother?"

He shook his head and pursed his lips. "I never should have shared that letter with you. One of my many drunken misdeeds. It's a fool's errand. You know that, don't you? I've tried to solve it for years with nothing to show for it. It was a riddle with no answer, created by a madman."

"But it does have an answer. There was a companion to that letter. That's why you and your mother were never able to decipher it."

He frowned at her. "I don't understand."

"I took the liberty of making a copy of your mother's letter one night before you and I parted ways. Please, don't be angry. You know that I have abilities along those lines, and I thought maybe I could help. But I made no more headway than you. Then I was in Siena and cared for a sick old woman who was a cousin of Matteo Dazzo, a squire of your grandfather."

Giovanni nodded. "I remember my mother mentioning him to me."

"She had kept a letter that Sir Domenico had sent him, and she showed it to me. I was amazed to see that it is a complement to the letter your mother had, not a duplicate. That's why you weren't able to solve the clues in her letter by itself. I copied the letter to Matteo and combined it with the one you had."

She proceeded to tell him a fanciful version of how she'd deciphered the clues. At first, he scoffed at her incredible tale, but by the end, his eyes went wide when her meaning registered.

"The Templar treasure?"

She nodded. "I have the way to find it. I just need a ship to take me there."

She withdrew the full combined letter from her kirtle and showed it to him.

He looked dubious as he took it and read it. But the farther he went, the clearer it was to Sofia that she was reeling him in.

When he was done, he looked up. "This is true?"

"I've already solved the first three clues. From Siena to Florence and now to Venice." She told him the meaning of the first three quatrains, convincing him even further, without mentioning her previous companions.

"Then the answer to the next clue must be in this city."

"It is. Once we solve it, we can set sail for the isle of our destiny, as the riddle says. Then we will have more riches than we could have ever dreamed of."

She had no intention of letting Corosi take all of the hoard for himself, though she didn't doubt he would try. She knew that at best, he intended to keep her as his mistress once he'd remarried and, at worst, was prepared to discard her as soon as he found the treasure. Even though Giovanni was a smuggler, she didn't believe that he would cheat her out of her rightful share. If he made a vow, he would keep it.

He considered her proposal, and she could see the doubt creeping into his eyes.

"Sofi, do you really think it exists?"

"Everything has proven correct so far. Why would your grandfather make up this quest if it didn't actually lead to the Templar gold?"

"I don't know. I was never really sure it was out there. Now it seems too good to be true."

"We have to take that chance," she said. "Think about your future. Do you want to be a ship's captain until the day you die? It's a difficult life."

When he hesitated, she added, "Think about your father."

"He disinherited me. He wants nothing to do with me. He told me himself."

"Exactly. You will never be his son again. But you can become even wealthier than he is. With that much money, your estate will be far grander than his."

"I don't need to outdo him."

"Then what about your mother? Give her a reason to defy Signore Corosi and come to you. With all that wealth, you both could live separate from your father."

Sofia could tell those words struck a chord. He inhaled sharply, then nodded. "I'll take you. When do we leave?"

"We still need to solve the clue in Venice. I have some matters to attend to first, then we can solve it together."

She knew Corosi and Armstrong would be arriving as soon as they had eliminated Luciana, Willa, and Fox, so she had to be ready to deal with them, and keep them far away from Giovanni.

She held out her hand for the letter, which Giovanni was reading again. Under his breath, he said the first line of the Venice clue out loud:

Where the patron saint is revered, study the embellishments of the golden veil.

When he was done, he gave the letter back to her, and she replaced it in her kirtle.

"If we're going to do this together, I'm going to need my own copy of the combined letter."

"You'll have it," she said, kissing him once more for good measure. "I'll return as soon as I can. Make ready to sail."

She opened the door, but before she could go, Giovanni said, "There's only one problem."

"What's that?"

"I've figured out where we need to go to solve the clue. We won't be able to see the golden veil again until Christmas."

46

The Road to Venice

Although Corosi's back ached from the fast pace they'd kept up from Florence, he wasn't going to be the old man asking Armstrong and his men to slow down, especially when they were so close to Venice. He adjusted his seat in the saddle, but his spine still sent a tiny jolt of pain into his neck every time his horse took a false step.

Armstrong rode next to him, and ten mercenaries followed behind. He looked over and noticed Corosi shifting uncomfortably.

"Do you need to stop for a rest, signore?" he asked.

"I'm fine."

"You don't look fine. You look like you have bees in your braies."

"I've ridden for a week without complaint. You'll be lucky to be as fit as I am when you're my age."

"I will admit that I had my doubts you'd make this journey."

"And let Luciana beat me in this quest? I think not."

"She must be arriving in Venice soon."

"I don't see how that's possible. We've been going from daybreak to sundown every day. There's no chance Luciana could keep up that kind of pace."

"You're doing it," Armstrong said. "Why can't she?"

Corosi scowled. He could be right.

"That would explain why we haven't caught sight of them."

"Which means they will have at least one extra day to solve the clue."

Corosi unfolded the copy of the letter that Sofia had transcribed for him. The script was larger so he could read it. Over the years his vision had become blurrier for close objects, particularly in dim surroundings. The morning sun, however, provided more than enough light.

> *Where the patron saint is revered, study the embellishments of the*
> *golden veil.*
> *Find the figure in white who resists all but the command of*
> *Christ.*
> *Among his four gilded cousins, the chosen one is closest to the basin*
> *of the city.*
> *Beneath, next to the source of the seed of life, is inscribed the isle of*
> *your destiny.*

"Does that mean the patron saint of Venice?" Armstrong asked.

"It must. Saint Mark. Everything in the city seems to be named for him."

"Then '*Where the patron saint is revered*' has to mean the cathedral. Is it as large as the one in Siena?" Armstrong had never been to Venice.

"Larger. Saint Mark's Basilica is one of the largest churches in the style of Byzantium. Although it isn't as modern or as tall or as well-lit as the Duomo will be when finished, it's an impressive piece of architecture all the same. Many of its elements are the spoils of the Crusades, taken from Constantinople during the sack centuries ago."

"Such as the statue of the Winged Lion of Venice?"

"No. That arrived earlier. But the bronze horses adorning the basilica's front façade were brought back by the Venetian Crusaders."

Armstrong shook his head. "An interesting history lesson. Does any of this actually help us solve the riddle? We're supposed to '*study the embellishments of the golden veil.*' What is that?"

"I believe I know. There is a famous golden altarpiece inside the basilica called the Pala d'Oro. This pall is made of gold instead of a cloth that is usually draped over the altar, and it holds the relics of Saint Mark. The embellishments are a series of enamel panels that decorate its front."

"So we need to find the man in white on this altarpiece. Have you seen the Pala d'Oro?"

"Only once. It's truly remarkable, but I don't remember it in detail. There are dozens of figures on it."

"Then we'll have to see it for ourselves."

"That's easier said than done. A wooden painting covers it at all times except during major feast days of the Church."

"Why would your wife's father give us a clue that we couldn't see?"

"The cover didn't exist in Ramberti's time. It was created sometime in the last decade when the Venetians decided they wanted a greater sense of drama, with the Pala d'Oro only to be revealed when they chose."

"We can't wait for the next feast. That would be Christmas. What about the four gilded cousins? Maybe we could figure that part out without the first sentence of the clue."

Corosi nodded. Armstrong had made a good suggestion for once.

"I'll ask my banking contacts in Venice if there are any golden paintings or statues of four family members. That could help us skip a step."

"And just in case that leads nowhere, I'll go to the basilica and see if there is another way to get a look at this…"

"Pala d'Oro. That will be a last resort. We will no longer be in friendly territory, so use discretion inside the church. Nothing like what you did in the Duomo."

"The Duomo hasn't been consecrated yet, so I wasn't committing sacrilege. But I'll be more cautious here. If we want to stay ahead of Luciana, we should try to get in and out as fast as possible."

"Perhaps Sofia has already acquired a ship."

Just before she had left Florence, they'd agreed that she would go to the Basilica of San Marco every day at the hour of terce so that Corosi and Armstrong could rendezvous with her when they arrived.

"Preferably a ship with the sort of men who will do what we need for this quest."

"I'd expect nothing less."

"Which presents a problem," Armstrong said. "My men are loyal to me."

"As you are to me." He had Armstrong swear an oath of loyalty to him before divulging the secret of the Templar fortune to him. "So what's the problem?"

"When we find the treasure, the cutthroats on the ship might decide to keep it for themselves."

"And do away with us. You have a point. Do you also have a suggestion?"

"I do. We don't tell them what we're looking for, and when we locate the treasure, we slay the crew in their sleep. Then after we load the gold onto the ship and hide it in the cargo space, we hire a new crew to sail the ship back to a safe harbor without them ever knowing what is carried on board."

Corosi had no doubt Armstrong and his men would slaughter an entire ship's worth of sailors to have a part of the riches they expected to discover.

"That's a good plan," he said. "Unless the island we are directed to is uninhabited."

"Then we'll only kill the most senior men and any of the roughest sailors. We keep enough of them alive as a skeleton crew. And we make sure they know it, so they'll be too terrified to rebel. Just enough of them to get us back to Italy."

But it wasn't the crew of this unknown ship that most concerned Corosi. It was his disowned son Giovanni. If by chance he were not at sea right now, surely Luciana would seek out his help.

She might even tell him the truth that she'd hidden from him all these years. Then Corosi would have to worry about yet another enemy.

VENICE

The voyage across the lagoon was short, but Fox's stomach still got queasy. He'd never been able to conquer his seasickness, but chewing on ginger kept the worst of it at bay. As usual, Willa enjoyed the jaunt, standing at the bulwark the whole way with Luciana, who didn't show any discomfort either. The fact that they were in a city that was literally built on the water—and the likelihood that they would have to travel to another island soon—meant that he'd have to secure a large supply of ginger.

They left the horses at a stable near the northern docks and made their way to the place where Luciana thought her son's ship would be moored. Fox didn't bring up the possibility that he might be at sea. They would deal with that complication if they came to it.

To his relief, the *Cara Signora* was berthed just where she thought it would be based on the letters she had received from Giovanni over the years. Luciana held Willa's hand tightly as they walked toward the ship.

The crew seemed to be loading supplies on board for another journey, so it was fortunate that they arrived when they did. Another day or two and they would have missed him.

"I don't see him," Luciana said. "It's been so long. What if he doesn't recognize me?"

She and Willa were both back to their original hair color, having stripped the dye out over the last few days.

Willa patted her arm. "A son will always recognize his mother."

Fox knew that to be the truth. The last time he saw his mother was as a child, and he remembered every curve of her face to this day.

Luciana tensed when she saw a handsome man in his thirties emerge from below deck. He apparently was the captain, ordering some of the men to carry out their duties with an air of authority.

Luciana cried out. "Gio!"

He turned his head and went slack-jawed. Then his face lit up in a huge smile, and he yelled, "*Mamma mia!*"

He ran down the gangway to pick Luciana up in his arms and twirl her around. She laughed with unbridled joy. They stopped moving and embraced tightly. Finally, Giovanni pulled away and held her at arm's length to look at her adoringly.

"I didn't think I'd ever see you again, Mamma."

"You almost didn't. But I'm thrilled to be here. You don't know how hard it's been to not see you."

The happy reunion caused Fox's chest to ache. For years he had hoped against all odds that the news of his mother's death in an attack by highwaymen had been a horrible mistake, that she would someday appear out of the blue just like this.

Giovanni looked at Fox and Willa curiously, then scanned around as if he were wary of a lynx on the prowl.

"Is Papà here?"

"I don't know."

"You don't know?"

"I hope he isn't."

"Why not?" Giovanni asked. "And who are these people?"

"Pardon me. Sir Gerard Fox and his… wife, Lady Fox, but I call them Gerard and Willa. They have served as my protectors."

Giovanni cocked his head at that, surely nonplussed that she would need protecting, and by a married couple at that.

"Can we speak in private?" Luciana continued. "I have something difficult to tell you." When it looked like he would take her alone, she added, "Willa and Gerard must be there with me."

"Of course." He ushered them up the gangplank. "I have some news as well. Remember that letter your father left you?"

Luciana had been paying close attention to her steps on the narrow board, but her head snapped up at that.

"You mean about the treasure?"

"That's the one." He looked back at Fox and Willa as he stepped on deck. "Are you certain you want to discuss this in front of them?"

"They know all about it."

"They do?"

"It's a long tale," Luciana said.

Once Fox and Willa were on the ship, he guided them all toward the aftcastle.

"Why do you mention the letter?" she continued.

"Because I believe the second half of it was recently discovered."

That caused all three of them to stop in their tracks.

"By whom?" Fox asked.

"By a woman I know named Sofi. She showed it to me, and I believe it's real."

"What does she look like?" Willa asked.

"She's got dark hair and…" Giovanni looked past them and pointed to the docks below. "In fact, there she is right now."

They all whipped around and there Sofia was fifty yards away, walking breezily toward the ship. She raised a hand to wave at Giovanni, then froze when she saw who else was with him. Without a moment's hesitation, she dashed into the closest alleyway and disappeared from view.

Fox made a move to give chase, but Willa grabbed his hand to stop him.

"You'll never find her in that maze of streets we just came through. Even if you did, she might be leading you into a trap."

As usual, Willa was right.

"Armstrong and Corosi will certainly know we're here now," Fox said.

"What in Satan's depths is going on?" Giovanni asked.

"We'll tell you now," Luciana said, "but make sure no one else gets on this ship."

He was puzzled by the request, but said, "All right. I'll have two men posted on watch."

"Are they capable men?" Fox asked.

"They're all former soldiers. We met on the battlefield. They decided to give up archery and sword fighting to join me at sea." He snapped his fingers and gave the orders to two of his biggest sailors. They immediately went over to the gangway and stood guard.

When they reached the cramped captain's quarters, he put Luciana in his chair, while Fox and Willa sat on his bunk.

"Now please tell me why you're all here and why Sofi ran at the sight of you."

"I know that woman as Sofia," Luciana said. "Until several weeks ago, she was my lady's maid, and she tried to kill me."

As the news sank in, Giovanni beat his fist against the wall. "That harlot! She told me nothing of you. How long has she worked for you?"

"Since not long after the Great Mortality."

His eyes suddenly turned regretful. "She came to you because of me. I talked to her often about you."

"Did you tell her about the Templar treasure?" Fox asked.

Giovanni still seemed awestruck that they knew about it, but he nodded. "She just told me yesterday that she'd acquired a copy of the letter for herself. I must have given her everything she needed to know to worm her way into your household. It's all my fault."

Luciana took his cheek in her hand. "Don't ever say that. You couldn't have known that she would take advantage of you. Of all of us."

"I should have seen her for what she is."

"I was fooled just the same. Only Willa suspected the truth."

"I simply recognized that she was not a loyal maid," Willa said.

Giovanni shook his head. "If you say that she tried to kill you, why didn't Papà stop her?"

Luciana choked up at trying to deliver the devastating news, so Fox spoke up.

"I'm afraid that he and Sofia are in league together. Signore Corosi was the one who hatched the plot to have your mother killed."

Giovanni tried to absorb that news and looked at his mother.

"It's true," she said. "We've been on the run from him ever since I went to carry out a task for him related to his bank."

"In a town called San Giuseppe," Willa said. "That's where we met."

Fox told the story beginning with the ambush on the town, with Willa and Luciana adding details as the tale progressed. The only parts he left out were anything about his excommunication. Giovanni listened in rapt horror, grasping his mother's hand as he heard of his father's depravity.

When they reached the end with their arrival in Venice, Fox said, "So that's why we need your help. Your mother figured out that the first clue relates to some famous golden altarpiece at San Marco, but we need to figure out how to see it without waiting for the next service where it's publicly shown."

"You mean the Pala d'Oro. I suppose we'll have to go to the basilica tomorrow to see if there is some way to get a look at it in secret."

"We must get to the treasure before Riccardo does," Luciana said. "It's the only way I'll ever be free of him."

"Because of the money?"

"No, there's something else that my father concealed along with the treasure. This won't be easy to hear."

"I have to know the truth," Giovanni said.

"I agree. It's time. Hidden in the treasure is a letter from the king of France to the pope. Before he died, my first love, Matteo Dazzo, told me about this letter. He and my father intercepted it before it could reach the pope in Avignon, who would have absolved Riccardo."

"Absolved him of what?"

"It may be hard for you to believe this, but Riccardo became a Knight Templar. He grew jealous of Matteo, angry with my father, and bitter against the Templars for the vows he could not escape.

So he betrayed the whole Templar order. He was in league with the king of France to ensure that the pope would issue the edict disbanding the Templars, dissolving all debts to them."

"If we can find that letter with the seal of the king of France on it," Fox said, "we can take it to the current pope and show him that Signore Corosi actually took vows of poverty and chastity."

"That would annul his marriage to your mother," Willa said. "And it would mean that his wealth would be handed over to the Knights Hospitaller as all of the other Templar holdings were. Except for your mother's dower lands, which of course would revert to her if the marriage was declared void."

"Signore Corosi might desire the hidden Templar gold," Fox said, "but he wants that letter even more. He would be left a penniless outcast if we were to find it first, and likely proclaimed a heretic for marrying despite his vows."

Giovanni had swiveled from speaker to speaker, disbelief and shock registering on his face. When they finished, he put his head in his hands, then ran his fingers through his hair as though he wanted to tear it out.

"This is incredible. My father, the king of France, and the pope involved together in a plot to overthrow the Knights Templar? Even though he disinherited me, it beggars belief that he would do all that."

"Will you help us?" Fox asked.

Giovanni threw up his hands. "How could I not? By all of your accounts, my father tried to murder my mother. I know whose side I'm on in that battle."

Luciana stood and sat a confused Giovanni down in the chair. She took both of his hands in her own. "Perhaps it would help you if you learned something else about Riccardo. You never knew the real reason he disinherited you."

"He claimed I stole from him. But I told you that wasn't true. Now that I look back on it, I realize I was disrespectful for many years leading to his accusation."

"Your adolescent rebelliousness had nothing to do with it. As you became a man, he recognized you for who you really are. I see it clearly today."

By now, even Fox was engrossed in the story. He and Willa had never heard anything about a disinheritance.

Giovanni, however, remained bewildered by her cryptic words. "What are you talking about?"

"I hope you will still love me when I tell you what you deserve to know."

"I will always love you, Mamma, no matter what you could tell me. It's my father that I hate."

Luciana shook her head. "Oh, my dearest boy, Riccardo isn't your father. Matteo was."

48

Eighteen years ago—July, 1333

Villa Ramberti, Tuscany

With the warmth of the afternoon sun on her face, Luciana sat in the solar cradling Tommaso, the miracle baby that had taken twenty years for her to bear for Riccardo. She still had trouble believing that he was in her arms after so many failed pregnancies and stillborn children. She'd almost given up the idea that she'd have any more, but here he was, perfect and calm and warm.

If possible, Riccardo had seemed even more overjoyed than she. He had showered both of them with gifts, including a magnificent birthing tray depicting the birth of Saint John the Baptist, another child miraculously born to elderly parents. Luciana was pleased to see how Riccardo delighted in the baby, often showing him off to his associates, although she had observed that the baby's arrival had seemed to increase tension in his relationship with his elder son.

Giovanni sat across from her, his long and lean body draped over the chair. With his dimpled chin, dark brows, and gray eyes, he bore a striking resemblance to Matteo. His behavior matched what she remembered of his father as well—a restless young man brimming with charm and confidence to the point of hubris, but with a depth of selfless loyalty underneath that she could always count on.

He was whittling a horse from a piece of willow, the knife moving easily in his hand.

"That looks quite good," Luciana said. "You have a talent for carving."

"I always loved the one you gave me. I thought my little brother should have his own. Of course, I'd rather be teaching him sword fighting and bow hunting."

"I think that's a few years off," she said with a laugh. "Thank you for sitting with me."

"I'm just happy to see you well. I remember some of the other times…" His voice trailed off.

Luciana knew what he meant. During several of her failed pregnancies, her life was in jeopardy. Her physician didn't know if she would live, let alone have another child. Gio had been by her side many of those long nights, one of the reasons she got through them.

She decided to change the subject.

"I remember sitting in this very room with you as a baby. Now you're a fine young man. Soon you'll have your own family as well."

"My baby brother is enough new family for me right now." Giovanni leaned forward and tickled Tommaso's neck. The baby rewarded him with a giggle.

His deflection irked her. Luciana had been dreading this conversation, but she supposed it was time.

"It's time for you to take some responsibility," she chided. "You'll have to stop carousing in Florence. This latest escapade cost you dearly."

"I don't know what you mean," he said with a sly grin.

"Don't try to fool your mother. I know how much you spend and what you spend it on—gambling, drink, and women."

"Father doesn't seem to mind."

"You never can tell what your father might know, but thankfully he is too busy with work to do anything about it. You're young now, but you'll take over the bank one day, and I intend to make sure you are ready for it."

Giovanni rolled his eyes. "His business is so dull. You handle his accounting. What does he need me for?"

"First, that arrangement is private, only for our family to know. I hope you haven't been spreading word that I work with your father."

"My friends couldn't care less about it."

"As long as you're free with the florins that keep them around you. Gio, the birth of your brother was difficult, and I'm just now recovered enough to help your father again in the business. But it showed me that you need to be more active with it. I will teach you."

Riccardo appeared in the doorway. Instead of his usual broad smile at the sight of the baby, a grim look dominated his face. In one hand, he held some sort of document.

"There you are. My son."

"Do you mean me or Tommaso?" Giovanni teased.

Riccardo stalked to him, unamused. He pulled Giovanni from his seat and raised an arm as if to deliver a blow. Luciana rose to her feet, alarmed at his manner.

"Did you really think I wouldn't find out what you did?"

Giovanni gave a worried look to his mother, who nodded for him to tell the truth.

"I'm sorry, Father. It was just me and a few of my friends at the tavern. We only wanted to play at dice. I…"

"I don't care about your childish amusements, embarrassing though they are."

"What is this about, Riccardo?" Luciana asked.

"While you've been away from your bookkeeping duties during your lying-in, I discovered that our son has been stealing from me."

Giovanni's mouth fell open. "Father, I swear to you that I don't know what you're talking about."

"That's how you fund your merriment, apparently. I trusted you with transferring those coins, and here I find out that you are taking a share before it reaches its destination."

"That's not true!" Giovanni protested. "Whoever told you that is lying!"

Luciana knew her son was careless and too taken with his revelry, but he wasn't a thief or a liar.

"There must be a misunderstanding, Riccardo…"

"I wish there were," he replied with an angry shake of his

head. "I saw the accounting myself. After all I've given you, you embezzle from me?"

Now Giovanni was desperately pleading. "I beg you, Father, you must believe me that I didn't do this."

"I *don't* believe you."

"*I* give him the money for his merrymaking," Luciana said. "If anyone should be punished for that, it should be me."

"Don't try to make amends for him, Luciana. He has committed a grave crime against me. If he had committed this kind of thievery against someone else, he could be hanged for it. But against his own father... because of my love for him and for you, I will only disinherit him."

Giovanni gasped in astonishment. Luciana could hardly breathe. She knew what a terrible sentence that was.

"Please, Riccardo, give me a chance to look at the records and prove to you that this is an error."

"I have had them checked—twice—by a notary. I've made my decision. I've already drawn up the paperwork with the lawyer and had it witnessed." He brandished a writ with his seal clearly visible as he faced Giovanni. Although he was several inches taller than Riccardo, Giovanni seemed to shrink under his father's gaze. "Your horse and belongings are being prepared as we speak. I won't send you off a pauper. You'll have enough to make a life somewhere else, but I expect you never to darken the door of my house again."

"Father, I didn't do this."

"It's time for you to be a man and face the consequences for who you are and what you've done." Riccardo threw a glance at Luciana. "I know you'll make something of yourself, but you won't contribute to the Corosi legacy."

Giovanni opened his mouth to defend himself again, but Luciana knew from long experience with previous altercations that Riccardo wouldn't yield. Protesting further would be useless. It seemed that Gio knew that as well.

"Don't worry about me," he said, straightening himself to his full height. "I'd rather live free to do what I want than spend another hour trying to become you." He went to Luciana and handed her the unfinished horse carving. "Tell Tommaso this is from his brother."

He stalked out, and Luciana raced after him, but Riccardo grabbed her arm to stop her.

She wheeled on him and spat at his feet.

"You know very well that he would never steal from you."

"I didn't want to hurt him any more than I had to, Luciana." For the first time, Riccardo looked regretful about his actions. "This was the only way."

"How can you say that?" Luciana shouted, beating on Riccardo's chest with her free arm. "You're driving our son out of my life."

"You mean, *your* son."

That comment made Luciana freeze. She could see on Riccardo's face that he knew who Giovanni's father really was. She couldn't speak.

"It was so apparent as he was growing into a man," Riccardo continued. "It was as if I were seeing Matteo brought back to life. Do you know how that made me feel, seeing him every day and knowing what you did?"

"I… I didn't know if he was yours… until much later. We married so quickly after you… after the duel. It was a mistake. An awful, girlish mistake. Don't make Giovanni pay for it."

"Until Tommaso was born, I didn't have a choice. I had to live with it. But now I have a true son to follow in my footsteps."

The implication slammed into her like a brick. "You've been planning this?"

"It's for the best." Riccardo stepped closer to her. "Now don't get an idea about telling him or anyone else who he really is. It won't do anyone any good. You have to think about *our* son. Tommaso will need you." She looked down at the baby, still asleep in her arms.

That was all Riccardo had to say. She knew how her husband operated. He would take Tommaso from her if the rumor got out that Giovanni wasn't his. He couldn't stand the embarrassment of being considered a cuckold.

Luciana shook her head in defeat. "No one will know. I swear."

Riccardo looked at her for a long while until he seemed satisfied with her answer.

"Good. We're going to have a good life, you and me and Tommaso. Now go tell your son *addio*."

He kissed Tommaso on the forehead and left Luciana there trying to catch her balance. Early in her marriage, Luciana had been a totally subservient wife, tormented by her night of weakness with Matteo and eager to prove to Riccardo that she had completely rejected her father's betrayer. She had wondered from before he was born whether Giovanni was Matteo's son, not Riccardo's, and she had become convinced that her years of losing babies afterwards was punishment for her sin. She thought she had kept it all secret from Riccardo, but she should have known better. Maybe this day was inevitable, but she knew she would never forgive him for driving Gio away.

Finally, her feet grew steady enough to take her out to the courtyard.

Giovanni was at his horse, strapping his bow and sword to the saddle already laden with bags. His face was etched with fury.

When he saw Luciana approaching, he said, "How could he do this to me? I'm his oldest son, and he just tosses me aside like I'm nothing."

Luciana held his hand. She desperately wanted to tell him the truth, but she had another son to think about, one who depended on her completely.

"You will keep in contact with me, Gio? Write to me however you can. Tell me where you are. Perhaps I can visit you."

"I'll do my best," he said with a catch in his throat. "I love you, Mamma."

"Oh, my sweet boy. I will miss you with every breath I take."

She embraced him tightly and kissed him on each cheek.

Giovanni bent down and tickled Tommaso's neck one last time and drew out a tiny gurgle in response.

"Be well, Brother. I'm sorry to leave our mother here with that tyrant, but you need her and our father would never let me take you both."

After climbing onto his horse, he looked up at the villa. "I hope I never see him again."

He kicked his spurs and took off at a gallop. In a cloud of dust, he was through the gates and gone.

Luciana hugged Tommaso close to her, her tears falling onto his swaddling clothes. She wiped them away from her face and took a deep breath. She had to be strong for her baby, and she drew comfort from her deep certainty that Giovanni was a capable young man who would find his path in the world. She reassured herself that one day they would be reunited. It was the only way she could live with his sudden loss.

49

October, 1351

VENICE

Hundreds of parishioners streamed into Saint Mark's Basilica for the midday mass. Armstrong would join them soon, after he was done inspecting the statue of the Four Tetrarchs at the south corner of the façade. Four figures, just as the clue said. Although the statue was made from purplish-red porphyry and not gold, Domenico Ramberti's clever riddle might have some other meaning Armstrong couldn't divine.

A passing priest told him that the statue of four Roman emperors had been taken from Constantinople during the Sack of 1204, so it definitely would have been there during Ramberti's time. He looked over the four-foot-tall quartet of men carefully for anything that would indicate an island. The clue mentioned that it would be near "the seed of life," but he didn't see any plants in the sculpture. One of the statue's feet was missing. Perhaps that was significant, but he didn't know why.

Unable to decipher an answer, he finally gave up. He would have to bring Sofia and Corosi back at a later time to see if they could spot something he'd missed. They were off inquiring about other golden statues and paintings around the city, in more of a hurry now that they knew that Luciana, Fox, and Willa had already arrived.

On the way to Venice, Corosi had told Armstrong the story of disinheriting his elder son for embezzlement. He was convinced that Luciana would seek out Giovanni. Armstrong thought he sounded like another ungrateful son who had thrown all his advantages away and deserved to lose everything. He and Fox should have plenty in common.

Armstrong was only slightly annoyed that Corosi had told Sofia about Giovanni long ago, and she hadn't shared it with him. He admitted she was clever to spy on Giovanni while she was at the docks securing a ship. She reported seeing him reunited with his mother, who surely would have told him everything and brought him to her side. He wondered what else Sofia might know about Corosi that she hadn't passed along to him.

If Corosi and Sofia's inquiries didn't lead to the solution of the clue about the four figures, Armstrong would have to come up with a way to get access to the Pala d'Oro. A speedy four-person caorlina was waiting nearby to take him back to the large privateer ship called the *Drago Marino* that Sofia had found for them to hire. Though the quarters were cramped, the captain, who indicated that he and his crew would follow any order if the price were right, had given Corosi the use of his cabin. They would be ready to sail as soon as they had solved the Venice clue. Now all they needed to know was the ship's destination.

Armstrong joined the throngs heading toward the gigantic basilica's main entrance. Directly across from it was the towering Saint Mark's Campanile, whose copper-topped spire had been visible all the way from the mainland. It dominated the expansive piazza packed with hawkers and beggars hoping to wheedle money out of rich merchants and pilgrims who came from the world over to see San Marco's wonders.

From its spot atop a tall pillar, the Winged Lion of Venice watched over the harbor—called the city's "basin," according to Sofia. With her knowledge of the city, she had immediately realized what this enigmatic clue meant. It wasn't a fountain they were searching for.

*Among his four gilded cousins, the chosen one is closest to the basin
of the city.*

So they now knew that the inscription they needed to solve this quatrain would be found on the cousin closest to the harbor.

Florence certainly had its share of wealth, but it seemed that Venice was virtually built out of money. Centuries as a center of Mediterranean trade had obviously made the city far richer than any he'd seen in his travels through England and France.

The basilica was the grandest example. The front façade was festooned with gilt mosaics, any one of which could provide the answer to the riddle. The solid bronze doors featuring lion-head knockers and two pairs of snorting bronze horses standing atop the loggia were taken from Byzantium as potent symbols of Venetian conquests during the Crusades. The cluster of onion domes on the top evoked the glamour and romance of the East, while the sheer size of the building and the many ornate spires, arches, and pillars represented prestige and power few other cities could hope to match.

When he entered the darkened interior, the evidence of wealth was even more awe-inspiring. Rare smoldering incense filled the space with a heavy scent, while hundreds of candles burned in every corner with no regard to expense. The vast interior soared to unimaginable heights and seemed to be completely encrusted in gold. It felt like entering the Heavenly Jerusalem. The thousands upon thousands of tiles forming the mosaics told the entire history of the world from the Bible. Gilt statues of seemingly every saint in Christendom stood on plinths, in chapels, and attached to columns. Without the Pala d'Oro to direct them, they could be searching just these images for weeks without knowing whether they were even looking in the right place.

Armstrong stood taller than most of the crowd, which gave him a good view toward the altar where he could see the panels of painted wood that concealed the Pala d'Oro.

It was clear that the only way to see under that cover would be to enter the basilica when no one was around. That meant sneaking into the cathedral at night and removing the panels. He looked up, but saw no way to gain entrance except for the sets of windows that ringed the domes. But even if he could get to that level from the outside, he couldn't see a way to get down to the floor of the nave.

He turned around and noticed a balcony running along the front of the church, with doorways piercing its walls at either end. That meant there must be stairways hidden in the walls to access the loggia that held the bronze horses overlooking Saint Mark's Piazza. Therefore, there had to be a way out, which meant there was also a way in.

If he could climb up to the loggia from the outside, he could get into the basilica. Then it would be a simple matter to get to the Pala d'Oro, remove its covering, and peruse its enamel images for the man in white who would lead them to the next clue.

Satisfied that he had accomplished his mission, he was about to exit before the service concluded when he saw another tall figure come out from behind a pillar to peer through the choir screen toward the altar. He instantly recognized Gerard Fox gesturing at the Pala d'Oro while speaking to a companion, who had to be Giovanni. Armstrong got up on his toes, and he caught glimpses of Luciana and Willa through small gaps in the crowd.

Fox's head started to turn, and Armstrong ducked down so he wouldn't be seen. Still in his crouch, he walked over to another pillar and hid behind it. He peeked out and saw that the four of them hadn't moved, so he was confident that he hadn't been spotted.

Armstrong had elected to come alone to the basilica so as not to draw attention to himself, but now he wished he had brought some of his men so he could have taken the four of them all at once. Since he was alone and without his sword, he decided to stay out of sight and follow them in the hopes that they would reveal something useful.

"It seems blasphemous to contemplate sneaking in here," Luciana said as they filed out with the rest of the flock after the services were completed.

Giovanni patted her shoulder, a reassuring feeling she'd missed all those years without him.

"Mamma, it's the only way to see the Pala d'Oro without waiting weeks for the cover to be opened. We will be careful not to disturb anything."

"I promise you, Luciana," Fox said. "We'll leave everything exactly the way we found it."

"You can get through a locked door? That seems like magic."

Willa looped her arm through his. "Gerard has many talents, including how to use metal prongs to pick locks."

"If it's not too complicated," Fox hedged. "And if I can't open it, we'll find another way in."

Luciana wagged her finger at Giovanni. "No broken windows. No son of mine will be responsible for desecrating a church."

She saw Fox's face tense. "Forgive me, Gerard."

"Why should he be insulted?" Giovanni asked.

"I have a complicated past," Fox said. "It's nothing you'd want to hear."

"It can't be any worse than what my father has done."

"Signore Corosi isn't your father," Willa reminded him.

"That's true. It will take more than a day to reject something that I've known for nearly forty years. But he *is* my father, legally. We have no proof otherwise."

"*He* has no proof otherwise," Luciana said. "But when he saw you growing into the likeness of Matteo as you matured, he had no doubt, so he had to come up with some excuse to make your younger brother his true heir. Accusing you of embezzlement was the easiest route to disinheritance."

"I want nothing of his. He used the income from your dower lands to fund his greedy rise."

"When we have time, I will tell you all about your real father. He was a special man."

"I look forward to that."

They walked out into the midday sun, and the bright light felt like a cleansing bath to Luciana after the darkened, scent-heavy interior of the cathedral that seemed to echo their grim conversation. Someday she hoped never to have to think of Riccardo again, but for now she could revel in the fact she was with her son instead of her husband.

Outside the basilica, they walked another hundred feet and stopped to look up at the loggia. Fox pointed out a door where he thought they could gain access to the cathedral after it had closed for the night. Giovanni agreed that would be the best way in, but they would need to figure out how to climb up there. Fox mentioned something about a special hook described in his personal manuscript called the *Secretum philosophorum*, and the three of them kept walking away from the basilica, animatedly talking about how to attach the hook to a rope.

Luciana didn't proceed with them. Something about the façade was nagging at her. It had to do with the clue. The figure in white and his four gilded cousins...

Then she realized what it was. The answer had been visible to them all along. If she were right, they didn't need to see the Pala d'Oro after all. She turned to tell her companions, but saw that they had continued to walk toward the waterfront.

Willa knew exactly what Gerard was talking about when he mentioned the grappling hook. An avid reader, she'd often studied his copy of the *Secretum philosophorum*, a prized book of tricks, ciphers, and special knowledge his mother had gifted to him with a loving inscription. Now it had given them a tactic to get into the basilica. She nodded along as Giovanni listened intently to the explanation.

"It describes a three-pronged piece of iron, like three clawing fingers," Gerard said, almost tripping over his words. "You forge it with a loop at one end and tie a rope through it. It's in the part of the book describing how to scale castle walls during a siege."

"How does it work?" Giovanni asked.

"I remember this now," Willa said. "It could be thrown up over the edge of the loggia."

"It has to snag on something and become taut," Gerard said. "You can then climb up the rope."

Giovanni nodded. "I would have to see this in practice, but I know a smith who can fashion something like that for us very quickly. He makes iron fittings for the *Cara Signora*."

"Then we come back here tonight," Gerard said. "Long after midnight to lessen the chance that we'll be discovered."

"I hope you're at ease with this plan, Mamma," Giovanni said, turning. "What do you…"

He stopped, and that was the first time Willa realized that Luciana was no longer with them. They'd been so caught up in the discussion that they'd lost track of her.

Gerard nodded back in the direction they'd come from. "There she is."

Luciana was waving to them and pointing at the basilica.

"I've got it!" she called to them from a hundred feet away. She followed that with something else, but it was torn away by the strong breeze.

"What did she say?" Willa asked as they started back in her direction.

"I think it was something about the clue," Giovanni said.

Luciana seemed just as excited as Willa had been a moment ago. Perhaps she had noticed an easier way to get into the basilica.

Her evident elation was cut short. Armstrong rose out of the crowd like a wolf among the sheep, snatched Luciana up, and threw her over his shoulder. She beat against him and screamed, but with her tiny frame, she looked like a child in his arms.

"No!" Giovanni shouted, and the three of them broke into a sprint to chase after Armstrong, who ducked into the closest alley leading out of the piazza and into the labyrinthine shadows.

 50

Fox saw the pain on Giovanni's face when Luciana was snatched away, and it was like a dagger to his heart. Seeing her taken in broad daylight brought back the sharp agony he felt at not being able to save his own mother Emmeline after she had been abducted. He vowed not to fail this chance to rescue Luciana.

They followed Armstrong into the alleyway. Despite Luciana's screams and struggles, no one stopped to help her, likely assuming it was a domestic issue. Instead, the crowd parted into an open path for Armstrong to run through. It seemed that Venetians were loath to get involved, but at least it helped show where Luciana had gone.

There was a canal straight ahead, and Armstrong descended a few steps.

Willa, who was trailing close behind Fox and Giovanni, said, "What's he doing?"

"He's getting into a caorlina," Giovanni said.

Four men with oars were standing on a boat that he boarded. As soon as Armstrong was aboard, they shoved off. Armstrong lifted Luciana from his shoulders and set her down roughly in the boat. He wrapped a rope around her hands and tied the end around one of the oar rests.

"Go, go!" he yelled.

The oarsmen paddled hard, taking the boat to the left, so that by the time Fox and Giovanni reached the edge of the canal, the caorlina was too far away for them to jump onto.

There was no walkway along this part of the canal, only the walls of buildings going straight down into the water. A gondolier idled nearby, but the gondola would be much too slow to catch the swift caorlina.

They'd have to run after it, but Fox knew that it would be difficult given the tangle of streets.

"Which way?" he asked.

"Down here," Giovanni said.

"Don't wait for me," Willa shouted from behind as they took off.

Giovanni sprinted back in the direction they'd come and took a right. They made two more turns in quick succession, and already Fox was thoroughly lost. If Giovanni hadn't been with him, he surely would have had to give up.

Fox glanced over his shoulder, but Willa was far behind. When she saw him look at her, she just waved her hands for him to keep going. As soon as they took another turn, she was out of sight.

They crossed over a bridge and spotted the caorlina cutting such a speedy course that gondolas were bobbing up and down in its wake. In the distance, the Grand Canal was visible.

"What now?" Fox huffed as he ran.

Instead of answering, Giovanni pointed and they turned left. When they turned right again, Giovanni cursed. They'd hit a dead end with steps leading down into another canal, and high buildings on either side. On the opposite side of the narrow canal, another few steps led up into what looked like a tavern. A plank of wood that could bridge the canal lay on the other side near the tavern, but it was useless to them.

"We have to go back," Giovanni said. He turned, but Fox grabbed his arm to stop him.

A gondola was slowly paddling by. It was piled high with crates.

"Come on!" Fox said and started running.

Giovanni didn't protest when he saw what Fox had in mind.

As the midpoint of the gondola passed the steps, Fox and Giovanni leaped from the pavement and onto the crates. Neither of them broke stride and took another jump off of them to the other side of the canal.

Giovanni landed on his feet, but Fox slipped on the wet steps and rolled through the door of the tavern. The astonished patrons who had been eating their midday meals were agog at the intrusion.

"*Scusi*," Fox said as he jumped to his feet and nodded to them. "*Buon appetito*."

He and Giovanni ran out the front door of the establishment and onto another street. To their left they could see that the caorlina had turned onto the Grand Canal and was heading north.

"We still have a chance," Giovanni said as he took off running.

Fox remembered how wide the Grand Canal was. If Armstrong's boat made it over to a canal on the other side, they'd lose it for sure.

"What's your idea?" Fox asked.

"The Rialto Bridge."

He didn't have to explain further. The large wooden bridge was the only one spanning the Grand Canal. If Armstrong passed underneath it, they could drop into it from above.

Again, Fox was completely confused by the maze of streets, but this time Giovanni seemed to know the correct path. He didn't hesitate at any of the intersections.

Finally, they came onto a wide street and went left. Up ahead, the Rialto Bridge rose up and over the water. It was full of city residents crossing it on their daily business. As they approached, Fox spotted the caorlina. It was only a few dozen feet from the bridge. Armstrong was in his seat next to Luciana, watching behind them to see if they were being followed by another boat.

"There it is," Fox said. "Hurry!"

They were both already breathing hard but picked up the pace. At the moment the bow of the caorlina was nosing under the bridge, he and Giovanni were pounding up the Rialto's wooden ramp.

They stopped in the center of the drawbridge section, waiting for the caorlina's bow to poke out. The boat was moving so fast that they wouldn't have time to hesitate, and misjudging the jump would put them into the water.

Then the boat appeared even faster than Fox had estimated. He jumped.

Willa had lost track of Gerard and Giovanni early in the chase, but she didn't give up trying to follow them. She got turned around several times and thought she'd lost them for good until she found herself on the walkway along the Grand Canal.

The caorlina with Armstrong and Luciana was just emerging from underneath the Rialto Bridge. She was trying to figure out what she could do when she was shocked to see Gerard jump down from above, landing right in front of Armstrong and Luciana. Giovanni followed a moment later, dropping in behind them.

Willa came to a stop at the edge of the canal and cursed her uselessness as she watched Armstrong leap to his feet, causing the boat to wobble to each side. He drew a dagger and launched himself at Gerard, but Gerard grabbed the wrist holding it and twisted until the knife dropped overboard. Gerard threw a punch at Armstrong's jaw, and Armstrong countered with a blow to the stomach.

While they were fighting, Giovanni sawed at the rope tying Luciana to the boat. Willa cried out when one of the oarsman lifted his oar out of the rowlock, but Giovanni couldn't hear her. The oarsman swung it around, catching Giovanni in the side of the head and knocking him over the side before he could finish untying Luciana, who screamed for her son as he fell in.

The oarsmen at the bow had a similar idea, but Gerard and Armstrong were now exchanging blows from such close quarters that the oarsmen couldn't get a clean swing at their target without hitting Armstrong.

Gerard got the upper hand and forced Armstrong against the edge of the caorlina, obviously trying to toss him into the canal. Armstrong scrabbled for purchase on the boat's frame but found only the rope used to tie up the caorlina to a dock. As he tumbled over, he still had a firm grip on Gerard's tunic with his other hand.

Armstrong screamed in terror when his legs flew into the air.

He tilted over the side, but he didn't let go of Gerard, pulling him into the water as well.

Willa couldn't just stand by and do nothing. She ran toward the nearest dock.

Armstrong had never felt such fear. He shrieked again as he went under, and the filthy water filled his mouth. His mind was purely focused on survival, so he released his hold on Fox. He hadn't intended to pull Fox in with him. He was trying with all his might to avoid falling in himself.

He did, however, keep his grip on the rope that he somehow remembered was still attached to the boat.

Armstrong didn't bother flailing his arms and legs in a futile attempt to swim. He had enough presence of thought to pull himself along the rope toward the caorlina, which was still dragging him forward.

His head broke the surface, and he sputtered as he inhaled a breath that he was worried would never come again.

By now the oarsmen were reeling him in, so all he had to do was hold on. When he was beside the slowing boat, they reached down and plucked him out of the water by his shoulders. He settled into the bottom of the boat, coughing up what he'd sucked into his lungs.

Luciana glowered at him. "Did you have a nice swim?"

Armstrong had the urge to strike her, but he didn't want to have to answer to Corosi for that. However, there was someone else toward whom he could direct his fury.

He shook the hair off his face and staggered to his feet, careful to stay in the middle of the boat.

"Turn around," he ordered the oarsmen. When they hesitated, he bellowed, "Turn this boat around!"

They did as he commanded, pivoting in the wide canal. Armstrong could see the heads of Fox and Giovanni floating in the water near a side canal not a hundred feet behind them. He picked up the hook used to pull the caorlina into the pier. On its tip was a pike that would do the job nicely.

He planned to spear the helpless Fox on his way past. Then he could do the same to Giovanni and make that disloyal shrew watch as he took the life of her son.

When Fox saw what he was doing, he yelled something to Giovanni, and they started swimming, but they were too far from any boat or stairs to escape before Armstrong ran them down.

Armstrong grinned as he balanced the pike in his hands. It was plenty long enough to stab down into the water from where he stood.

But when his boat was halfway to Fox, he was shocked to see a gondola shoot out from a side canal. The solo oarsman was paddling as hard as he could, directed by Willa, who was perched on the bow of the boat.

Before the caorlina could get there, the gondola was beside Fox, who clambered over its side. Then he helped Giovanni up after him.

Armstrong was just twenty feet away when he passed them. He ordered the oarsmen to keep going. There was no way the gondola with a single oar would be able to keep up with them. Both Fox and Giovanni, who dripped water just as he did, remained silent, obviously realizing that they'd lost their chance to retrieve Luciana. She clasped her hands together and mouthed a silent prayer, but Armstrong didn't know if it was because she was praying for her life or thanking God that her son was unharmed.

As Armstrong's boat went by, he sneered at them.

"Don't you have anything clever to say, Sir Gerard?"

It was Giovanni who spoke. "If you hurt her, you'll wish you were dead."

As the caorlina sped away, Armstrong called back, "If you want her back, stay by your ship. We'll send a message."

He waved at them, and soon they were lost in the distance.

 51

Aboard the *Drago Marino*, Corosi stood with Sofia in the corridor outside the cabin where Luciana was being held.

"You shouldn't trust anything she says," Sofia warned.

She'd seemed on edge ever since he'd arrived in Venice. She had shed tears when she described her narrow escape after an ill-fated encounter with Fox on the road outside Venice and how he had killed the two guards sent to protect her. Corosi could tell that she was still uneasy. At least she had warned them that Giovanni was in the city and had joined forces with his mother and her two guardians.

"Giovanni could use his own ship to go find the treasure," Corosi said, "helped by that heretical duo. Ours is slower than his carrack. He could be gone with the treasure before we even arrive at the correct island."

"What do you plan to do with her?"

"She makes attractive bait. Besides, I want to see what she'll agree to in order to save her life. Failing that, to see what she's willing to do to save her son's life."

Corosi would eliminate Giovanni if he had to. His pride in his elder son had turned to outrage as Giovanni grew up. Corosi had found himself looking into the unmistakable visage of Matteo and realized Luciana had deceived him, bearing a son that did not carry his blood. He'd prefer to avoid killing Giovanni if possible, but not if his former son got in the way of finding the treasure and destroying the letter that could spell disaster for his plans.

"You have no way of getting to him," Sofia objected. "You said assaulting Giovanni's ship while it's docked in Venice is impossible."

"The doge would see it as an attack on the city itself if it happened within the harbor. I could be strung up if they learned I was responsible. Better to figure out a way to do it at sea."

"And that's when you'll do away with her?" Sofia asked.

Corosi caressed her head and kissed her lightly. "Just as soon as possible, my dear. Then there will be nothing in our way."

She seemed soothed by that and left as he opened the door to the cabin.

Armstrong was inside standing watch while Luciana sat at a small table, a full dish of food in front of her.

"She won't eat," Armstrong said.

"Are you worried it's poisoned?" Corosi asked in amusement. "Why would I do that when I could have Armstrong here slit your throat?"

"I tasted the food to show her it was safe. She still won't touch it."

Corosi took the seat across from her and pulled the plate to him. "That's your choice. I'm starving." He tore into the crispy chicken and bread. Through a full mouth, he ordered Armstrong, "Leave us."

Armstrong nodded and closed the door behind him as he exited.

"Your friend Gerard Fox killed two of my men on the road to Venice. Sofia told me. He's been quite a thorn in my side."

Luciana shook her head. "I don't know what you're talking about."

"Of course. I guessed that you'd deny it."

She looked at him thoughtfully for a moment before she shook her head and said, "It seems so naïve of me now. How could I have been taken in by your lies all those years ago? My only excuse is that I was so young. You certainly took advantage of that."

Corosi dropped the chicken leg he was holding. "Apparently I was the one who was naïve, expecting to bring a virgin to the marital bed."

Ignoring his comment, she continued, "But it wasn't just your lies that fooled me. You really were different then. Your gallantry was, of course, already compromised, but when Giovanni was born, you truly loved him, and even me, I think. It's the years that have hardened you."

"And why shouldn't they? Learning Giovanni wasn't my son paled in comparison to losing Tommaso and finding out that my wife was conspiring against me with a competitor. You're the one who made me change. Your betrayal. What do I have left except my name and the hope of a legacy?"

"You've abandoned your last shred of honor in this quest for your so-called legacy."

The remark made him flinch, but he soon recovered himself. "If I don't have any honor left, then perhaps I should just do away with you right now."

Luciana replied, "You won't kill me."

"I've already tried twice. What's to stop me from making a success of it the third time?"

"That would be a stupid idea."

Corosi chuckled. "And why is that?"

"Because then you'll never find the treasure."

"I think we've done quite well so far. We're here in Venice, aren't we?"

"You won't get much farther," she said with certainty.

"Don't underestimate us."

"I'm not. Your problem is that you don't have the clue you need to solve the final riddle."

Corosi stopped chewing. "What do you mean?"

"You have the copy of Matteo's letter from my father that I transcribed, yes?"

"Of course. Sofia found it in your clothes chest. Thank you very much, by the way."

"Do you think I would let her find a true copy?"

"Let her find? Sofia stole it from you."

"As I knew she would. Willa suspected from the time of the attack that Sofia had betrayed me. That's why I left a copy so conveniently to be found. But of course I changed some words when I transcribed it from the original."

Corosi pushed the plate away. He'd lost his appetite.

"All of the clues have proven correct so far."

She leaned toward him and spoke with satisfaction. "I just needed to adjust a few of them at the end to throw you off the track."

Corosi's heart beat faster at her revelation. He couldn't be sure she was telling the truth, but Sofia had told him about the test with the broth, and altering the letter was just the kind of thing Luciana would have done if she'd had any inkling Sofia would betray her.

He glared at her. "What are you proposing?"

"I'm not proposing anything. I just wanted you to know before you killed me that you'd already lost. I'll die knowing that Giovanni will carry out my final wish and ruin your life."

Corosi reached across the table and slapped her hard. She didn't cry out. She just massaged her cheek and stared at him, which infuriated him all the more. He stood up and wagged a finger at her.

"If I'd known you for the whore you are, I never would have married you in the first place. And now you're too old to be any good to me. I promise you that you'll see Giovanni die before I put you to the sword."

He stormed out of the chamber and slammed the door behind him.

Armstrong was still there waiting for him and frowned. "What did she say?"

Corosi took a breath to calm himself. When he'd regained control, he said, "That the letter we have is a fraud." He explained that part of the conversation.

"Do you think she's telling the truth?" Armstrong asked.

"I don't know. She's almost as skilled at deception as I am."

"Then the clue about Venice might be incorrect as well."

Corosi hadn't thought of that. Now his stomach roiled even more.

"I'll torture the truth out of her."

Armstrong shook his head. "In my experience, torture only

works when you want to get a prisoner to admit something you already know to be true. She might tell you another lie about the clue just to get the torture to stop, and we'd be in a worse situation."

"Then we need the original letter to be sure."

"I agree. The only way we'll get it is if we trade your wife for it."

"What? Absolutely not!"

"Is there anything else Giovanni would give up the original letter for?"

To Corosi's dismay, he realized Armstrong had a point.

"You're suggesting that we make the trade now?"

"No. We need to ensure that the Venice clue is correct first. For all we know, Fox has already deciphered it. Then they would have a head start."

"We need a way to keep us even."

"Exactly."

"And you have a plan to do that?"

Armstrong thought for a moment before saying, "We have to get a note to Giovanni. But let Luciana write it. He would recognize her handwriting, and that will prove that she's still alive, which is important to make this work."

"To make what work?" Corosi asked.

"Ensuring that the Venice clue is correct. Fox and I are going to solve it together."

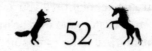

52

Fox thought Giovanni might go mad after reuniting with his mother only to lose her again the next day. He was alternately railing at Corosi in a frenzied state and then suddenly sinking into a morass of despair. Fox and Willa tried to calm him, but without knowing where she had been taken or even if she were still alive, they convinced him that the best thing they could do was prepare to solve the next clue in Ramberti's riddle.

Giovanni's smith had crafted a hook to the specifications in the *Secretum philosophorum*. Finding a length of rope long enough for their purposes on a sailing ship had been easy enough. The three-pronged iron device was now attached. All they would need to do was throw it high enough to secure it to the railing along the basilica's loggia before scaling the wall. It would then be a simple matter of sneaking along the walkway to the door that would give them access to the interior.

Fox was practicing twirling it around and tossing it up to the main mast's yardarm while Willa recited the Venice quatrain for him and Giovanni, who was back to his sulking phase:

*Where the patron saint is revered, study the embellishments of the
    golden veil.*
*Find the figure in white who resists all but the command of
    Christ.*
*Among his four gilded cousins, the chosen one is closest to the basin
    of the city.*
*Beneath, next to the source of the seed of life, is inscribed the isle of
    your destiny.*

"And you have never looked at the Pala d'Oro in detail?" Willa asked, trying to prod Giovanni out of his stupor.

He shook his head. "I've seen it, of course. But inspected it closely? No. We're only allowed to be close to it on special feast days. For all that I could tell you, our Lord Jesus Himself might be dressed in white on that panel."

"He could be," Fox said as he reeled in the rope for another swing of the hook. "The Church teaches that the 'brothers of Jesus' mentioned in the Gospels are really his four cousins James, Joseph, Simon, and Jude. But they don't sound like a likely grouping to be depicted anywhere else."

"Who in the Bible did have cousins?"

"Too many to count, especially in the Old Testament," Willa said. "Once you see the figure, you may need to consult the Bible for the answer."

Giovanni's attention was caught by the two guards watching over the gangplank. He leaped to his feet and went over to them. A boy was running up the gangway and calling, "Master Giovanni?"

"Here."

"I was sent to give this to you." The boy handed him a piece of paper, then scurried back down to the dock and out of sight before Giovanni could stop him.

He opened the folded note eagerly as he walked back to Fox and Willa. His eyes lit up when he started reading.

"She's alive!" he exclaimed.

"It's from Luciana?" Willa said.

"What does it say?" Fox asked.

"It's in my mother's handwriting. I'll read it. 'To my son, this edict must be obeyed or I will die. Sir Gerard will join Sir Randolf in deciphering the relevant clue together this evening.'"

Fox saw Willa's face stricken with fear.

Giovanni went on. "'I have seen all parties swear before God to a truce for this occasion. When this matter is settled, we will arrange for an exchange—me for my father's original letter to Matteo. Be at the campanile when the moon is at its highest.'"

"It sounds like Corosi dictated it," Fox said. "You two should stay here."

Willa was aghast. "You're not actually going, are you?"

"Do we have a choice? Luciana said they swore to a truce. I don't think she could have been forced to write that if they hadn't. Besides, they want the letter."

"Why?" Giovanni asked. "They already have it."

"I don't know. Maybe theirs was destroyed."

"They could just have one of us recite the clues. I feel like this is important. My mother is clever, so if Corosi is asking for the original letter, then it's because she somehow convinced him that he needs it."

Fox nodded. "The note is very specific, isn't it? But for what reason would he want the original?"

"Because they have only a *copy*," Willa answered.

After a long moment's thought, Fox said, "Perhaps she told them that something is wrong with the copy."

"That would explain why they'd want the original."

"*Is* there something wrong with it?" Giovanni asked.

"I don't think so. But maybe your mother is fooling them. If that's the case, then it's also why they want me along to solve the Venice portion of the riddle. They don't trust their version of the letter."

Willa came to Fox and held his hand. "What if they go back on the truce?"

"Then they won't get the letter."

"That's not a very reassuring answer."

"Don't you think we should accompany you?" Giovanni asked.

"No," Fox replied. "It's safer for me if you remain on the ship. If they think there is any chance that you'll destroy the letter or sail off on your own, it will improve my chances of staying alive."

Willa nodded reluctantly. "If they saw all three of us, they would certainly consider violating the truce to capture us."

Fox took her hands in his. "I'll be on watch for any trickery, though I believe I'll be unharmed. Armstrong may be a brute, but he seems to hold to his vows."

Fox put on a brave face for Willa, but he wasn't really sure he believed his own words.

A three-quarter moon was high in the sky near the midnight hour. The streets were quiet as Fox emerged into the north end of Saint Mark's Piazza with the rope looped over his shoulder and the hook dangling by his waist. There was enough light for him to see two men standing at the base of the bell tower.

He checked the perimeter as he crossed the vast square, his footsteps on the stone announcing his presence. When he was within fifty feet of them, he stopped. He could now tell it was Corosi and Armstrong. If the parley was nothing but a ruse, Fox was prepared to run and had already gotten suggestions from Giovanni about several routes that he could take to evade them.

"We have a truce?" he demanded.

"Until sunup," Corosi said.

"Call me untrusting, but I'd like to hear you say it."

"I swear to Almighty God that all hostilities will cease between us until the sun rises."

Fox nodded at Armstrong. "Him, too."

Although it sounded as if the words were being dragged out of him, Armstrong said, "I swear to Almighty God that all hostilities will cease between us until the sun rises."

After Fox repeated the phrase himself, he approached them. "Is Luciana all right?"

"She is," Corosi said.

"Let's get on with this," Armstrong growled. "I don't want to spend any more time with him than I have to."

"What is that you're carrying?" Corosi asked.

"Our way into the basilica."

"We already have one," Armstrong said. "We built ladders that will take us up to the loggia."

Fox laughed. "Ladders? Would you like to announce to anyone who might pass by what we're doing?"

"And your solution is a rope?"

"With this." Fox showed them the hook. "Then we can pull the rope up behind us and no one will know we're there."

"Sounds risky to me, but I'm willing to give your foolish idea the chance to fail."

"I have torches."

"We have lanterns," Armstrong said.

Corosi was growing impatient. "Stop wasting time squabbling like two old women and get on with it. When you've deciphered the clue, come right back here."

"And then we'll make the trade? The letter for Luciana?"

Corosi nodded. "I already told you the arrangement."

Fox still didn't trust him, but at least he had their oaths that he would be alive until morning.

"Let's go," he said. "We're least likely to be seen on the north end, shadowed from the moon."

Armstrong picked up the two unlit lanterns behind him and followed Fox along the basilica's façade and around the corner, where the darkness enveloped them. They looked in all directions, but they were alone.

"Stand back," Fox whispered in English. If nothing else, he could finally use his native tongue with a fellow countryman.

"Why?" Armstrong replied in English as well.

"If I have to explain everything to you, we very well might be here until sunrise, and then I'll have to kill you."

"I would enjoy it if you tried."

Fox sighed. This was going to be a long evening.

"I have to swing this around so that the hook will have enough speed to fly over the railing and latch on. Do you see?"

"No."

"Then stand back and watch."

Armstrong grudgingly backed away, and Fox laid out the thin rope so that it wouldn't tangle. He picked up the hook and began swinging it around in wider and wider circles until he estimated that he had the appropriate speed. He heaved it up and let go of the rope.

Just as he'd perfected in practice back at Giovanni's ship, the hook grappled onto the stone railing above. Fox pulled down on the rope to test it, and it seemed secure.

"*Et voilà.* Do you need a demonstration for how to climb?"

Armstrong grunted. "Out of my way."

He put his hands on the rope, then braced his feet against the wall and began walking up with ease, the lanterns on his hip. Fox was impressed with his skill, though he'd never tell Armstrong that.

When Armstrong was up and over the railing, Fox followed. At the top, Armstrong made no offer to help him up the last few feet.

"Thanks," Fox said sarcastically, trying to keep any effort out of his voice, "but I'm able to do it on my own."

"You'd be pathetic if you couldn't," Armstrong shot back.

When Fox was safely on the loggia, he reeled up the rope behind him, detached the hook, and set them aside for the climb back down. They made their way along the balcony overlooking the piazza and found the door between the bronze horses standing guard over the basilica.

Fox removed the lock-picking tools he'd hidden up his sleeves.

"What are you doing now?" Armstrong asked in exasperation.

"I have a way to unlock doors known to few."

"You mean that you're a common thief?"

"I've found it useful in many situations."

"A thief and an excommunicant. You're full of great qualities."

Armstrong reached out and twisted the handle. The door popped open. He smirked at Fox.

"Do you really think they would lock a door up here?"

"Obviously, they should."

He tucked away his pick while Armstrong took out a fire steel and lit the two lanterns before going inside.

They searched around until they found stairs that could take them down to the nave. The light streaming through the windows from the moon was the only other thing besides their lanterns keeping the interior from being pitch black. A thousand golden sparks from the mosaics met them wherever they turned, but otherwise the vastness of the cathedral seemed to envelop them.

When they reached the floor of the nave, they stopped to listen for sounds indicating another person's presence. A chill went up Fox's spine at the eerie silence. They might as well have been in a tomb. No moving light betrayed a priest checking in on the cavernous space.

"We're alone," Fox said, keeping his voice low so that it wouldn't echo.

"Then let's make this quick. Being in here with a heretic is worse than I expected it to be."

They kept to the side of the basilica as they made their way toward the altar.

"Why did you agree to this if you're so disgusted to be with me?"

"I was the one who suggested it."

Fox looked over at him in surprise.

"We needed to be certain that the clue we have is correct," Armstrong went on.

"I thought you would have tortured the information out of Luciana."

"You think I'm some kind of beast, don't you?"

"You did ambush an unsuspecting group of innocent men and then tried to kill Corosi's wife."

"I attacked my lord's enemies, as any knight is obligated to do."

"His wife is his enemy?"

"If he says she is. And who are you to talk? You didn't just attack a priest or a monk. You set yourself at a cardinal."

"I had my reasons," Fox said.

"As do I. I am making something of my life. I am seizing an opportunity before me. What else is there to do?"

"I suppose we have different ideas about what honor means if that's the opportunity you would seize."

"I honor my lord and the Lord. Anything beyond that is fair

game based on the natural division between the strong and the weak."

"Knights are required to defend the weak."

Fox hadn't heard Armstrong laugh until now. It echoed harshly against the stone walls. "If you adhere to that naïve notion, you're simpler than I thought. God favors the strong."

"Then he must favor you. It's right there in your name."

"He does. If you were as smart as you seemed, you would join me. I don't want to be in a church with you, but I must confess that you're a good fighter and a clever tactician. We could create the greatest army on the Italian peninsula. It would be ours for the taking."

Now Fox understood why Armstrong wanted to have time with him. It was a chance to recruit him.

"Why would I do that?"

"Given your situation, your prospects are limited, and you need to provide for your wife and future children. We both know you can't return to England. What else would you do?"

It was nearly the same point made by Willa. He had to admit that Armstrong's skills as a warrior would make him a powerful ally.

"That's a generous offer, Sir Randolf. But would you be comfortable riding with an excommunicant?"

"Your victory in the Palio convinced Barbieri of your innocence, so your name would be clear in Italy. We all have to make compromises, Sir Gerard. If I could see fit to team up with you, perhaps you would be able to put aside our differences."

Fox's fellow soldiers had done unspeakable things during England's invasion of France amidst the ongoing war between the two nations, but he had still defended his comrades-in-arms with his life against their enemies. Was Armstrong so unlike them? He did present a tempting proposal. It would give him and Willa a chance for some stability to build a life together.

In the end though, Armstrong's code of honor and loyalty, albeit resolute, was warped. He had chosen to join with a man who would murder his own wife and agreed to carry out the task for him. That, Fox couldn't abide.

He shook his head. "My goals are more modest than commanding an army."

"Such as riding around with a helpless woman, landless and with no future?"

"It has its benefits."

Armstrong shook his head. "So be it. Just know that if you reject my offer, I won't hesitate to kill you when this truce is over."

"And after such a pleasant time together?" Fox jested.

"Maybe I should be glad about your decision. Your attempts at wit are already tiresome."

They reached the altar, and the figures painted on the wooden cover of the Pala d'Oro seemed to dance in the flickering light of the lanterns, which they set on the altar. The cover was constructed of two horizontal wooden panels. The top one featured half-length portraits of Christ, his mother, and other saints, while the lower one depicted the life of Saint Mark in seven scenes.

"Do you know the story of how Saint Mark's relics got to Venice?"

"No. Do I care?"

Ignoring him, Fox continued, "Luciana told me yesterday. Hundreds of years ago, Venetian merchants slipped the bones of Saint Mark out of their resting place in Egypt by putting them in barrels of pork, which the Muslim guards refused to search. If either of us can be that clever tonight, we should have that clue solved and be on our way in no time."

As Fox was talking, they slid the panels out of their grooved slots and set them aside.

"You start on that end," Fox said, pointing to the left. "I'll look at this end. Remember, we want the figure in white."

"'*Who resists all but the command of Christ.*' Yes, I know what to look for."

Armstrong seemed annoyed at having his offer to join forces rejected.

Fox carefully went over the small enamels one by one. Despite the tension of the situation, he couldn't help but admire their exquisite beauty. The colors glowed like jewels set into golden mounts. Trying to focus on the task in hand, he saw that there were many men depicted in them, but not a single one wore white. He checked again in case he'd been deceived by the dim light of his lantern, but he confirmed that no figure was in white.

He went over to Armstrong.

"Anything?" Fox asked.

"Nothing," Armstrong replied. "There's nobody in white anywhere. I'm looking again to be sure, but I don't think I could have missed it."

"I didn't see one, either."

"Do you think it could have been removed since Ramberti saw it? That was more than three decades ago, and Corosi mentioned that it has been remounted since then."

"I suppose it's possible, but Luciana didn't think…"

Fox stopped speaking when a flash of white lit by Armstrong's lantern caught his eye.

"Go back!" Fox said.

"What?"

"I saw a figure in white."

Armstrong moved the lantern back. Fox pointed out what he'd seen.

"There." He pointed to the enamel at the far upper left.

Armstrong scoffed. "Those aren't clothes. That's a white donkey."

He was correct. It was a donkey carrying Jesus into Jerusalem. The donkey was a bright white. Fox muttered the line he'd memorized:

Find the figure in white who resists all but the command of Christ.

"Don't you see?" Fox said.

"No. I thought we were looking for someone in white robes."

"The clue says it's a *figure* in white. We just assumed it was a person."

"Ramberti meant for us to find a donkey?"

"According to scripture, Christ commanded the disciples to go find a donkey that would carry him into Jerusalem. Donkeys are notoriously stubborn, but the donkey carried him willingly."

Armstrong was dumbfounded. "Then we're looking for a donkey's cousins?"

Fox recited the clue:

Among his four gilded cousins, the chosen one is closest to the basin
   of the city.

"Horses," Armstrong said. "The donkey's cousins are horses. We passed the clue on the way into the basilica."

"Those four bronze horses outside?" Fox asked.

"They're cast from bronze, but Signore Corosi told me they're gilded. I could see them glinting in the sun today. The answer was staring us in the face all along."

They quickly and carefully replaced the covers on the Pala d'Oro and raced back the way they'd come. When they returned to the loggia, they cloaked their lanterns so only a modest amount of light shone through. Armstrong immediately headed to the horse closest to the Bacino San Marco, the waterfront next to the cathedral called the Basin of San Marco.

Beneath, next to the source of the seed of life, is inscribed the isle of
   your destiny.

Fox pulled himself up onto the pedestal underneath the horse's hindquarters.

"The source of the seed of life?" Armstrong asked.

Fox nodded. "Where a steed's bollocks are located." He held up the lantern, not knowing what he was looking for. Armstrong climbed up next to him. The close proximity was unsettling, but he'd sworn no violence before daybreak.

"There's some writing," Armstrong said, pointing at the left inner thigh of the statue.

Fox held the lantern closer until letters painted in blue

ultramarine resolved. The position was well protected from the weather, so the writing was still legible enough to discern.

Colossus.

The next line in the clue mentioned the *isle of destiny*. There was only one isle associated with the Colossus.

"The treasure is on Rhodes," Fox said, climbing down from the pedestal. Armstrong remained behind to be sure that's what it read.

When he came down as well, he said, "Why would a Knight Templar hide the treasure of his order on the island that serves as the headquarters of the Knights Hospitaller?"

"I think the Hospitallers were still establishing their foothold on Rhodes at the time Ramberti arrived. But who knows? Maybe he was attacked and had to improvise a hiding place. And what better place to hide the treasure anyway, than right under the Hospitallers' noses?"

"At least we know where our journey will end," Armstrong said. "Are you certain you don't want to reconsider my proposal?"

"I can't forgive what you've done to Giovanni's mother. When this night ends, we will be mortal enemies again."

"Sympathy for the weak will be your downfall."

"If it is," Fox replied, "then I'll have gone down on the right side."

They shimmied back down the rope, but with no way to detach the hook from below, they had to leave it where it was for some alarmed and confused priest to find in the morning.

They met Corosi back by the campanile.

"Did you find it?" he asked eagerly.

"Rhodes," Armstrong told him.

Corosi nearly clapped his hands together in delight, then his face darkened at a thought.

"Fie on it!"

"What's the matter?"

"The captain of the *Drago Marino* said that Hospitaller ships have been leaving Venice for the past week heading to Rhodes."

"Why?" Fox asked, switching back to Italian.

"He said the other captains told him the Hospitaller Knights have been recently recalled back to the grand master's palace for an assembly to discuss future plans to continue the Crusade and guard the order. The island's city will be swarming with armed knights."

"Perhaps we should wait until their meeting concludes," Armstrong said.

Corosi shook his head. "I'm not waiting. We'll figure out how to manage it on the way. We'll be off as soon as we can."

"What about Luciana?" Fox said. "You said that we'd make the trade—her for the letter."

"That's exactly the arrangement I promised. I didn't say when."

"What do you mean?"

"Do you think I'd let you get to the isle of my destiny ahead of me? Now that we both know it's Rhodes, you might outrace me there. I can't have that."

Fox forgot that Corosi was an expert with the specifics of contracts. He had only promised to make the trade after the clue was found. He didn't say how long after.

"I suppose you have a proposition?" Fox said through gritted teeth, galled that he'd been tricked.

"I do. Your ship is faster than ours. To prevent you from getting there first, we will sail all the way to Rhodes in sight of each other. Since you have the letter and we have Luciana, we are at a draw. That will keep us together until we reach the island, where we will make the trade."

"We'll make the exchange as soon as we arrive there?"

"Yes."

"And we'll have a truce there to make the trade?"

"I swear to it, as God is my witness."

Oddly enough, Fox put more faith in Armstrong's oath than Corosi's. Still, it would be the best agreement he'd get.

"I'm sure I can convince Giovanni."

"You'd better," Corosi said. "Tell him to meet our ship in the harbor tomorrow at midday. It's called the *Drago Marino*. You won't be able to miss it. It will be the biggest one out there."

"We'll be there." He looked at Armstrong. "It's been an interesting evening, Sir Randolf."

"That it has. I don't understand you, Sir Gerard, but I respect you. It will be a shame to kill you."

"Until our battle to the death."

"I look forward to it."

Fox turned and walked away as casually as he could, wondering how he was going to tell Giovanni that his mother would be held hostage until they arrived on a Greek island at the far end of the Mediterranean.

 53

After the events at the basilica and the hurried preparations to leave Venice, Armstrong was tired, but he would have plenty of time to sleep now that they were on the *Drago Marino*. The captain told them to expect a voyage of anywhere from a week to a fortnight to get to Rhodes. Staring out at the vast stretch of water made him uneasy.

They were at anchor between Venice and the barrier island called the Lido, awaiting the *Cara Signora*. The sun was nearly overhead, but Giovanni's carrack had not yet arrived. Corosi leaned on the bulwark of the forecastle watching for any sign of them.

"He'll come," Corosi said, but he didn't sound as confident as he wished to be.

"He has to," Armstrong replied.

"I wish we could attack them right here. Finish this here and now. The captain said his men are skilled with the crossbows in the armory. That's how they wipe out crews on other ships before boarding them."

As a licensed privateer, the *Drago Marino* had permission from Venice to intercept any ship flying a foreign flag. Genoese trade ships were frequent targets, and the captain was well known for his ruthless methods and high success rate, having commandeered five ships this year alone.

"Giovanni would destroy the original letter before we could board them. It's a big risk if your wife is telling the truth that she altered the contents in the copy."

"Believe me, I've considered that she's bluffing. And though the Venice clues proved true, you're right. We can't take the chance."

"Once we're under way," Armstrong said, "we need to start planning how we'll make the exchange. You'll honor the truce?"

Corosi sounded insulted. "You heard me swear to it, didn't you?"

"Of course."

"However, after the exchange the truce will be over."

"Still, Fox and Giovanni won't want to make the exchange in private. They'll want to do it somewhere they consider safe."

"I have an idea about that," Corosi said. "Before we set sail, I heard that all those knights gathering on Rhodes are invited to a feast for the entire city at the grand master's palace. If we arrive in time, that will be the ideal place for the trade, right under the noses of the Knights Hospitaller."

"And how do we prevent the *Cara Signora* from escaping with the treasure?"

"The Hospitallers' fortress city and harbor will be heavily guarded, but they won't care what happens once the *Cara Signora* leaves port. That will be our opportunity to put the crossbowmen to use. This time, our ambush will work."

Armstrong knew nothing about naval tactics, so he would leave that to the captain. But the reasoning seemed sound.

"Now that the end of our search is in sight," he said, "I have a request."

"A request?"

"When you make me commander of Florence's armies, I believe I should have an estate deserving of such a title."

"If the treasure of the Templars is as large as the legend says, we will have enough riches to supply you with a vast tract of land."

"And a tower in Florence?"

"If you desire it."

"I think it would only be fitting for someone of my stature."

"Then you shall have it."

Armstrong nodded. It would be well within Corosi's power to bestow those benefits on him. The question was whether he would follow through on his promise.

If he didn't fully trust Corosi to live up to his commitments,

Armstrong had another alternative to consider. Although it would require breaking his oath of loyalty, he could kill Corosi, have Sofia for himself, and use the treasure to build a powerful mercenary army. Had Fox, who was a worthy foe and an accomplished fighter, joined forces with him, it would have been easier to envision.

It seemed odd that an excommunicant would take such a self-righteous stance on the role of a knight, but Armstrong concluded that their competing codes of honor would never have worked together. Armstrong valued loyalty and commitment to one's word, while Fox idealized some higher-minded duty to protect the weak. Inevitably, it would have led them to clash, so perhaps it was fortunate that Fox turned down his offer.

Without Fox, the idea of striking out on his own was fraught with danger. If it were suspected that he had murdered Corosi—his lord—no one would trust him as a commander to carry out their schemes. And he would forgo any chance of acquiring land. He would be an itinerant mercenary the rest of his life, unless he returned to the cold of England, which was a distasteful prospect now that he'd gotten comfortable with the sun-kissed Tuscan climate and the riches to be made there.

Armstrong's thoughts were interrupted by Corosi pointing excitedly.

"There they are!"

The prow of the *Cara Signora* nosed into view as it passed the small island between them and Venice. It slowly came around and heaved to, not a hundred feet away.

Giovanni stood on the forecastle of his ship beside Fox and Willa.

"It's good to see you, son!" Corosi yelled.

"You have no right to call me that!" Giovanni shouted back. "I know the truth about my real father. I will never call you Father again. From now on, you are a stranger to me, Signore Corosi."

"You'd have been better off not knowing your mother's a harlot," Corosi snarled.

"And she would have been better off staying with my father

instead of marrying a heartless philistine. Now where is she?" Giovanni called out.

"She's below deck!" Corosi answered.

"I won't set sail until I see that she's all right!"

Corosi sighed. "I suppose we need to show him. Go get her and bring her up here."

"Yes, signore."

Armstrong left and went to their accommodations in the stern. Luciana was kept in a cabin that was barred from the outside. Corosi was concerned that if she were allowed to roam the ship that she might throw herself overboard in an attempt to escape or die trying, especially with her son's ship sailing nearby.

Her tiny cabin was at the end of the empty corridor. Armstrong had a stop to make first. He might not have another chance during the entire voyage.

He opened Corosi's cabin door, and Sofia, who was dressed only in her underclothes, gasped as she turned at the abrupt entrance and scrambled to cover herself with her kirtle. But when she saw who it was, she dropped the kirtle and jumped into his arms, kissing him passionately.

When she pulled away, she said, "I don't think I'll be able to keep myself away from you for a two-week sailing."

"You'll have to. We've been able to deceive Corosi for this long in part because we pretend to snipe at each other. We'll have to maintain it for the duration of the trip."

"But I hope not much longer."

"Not after we've found the treasure."

"What if we killed Corosi during the voyage? Perhaps he could have an unfortunate accident and fall overboard in the middle of the night."

Even though he had just been thinking the same thing, hearing such blasphemy against his lord spoken aloud made him catch his breath. He couldn't let her see his hesitation, so he replied nonchalantly, "That would be unwise. I don't know how the captain and his men would react if Corosi were gone. They might turn around and head back to Venice."

"Or they might continue on to the treasure with us if they knew about our quest."

"They might also kill us all and search for it themselves."

Sofia seemed put out. "Very well. Then we stay with our plan."

He silently peered down at her. She was incredibly beautiful, far more than any other woman he'd ever been with. But it bothered him that she was so nonchalant about the plan to betray Corosi once they had the treasure in hand. If he chose not to breach his code of loyalty and sided with Corosi instead of her, she could easily turn his lord against him. Could she even attempt to murder Armstrong as well?

He now understood that she had cleverly maneuvered him into an impossible situation by making him choose between her and Corosi.

"With the financial knowledge I acquired from Luciana," Sofia said as she stroked his arm, "I will help you build a military the king of France will envy and fear. You'll be able to dictate your terms to any of the cities in Italy. Think about what it will be like to command thousands of men."

Her vision was tempting. Without Corosi, he wouldn't have his own land, but he would have freedom from being at his lord's beck and call.

"Did Giovanni come as we thought he would?" Sofia asked.

"He's here now. He wants to see Signora Corosi before he goes any further."

"Ah, the devoted son," she said disdainfully. "I knew he wouldn't abandon her."

"How did you know that?"

Something flashed in her eyes before she smiled and said, "You men are all the same, so enthralled by your mothers. Italians are even more so. He's predictable."

Armstrong saw more there, but he let it go. Sofia was such a skillful liar that he'd never get the full truth from her anyway, and that was something that also troubled him.

He kissed her one more time and was tempted to bed her right there, but Corosi was waiting.

"I have to go."

"This voyage will be excruciating without you lying beside me. I'll see you on deck when we set sail."

Armstrong closed the door behind him and went down the narrow hall to the last door. He knocked and unlatched it.

Luciana was sitting on her cot.

"What do you want?" she said.

"Your son demands to see you."

She jumped to her feet. "My son?" Her voice was tinged with both hope and worry.

"He's waiting on his ship. Come with me."

He led her out onto the deck. The *Drago Marino*'s sailors glared at her. They felt it was bad luck to have any woman on board, let alone two, but they obeyed their captain and put up with them.

Armstrong took Luciana up the stairs to the forecastle. When she saw Giovanni across the way, she tried to rush over to the bulwark, but Armstrong kept hold of her arm and guided her to Corosi's side, remembering his concern about her jumping off the ship.

"Let go of her!" Giovanni shouted. "Have they hurt you, Mamma?"

"I'm unharmed, my dearest! Don't fear for me! Leave now!"

Corosi laughed at her. "He'll do no such thing." He turned toward Giovanni and called across the water, "You know the rules! Stay in sight of the *Drago Marino*. If I believe you've gone ahead without us, you'll never see her again."

Giovanni smoldered. "I understand. I expect to see her every evening without a scratch on her."

"So be it. Are we ready to sail?"

"Lead the way."

Armstrong watched Fox with his wife. Despite his contempt for the pair, they did seem to make an effective couple, which made him think about himself and Sofia.

Then he looked over at Corosi, a powerful ally who could give him everything he'd ever wanted as a boy growing up in England.

It was a dream that was out of reach as a second son but now tantalizingly close in Italy.

He would soon have a choice to make between them—either an estate and a command, or the freedom to marshal an independent company that had the potential to make him more powerful than a lord. The Templar treasure on Rhodes would force a selection, even if the correct one was not obvious yet.

But one thing was certain. It was either Sofia or Corosi. One of them would have to die.

THE KNIGHT'S HOUR

The Eastern Mediterranean

54

THE GREEK ARCHIPELAGO

Willa was grateful for the strong breeze snapping the sails of the *Cara Signora*. They'd been traveling during the day so that the *Drago Marino* could keep them in sight and heaving to at night. Thankfully, the weather had been calm, so there had been no worries about losing each other in heavy seas. According to Giovanni, the favorable winds meant they were a week from arriving in Rhodes. She would be delighted to be off the ship—as would Zephyr and Comis—but not as thrilled as Gerard would be.

She found him amidships as usual since it was the most stable part of the ship. His *mal de mer* was kept in check by the generous portion of ginger they'd purchased in Venice before leaving, but he still didn't enjoy the voyage. She sidled up beside him at the bulwark as he watched the *Drago Marino* maintaining a parallel course several hundred yards off the port beam.

"Thinking about her?" she asked.

Gerard nodded. "Luciana is a strong woman, but I don't trust Corosi to treat her properly."

"Imagine how Giovanni must feel."

"He has the running of the ship to keep his mind busy."

"A ship he named after his mother."

"At least we've been seeing her every evening."

"We'll find a way to free her," she said.

Gerard smiled at her. "There's that ray of hope you always have."

"I'm not unaware of the danger we're up against, but I have to believe that things will turn out all right. Otherwise, why go on?"

"And that's exactly why I want you beside me as my wife." He took her hand. "I've been thinking about our wedding. Perhaps we've been trying to go about it the wrong way."

"What do you mean?"

"Do we really need a priest to marry us?"

"Of course we do."

"What about a handfasting? Just you and me vowing our commitment to each other. It's frowned upon, but it's still legally binding in the eyes of the Church."

"But we wanted a priest's blessing."

"Is that so important?"

"I'd never considered marrying without it."

"We can be wedded in the Church someday, when my excommunication is resolved, but why should we wait until then to be husband and wife?"

It took her a moment to respond because she was stunned, and she saw him deflate from her hesitation. She squeezed his hand and beamed at him.

"I think that's a wonderful idea. But when?"

Gerard looked elated. "The sooner, the better. Perhaps even on Rhodes. We can recite our vows together beneath a beautiful tree under a bright blue sky."

"That sounds so romantic."

"Then it's set," Gerard said with a grin. "After this quest is over, the wedding will be our reward."

"Don't you think the wedding night will be the true reward?"

Gerard seemed bemused but appreciative. "I didn't know women said such things."

"I thought we established long ago that I was not like most women."

"You have me there. Am I like most men?"

"You are nothing like most men. That is precisely why I want to marry you."

They held hands while looking at the sea until they were interrupted by Giovanni.

"I'm sorry to disturb you," he said. "But I have some information that might be helpful."

"What is it?"

"I prefer to show you."

Giovanni took them back to his cabin. A chart lay on his desk next to a piece of paper. The large chart was marked "Mare Mediterraneum" and consisted of the sea and its surrounding lands, crisscrossed by countless lines that must have somehow helped with navigation. The drawing on the paper next to it was a simple hand-drawn copy of the island labeled "Rhodes." All around the island, dots had been added with names next to them, including one at the north tip that seemed to be the main city.

"I spoke to my crew about what we will be looking for on the island. I thought they deserved to know that we may be going into harm's way, and to a man they agreed such a treasure was worth the risk, although I have no doubt they wouldn't have hesitated to help me even if it was only to retrieve my mother."

"I've seen how loyal they are to you," Gerard said.

"They've followed me into battle before," Giovanni said, "so this is nothing new to them. We all threw our lots together as sailors in the hopes of just such an opportunity as this."

He opened the letter and placed it on the table for them to read.

At the palace gate the sun's shadow will point to the knight's hour.

Follow the cast line to the word that begins the name of the sought-after stronghold.

There, circle west from the stairway to a faithful rock in the Templars' true colors.

Disturbing its peace will lead to proof of the king's duplicity and fortune's fate.

"My crew has been sailing the Adriatic and Aegean for many years," Giovanni said, "and Rhodes has been one of our frequent stops. Since we're looking for a stronghold, all of us pooled our knowledge to recall as much as possible about Rhodes. These are all the castles and forts we could remember on the island. I wrote them down on the map."

Willa read off the names on the list: Feraklos, Monolithos, Kritinia, Lindos, Asklipio.

"There could be others in addition to these," Giovanni said. "Many of them were abandoned once the Hospitallers concentrated their forces in Rhodes City. Others are castles built by the Hospitallers, but may have older structures beneath that were there in my grandfather's time. In addition, there are lookout towers all over the island, and we have no idea how long they've been there."

"And you mentioned the Palace of the Grand Master," Gerard said.

Giovanni shook his head. "The construction work for the defensive walls is enormous. If the treasure had been buried in that stronghold, it would have been discovered by now. Besides, at the time he delivered the treasure to the island, the Knights Hospitaller had already taken over the city. It would have been impossible for Templars to hide such a fortune there without it being seen, so it must be somewhere else on the island."

"But we still need to go to the city," Gerard said. "The palace gate is there."

The three of them had discussed this clue. They'd quickly decided that the palace gate referred to the Palace of the Grand Master, but the rest of the meaning had eluded them. After going around and around, Fox had finally suggested that the clue might refer to a sundial. But none of them could guess what any of the hours might have to do with a knight.

"I believe I know the sundial we're looking for," Giovanni said.

"On the wall of the gate?" Willa asked.

"Not on the gate. In front of the gate. At least it used to be."

"Used to be?" Gerard asked. "Where is it now?"

"There is an ancient Roman sundial that was mounted on a pedestal in front of the existing Byzantine palace's gates when the Hospitallers conquered the island. It's a huge round piece of marble with a bronze pointer that casts a shadow toward the markings indicating the hours of daylight. Once the Knights of Rhodes took over the city as their main seat, they enclosed that area to form a huge forecourt, but they moved the sundial so that it now sits inside the palace itself in the inner courtyard."

Gerard nodded his head in approval. "That has to be it. If Luciana and Matteo had completed this quest when her father thought they would, they could have walked right up to the area outside the old palace gate to decipher the clue."

"Now someone has to actually get inside the inner courtyard of the Palace of the Grand Master to look at the sundial," Willa said.

During their regular stop two days ago, Corosi had proposed trading Luciana for the letter at the upcoming town feast for all of the knights who would be converging on the island. It was to take place in the palace's forecourt. Such a public place would make the exchange safer, but it wouldn't necessarily help them with the clue.

"The entrance to the palace is guarded at all times, and only knights are permitted beyond the main door. That's why the feast for the townspeople is being hosted in the forecourt."

"Then someone has to pretend to be a Hospitaller to get through the entrance to the palace and access the inner courtyard," Willa said. "During the feast, when it's most crowded with plenty of distractions will be the best time to do it."

"Giovanni and I will be making the exchange with Corosi and Armstrong," Gerard said, "so we won't be available to do that."

"But Corosi won't expect *me* to be at the exchange."

Giovanni frowned at her. "You can't possibly mean you'd pretend to be a knight."

"I read a history of the Crusades that told of the consorors of the Hospitallers, lay sisters who aid the knights in their endeavors, especially as nurses to help with the pilgrims."

"You're going to steal into one of the most heavily fortified locations in all of Christendom?"

Willa shrugged. "Why not?"

"Because you're a woman," Giovanni sputtered.

Gerard smiled at that stupefied response. He remembered feeling the same way at one time, before his adventures with her.

"There's something you should know about Willa," he said. "She's not like most women."

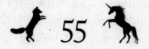

55

RHODES

The cabin that Luciana had been locked in for two weeks had only a small porthole high on the wall to let light through, so the sole time she got to see anything besides her three walls and a door were during her evening excursions on deck where Riccardo paraded her to show Giovanni she was still alive. Her husband acted as if he were worried she would throw herself over the side of the ship, but she had no intention of doing that, not when she was given daily hope from seeing her son, Fox, and Willa nearby.

She kept herself occupied during the long voyage by envisioning her life free from her husband. Revenge was not on her mind. She simply wanted to have her lone surviving child back with her, and the only way that could happen was to ensure that Riccardo was stripped of all his wealth and power. How he dealt with that outcome was up to him.

It had only been light for a few hours when the ship stopped moving and there was more shouting than usual. Her door opened, surprising her, since normally she was brought out only in the evening. Armstrong was standing in the doorway.

"It's time to go, Signora Corosi."

"Where are we going?"

"Put your shoes on. We've arrived."

He took her up the familiar route to the deck, and she blinked in the bright sunlight. Canvas covers were laid out on the deck. A corner flapped up in the breeze, revealing a crossbow already cranked and loaded with a bolt. Luciana had a good guess what they were for.

Looking out over the water, she saw two protective barriers

made of stone reaching toward each other to form the entrance to the harbor of Rhodes. It was filled with ships, some anchored and some docked while others were coming in through the harbor's mouth. She imagined the great bronze Colossus of Rhodes bestriding the entrance—so tall an entire ship could pass safely beneath his legs—with a torch lifted in one hand to serve as a beacon to sailors and a spear in the other to warn off invaders. It surely must have been the largest statue ever created. Now there was no trace left of that Wonder of the World.

Armstrong led her to the forecastle, and as she climbed the stairs, she took in the great walls of the city. They were as massive as any she'd ever seen, a reflection of the awesome wealth of the Knights Hospitaller, although many called them the Knights of Rhodes now that they had made the island their bastion.

She'd heard about them as a child from her father, for they had been the main rivals to the Knights Templar. Both were military orders deeply involved in the Crusade to capture Jerusalem, but the Templars had been founded to protect pilgrims traveling to the Holy Land, while the Hospitallers had focused on their health and welfare.

She couldn't blame them for the Templars' downfall. That was the doing of King Philip of France and Pope Clement. The Hospitallers had merely been the beneficiaries of the Templars' demise, having inherited the Templar wealth and properties after they were destroyed.

Ever since she'd discovered that they were headed to Rhodes, Luciana thought it odd that her father's order had chosen their rivals' island for safeguarding the treasure. She always considered Cyprus the likeliest candidate. She supposed she'd never know the details of her father's final voyage, but she was somewhat comforted by the fact that she was now following in his footsteps.

Her eyes continued along the wall to an incomplete watchtower next to a mass of piled stones, scaffolding, and cranes. Hundreds of men were busily adding on to the impressive battlements. It must have taken decades to build the walls already there and would take more decades still to finish them. But once complete, this island would surely never be conquered.

She continued turning to take in the view but stopped abruptly when she saw the *Cara Signora* docked not a ship's length away. Giovanni and Fox stood on the aft deck watching her. Her son waved, and she smiled and waved back.

Riccardo came up beside her as Armstrong stepped away.

"At last we're here. Will you be as glad to be off this boat as I am?"

"I'll be glad to be away from you."

Riccardo nodded at Giovanni. "But isn't it wonderful to have the family together one last time?"

"Giovanni is no longer your family, and neither am I. You made it clear that's what you want."

He rounded on her, spitting his words. "You were the one who betrayed me, Luciana. You gave me a son who was someone else's. Do you have any idea of how that made me feel? I loved Giovanni as my own flesh and blood. But once I realized the truth, I could see him developing into the same heedless scoundrel that his true father was. How long was it before he would betray me, just as you and Matteo had? When Tommaso was born, I took it as a sign that maybe you and I could start afresh. And when the Pestilence took him, I mourned his death as much as you did, likely even more. Now I need a new family. One that is truly mine."

"Don't you dare claim that Tommaso's loss meant more to you than me. After you banished Giovanni, Tommaso was all I had. After the Great Mortality, I was left with nothing. And now all you want is my death."

"Do you think I wanted any of this? You are the one who went behind my back to start this quest again. You know what's at stake for me. My only choice is to try to restore my life to what it should have been."

Although Luciana knew the real reason that Riccardo had banished Giovanni, they'd never discussed it before. Now there was no reason to hold back.

"Giovanni would have been as faithful to you as your own

blood," Luciana said, "just as Matteo was to my father. It was your jealousy that destroyed our family."

"My jealousy?"

"You could never live with the idea that my father loved Matteo more than you. I didn't see it then, but it's so clear to me now. When you saw that your mentor favored my true love, you couldn't abide it. You wanted to punish Papà, so you betrayed him and you lied about Matteo to me. I didn't ruin your life. You ruined mine."

Riccardo raised a hand as if to strike her, but he restrained himself and smiled.

"I've never told you how your father really died, have I?"

Luciana didn't like his smug expression. "You couldn't know. He disappeared after he hid the treasure, long after we married."

"No, he returned from his journey to give a final message to the Templar grand master. I knew he would. You remember my journey to Paris soon after Giovanni was born, don't you?"

Her breath caught in her throat. "You saw Papà?"

"Not only did I see him, but I was the one who put him to the sword."

His words were so awful that she didn't want to believe them. But she could see the horrible truth in his gloating eyes. She'd been married to her father's killer for nearly four decades. The revelation made her ill.

As Riccardo stood there with smug satisfaction, the rage built up until she couldn't contain herself. She threw herself at him, her fingers ready to claw his eyes out. Only Armstrong's hold kept her from blinding him.

"You'll burn in Hell for what you've done," she growled.

Riccardo regarded her calmly. "I tell you this to show you that we've both done what we had to do. But I need to look to my future. I think you know you can't be part of it."

"And why would I want to be, you murderer!" Luciana snapped. She was desperately trying to keep from breaking down into sobs of grief.

"Perhaps this will help you understand the pain I felt when I realized your father favored Matteo over me. Now I will return you to Giovanni and he will give me the letter."

Luciana's body went numb at the thought of her son walking into a trap. "Don't kill him, please. He's all I have left."

"Don't look so worried. I've agreed to a truce for the exchange. We're going to make the trade at the Hospitaller feast. You'll both be safe. I wouldn't dream of starting a fight in the midst of hundreds of knights."

He nodded to Armstrong, and they walked toward the gangway. But Luciana's worry wasn't about what would happen at the feast. It was about the array of crossbows on the deck of the *Drago Marino*.

56

Once Fox and Giovanni were off the carrack, they walked quickly toward the nearest city gate. They were dressed in their finest clothes in order to blend in as noblemen attending the feast. Giovanni was preoccupied with the fact that Armstrong and Corosi were behind them. Fox had seen both of them walking down the gangplank of the *Drago Marino* with Luciana.

"Don't look back," he said. "Your mother is with them."

"I'm more concerned about their men coming after us. During the past two weeks, I've counted ten of Armstrong's men. In addition to their ship's crew, that doubles what we have."

"They won't attack before they get the letter. We have a truce until then."

"And if they don't honor it?" Giovanni asked.

"They have no reason to break it. The attack will come far away from the grand master's palace, after the truce has expired and we reboard the ship."

"You think they won't attack us while we're still in the city?"

Fox shrugged. "It would be dangerous for them to do so. There are sergeants guarding the walls and gates. An alarm would get a hundred knights from the feast to come running. They'd put up a good fight even if they were drunk. Maybe even better than good."

"So they'll attack us outside the harbor?"

"Does it matter?"

"Not if our plan works," Giovanni answered.

"Then stop looking over your shoulder."

Both of them were without their swords and were waved through the harbor gate without incident. They followed the crowd of townspeople heading toward the feast.

Fox checked behind them and saw only Luciana, Corosi, and Armstrong a safe distance back. He would recognize any of Armstrong's mercenaries, and nobody else nearby looked familiar.

"We're not being stalked," Fox said.

"I thought you said they wouldn't attack us before the feast."

"I'm not perfect, and it doesn't hurt to be careful."

The city bells sounded for the hour of sext, the signal for the feast to begin. All who had been dawdling now made their way toward the palace so they wouldn't miss the festival.

Giovanni patted his chest where he had the letter stowed as they reached the city's main street. It was steeply sloped up from the hospital at the base of the hill. Several lay sisters of the Hospitaller order on duty waved to others as they left for the feast, promising in French to return in time to relieve them so that they could also partake in the festivities.

As Fox and Giovanni walked up the street, they passed buildings called *auberges*, or inns, marked with the arms of each of the eight *langues*, or tongues, representing the various languages spoken by Hospitallers throughout Europe. Houses related to England, France, Italy, Provence, and four other regions hosted the knights who had descended on Rhodes from all over Europe for this gathering. Each *langue* had a head called a pillar, who was responsible for a specific area of the Hospitaller organization. That of Provence was in charge of all the order's properties, while the Italian pillar served as the commander of its fleet. Above all the pillars was the grand master, whose palace stood at the top of the street. An open vaulted archway indicated the entrance to the palace's forecourt. Even now they could hear the raucous commotion from hundreds of people celebrating.

When they crossed under the honey-colored stones of the archway, they saw people milling about in the expansive forecourt enclosed by an imposing wall. Almost directly opposite the archway, thick turrets flanked the guarded entrance to the palace and its inner courtyard. A few knights could be seen exiting the palace proper into the forecourt, but most of the movement was restricted to servants going in and out, some of them carrying platters heaped with food and drink.

"The grand master's palace," Giovanni said.

As attendees entered, musicians, acrobats, and fire-eaters entertained them to appreciative shrieks of joy and applause. It was only when Fox and Giovanni went all the way in that they saw the full extent of the event.

Rows and rows of trestle tables had been set up for the feast, extending all the way to the far end of the forecourt a hundred yards in the distance. Some of them were occupied with the city's residents talking and preparing to partake of the grand meal provided to them courtesy of the knights. Many of them were standing and moving about to visit with their neighbors while the servants laid out an array of delicacies.

"Where are all the knights?" Giovanni asked.

Among all the tables, most of the attendees were dressed as commoners. If there were truly hundreds of knights in attendance, they were nowhere to be seen.

"They must have a separate feast going on inside the palace."

"Then this is merely to provide a festival for the citizenry. Will that hurt us?"

"I don't know," Fox said. "Corosi said to meet us out here."

Though there were few knights visible, there were plenty of sergeants of the order walking around with pikes to keep the drunken bacchanalia peaceful and orderly. At least that made Fox feel more comfortable with the truce Corosi and Armstrong had promised.

Fox and Giovanni walked farther into the crowd to wait. It wasn't long before Fox spotted Armstrong's tall form towering over the other attendees.

"There they are," Fox said.

He gestured ostentatiously to Corosi and Armstrong so that they would focus attention on him and Giovanni instead of noticing Willa sneaking into the grand master's palace right behind them.

57

As soon as she had seen Luciana being taken through the town gates by Corosi and Armstrong, Willa unloaded Comis and Zephyr from the ship, already saddled, and rode into the city. She tied them up outside of the house of the English tongue. Anyone passing would assume they were owned by the knights inside and wouldn't dare touch them. She had planned to go to the hospital and claim that she was a new sister in need of clothing so she could get the outfit she required for her plan. But when she saw the black habit and wimple of a nun on a drying line, she decided it would be easier to simply borrow them. Suddenly she was transformed into a lay sister of the Hospitaller order.

When she arrived at the feast, Corosi was just in front of her, so she held back until she could slip into the palace entrance. She was stopped by one of the two sergeants guarding the doors.

"What's your business here?" he asked in French, the traditional language of the Hospitallers.

"I was asked to deliver some healing herbs," she answered in fluent French.

"By whom?"

"A knight of the English tongue requested them. The spicy food has apparently not agreed with his innards."

The guard raised an eyebrow at his comrade, who snickered. They didn't seem surprised that an Englishman had trouble stomaching the Mediterranean fare.

The guard waved her in. "Next time tell him to stick to the bread and frumenty." That got a laugh from his companion as she walked through the towering entrance hall. On the opposite side, a vaulted archway opened out into the inner courtyard, paved in gray stone and white marble set into a pattern of large squares not unlike those on a chessboard.

A raised dais had been constructed along the west wall of the courtyard, and the grand master himself presided over the affair from his chair of honor in the center. Presumably the men seated on either side of him were the pillars of each of the tongues. In front of them, the tables were occupied by hundreds of men identically dressed in black tabards emblazoned with white crosses, all of them of the Hospitaller order. Willa had never seen so many knights outside of a tournament.

The free-flowing wine and ale had already taken effect, for there was much singing and carousing. Many of the guests, especially those far from the head table, were pinching and grabbing at the servant women as they laughed. Though they had taken vows of chastity, Willa knew that some of the knights considered it more of a promise not to take a wife, privately enjoying the company of ladies as much as any other noble, so long as they were discreet.

Since Willa was dressed in a lay sister's habit of their own order, she hoped she would be undisturbed by any wandering hands. Still, she kept her head down as she walked quickly to the north end of the courtyard.

Her aim was the Roman sundial that sat on a pedestal in the location where it would receive direct rays from the sun and not be blocked by the high south walls of the palace. As she approached it, she repeated the first two lines of the clue in her mind.

At the palace gate the sun's shadow will point to the knight's hour. Follow the cast line to the word that begins the name of the sought-after stronghold.

The sundial had been formed out of a huge piece of stone. Etched into its face were Roman numerals signifying daylight hours from VII to XVII, with lines going from each number to the bronze pointer in the middle. Beneath the numbers was some kind of battle scene. On the right side was a horse-mounted soldier leading men on foot into a fight toward their foes on the left, including soldiers, animals, and what looked like storm clouds with lightning.

Around the edge under the battle scene was an inscription in Latin.

For the glory of Rome, we will not be deterred by evil men, nor wild beast, nor ferocious tempest.

That was the only writing on the face, so one of them had to be the word she needed. Willa studied the sundial looking for something representing the "knight's hour." There was no specific canonical hour referring to knights, so perhaps one of the Roman numerals was the clue.

But none of them seemed to have any relation to a knight. She remembered back to the marble carving in Florence depicting the war of the Titans and realized that Ramberti might be using the same type of puzzle here.

She studied the battle scene, and as she came to the hour marked "X" for ten, she found what she was looking for. Directly beneath the numeral, there was a figure that looked remarkably like a knight.

Even though the man on the horse must have been a Roman soldier, he held a sword high in one hand and a shield in his other as he bravely led his men against their enemies. Ramberti no doubt would have considered him representative of a courageous knight.

She looked around to make sure no one was watching, then traced an imaginary line from the bronze pointer toward the Roman knight, continuing past him to the saying below it.

She stopped when her finger landed on the Latin word for "wild beast." *Fera.*

She mentally ran through the list of castles and fortresses that Giovanni had told them about. There was one that started with "Fera." What was it? Ferakos? Feralos? Whatever it was, she was sure that was the one.

There was a commotion behind her, and she whirled around,

fearing that she had been discovered or that Armstrong had found a way in. Instead, some of the knights were surrounding one of their comrades, who was holding his throat. He pounded on the table and then fell onto his back, clawing at his mouth and neck.

One of the knights shouted, "What happened to him?"

Another responded, "He was eating and then suddenly seized up like this!"

They were kneeling beside him while others surrounded them to watch, but everyone was paralyzed into inaction.

"What should we do?"

"I don't know!"

Willa should have simply left. Getting involved would put her in danger of her identity being revealed as false. But she knew what was happening. She'd seen it once before when she was at a dinner back in England.

The man was choking. If he didn't expel what was blocking his breathing, he would surely die.

The problem was that she also knew a way to eject the piece of food. A priest in attendance at that dinner had cured the choking man.

Willa thought back to how Gerard had come to her rescue the day they had met, at great risk to himself because it was the right thing to do. She knew how to save this knight.

In the moment that all of these thoughts flashed through her head, she'd already made up her mind and rushed toward him. If she had the means to save the poor man, she wasn't going to let him die.

 58

Corosi studied Giovanni as he stood face to face for the first time in almost two decades with the man he had raised as a son. Even though Matteo had died when he was half the age of Giovanni now, a more weathered version of the same face stared back at him. And it brought the same feelings of envy and betrayal back to him as stinging as ever.

"*Buongiorno*, Giovanni."

"Signore Corosi."

Armstrong and Fox watched silently. Corosi held Luciana, who strained to run to Giovanni.

"It seems you've fared well in Venice," Corosi said.

"Why are you even trying to be civil? I know very well what you did to my mother. What you tried to do."

"Then you also know what she did to me."

"You deserved it for betraying my real father."

"I raised you as my own son."

"And then you threw me out. What do you want from me? Gratitude?"

"It wouldn't be unfounded. You lived in luxury until you became a man."

"You kept me from ever knowing my father."

Hearing Giovanni refer to Matteo as his father for the first time stoked a fire in Corosi's chest.

"Your father was half the man that I am. Domenico Ramberti was too blind to see that."

"Or perhaps he saw the selfish louse you really are."

"Stop!" Luciana yelled, drawing looks from some of the more sober feast attendees. "This bickering serves no purpose."

"She's right," Giovanni said. "We've come to make a trade. Let's be done with it."

Corosi tamped down his anger. At least this interaction would make doing away with Giovanni that much easier.

"You have Ramberti's letter?" he asked.

Giovanni removed a parchment sheet from his tunic. He held up the folded note so that Corosi could see the broken wax seal. Since he had used it himself, Corosi recognized the stamp from Ramberti's signet ring, an eagle with its wings spread and talons bared surrounded by the words *SIGILLUM FRATRIS RAMBERTI*—Seal of Brother Ramberti.

"Now let her go," Giovanni said.

Corosi took the letter and released Luciana, who dashed to Giovanni's side. Corosi flipped open the letter to read the last clue.

When he saw what it said, he looked up in fury.

"You tricked me!"

"What does it say?" Armstrong asked.

"The same thing your letter says," Fox replied.

"I knew you couldn't take the chance that I was bluffing," Luciana said with glee.

"We'll still have a truce," Fox said. "We made the trade as promised."

"It's true," Armstrong said. "But as soon as we all leave here, the parley is over."

"Then I think we might stay for the meal. It's such a lovely day, it would be a shame to leave the party early."

Corosi drew his dagger and sliced up the parchment letter in front of Luciana. To his frustration, she didn't reveal any emotion at seeing her father's precious memento sliced to pieces.

"You'll regret deceiving me," he snarled.

"I sincerely doubt that," she replied.

Corosi wanted to kill them there and then, but committing murders in the middle of the Hospitallers' fortress would no doubt turn out… badly. He would have to stick with his plan to intercept them as they sailed out of the harbor. Wherever the final destination was, they would need the ship to haul the treasure away.

"Come," Corosi said to Armstrong and turned on his heel.

Armstrong followed, and as they passed the guarded entrance to the palace, out of the corner of his eye he caught a glimpse of Sofia's hood as she went through it.

"You're no servant," the sergeant said to Sofia in the familiar French she'd learned from traders who'd come through Venice.

"I'm a servant of a kind," she replied.

"To do what?"

"Are you dense? Would you like me to bring the Pillar of the Tongue of Italy back here to explain that he requested my presence?"

The other guard shrugged at the sergeant. Neither of them relished being chided by one of the most important Hospitaller visitors in the city and endangering their sought-after palace positions.

The sergeant waved her through. She smiled at them and went in.

When she entered the courtyard, she noticed a cluster of knights near one of the back tables blocking her path to the sundial. She stayed back to wait for whatever was happening to end.

She caught a glimpse of a woman, possibly a nun, on her knees over a man lying on his back. The woman thrust both her hands upward into his belly in a swift motion. The men around her looked concerned.

The knights were crowding so closely that the nun looked up and motioned for them to stand back, and that's when Sofia caught sight of her face. It was Willa in disguise.

Despite her surprise, Sofia grudgingly respected the woman's daring and ingenuity for sneaking into the palace as she had, only under different circumstances.

Willa pushed again, and suddenly an object flew out of the distressed knight's mouth. It landed on the ground nearby, recognizable even at this distance as a half-chewed date. Sofia realized that it must have gotten lodged in the man's throat.

The knight coughed and rose to his feet. His compatriots applauded and cheered, patting the man on the back as Willa stole away quietly.

Sofia watched to see which way she would go. Had she already solved the clue or had she been on her way in when the crisis occurred?

She saw Willa head back toward the palace entrance and realized that she must already have the answer. Sofia had to know what she'd learned. She drew a dagger from her sleeve and angled to intercept Willa.

Willa was in such a hurry to depart that she didn't notice Sofia coming up behind her. Sofia grabbed her arm and put the point of the dagger in her back.

"Cry out and I'll cut you down right here."

Willa turned her head to see who had accosted her.

"No, you won't, Sofia, or you'll have a hundred knights recently grateful for my services string you up before night falls."

"Try me. I'll be gone before they know what's wrong with you."

"A hasty departure means that you won't be able to solve the clue."

"And you did?"

"I'm not very bright," Willa said. "It will take a man to figure it out."

"Save that nonsense for these fools. We both know how ignorant men can be. You, on the other hand, are clever, aren't you?"

"That's quite a compliment coming from a woman who deceived her lady for years."

"It's a plan I won't let you ruin at this late stage."

"So what do we do now?"

"Signore Corosi has just given up Luciana, but now we have you. I'm sure that Sir Gerard will do anything to get you back, even if he isn't really your husband. Sir Randolf told me you're living in sin. It seems we have a lot in common."

Willa scoffed. "I pray to God that's not so."

"I'm sure there are some differences between us. For instance, I have a knife in your back. Now, we are going to walk out past those guards and straight back to the *Drago Marino*. You'll find out how quick I am with this dagger if you attempt to flee."

"You see? My prayer has already been answered. You've shown just what a harpy you are. I'm so relieved."

"Enough. Start walking. Slowly."

Sofia kept a firm grip on her arm and the tip of the blade pricking the small of Willa's back. A quick thrust in that spot would lead to a slow, painful death.

Willa walked calmly and deliberately forward.

"Any word to the sergeant at the front entrance, and I'll drop you right there."

Willa nodded and kept going. They were nearly at the exit when from behind her came a shout in French.

"Sister! Sister!"

She turned to see the knight who'd nearly died hurrying toward them. He stopped in front of Willa.

"Sister, my name is Harold Wentworth. I wanted to show my appreciation for your assistance. I would have died had you not intervened."

"It's quite all right," Willa replied. "I'm just glad my experience at the hospital was useful here."

"I don't even know your name to properly thank you."

"That's not necessary."

"I believe it is. Please, I insist."

"It's Sister Willa. You're English, are you not?"

He nodded. "From London."

Then Willa said something in English, a language Sofia had never spoken. Harold's eyes went wide at the same time that Willa lunged to the side.

The movement caught Sofia off guard. She thrust forward with the knife, but missed Willa by a hair, slicing only her thick nun's habit. Instead, the dagger kept going and slashed the knight in the arm.

Sir Harold was so surprised at being stabbed by a woman in the Palace of the Grand Master that he was slow to respond, which was the only thing that saved Sofia. She dashed toward the front entrance. The guards were posted to keep people out, not in, so she was able to run by them even as Harold was calling for them to stop her.

They reached for her but were too late. She didn't look back as she ran through the forecourt and out into the street, cursing her bad luck all the way back to the ship.

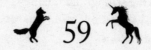 59

Fox had been watching for Willa to exit the palace, so he was shocked to see Sofia come running out instead holding a bloody dagger. He hadn't even realized she was at the feast.

Fox jumped up from the table where they'd been eating and sprinted over to the palace entrance with Giovanni and Luciana close behind.

As they approached it, two guards ran out in pursuit of Sofia, but they were too far behind to catch up with her.

"What's going on?" Giovanni asked.

"I wish I knew," Fox replied.

"I hope Willa is safe," Luciana said.

So did Fox. He breathed a sigh of relief when he saw Willa just inside the palace entrance tending to a Knight Hospitaller whose arm was bleeding. The two of them had a short conversation as she wrapped his wound with a linen cloth. When she was finished, she quickly made her way past the sergeants at the entrance, who were soon joined by two more guards.

"Are you all right?" Fox asked as she stopped in front of him. He desperately wanted to embrace her, but it would be unseemly for a nobleman to clasp a nun to his chest in public.

"I'm unhurt. That knight took the edge of Sofia's knife instead of me. Thankfully it's a minor wound." She grasped Luciana's hands. "I'm so relieved to see you, Luciana."

"And I, you," Luciana said.

"We must go now," Giovanni said. "Signore Corosi will be mustering his troops to intercept us."

They walked quickly from the outer courtyard toward the English *langue*.

"Did you solve the puzzle?" Fox asked.

"Yes. The start of the stronghold's name is Fera."

"Feraklos Castle," Giovanni said. "It's on the east coast of Rhodes just north of Lindos."

"How long will it take to sail there?" Fox said.

"It depends on the wind. We'll likely be there by nightfall."

"If Willa and I ride hard, we can be there before you. That should give us a good head start as long as Corosi doesn't know where to go yet." He turned to Willa. "Did Sofia find the clue?"

"I don't think so. I was distracted, but the sundial was in my sight the whole time. They certainly won't be able to get back in to see it now. I told the knight she stabbed that she might have been a spy for the Turks. They're doubling the guard and will deny entry into the palace for anyone they don't already know."

"Well done," Fox said. "That should slow them down a bit."

They reached the horses just in time. Armstrong and his men were running toward them up the street from the direction of the harbor. They must have discovered Fox and Giovanni's plan. Though they weren't armed with swords, they were a daunting force.

Fox and Willa climbed onto Zephyr while Giovanni and Luciana rode on Comis. Armstrong was still a hundred feet away when they took off. Instead of riding east to the harbor where they suspected Corosi's troops awaited them, they galloped toward the city's west gate, leaving Armstrong shouting at them until he was out of sight. They rode fast for the inlet that they'd already selected on the way into Rhodes.

As soon as Willa left the ship, Giovanni's first mate had cast off from the dock and departed the harbor. It was part of the ploy hatched by Fox and Giovanni. They had decided either that confusion on the *Drago Marino* about this unexpected move would delay response until they could get orders from Corosi and Armstrong, or possibly that the crew of the *Drago Marino* would simply assume the *Cara Signora* was abandoning her captain. Either way, they figured the *Drago Marino* would not follow.

When Fox and Willa arrived at the pre-selected beach, a dinghy from the *Cara Signora* was making its way from the anchored ship.

As they dismounted, Giovanni gripped Fox's hand in a firm shake.

"I can't thank you enough for helping us. Both of you. You're quite brilliant."

"It's not over," Willa said. "We haven't actually found the treasure."

"Yet," Luciana said. "I can't believe we're nearing the end of a quest my father set me on nearly forty years ago."

"Be wary of Corosi," Fox said. "He's just as clever as your father. So is Armstrong."

"And don't forget Sofia," Willa added.

When the rowboat arrived on the beach, one of the rowers held out Fox's weapons. He strapped Legend to his waist and put his bow and arrows on Zephyr's saddle.

They also got the drawing of Rhodes.

"Here is Feraklos Castle," Giovanni said, pointing to a spot halfway down the island's east coast. "You can take the eastern coast road directly south."

"Have you ever seen Feraklos Castle?" Willa asked.

"Yes, when we've docked in Lindos. You'll see the fortress atop a promontory. There is a half-moon bay beside it. The promontory beyond it is topped by the Acropolis of Lindos. If you can see both, Lindos is the one with an ancient temple on top and Feraklos is the castle to the north."

She and Fox mounted their horses while Luciana and Giovanni climbed into the dinghy.

"If we're fortunate," Fox said to them, "we'll have the treasure loaded onto the *Cara Signora* and be gone long before Corosi even discovers where it is."

They waved and pushed off from the beach. Fox looked at Willa.

"Are you ready?"

"I'll race you."

He smiled. A woman after his own heart. Side by side, they set off at a gallop for Feraklos Castle and one of the greatest treasures the world had ever known.

 60

It wasn't until later that evening that Corosi was able to charm the Pillar of the Tongue of Italy into escorting him into the palace to inspect the sundial. With vespers coming shortly and the sun already descending over the city walls, the revelers in the forecourt had dispersed, so Armstrong and Sofia were alone and out of sight of the palace guards while they waited for him to come out.

"Once we learn where to go from Signore Corosi," Sofia said, "we can solve the last clue on our own."

Armstrong glanced at the entrance to the palace. "What are you saying?"

"We don't need him anymore."

"You'll poison him?"

She shook her head. "I have no more. You'll have to kill him."

When he hesitated, Sofia put her hand on his chest and looked up at him lasciviously.

"I know you don't want me wasting my bedchamber talents on him instead of you."

"I swore an oath of loyalty to Signore Corosi. To go back on that oath by murdering him with my own hands would be a sin."

Sofia backed away with a disgusted look. "Knights break oaths all the time. Half the men in that palace would bed me in an instant despite their vows of chastity. The other half would probably like to but wouldn't be up to the task."

"It's a difficult decision." And it was, now that he was at the actual point of action. Although Armstrong was willing to kill in the service of his lord, turning his sword on that lord would be a step from which there was no going back.

"I thought we were partners in this," Sofia said. "We seize the treasure and then go wherever we want. Venice, France, even England, though from what you've told me of it, it's so cold and dreary for much of the year that I might go mad."

Her utter determination and ruthlessness were as convincing as her seductiveness was intoxicating. She would not stop until she had what she wanted. It made his decision easier than he thought it would be.

"When do we do it?" he asked.

"This is the time. We kill him now."

"Right here? I think the grand master and his knights would take offense."

"No. Back on the ship. Then we can throw his body overboard."

"And the crew?"

"Do I have to think of everything? You're a big, strong knight with ten hardened soldiers at your side. They'll follow you, and if they don't, you can make an example with some of them. Besides, once they see the size of the Templar fortune, they'll drop to their knees and thank you for leading them to it."

"If the fortune really is there." Armstrong still feared that it could have been looted after all these years.

"I believe. You should, too."

"Then I think you should be the one to kill him. He won't be suspecting it."

Exasperation tingeing her voice, she said, "Since you're so squeamish about your oath, I suppose it's up to me. I was prepared to use my dagger once today. This time I'll finish the task. But I will only do it when the three of us are alone, just in case something goes wrong, so that you can help me. You'll have to dispose of the body anyway."

Before Armstrong could say more, Corosi exited the palace alone with a smile on his face.

"Do you have it, signore?" Armstrong asked.

"I do." Corosi looked around to make sure they wouldn't be heard as they began walking back to the ship. "Once I figured out the clue, I got the pillar of the tongue to tell me the name of the castle and its location. We'll set sail for Feraklos Castle the moment we step onto the *Drago Marino*."

"The *Cara Signora* may already be there."

"They're not that far ahead. We'll surprise them the way we discussed. After that, nothing will stop us from taking the Templar treasure for ourselves."

Sofia put her arm through his. "My love, you are positively giddy with excitement."

"And so I should be, no? We are a hair's width away from the end of our quest."

"Of course. I believe wine will be in order to celebrate our coming victory."

"And the bold new future that awaits us all."

Sofia turned and flashed a brief smile at Armstrong. "I heartily agree. Don't you, Sir Randolf?"

Armstrong nodded with both unease and resignation about what was to come. "It is truly a momentous occasion."

Corosi couldn't help but feel a charge of anticipation at not only discovering the vast treasure hidden by the Templars but also the prospect of destroying the letter from the king of France that had been hanging over him like the Sword of Damocles for almost forty years.

Now that the *Drago Marino* was under way with an estimated arrival at Feraklos Castle by morning, Corosi was in his cabin with Armstrong and Sofia, ready to toast their accomplishments with a special wine from Bordeaux that he had acquired in Venice before departing. He held his cup high.

"To Sir Domenico Ramberti. If not for my old master leaving these clues, we would never have been able to take the Templar treasure for ourselves."

"To you, my love," Sofia said. "Without your guidance, we would not be in this position."

"I can't argue with that." He looked to Armstrong, who had a dour look on his face.

"And you, Sir Randolf? What would you like to toast?"

He raised his cup. "To a new beginning."

"I'll second that."

After they all drank, Sofia came closer to him, her expression uncharacteristically sharp.

"I suppose I should be grateful for what you've given me. And now I have something to give to you."

He smiled down at her. "And what's that, my dear?"

The blade appeared out of nowhere, aiming straight at his throat. Corosi dropped his cup of wine and staggered back, blood spattering his face.

Sofia looked down and gaped in surprise at the tip of a sword protruding from her chest. Her mouth moved silently as she looked back up at Corosi. The dagger that had previously been hidden in her hand dropped to the floor.

Armstrong yanked his sword out, and Sofia collapsed to the floor. She stared up at Armstrong with blood oozing from her lips and shook her head in disbelief. He watched her dispassionately as he wiped his sword on a rag and sheathed it. He stayed silent until she went still with glassy unblinking eyes.

"What is going on?" Corosi demanded, his heart hammering in his chest.

"I'm sorry, signore," Armstrong said, handing over another clean rag. "I didn't think she'd actually go through with it."

Corosi wiped his face with the rag. "Why didn't you come to me before this?"

"She made her proposal for me to team up with her and kill you while you were inside the Hospitaller palace. Had she not gone through with her attempt to murder you, I would have told you this evening."

"She thought you would betray me?"

Armstrong nodded. "Because of greed. She didn't want you to take all the treasure for yourself. I tried to convince her that you wouldn't, but as you can see, she didn't agree."

"Then I owe you my life."

Armstrong stepped toward him and took the rag back.

"We still have a bargain, do we not?"

Armstrong suddenly seemed very large in this small room. Corosi was fit for his age, but no match for a knight in his prime. For a moment, he wondered if this Englishman would complete the murder that Sofia had attempted.

"You want land and you want command of a company of men," Corosi said quickly but as calmly as he could so as not to reveal that Armstrong intimidated him. "I can ensure that you will get both in Florence."

"If we find the treasure."

"Even if we don't. You have proven your loyalty to me. I will make sure you are my trusted commander when I become leader of Florence. In truth, I will become leader of Florence because I have you at my side."

Armstrong regarded him for a long moment, then stepped away. Corosi let out a breath of relief as Armstrong wrapped Sofia's lifeless corpse in a blanket and threw her over his shoulder.

"I'm glad to hear you say all that, Signore Corosi."

Then he was gone with Sofia's body. Corosi fell into his bed, his stomach roiling over how close he'd come to death, the feeling identical to when he'd been saved in the same way from Domenico Ramberti's blade nearly four decades ago. It was only by thinking about the treasure that he was eventually able to calm his nerves.

61

FERAKLOS CASTLE

Other than stopping at a creek to water the horses, Fox and Willa had cantered most of the way down the east coast of Rhodes. The road was little more than a dirt track, but it was easy to follow. Though they'd passed small stands of trees, the dry terrain was comprised mostly of spindly bushes.

When they exited a ravine with the sun low in the sky, two fortresses came into view. In the distance was the Acropolis of Lindos hovering over a town of houses all painted white. Nearer to them was a stone castle built atop a lonely promontory.

There was not a single homestead in its vicinity. Parts of the walls were already crumbling, evidence of its neglect. According to the brief talk Willa had with Sir Harold while she was bandaging him, the Hospitallers abandoned Feraklos soon after they'd conquered the island in 1310, concentrating their forces in Rhodes City while they established their newfound foothold. That meant when Domenico Ramberti arrived on his ship three years later, there would have been no Hospitallers in the vicinity to observe his Templars hiding the treasure. The castle looked as if it had been deserted since then.

They rode up to the base of the outcropping, the castle high above them and the sea far below.

"It could be any stairway associated with the castle," Fox said as they dismounted. "The clue isn't specific enough to tell us." He had memorized the final two lines and said them out loud:

There, circle west from the stairway to a faithful rock in the Templar's true colors.

Disturbing its peace will lead to proof of the king's duplicity and
fortune's fate.

"Do you really think Ramberti would have hidden a treasure inside a castle of his rival?"

Fox shook his head. "The whole thing seems strange. The castle must have been abandoned when Ramberti hid the treasure, but he'd know they might come back. He must have had no other choice. Hiding it inside the castle would seem much riskier than outside, so let's start by going around the base."

Fox took the spade he'd brought in case the treasure was buried underground. They walked west looking for a stairway, but when they reached the north side, the slope of the outcropping was nearly vertical all the way to the water below, and no stairs were visible.

Looking out at the water, Fox could see they were still more than a hundred feet above sea level. Below them was the half-moon beach Giovanni told them about. A rickety old rowboat was the only object on the sand.

"Look," Willa said, pointing to the north. "They've arrived."

Fox followed her gaze until he saw a ship far in the distance past the headland. He couldn't make out any details, but it had the same size, shape, and number of masts as the *Cara Signora*. In any case, it was too small to be the *Drago Marino*.

"If that's really them," Fox said, "they won't be here until sundown. Let's continue our search. Otherwise, we'll have to wait until morning."

They walked around to the other side of the promontory.

"There are the stairs," Willa said.

They hadn't been visible until now because the lower section was in disrepair. Fox could just make out weathered stones winding upward to the castle above.

"I see why the Hospitallers no longer use Feraklos," he said. He pointed at the Acropolis of Lindos to the south. "That fortress has nearly the same view and a nice town below to supply it."

"Will the people in Lindos be able to see us retrieving the treasure?" Willa asked.

"Not if Giovanni anchors the *Cara Signora* on the north side of the promontory. Their view of the ship will be completely blocked."

"Good. The clue says we must circle west to find a rock in the Templars' true colors."

"Red and white. They were known for going into battle wearing white tabards with red crosses on them. But what does it mean to be a faithful rock?"

Willa shrugged. "It's godly in some way?"

"I've never heard of a pious stone."

"Perhaps we'll know it when we see it. Look for anything unusual."

They began walking around from the base of the stairs toward the western side of the outcropping. Fox took the more treacherous path higher up while Willa took the lower area.

"We must have passed it already or we're wrong about the color," he said, inspecting every rock as he walked. "I don't think it will be small. It would have to be large enough to spot."

"But not so unusual as to stand out as valuable. Ramberti wouldn't want to risk someone taking it."

"Right. So it won't be gold or obsidian or anything else precious."

"What if it's covered in dirt after all this time?"

"If we can't find it tonight, we'll bring a broom tomorrow and sweep clean every rock on this hill."

They crisscrossed back and forth in their search. Fox nearly wrenched his ankle several times when he misplaced a foot. Ramberti certainly hadn't made it easy on them.

Twice he passed the remnants of an old rockslide, worried that it had covered up the stone they needed to find.

The sun was now descending rapidly. They would have to end their search soon.

"I don't see anything strange or distinctive," Willa said. "Certainly no '*faithful rock*.'"

"I don't, either."

"Do you need help looking over that large pile?" she asked, indicating the rockslide.

"I suppose it can't hurt. Perhaps a portion of the rock will still be identifiable under all of that."

He gave her a hand up to it, and they began looking at each rock from opposite sides. But they all seemed like unremarkable stones that had cascaded down from above.

When he got to the base of the rockslide, a white flash caught his eye.

"I think I might have something." He waved Willa over as he bent down to look more closely.

Willa kneeled beside him and used the edge of her kirtle to wipe off a rock the size of a platter that was wedged into the pile. When she finished, she gasped.

The rock was now clearly revealed as made of some kind of white mineral with veins of dull red running through it. The veins crossed each other in the center in a manner reminiscent of the Templar cross.

"*A faithful rock in the Templars' true colors*,'" he said in wonder.

"This is it!" Willa exclaimed. "Now we just need to disturb its peace."

"It seems like the rockslide has already done that."

"Perhaps a message on the underside of the rock will show us the way into the place where Ramberti hid the treasure. This is the final clue. It has to be in the side of this hill somewhere."

Fox put his hand around the stone, but it was firmly wedged in by the surrounding rocks. He couldn't budge it with his fingers.

"I'm glad we brought this spade," he said. "We'll need many more when Giovanni and his crew arrive. But if we have to dig out this entire hillside, I don't know how we can get it done before Corosi and his men arrive."

He stood and pushed the spade into the crevice underneath the stone so that he could lever it out. Even with the tool, the rock didn't want to move.

With a great heave, Fox pressed down on the end of the spade with all of his might. The rock finally slipped out and tumbled down the hill.

"I'll get it," Willa said and was about to follow it down, but Fox grabbed her arm. The rocks above were groaning and creaking, and he suddenly realized that they weren't the remains of a rockslide at all. They had been stacked there in that exact manner.

"Hurry!" he yelled, yanking her to the side. "It's coming down!"

They ran out of the way as the stones began to follow the "faithful rock" down the hill. They fell with a tremendous thunder, kicking up a cloud of dust that obscured the sky.

When all was still again, Willa said, "What happened?"

"That rock was like the keystone in an arch. Without it in place, the entire pile of carefully placed rocks was designed to fall."

"Designed?"

"The Templars were known to have master builders among them. Ramberti must have brought one with him when he stashed the treasure away. Imagine if an earthquake had jostled the stones loose. Someone else would have found the treasure long before us."

After the dust cleared, an opening in the hill taller than a man was revealed. With the sun so low, they could see nothing but darkness in the cave.

Fox ran to Zephyr and got two torches. He brought them back and gave one to Willa before lighting them with his flint and some kindling.

Willa looked at him with both apprehension and wonder. "What do you think is in there?"

"Let's find out."

"You don't think there are... dead bodies?"

Fox shook his head. "Don't worry. This isn't consecrated ground. Even if some of his companions had died along the journey, Ramberti never would have buried them here." That seemed to put her at ease. "Are you ready?"

She nodded. Fox led the way inside. The gloom soon swallowed them, and only the barest hint of light from the setting sun followed them in. The walls and ceiling had been carved by manmade tools, and the pathway had been pounded flat.

Something glinted in the flickering light of the torches.

"Do you see that?" Willa asked in a hushed tone.

"I see it," Fox said, "but I can hardly believe it."

Ahead of them was a huge box overflowing with gold coins. French livres, Florentine florins, Byzantine bezants, and Venetian ducats littered the ground around it.

Willa ran her hands over the bright pieces of gold that still looked as polished as the day they were minted.

"There must be a fortune here. But where's the letter about Signore Corosi? Is it buried among the coins?"

"This can't be all of it," Fox said.

"You sound disappointed. We're looking at a king's ransom here."

"The Templars were supposed to be the richest organization in history. Remember, the reason they were destroyed was because they had lent the king of France a sum so exorbitant that even he couldn't pay it back. I don't think Ramberti would have sailed halfway across the world to stow this one box here."

He held the torch higher, but the blackness receded into the distance. He could tell from the echo of his voice that the chasm went far deeper into the mountain.

"You really think there's more than this?" Willa said.

"I'd wager it."

They walked another step and Willa pointed at an object jutting from the wall.

"That looks like another torch. Do you think it still works? It might provide us more light."

"Let's try it."

Fox touched his flame to it. The torch must have been covered in pitch because it lit up immediately.

Then something else happened that surprised Fox.

A sizzling set of sparks raced from the torch along the wall until it reached another torch ten feet away. That one lit as well and the sparks continued down the cave, which was now revealed as a tunnel.

One by one, torches blazed to life, lighting up all the way around a curve in the passage and beyond.

Willa gasped as the full scope of what Ramberti had hidden

was now visible in front of them. Fox's jaw dropped as he took it all in.

Gold, jewels, and priceless objects filled the entire cave to bursting. Centuries of accumulated wealth lay before them.

And somewhere in all of that was the letter that would set Luciana free.

FORTUNE'S FATE

Rhodes

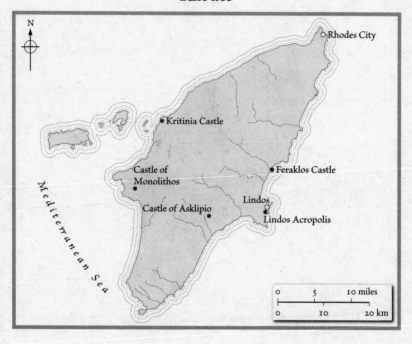

62

Now that the tunnel was well lit by the torches, Willa could extinguish her light and wander down the narrow path through the lavish array of invaluable artifacts, precious gems, awe-inspiring objects, and bright gold in every form. She could barely catch her breath with each new discovery.

"Do you think we'll even have space on the *Cara Signora* for all this?" she asked Gerard, who was just as in awe of the hoard as she was.

"I'm sure we'll find a place for everything, even if we have to pile it up on the deck. I just hope the ship doesn't sink under its weight."

Willa ran her hand over an ornate golden shrine shaped like a cathedral that rivaled the Pala d'Oro for opulence.

"Where did this all come from?"

"It was all donated to the Templars," Fox answered as he picked up a clutch of gold coins and let them slip through his fingers. "Some of it by nobles who joined the order, some from families who believed in their mission of Crusade, some by pilgrims who deposited their money with the Templars to protect their fortunes while they traveled but never returned."

"No wonder the French king wanted to seize this treasure for himself."

"These riches are the reason why kings, dukes, and earls from across the continent funded their armies and acquired holdings by borrowing from the Templars."

"I see why Signore Corosi was eager to learn from them. He seems to be on his way to replacing the Templars as Europe's preeminent banking empire."

"With all this, he would become the most powerful man in Europe. Even the pope himself would come to Corosi for money to expand his palace in Avignon."

They kept moving along the treasure trove looking for anything that might contain a letter, with Willa taking the right side and Gerard the left.

She marveled at every new discovery. A row of crates was filled with all manner of serving dishes and utensils fit for a royal banquet—plates, beakers, flagons, tankards, goblets, bowls, and platters of all shapes and sizes made of silver, gold, bronze, and pewter, steel knives with carved ivory handles, a golden tureen crafted to resemble a ship in full sail, rock crystal ewers carved with climbing vines, drinking horns with gilded mounts.

The next set of crates was just as incredible. They contained liturgical objects of all types, including crosses, pyxes, chalices, and pattens. Beside them were piles of aquamanilia—pouring vessels for wine and ale, all of them made of precious metals and shaped into creatures of various kinds. Lions, dragons, unicorns, eagles, and beasts that Willa had never seen before made her realize that the privileged life of the lady she had served did not touch on the wealth that the truly rich possessed.

She was so taken by each item that Gerard's muted "hmmm" from behind her barely registered. She turned to see him standing over a vast array of gems and jewelry. He had something in his hand that he quickly stuffed into the purse under his tunic.

"What do you have there?" she asked. "I think there's enough to go around. You don't need to steal anything."

He whipped his head toward her in surprise, as if he'd been caught at something naughty.

"Oh, it's just something that I might want for later."

"A brooch?" she teased. "Or perhaps a golden coronet studded with rubies?"

"You know how difficult it is to find one to fit my head."

"So you're not going to tell me what that was?"

"I'll show you when the time is right," he said with a conspiratorial smile.

He seemed pleased with himself, so she didn't press him further. Though her curiosity was piqued, she changed the subject.

"Why do you think all of this is on display? Wouldn't it have been easier to simply stow it away in the manner it was transported, packed away in these crates, boxes, and bags?"

"Perhaps Ramberti was trying to take inventory of everything after the mad dash to get it all out of France. The Templars were legendary record keepers."

"And then he didn't bother to pack it all away again?"

Gerard tilted his head to acknowledge the point.

"Maybe he wanted to make an impression on Luciana and Matteo," Willa continued. "He expected them to find all of this just a few years after it was hidden, and he wanted them to think that these immense riches meant the restoration of the order was possible. Given his obsession with the glory of the Templars, he strikes me as someone who would make a grand gesture like that."

"That would explain the torches set up to light all at once."

Willa glanced at the string of torches and the novel method for connecting them.

"I've never seen that type of sparkling fire before. Do you know what it is?"

"I believe the answer is here," Gerard said, moving on from the jewels. He pointed to a dozen barrels lined up against the wall. One of the lids was off. Gerard dipped his hand into it, and black powder poured through his fingers. He put his hand up to his nose, then held it out for her to sniff. She recoiled from the acrid odor.

"I remember the smell from the battlefield at Crécy," Gerard said. "Our side had weapons called cannons that shot iron balls at great speeds. This powder was used as a fuel to propel them."

Unusual characters were scrawled on the side of the barrels.

"Is that writing?"

Gerard peered at it. "That looks like the language of the Far East. These barrels must have been transported over the great trade routes from China. This powder is worth its weight in gold."

Willa couldn't imagine how far the barrels had traveled. She was in awe at seeing something from the other edge of the world, created by foreign peoples she would never meet.

"Do you think we might go there someday? Isabel and I read the tales of Marco Polo, and he traveled there."

"Who knows where our travels will take us?" Gerard said.

Her eye was distracted by the cache of weapons beyond the barrels. She hurried over to them and looked wide-eyed at swords of different curvatures and lengths, maces, pikes, axes, and daggers with bejeweled hilts and sheaths.

But it was the bows and arrows that intrigued her. There were dozens of bows and a crate of arrows. The bows were reminiscent of Gerard's recurve bow from the Holy Land, and all of them were as expertly crafted. She plucked the one she admired most— inlaid with a dense black wood and ivory to create a pattern of delicate leaves—and felt the finely balanced heft. The grip fit her hand perfectly.

"You've always wanted one of your own, haven't you?" Gerard said.

"It's beautiful."

"It's meant for you. Take it."

She looked at him in surprise. "Do you think so?"

"Why not? There are plenty more if Giovanni's crew wants them. But you deserve your pick of them." He picked up an arrow bag and stuffed it with shafts and a bowstring, then handed it to her.

Willa could hardly withhold her excitement at having her very own bow. She threw her arms around Gerard's neck and kissed him passionately. It was a long time before they pulled themselves away.

"Have as many of the bows as you like," Gerard teased.

"No, I only need one. The right one." She couldn't wait to try it out.

They continued their search for the letter. More unique and beautiful objects awaited them—shrines and reliquaries that might have been holding anything from pieces of the true cross to locks of the Virgin Mary's hair, thick manuscripts with ornamented covers, finely woven tapestries, painted stone statues of kings, saints, and the Virgin and Child. It would take weeks just to count up all the riches that the tunnel contained, and they hadn't yet explored the entire length of it.

"I've found something," Gerard said.

Willa rushed over to him. Set on top of a finely carved wooden chest covered in a rich figured silk, as if on display, was a small box no bigger than a loaf of bread. Its sides were entirely composed of delicate gold filigree filled with lustrous blue enamel and studded with gems. Gerard pointed at its lid. It was inlaid with an emblem of two riders on a single horse carrying shields showing the Templar cross.

"Those are the arms of the Knights Templar."

He unlatched the clasp and lifted the lid. Inside was a parchment letter with a broken seal showing an enthroned ruler holding a scepter topped with the fleur-de-lis, the symbol of the French king.

The letter that Corosi feared would destroy him was now in their hands.

63

After the *Cara Signora* got as close to shore as she could without fear of running aground, Giovanni dropped anchor and had his men prepare their two skiffs while Luciana eagerly looked to the beach for signs of Willa and Fox. She had to keep pushing strands of hair out of her face, loosened from her braids by the breeze blowing in toward land. The dusk made it hard to tell if anyone was in the vicinity of the beach, but she couldn't see any horses.

She insisted on being in the first boat to shore, climbing down the rope ladder despite Giovanni's protestations. They pushed off with two rowers, giving room for the rest of the crew to lower the second skiff.

Halfway to shore, she spotted someone at the base of the promontory supporting Feraklos Castle waving a torch back and forth, and she caught a glimpse of Fox's distinctive horse. Apparently they had found something, but she didn't want to get her hopes up too much just to have them dashed.

As soon as they landed, Giovanni helped her from the boat, and they climbed the hill, where they met Fox and Willa. Both of them were beaming.

Luciana felt the first flutters of excitement. "You found it?"

Willa nodded. "We found everything."

"The letter?"

"Come and see," Fox said.

"And the treasure?" Giovanni asked.

"If you don't lay eyes on it yourself, you won't believe it."

Luciana held Giovanni's hand as they walked toward the hill, with Fox explaining how they uncovered the opening to the cave that she could now see was brightly lit.

The moment they saw the first glimmers of gold, she and Giovanni halted in disbelief. The two crewmen with them whistled and shrieked, running toward the chest of gold coins.

Luciana was so overwhelmed at the sight that she felt lightheaded, but she drew strength from Giovanni's grip. Willa took them on a tour of what they had found so far.

Giovanni turned to his two crewmen and said, "Get every man we can spare from the ship over here now and begin loading everything on the ship immediately. I want it all on board by the time the sun rises."

The two crewmen whooped and sprinted back down to the beach.

"We should leave by then whether we've moved it all or not," Fox said. "Corosi will be coming as fast as he can once he discovers the location."

"The wind is high tonight and there's only a quarter moon. It's enough light for us to row by, but sailing in these conditions along the coast will be hazardous for a ship as large as his."

"He might risk it."

"We'll keep watch. Any lights on the horizon, and we'll set sail."

Fox nodded. He tapped a barrel. "Take care with these."

"What are they filled with?"

"Black powder. Used to fire cannons."

Giovanni looked at them warily. "I'll tell my men."

Willa guided them past all manner of gold, jewels, and assorted weapons, coming to a stop in front of a jewel-encrusted box inscribed with a seal Luciana recognized as belonging to the Templars. She looked at Willa.

"Is this…?"

"Open it," Willa said.

With trembling fingers, she lifted the lid and saw a parchment within. There it was, the letter she had been dreaming about. She only hoped it would be her deliverance.

She picked it up and unfolded it. Her hands were shaking so much that she was having trouble reading the words in the soft light. Fox saw her distress, gently took the letter from her, and read aloud:

Philip IV, by the grace of God, august king of the French, to His Holiness Pope Clement V.

We have been sorely disappointed that the Ecumenical Council in Vienne, convened by Your Holiness for the sole purpose of hearing testimony against the Poor Fellow-Soldiers of Christ and of the Temple of Solomon, has failed to make a finding necessitating the dissolution of the order. We therefore send our servant, Sir Riccardo Corosi, to share that a written confession has been devised as a declaration that not only are the loathsome crimes of which the Templar knights have been so publicly accused true, but also that they were committed with the full knowledge and complicity of Your Holiness. The confession is properly sealed under the name of one of the highest-ranking knights of the order, Sir Domenico Ramberti, to which my servant, Sir Riccardo, can personally swear when he delivers this message. We hope that Your Holiness will consequently see the benefit of convincing the hallowed Council that the Templar order should be dissolved and its knights condemned, without the aforesaid letter ever being brought before the council.

In a gesture of good faith, we beseech you to absolve the messenger who has carried this communication, Sir Riccardo, of his vows of poverty and chastity taken as a Knight Templar. We hope and expect to see Sir Riccardo return to Paris with the information that Your Holiness has acted in accordance with the grace of God in attending to all the matters imparted in this letter.

Given in Paris on 25 January in the year of grace 1312

Giovanni was slack-jawed as he spoke. "Then Signore Corosi actually *is* a Templar knight?"

Fox nodded. "This letter was intercepted by your father and your grandfather before it ever made it to the pope. My guess is that Corosi didn't dare tell the French king that the letter had been intercepted, let alone ask for another. When the king never heard back from Corosi or the pope, he must have decided to take his army to Vienne to force the pope to disband the Templars. Corosi, meanwhile, simply acted as though the pope had absolved him and never told anyone the truth."

"But he knew the danger that my father posed," Luciana said, "since he could swear that he had not written the letter, but rather could testify that my husband had colluded with the king of France against the pope. That's why Riccardo killed my father."

"What?" all three of her listeners said in unison.

"Yes, just before we left the ship in Rhodes City, my husband admitted it. When my father's puzzle arrived, he feared that my father would eventually come to Italy and reveal all of Riccardo's lies. So he went to Paris and killed him. Now that we've found the king's letter, we can finally avenge my father by taking away all my husband holds dear."

Giovanni seemed dumbfounded to hear that the man whom he had used to think of as a father had actually murdered his grandfather. "Then everything Signore Corosi owns would be…"

"Forfeit the moment this letter makes it to Avignon. The pope can rightly claim that the king unsuccessfully threatened his predecessor and that Corosi was never absolved of his vows, allowing the Church to seize everything Corosi owns. The current pope is deeply in debt to Corosi and would only be too overjoyed to have an excuse to take possession of his estate," said Luciana.

Giovanni looked alarmed. "Even your dowry?"

"I shouldn't think so," Willa said. "If he took the order's vows, including that of chastity, then the marriage to your mother would be annulled as if it had never happened. Any property included in her dowry before the wedding would be returned to her."

Luciana took the letter back from Fox.

"Thank you both for what you've given me. You can never know what difference this will make in my life and for my only remaining son."

Willa took her hands and said, "It's our pleasure. We hope this frees you to live out the rest of your life in peace."

Giovanni gripped Fox's hand. "You are an impressive knight, Sir Gerard, blessed with resolve, intelligence, and kindness."

"I'm only happy to see you and your mother reunited. I hope you see that she will need you now more than ever."

"And I, her."

Luciana thought she saw Fox's eyes dampen, too, before he looked away.

"There's something else," Willa said. She nodded down to the box.

There was another letter inside. Luciana had been so focused on the king's missive that she had overlooked it.

The seal on it was her father's. It was unbroken. On the front it read in Italian, "*For Luciana and Matteo*."

She picked it up, afraid to break the seal. Willa and Fox moved discreetly away, while Giovanni stepped toward her.

"Open it, Mamma."

Luciana took a deep breath, her hands now steady, and cracked the seal in half.

As she unfolded it and began to read, she could hear her father's voice, as if he were there with her.

To my dearest daughter Luciana and my faithful squire Matteo,

As you are reading this letter, together you have successfully deciphered the clues I sent you as I fully expected you would. I sincerely wish I could be with you here now, but I fear that my fate lies elsewhere. Our ship was sighted off the coast of Rhodes after it was damaged in a storm, and we knew the Knights of the Hospital of St. John would soon find us. Our only chance was to offload the treasure under this forsaken castle and sink the ship. But I know that our efforts will not have been in vain, for surely the letter from King Philip will reveal to His Holiness the Pope that he was threatening my brethren for his own ends and that they are wholly innocent of the slanderous charges against them. Thus this treasure that I entrust to you will be used to re-establish the Order of the Temple of Solomon for the benefit and the glory of the Lord.

I am most proud of you, my lovely and clever Luciana, and I so desire to see the lady that I know you have become. I take solace in the thought of you and Matteo joining to produce a legacy and love that will endure.

Given in Rhodes on March 23 in the year of Grace 1313

Luciana lifted her eyes from the letter, this time with tears streaming down her cheeks. She cupped the face of Giovanni, who had been reading beside her.

"You are our legacy and our love," she said.

"I wish I could have met him."

"Every time I look at you, I see both of them. Your father and my father would have been so proud to know what kind of man and leader you've become. I think my father was mistaken in his belief that anything could have saved the order, but it was his idealism and honorable conduct that made me love him so much." She smiled at Giovanni. "I can see both of those qualities in his grandson."

After they shared a silent moment together, Fox approached them while Willa began placing objects back into their containers for easier transport.

"Pardon my intrusion," Fox said, "but I believe we are pressed for time."

Giovanni kissed his mother's hand and nodded. He rose to his full height and his face set into a look of iron will. He stalked toward the cave entrance and barked out orders to his crew who were just arriving.

"Men, time's a-wasting! Don't spend precious moments gawking. You'll get your fair share. Close up these crates with whatever you can fit inside and start moving them down to the beach."

Luciana put the letters into her kirtle. Until the king's letter was in the hands of the pope himself, she didn't plan to let it out of her sight. The second one she placed close to her heart.

64

After the four of them and the crew worked furiously all night to empty the cave, there were only a couple of chests of gold left inside. The holds of the *Cara Signora* were jam-packed, with crates on her deck still to be stowed. Fox, exhausted from lack of sleep and the nonstop transfer of the cave's contents to the beach below, was fastening the lids of the last chests as the first rays of sunlight were peaking over the horizon.

Willa returned from watering the horses at a nearby stream.

"How much more is there?" she asked as she led Zephyr and Comis to stand by their saddles.

"Only these two chests."

"Only?" Willa said with a laugh. "They hold more gold than we've ever seen in our lives. The sole reason they didn't use larger ones is because they'd be too heavy to carry."

"I suppose one loses perspective after seeing the vast amount of riches that we've moved tonight. Did you see if either of the skiffs are on the way back yet?"

She shook her head. "They're still unloading them at the ship. But it seems like everything we've carried down to the beach has been taken away."

"Giovanni said there's barely room to move around below decks. The only spot open is the stall for the horses."

"Where will we load Zephyr and Comis?" Willa asked since the skiffs were too small to carry horses, and they'd have no way to get them from the small boats onto the ship anyway.

Fox nodded to the town situated under the acropolis. "There is a dock over in Lindos. We'll ride over there and the *Cara Signora* will meet us." He secured the lid on the final crate. "That's it."

"I didn't think we'd get it all done in one night."

"Money and fear are two great motivators. Now that the crew has seen all of this, they're afraid to lose it."

"This amount of money can make people do awful things as well."

"Which is why we can't let Corosi get his hands on it."

"We won't keep the reliquaries, crosses, and other liturgical artifacts, will we?"

"We can't sell them, and melting them down for the gold would be a sin. They'll make fine donations to needy parishes."

The relics in their golden and gem-studded housings would be especially welcome. They'd draw pilgrims who would then donate money to the local church as an offering.

"Don't you loathe giving anything back to the Church?" Willa asked as they began to saddle the horses.

"To the Church, yes. To churches, no. But I don't think they deserve anything that isn't religious in nature."

Willa looked as if she'd had a sudden thought. "Would the return of all these religious objects be enough to convince the Church to absolve you?"

That brought Fox up short. He hadn't considered that possibility.

"I suppose it could. As much as the Church professes not to compromise its principles, the restoration of these sacred treasures might sway the pope to rescind my excommunication."

"Luciana already made clear that she only wants enough of a share of the treasure to start over with her son and her freedom. The rest of the gold coins and gems will be split by the crew. I'm sure Luciana would let us turn these riches over to the Church. When we return to Venice, we'll transport everything to Avignon. The pope will *have* to pardon you!"

"I don't know if it will be that easy. I was excommunicated for assaulting a cardinal. The pope may not take so kindly to absolving me for that. He might think it sets a poor example."

"We have to try it."

Gerard opened his mouth, but Willa interrupted him.

"If you're going to continue to protest, you can stop right now."

Gerard's mouth snapped shut. He gave her a smile and nodded.

"Good, then we'll talk to Luciana and Giovanni about it. I'm sure they'll agree. It does seem a shame that after everything Luciana's father went through, his dreams for the Templars are lost," she said.

Fox buckled Zephyr's reins and shrugged. "There are none left except for Corosi, and he's definitely not who Luciana's father had in mind when he foresaw the Templars rising again. I think Luciana knows that her father's vision for resurrecting the order was always impractical, even if it kept him going for so long."

"But lawfully, doesn't this all belong to the Hospitallers now?" Willa asked.

"Did it look like the Hospitallers need this money?"

"You're probably right. I do want to send something back to Mother Catherine at La Sacra di San Michele. They certainly could use the funds."

"That's a fine idea," Fox said. "What about a reliquary and one of those golden shrines?"

Willa smiled and nodded. "You're a generous man."

"After what we brought upon the abbey, it's the least we could do."

Now that the horses were saddled and their bags attached, Fox looked south toward Lindos. He estimated they'd easily be there by mid-morning and away long before…

A ship was rounding the point below the acropolis, coming their way fast thanks to the brisk wind blowing this direction. Fox's stomach sank when he recognized it.

Willa came up beside him. "Is that…?"

"The *Drago Marino*. They must have sailed far off the coast overnight to avoid any chance of running aground and overshot the mark."

Corosi's ship was hidden from the view of anyone on the *Cara Signora* by the promontory crowned by Feraklos Castle. At this rate, she'd arrive before Giovanni could even raise sails.

Fox ran around the hill with Willa on his heels. When he finally could see the *Cara Signora*, it was as he feared. Her sails were stowed, and they were still hauling crates up from the two skiffs. No one on board could see the approaching danger.

Fox jumped up and down, shouting and waving his arms, but it was clear they were too far away to be understood even if someone spotted them.

"Come on," he said.

He ran back to Zephyr and leaped on. Willa did the same on Comis. They raced down to the beach.

As soon as Zephyr's hooves splashed into the water, Fox jumped off. He shouted his warning, but they were still too far away to be understood. By the time a skiff returned to shore, it would be too late to do anything. Corosi and his larger crew would massacre everyone on the *Cara Signora* and get away with the treasure.

The rowboat that had been abandoned on the beach was their only hope.

Fox strapped on Legend, took his bow and arrows from Zephyr's saddle, and pulled the boat into the water. Before he could stop her, Willa climbed in holding her bow and arrows from the treasure.

"You're staying here," he said.

"By thunder I am," Willa replied, picking up one of the oars. "You'll get to the ship faster with both of us rowing."

Fox got into the boat with her. "You're going to hit me with that oar if I continue to argue, aren't you?"

"Only if I don't shoot you with my new bow first."

"You make a persuasive case," he said, pushing them off the beach with his oar.

They both began rowing as hard as they could. Comis whinnied as they left, while Zephyr stamped his feet and chuffed.

"Do you think they'll be all right?" Willa asked. She didn't say it, but her implication was clear.

If we don't make it back.

"Of course, they will be," Fox said with a glance at his beloved. "They have each other."

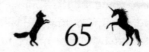# 65

With the *Drago Marino* bearing down like an onrushing leviathan, Willa and Gerard pulled on the oars as hard as they could to get to the *Cara Signora* and raise the alarm. Once they alerted Giovanni to the danger, he ordered the crew to weigh anchor so they could get underway as quickly as possible. They didn't bother to raise the skiffs, extinguish the lanterns that had been lit for their late-night endeavors, or stow the netting and ropes they'd been using to bring the cargo aboard. It was a race to raise the anchor and sails, though Willa worried that it was already too late.

She strung her new bow and took a test shot at the mast, hitting it dead center. This bow had a different feel from Gerard's, but the weight and the draw were perfect for her smaller hands. The refined decorations and lighter heft made her wonder if this might have been a woman's bow before it came into the Templars' possession.

Giovanni approached her and Gerard and spoke in a low voice.

"We won't be able to outrun them, not with this wind. We'd have to try to tack out of the cove right past them."

"Would they be able to intercept us?" Gerard asked.

"I know this captain's strategy. He'll get close enough to rake our deck with crossbow bolts. I'll lose half my men in the first volley."

"What about grounding the ship?" Willa said. "Then we could flee on foot."

"No," Luciana said as she walked up to them. "I won't run from my husband anymore, and I won't let him have the treasure."

"But you can take the king's letter and free yourself."

Luciana patted her chest. "The letter stays with me from now on. If Riccardo wants it, he'll have to rip it from my dead body."

"Fleeing on foot wouldn't matter anyway," Giovanni said. "We don't have enough horses for everyone and my fath… Signore Corosi would send every man on his ship after us. We wouldn't get very far."

"You go," Luciana said to Willa and Fox. "This is no longer your fight. You've done more than enough for me."

"We're not leaving," Gerard said. "And I think there's a way we can improve our chances in a battle."

"How so?" Luciana asked. "I saw the crossbows that Giovanni mentioned."

Gerard looked at Giovanni. "You said your men used to be soldiers."

"That's true. They'll fight well, but we are outnumbered more than two to one."

"Do they know how to use a bow?"

Giovanni nodded. "They are experienced archers."

"Then drop anchor again. Although we only have enough arrows for a few volleys, our best chance is to arm all of your men and let Corosi come to us."

"But we won't be able to maneuver."

"If your men are busy operating the ship, they can't fight. The bows and arrows from the Templar hoard give us our only advantage."

"What's that?"

"Surprise."

From his perch on the forecastle of the *Drago Marino*, Corosi rested his hand on the hilt of his sword, peering at the *Cara Signora* as his ship sped toward her. The captain had strategically sailed farther out to sea so that they could come at Feraklos from an unexpected direction to ambush them before they could attempt an escape, and it seemed that his strategy had worked perfectly.

"We've caught them by surprise," said Armstrong, who was standing beside him with a sword on his belt and a crossbow in the crook of his elbow. "The sails aren't even half raised, and it's still at anchor."

"Giovanni must not be as competent a sea captain as I thought," Corosi said. After almost two decades of being apart, he only saw more and more evidence of Matteo's parentage in Giovanni's unthinking actions.

They were still three hundred yards out, so he couldn't see any faces clearly yet. Every man on board the *Drago Marino* not actively running his ship was equipped with a loaded crossbow like Armstrong. As soon as they closed within a hundred yards, they would launch their bolts, taking out as many people on deck as possible before boarding. Then they'd drop sails, and it would be a simple matter to execute anyone left alive. If they were lucky, his opponents had already found the Templar treasure and had loaded it on board.

He supposed Luciana would be below decks, out of the danger from the crossbow bolts. That would leave him with the distasteful task of killing her, but he was ready to do what needed to be done. She had defied him long enough.

Armstrong leaned forward and squinted at their target. "Where is everyone?"

Not only was the deck of the *Cara Signora* empty, but there were no men working the rigging or doing any of the other normal tasks to get a ship ready to sail. In fact, Corosi couldn't see a single person.

"Perhaps they fled in their skiffs."

Armstrong shook his head. "We would have seen them rowing to shore. Something's wrong."

"Then they're either cowering in terror or waiting until we've boarded to fight back, which is a fool's game. With our superior numbers, we'll have no problem defeating them."

"Perhaps. But I want to be ready for them to appear just the same." Armstrong yelled to the crew. "Crossbows at the ready!"

Armstrong's mercenaries and the available *Drago Marino* crew lined the bulwarks and raised their crossbows to shooting position.

Corosi called back over his shoulder to the captain who was standing near the aftcastle at the helm.

"Get us as close as you can!"

He waved back his acknowledgment. The *Drago Marino* stayed on course directly at the *Cara Signora*.

When they were within two hundred yards, every person on Giovanni's carrack rose in unison. They must have been lying on the deck out of sight. He even spotted the two women in their brightly colored gowns.

"What are they doing?" Corosi wondered.

He went cold when he heard an unintelligible shout and every man plus Willa raised bows, drew back, and loosed a hail of arrows in their direction. The shafts flew up high in an arcing trajectory.

"No!" Armstrong cried out. "Everyone down!"

But Corosi knew that it was too late. Some of the men shot their crossbows even though they were still too far away for the bolts to reach their mark. Others did as Armstrong instructed and lay flat on the deck, while a great portion of them ran, looking for somewhere to hide.

Corosi ducked down and pressed himself tightly against the bulwark just as the arrows rained down on them. Armstrong did the same.

Arrows smacked into the *Drago Marino* with the sound of a hailstorm. Half of them seemed to find a victim, with men crying out in agony as the points pierced their unarmored bodies. Corosi saw one of the arrows hit the captain in the center of his chest, and he fell backward with his mouth formed in a silent scream.

The first mate should have taken command, but he was frozen in horror at something in the sky.

Corosi peeked out and saw another volley of arrows coming toward them. They must have shot the next round before the first ones had even landed.

The first mate died as the next arrows came down, taking one through his neck.

Men lay dead and dying across the *Drago Marino*. Corosi could see that their numbers were already cut down by more than a third. Then another volley of arrows fell from the sky. Now their numbers were halved.

He looked over the bulwark again. The arrows had stopped falling. The crew of the *Cara Signora* had instead armed themselves with swords, maces, and hammers.

They were only fifty yards away and closing fast. To Corosi's horror, no one was manning the *Drago Marino*'s tiller, and they were locked on a collision course with the *Cara Signora*. Nothing would prevent their impact with the stern of Giovanni's ship.

Armstrong grabbed the bulwark and jumped to his feet. He leaned over to yank Corosi up by his cloak.

"How dare you!" Corosi snapped at the disrespectful behavior.

"We're all fighting now," he growled. Then he yelled to the men. "Get to your feet, you dogs! Draw your swords and prepare to board them!"

He raised his crossbow and loosed the bolt. It missed Fox by inches.

In turn, Fox raised his bow and shot. It was a perfect aim. If Armstrong's crossbow hadn't deflected the arrow, it would have gone right through his heart.

Fox didn't have time for a second shot. Everyone on the *Cara Signora* scrambled to hold onto anything they could as the *Drago Marino* plowed into her stern. A terrible crack sounded as splintered wood flew into the air.

Armstrong and Corosi were nearly thrown over the bulwark as the *Drago Marino* jolted to a stop, her bow firmly lodged into the carrack. But now all they had to do was leap over the side to get onto the *Cara Signora*.

Corosi noticed that the impact had upended a chest that had been lying on the deck, and its contents had gone flying. Gold was scattered across the wood planking.

He nearly stopped breathing. Luciana had actually found the

treasure. It was his for the taking. Now he had to get that letter and incinerate it, which looked like it would be easy enough, since a lantern had fallen to the deck, igniting the oil inside that spilled. The fire was immediately snuffed out by the nearest crewman, but there were plenty more lanterns still burning where they hung.

He saw Luciana, whose hand was tight on her breast. If she held the letter, that's where it would be.

Armstrong was the first over the side. He turned back to the surviving mercenaries and *Drago Marino* crew.

"If you want to be rich," he shouted, pointing at the gold littering the deck, "come with me and wipe them out!"

Then he sprinted toward Gerard Fox.

66

The volleys of arrows had managed to keep the *Cara Signora* from being overwhelmed immediately, but Fox knew that they were still outnumbered. From her position on the forecastle, Willa was able to pick off several of the *Drago Marino* crew as they rushed across, but they took down an equal number of Giovanni's men with their remaining crossbows.

Fox concentrated on Armstrong, who stalked toward him with his sword in one hand and a wicked dagger in the other.

"You don't have armor this time," Fox said.

"I don't need it," Armstrong replied and slashed at Fox with a vicious series of strikes.

Fox countered each one, but he was in the thick of the battle raging around him. He simultaneously had to fend off blows from several of Armstrong's men who were swinging wildly at any enemy around them. That gave Armstrong an opening to press forward, striking at Fox with unrelenting ferocity.

One stroke of the dagger got especially close and sliced a ribbon from Fox's tunic.

"We could have been comrades in arms," Armstrong said, twirling the blade in his hand.

Fox shook his head. "This was always the way it was going to end between us."

He charged at Armstrong again.

Willa had one arrow left, and it was trained on Gerard and

Armstrong as their swords clashed. She had a high position on the forecastle that gave her a clear view, but they were twisting and turning so fast that she couldn't get a clean shot at Armstrong without fear of hitting Gerard.

He swung Legend around in an effort to finish the fight in one stroke by taking off Armstrong's head, but his adversary ducked under the blade so that the only thing it caught was his ear.

Armstrong howled in pain and staggered to the side. He flailed wildly, his sword striking a lantern that cast burning oil onto a partially folded sail. The canvas erupted in flame, adding to the madness.

"Get out of the way, Gerard," Willa muttered, but he kept interposing himself in front of Armstrong.

Screams from below distracted her. Giovanni was attempting to fend off two attackers who were trying to get to Luciana. The men had backed the mother and son against the wall of the forecastle. If Giovanni went down, his mother was dead.

She didn't hesitate and used her last arrow on one of the men attacking them. Luciana looked up and mouthed her thanks, but Giovanni was still fighting for his life. He pressed his attack forward with a flurry of sword swings, leaving Luciana behind.

Only now did Willa see that Corosi had been waiting for his chance to strike. He raced toward Luciana, and Willa was helpless to stop him.

Before he could reach her, Luciana flung open a door and fled into the ship's interior. Corosi followed her in.

Willa yelled to Giovanni, but he was still engaged with his foe. There was nothing she could do to assist Gerard, so Willa ran down the stairs to the deck. She picked up the sword of the man she had just killed and darted after them.

Luciana saw the pure hatred in Riccardo's eyes as he stalked her. He would gut her for the letter she carried.

She scrambled down the ladder into the main hold. She knew they had stored the rest of the weapons down there, but it was so dimly lit that she couldn't see them. Crates and boxes were piled high, while valuables too large to fit inside them such as the shrines were stacked on top of them.

"Come back here, Luciana!" Riccardo screamed. "I know you have the letter."

Smoke from the fire on the deck above was already wafting down, and bits of flaming canvas floated through the hatches that were still open. She thought it was only a matter of time before the hold was engulfed.

She turned a corner and found herself at the stall where Zephyr and Comis were to be stowed for the trip back to Venice. Even though it had been mucked out, it still stank of manure and hay.

She thought about closing the door behind her to hide, but there was no way to lock it from the inside. She kept going.

Finally, she reached the cache of weapons. She wasn't strong enough for a hammer or mace, and Riccardo was skilled with a sword, so equipping herself with one as well would be foolish.

She took a pike from the pile and turned to face her husband.

When he came around the corner, she thrust the pike at his face, but he dodged the tip and knocked it to the side with his sword. Luciana was barely able to hold on to it and backed up.

"All I want is the king's letter, Luciana."

"All you want is everything in the world."

"That's not true. I don't want you."

Even now, his words stung her.

"You're a pig," she snapped. "I can't believe I was deceived into marriage with you."

"That will end soon enough. Sofia tried to betray me and paid with her life. The same will happen to you."

Even though Sofia had betrayed her mistress as well, Luciana couldn't help but gasp in shock at his callousness. Corosi was so satisfied with her reaction that he didn't hear Willa creeping up behind him with a sword in her hand. Luciana saw her and knew all she had to do was hold his attention a little longer.

"Your cruelty won't pay off. You've lost. This ship is going to the bottom of the sea with your precious treasure on it."

"As long as you and that letter go down with it, it suits me. I'll still be one of the richest men in Florence, ready to wed a new wife, and bed a new mistress."

"Not if I'm still around."

"You won't…"

Luciana didn't know what alerted him—a sound, a shadow, a faint smell even. But he was able to turn just in time to parry the blow from Willa's sword.

He knocked it aside and raised his own weapon. At that moment Luciana rammed her pike forward, piercing Riccardo in his side.

He let out a high-pitched shriek and whipped around, tearing the point from the wound. He grasped his injury and looked genuinely surprised and hurt.

"You stabbed me!" he wailed like an aggrieved child.

Off-balance from the dual attack, he stumbled backward as both Luciana and Willa advanced on him with their weapons. He retreated into the stall where he could defend the entryway.

Luciana didn't think he was mortally wounded, and once he regained his composure, he might find new courage to use his sword as he'd been trained. Better to leave him here.

She slammed the door shut and latched it.

"Hurry!" she said to Willa as she cut the rope securing a stack of crates. "Help me!"

Riccardo rammed the door. The latch barely held.

"Let me out of here, you witch!"

Willa hacked at the rope, too, and it split apart. With their combined efforts, they leaned into the crates and pushed, toppling them over in front of the door. The heavy metal objects inside would hold the door shut long enough to let them escape.

The smoke was building and more burning canvas was landing around them. She could already feel the heat from above.

"We have to get off this ship," Luciana said.

"I know," Willa replied.

Luciana threw the pike down and gave one last look at the door that her husband continued to pound against in abject fury.

"*Addio*, Riccardo."

She and Willa ran to get out of the deathtrap her namesake ship had become.

 67

Fox was breathing hard, which gave Armstrong hope that he was wearing down. He had to admit that Fox was the more accomplished swordsman, but the heretic wasn't used to fighting off an opponent with two blades. The dagger in Armstrong's left hand evened the fight, and all it would take would be a single distraction for him to strike the killing blow.

They ranged around the deck, sometimes clashing with other battling sailors. Despite Fox's attempt to whittle their numbers with the archery attack, Giovanni's crew was close to losing the battle, especially with half of them at the bow being cut off by the fire that was raging amidships.

The two of them circled each other, the fatigue starting to show on both of them.

"You should join your shipmates," Fox said, nodding at the *Drago Marino*. "They see there's not much time left for the *Cara Signora*."

It was apparent that the *Cara Signora* was going down, and the crew of the *Drago Marino* knew it. Though a few were still fighting, a number of them were frantically chopping away at the ship's bow to free it from the *Cara Signora*'s stern before the fire leaped to the other ship. The rest were dashing around the deck and into the holds to carry as much of the treasure back to the *Drago Marino* as possible.

"I'll join them when you're dead," Armstrong said.

"You're a stubborn man, aren't you?"

"It's one of my best qualities."

Armstrong launched himself at Fox, but he misjudged the angle and was off-balance, swinging his sword while supported on his back foot. Fox was able to duck back from the strike and flip his sword up, catching Armstrong on the side of his hand. He cried out in agony, and the sword went flying over the side of the ship, leaving just the long dagger in his left hand.

Armstrong didn't give up, switching the knife to his right hand even though blood was coursing from under his glove. He continued to press the attack using the dagger, but he was at a severe disadvantage. Fox reared back with his sword when someone jumped on his back. It was a huge sailor from the *Drago Marino*. He ripped at Fox's sword arm, and the Damascus-steel blade clattered to the deck.

Armstrong saw an opening and thrust his dagger at Fox, who pivoted using the sailor's arm, resulting in the man taking the point of Armstrong's blade in his side.

Fox bent down to retrieve his sword, but Armstrong kicked the hilt just before he could grab it so that the blade went spinning toward the bow through the raging fire. Armstrong swung his knife in an attempt to slash Fox's throat, but Fox rolled under the blade, snatching his own dagger out of its sheath and slicing Armstrong across the thigh. Despite the injury to his leg, Armstrong did his best to ignore the pain. It was time to finish this.

They both drew their daggers back for a killing blow at the same time, and each of them grabbed the wrist of the other with his free hand as the daggers came forward. They were locked together, spinning around until Fox was pinned against the bulwark, his back arched over the water. With the better leverage, Armstrong was slowly moving the dagger closer to his neck.

Someone called Fox's name. Out of the corner of his eye, Armstrong saw Willa through the fire next to Luciana and Giovanni. She had picked up Fox's sword and obviously wanted to help him somehow. Armstrong wished he could get hold of it. He'd kill Fox with his own sword. What did he call it? Legend?

"Willa, go!" Fox shouted. "Leave now!" His lapse in attention allowed Armstrong to slam Fox's wrist against the wooden bulwark, causing his dagger to fall into the water below.

Now Armstrong didn't need the sword, as he pushed Fox farther down. His dagger would do the job just as well. Perhaps he'd give it a name after he killed Fox with it. "Slayer" had a nice ring to it.

The edge neared Fox's skin. The blade was honed to such a sharpness that his life would be gone in moments once it made contact.

"That's far enough," Fox grunted.

"Are you begging me to stop?" Armstrong asked with a grin. "You're asking for mercy?"

"I want to go for a swim."

Armstrong suddenly realized his mistake and began to panic. They were both cantilevered out over the water, and Fox, merely pretending to be desperately holding him back, now had a tight grip on his wrists.

With a push off the deck, Fox pitched them backward over the bulwark. In a mirror of Armstrong's tumble off the gondola in Venice, Fox yanked Armstrong's hands down so that he had no way to arrest his fall.

Armstrong screamed in terror as the two of them plunged over the side.

All Fox could think about as he plummeted was keeping Armstrong's dagger away from his neck so that it didn't impale him when they hit the water. As soon as they were falling together, he twisted in mid-flight and dropped feet-first into the sea.

He shot down under the water with his neck intact. He kicked for the surface and inhaled a huge breath when he emerged.

Fox saw Willa, Luciana, and Giovanni at the bow climbing down into the rowboat, so he began to paddle in that direction when something caught his boot. At first he thought it might be a deadly sea creature, but then he felt hands clawing their way up his body.

Armstrong pushed himself up in a frenzy, sobbing as he came to the surface. He was in so much terror that he was trying to use Fox to support himself while he struggled for breath.

Fox's head was pushed under, causing him to swallow seawater. In an attempt to escape, he pried Armstrong's hands from his shoulders and dived farther down to get away.

When he surfaced a mere body length away, Armstrong was splashing wildly as he tried to keep his head above water.

"Help me!" he screeched between coughing up water. "Help me!"

But even if Fox were inclined to assist him, he'd only end up drowning himself as well. Armstrong's pleas became terrified gurgles as he sank into the water, and then there was nothing but bubbles as he disappeared below the surface. Finally, even the bubbles stopped. His motionless body slowly floated up with his hands and legs dangling beneath him.

Turning his back on the dead man, Fox swam as fast as he could toward the rowboat. It was just a matter of time before the fire reached the black powder stowed below deck. If a few handfuls of the stuff could propel a heavy iron cannonball at deadly speeds, Fox could only imagine what nearly a dozen full barrels would do to a wooden ship.

When he reached the small rowboat that he and Willa had commandeered from the beach, Giovanni pulled him in. He flopped into the boat, exhausted. Willa bent over and embraced him.

"I thought we'd lost you."

Fox coughed up some water. "Still breathing."

The other two skiffs with the surviving crew of the *Cara Signora* had picked up the few able to jump to the water from the forecastle and were already halfway to the beach. He took a seat beside Willa. By his feet were Legend and his bow, as well as Willa's new one.

"I couldn't leave them behind," Willa said.

Nearly the entire front of the carrack was ablaze. Giovanni shook his head as he watched his beloved vessel burn up, his face scored with pain.

"How long before the powder ignites?" Luciana asked.

"Hopefully long enough," Giovanni answered. He handed an oar to Fox, who began pulling as hard as his arms could manage.

68

Corosi's side ached from the wound that Luciana had inflicted as he hacked away at the door with his sword. Blood dribbled down his leg and onto the floor. He still couldn't believe she had stabbed him. What kind of wife did that to her husband?

The smoke seeping in through the cracks brought on a coughing fit as well as a sense of increased urgency. The fire seemed to be getting closer, and he had no intention of burning up on this ship.

He redoubled his efforts and carved out an opening big enough to push the blade through and tilt the outside latch up. Still, the door wouldn't move. He peered through the hole and saw that there were crates piled up against it.

Using his shoulder, he shoved the door, but he didn't have the right angle. Instead, he kicked at the base, a jolt of agony radiating from his injury with each impact.

Finally, the door started to inch forward. He kicked even harder, and on the last one it created an opening just large enough to barely squeeze through, but at the expense of hurting his foot in the process.

He wedged himself through the door and saw that the fire was blocking the way forward, the flames licking at a row of barrels with odd characters on the side.

His chase through the hold had taken him closer to the stern. He could see the *Drago Marino*'s bow embedded into the hold and heard the chopping of axes from the crew trying to dislodge it.

When he reached the aft end, two men were stuffing gold coins into their clothes.

"Stop that, you imbeciles!" Corosi yelled. "Help the rest of your crew get our ship away before this one ignites it."

The two sailors grimaced at him, but they followed his orders, and ascended the stairs with their loot. It was obvious to Corosi that he'd have to take command of the *Drago Marino* now that her captain was dead.

He exited onto the *Cara Signora*'s open deck and saw that his ship was nearly free of her. Heaps of gold coins and anything made of precious metals had already been tossed onto the *Drago Marino*, and he knew the crew would keep bringing more over until the last possible moment.

The fire had already consumed all the masts and a good portion of the bow section of Giovanni's carrack, but it hadn't yet spread to the *Drago Marino*. Once they were free, Corosi would take the remaining men and see if any of the treasure had yet to be moved from its hiding place on shore.

But first, he needed that letter. If he had any luck, Luciana and the king's missive to the pope had been burned up in the fire, but he didn't see her body in the maelstrom of flames.

He went to the bulwark and looked down to see if she had jumped overboard. The only body he saw was Armstrong's corpse floating face down. While Corosi regretted losing such a loyal servant, perhaps Armstrong's defeat showed he wouldn't have been capable of commanding an army after all.

Farther out toward the beach was a rowboat with two oarsmen pulling as fast as they could to get to shore and join the skiffs that were already there. At the back of the rowboat, he spotted Luciana watching the interlocked ships. The wench actually waved to him, as if she were casually dismissing him. He vowed that she would pay dearly for denying him the treasure that he had spent a lifetime pursuing.

"I will get you for this, Luciana!" he shouted, shaking a fist at her. "You can't run from me! I will find you wherever you go!"

He would take every man on his ship and hunt her down if it took his last breath.

"What's he shouting?" Willa asked.

Luciana shrugged. "I don't care." She couldn't hear a word he was screaming over the rampaging inferno on board the *Cara Signora*. There was no doubt, though, that he was incandescent with rage.

Then it seemed as if a volcano erupted from the sea. A massive explosion tore the *Cara Signora* in half with a deafening thunderclap so loud that Luciana's hands flew to her ears to cover them. Riccardo vanished, incinerated by the fireball.

The blast was so powerful that it ripped the bow of the *Drago Marino* apart, sending the few sailors who weren't consumed in the explosion flying hundreds of feet into the air. Gold and silver objects of all kinds flew with them at incredible speed.

"Get down!" Fox yelled.

They all ducked as bits of both ships rained down around and in the rowboat. One flaming piece of wood landed in front of Luciana. She smothered it with her skirt and pitched it over the side, while a gold coin moving as fast as a missile just missed Fox's ear.

Once the worst was over, they raised their heads. Flames were racing across both ships, accompanied by the sound of cracking wood and sizzling water. The blast must have killed everyone still aboard either vessel because Luciana couldn't hear even a whimper from a single survivor.

Water rushed in the gigantic holes blown in each ship. The *Cara Signora* was first to go down, as the two halves of her keel settled into the water. The stern and bow tipped up, then disappeared.

The *Drago Marino* was slower to sink, but she was just as mortally crippled. Her shorn bow dipped into the water, and it didn't take long for the ship to turn over like a turtle flipped onto its back, exposing the barnacle-encrusted hull of the stern. She stayed like that for a few breaths, then she sank bow first into the

Mediterranean. Only pieces of floating wood and bodies remained to mark the destruction of both ships.

Luciana turned in her seat.

"I'm so sorry about your crew, my dear," she said to Giovanni.

Her son shook his head with sadness. "I lost some good men today."

Fox counted out the ones who'd made it to the beach.

"Eight of them survived."

"I'm thankful for that. The rest of my crew deserve a proper burial."

"We'll bring as many of them as we can to shore," Fox said.

"Thank you."

"My condolences about your ship."

Giovanni nodded and looked at his mother. "It was a high price to pay, but the outcome was worth it."

Giovanni and Fox continued rowing to shore.

"Nothing remains of the Templars now," Luciana said.

"The Templars have been gone a long time," Fox said.

"I know. Although Riccardo was the lone remaining member of the order, the Knights Templar truly died the day he killed my father."

"And now their treasure is at the bottom of the sea," Giovanni said.

"Not all of it," Willa said. "There are still two chests full of gold coins up by the cave."

"Split between all of us, that's not a bad haul," Fox said. "And your surviving men along with families of the dead will get full shares." He focused on Luciana. "I'm just glad you're finally free of Corosi."

"What happens if that letter from the French king goes to the pope now?" Willa asked.

Luciana hadn't thought about that. She pulled it from the breast of her kirtle and opened it.

"Riccardo took vows of chastity and poverty," she said. "According to this, everything he has would either go to the Church or the Knights Hospitaller."

"And if no one but us knew about it?" Fox asked pointedly.

Luciana held out her hand to Giovanni, who squeezed it and nodded for her to do what she must.

"After everything we've gone through to get this letter," she said with a rueful shake of her head, "it's now worse for us to keep it."

She tore it up and tossed the pieces into the water. With Riccardo's death, she would inherit the entire estate from him as his wife.

"You may have been disinherited by Riccardo," she said to Giovanni, "but I will reinstate you as my heir."

"That's fortunate," he replied with a smile, "since I no longer have a ship."

Luciana released Giovanni's hand and took Willa and Fox's in each of hers.

"I can never repay you for what you've given me. Without your help, I would not be unshackled from my husband or reunited with my son. I hope it's not too bold to say that I consider you like my own children."

Willa reached across and hugged Luciana tightly. "You are a remarkable woman, Luciana. If only I were so lucky to be your daughter."

Fox swallowed hard, obviously having difficulty holding back his emotions. Finally, he said, "I am honored that you think of us that way. I feel the same toward you."

"You will always have a place in my home," Luciana said. "And if there is anything I can ever do for you, you've only to ask."

"There is one thing," Fox said, taking Willa's hand. "I think we would both be delighted if you would attend our wedding."

 69

LINDOS

Although the breeze was cool and the shade from the tree kept the midday sun off him, Fox's hands were sweating and his knees were shaking. He had his fist clenched tightly to keep what he held from slipping out.

Willa had picked this spot with the Acropolis of Lindos high above on one side and an azure cove on the other because it was away from the center of the bustling town. Except for Luciana and Giovanni standing on either side of them and Zephyr and Comis tied to the tree under which they all stood, they were alone.

It had been a whirlwind since yesterday to get the chests of gold back to Lindos where they were currently guarded by Giovanni's men. The townspeople had seen the smoke from the fire and explosion, so Giovanni had told the local magistrate that his ship had been boarded by pirates and that both ships had been lost in the ensuing battle.

Fox had been so busy with all those arrangements that he hadn't been able to get nervous thinking about their wedding, but now that it was time, he was surprised at how tense he felt.

Willa, on the other hand, was calmer and more beautiful than he'd ever seen her, with strands of her golden hair swaying free from the elaborate braids pinned in loops at either side of her head and a new gown of crimson velvet silk with gold cording that made her look like a princess. She seemed amused by Fox's nerves and exchanged a knowing glance with Luciana. Giovanni swallowed a chuckle. Even Zephyr sensed his comical unease and snorted.

The handfasting ceremony would be simple. In the presence of witnesses, they would recite their vows to each other. Although they wouldn't have the sacraments and blessings of the Church, they'd be considered wedded as soon as the marriage was consummated. Then they would be honestly able to tell anyone they met that they were husband and wife.

But Fox had one other element of the rite that he hadn't shared with Willa.

"Before we begin," he said, "you asked me the other night what I had taken from the box of jewels in the cave."

Her lips curled in a smile. "I remember. What is this about?"

Fox held out his hand and opened his palm. On it were two gold rings. The larger was a simple band while the smaller had two hands intertwined to signify a pair of lovers.

Willa gasped in delight when she saw them. Then she looked closer.

"Are they poesy rings?"

Fox nodded. The rings were so named because they had poetry inscribed on the inside of the bands.

"I chose ones with the sentiments that seemed to fit us the best."

He pointed to the one he would wear. It had the inscription etched in Latin.

UBI AMOR IBI FIDES.

"Where there is love, there is faith," he said. "I learned that from you."

Willa's eyes teared up at that, and Luciana cooed softly at the romantic sentiment.

"And mine?" Willa asked.

Hers was in French. "*Avec tout mon coeur.*"

"With all my heart," she said with a smile that melted Fox's. "So true. I love it. And I love you."

Luciana clapped her hands eagerly. "Well, go on, you two."

Fox gave the larger wedding band to Willa, then held her left hand in his and looked deeply into her eyes. It was said that a vein ran directly from the heart to the fourth finger of the left hand, on which he would place the token of his devotion. Suddenly he was no longer trembling.

"Here I take you, Willa, as my faithfully conjoined wife to have and to hold until the end of my life, and I give you my word on this."

He slipped the ring onto her finger. It fit perfectly.

Now Willa took his left hand.

"Here I take you, Gerard, as my pledged husband to have and to hold until the end of my life, and I give you my word on this."

She put the band on his finger. It felt so right that he silently vowed never to take it off.

They were frozen for a moment before Giovanni broke the quiet.

"Kiss her, you fool."

Fox took Willa into his arms and kissed her so long and passionately that Giovanni had to break them up with his words.

"I think you've adequately sealed the pact."

Fox pulled away, and as he took in her lovely face, it was as if his chest would burst with the happiness welling within it.

She peered up at him with a look of recognition.

"You feel it, too?"

Fox nodded. "Everything seems right with the world."

For the next two days, they barely left the tavern chamber they had rented. Although Willa had been unacquainted with physical love before their marriage, she quickly came to the conclusion that the life of a nun would not have suited her at all. Gerard seemed to agree, for they ventured out only to eat, and even then not for long.

When they finally emerged, it was because it was time for the burials of Giovanni's crew in the graveyard of a small church.

After the services, Fox and Willa met Luciana and Giovanni near the Lindos dock where Zephyr and Comis were already loaded onto the ship that would take Willa and Gerard away from Rhodes.

"What is your destination?" Giovanni inquired.

"We're heading back toward France," Gerard replied, glancing at Willa. "I promised my wife that I'd attend to some unfinished business we have there."

"And you're returning to Italy?" Willa asked.

Luciana nodded. "We should be able to find a suitable ship in Rhodes City. The wagons are already loaded for the trip there."

"Your men will go with you?" Gerard asked Giovanni.

"They all agreed to accompany us back to Florence," he replied, "where they can either serve our estate or find their own fortune. I have a feeling our city will experience a renewed life now that Signore Corosi is gone. Someone has to run his banks."

"And I have a feeling that my son will have his choice of eligible ladies after we arrive. I've already told him about Count Russo's daughter Veronica."

"She sounds like a woman with spirit," Giovanni said.

"Oh, she is," Willa said with a smile. "I believe you will enjoy her company."

"My father's dream wasn't realized," Luciana said, "but at least his line will go on. He was a brilliant, strong, and kind man. Even after all these years I still miss him. Going on this quest with you was a gift. By deciphering the message he left for me, it was as if I were spending time with him all over again."

"Sir Domenico sounded like a true knight," Gerard said. "Just to speak to him once about the Templars would have been astounding."

"I'm sure he would have been just as impressed by your accomplishments as I am. One of the things I always loved about my father was that he had a strong moral center." She took his hand. "I see much of him in you. There are very few knights left who are true to the old ideals, but you are one of them."

Gerard blushed at the compliment and nodded his thanks.

Giovanni broke the extended silence. "I'm sorry to say that it's time to get on our way."

"I don't want this to be a goodbye," Luciana said, "so I will wish you safe and wondrous travels with the hope that you will one day make your way back to my home."

Giovanni took Gerard's hand in both of his for a friendly shake. "Godspeed, Sir Gerard and Lady Fox."

"Godspeed to you," Gerard replied. "You'll both be in our memories forever."

Willa embraced Luciana one last time. "You'll be with me always."

"As will you."

Luciana and Giovanni mounted the horses that they'd hired along with a wagon for the treasure chests and joined the rest of the surviving crew to ride up the long hill back toward Rhodes City.

Gerard turned to Willa and sighed with obvious contentment as he regarded her. "It's just us again."

The way he looked at her sent her insides aflutter. "Yes, it is. I'm so glad it's you."

As they walked to the ship hand in hand, she said, "Do you have your ginger?"

"In Zephyr's saddlebags. I don't think there is any ginger left in Lindos."

They climbed the gangway and went up to the forecastle bulwark, where they could see Luciana and Giovanni just before they rounded a corner, waving to them until they were out of sight.

They stood there holding hands, enjoying the pleasant sunny day, and taking in the beautiful scenery all around them. The serenity of the moment made Willa believe that she and Gerard would eventually find the evidence they needed to reverse his excommunication. She truly felt that they were destined to be together in a loving home surrounded by children, living in peace with a bright future free of the Church's condemnation. And until then, she couldn't imagine anyone else she'd want by her side adventuring with her and seeing the wonders of the world.

The serenity of the moment was broken by the sounds of soft

sobbing. Willa turned to see a couple huddled nearby. The man was speaking quietly as he comforted the crying woman.

Willa couldn't bear to see someone in distress and guided Gerard over to them.

"I'm sorry to intrude," Willa said, "but are you all right?"

The man looked up at her with an anguished expression.

"Thank you for asking, but I'm afraid it's not a problem that anyone can solve."

Willa looked beseechingly to Fox, and he nodded without hesitation in answer to her unspoken question.

"Tell us about your troubles," Willa said, gently taking the woman's hands in hers. "Perhaps we can help."

Afterword

By Beth Morrison

One of the most frequent questions that Boyd and I received after the publication of our prior novel *The Lawless Land* was whether Fox and Willa's adventures would continue, so we were thrilled to begin work on the second installment, which takes place directly after our intrepid couple heads off into the Italian countryside. Boyd and I wanted the second book to have its own distinct character that would impart a different view of the medieval world, and Italy was the perfect setting.

Certain aspects of the fourteenth century will continue to pervade the Tales of the Lawless Land series, such as the societal changes brought on by the Black Death, the influential role of the Church in daily life, and the family ties that were at the heart of the medieval world. Italy in the period, however, was quite different from northern Europe, which served as the primary backdrop for the first novel. In fact, the term Italy is itself a bit of a misnomer. Unlike the centralized authoritarian monarchies found in countries such as England and France, northern Italy in the fourteenth century was composed of a patchwork of independent city-states, economic powerhouses that were constantly vying against each other for money and power.

These city-states were overseen by various forms of governance: Siena by the Council of Nine drawn by lot from the citizenry, Florence by the Signoria chosen from the members of the guilds of merchants and artisans of the city, and Venice by the doge, who was elected for life by the nobility. These city-states functioned more like separate nations, as many not only issued their own currency, but they even spoke versions of Italian that could be considered closely related descendants of Latin rather than dialects of the same language. For ease of storytelling, we have Fox and Willa learn a version of Italian that is intelligible across the different regions.

A number of characters in this novel are involved in banking, perhaps the most important aspect of medieval business in the Italian peninsula during the era. Because Italy was the center for the lucrative European trade in items such as silk, wool, and gems, it was the ability to store, move, and earn wealth that became preeminent. At the time, the Church forbade the practice of charging interest on loans, called usury, so medieval Christian bankers had to create other methods to make finance profitable. Two prime ways were currency exchange and investment, both of which were dependent on the vast seagoing trade that made Italy the center of international commerce. Just as today, when monies move across currency boundaries, it has to be exchanged into a new monetary unit. Bankers were allowed to charge a fee for that exchange, and given the large amounts of money moving through Italy, this process was very lucrative. Many merchants at the time also needed up-front capital in order to fund new ventures, at which point bankers would invest in the enterprise and take part of the profit afterwards. The bankers could then use this capital to lend to everyone from kings to the pope, a further road to wealth, as bankers were allowed to charge late fees for these loans.

We modeled the career of one of our main characters, Riccardo Corosi, on that of Giovanni di Bicci de' Medici (ca. 1360–1429), founder of the famed Medici banking dynasty, through means like those described by Niccolò Machiavelli (1469–1527), whose work *The Prince* was regarded as a template for tyrants to gain and maintain power (hence the word we still use today: Machiavellian). The Medici used the growth of their banking empire to dominate Florentine politics by the early fifteenth century, so Corosi was simply a bit ahead of his time. The henchman who carries out Corosi's dirty work, Sir Randolf Armstrong, was also based on a real person. Sir John Hawkwood was an English knight who rose to fame in Italy as the commander of a roving free company of mercenaries who sold their services to the highest bidder, including nobles, city-states, and even the pope.

Another central aspect to the novel is intimately tied to the medieval banking industry, the Knights Templar. Officially known as the Poor Fellow-Soldiers of Christ and of the Temple of Solomon, the Templar order has become synonymous in contemporary culture with intrigue and treasure (a reputation to which we ourselves are now contributing!). But the Knights Templar were originally founded as an order of military monks, sworn to regain the Holy Land in the name of the Church and to protect pilgrims traveling to sacred sites. They soon found that one of the main reasons pilgrims were attacked was for the large quantities of currency they needed for their journeys.

In an effort to minimize these kinds of thefts and robberies, the Templars became the first international bankers, setting up a system of letters of credit that essentially served as the medieval version of an ATM. Pilgrims would deposit cash or valuables at the Templar commandery in their home location, and carry with them a letter of credit, redeemable at a Templar commandery at their destination. We unfortunately don't know much about the actual form of these letters of credit, but we can imagine that the Templars would use the sophisticated codes and ciphers they were known for to authenticate them. The fiscal practices invented and disseminated by the Templars became a model for bankers and the financial industry in the fourteenth century.

The king of France himself held his funds at the main Templar headquarters in Paris, besides borrowing vast amounts from them. This fiscal relationship between the king and the Templars turned out to be the genesis of their downfall. Instigated by the French king, Philip IV, who was eager to have all his Templar loans canceled outright through the dissolution of the order, false accusations of corrupt initiation practices led to the arrest of all the Knights Templar across Europe on Friday, October 13, 1307 (often mistakenly thought to be associated with the unlucky reputation that Friday the 13th has today). The knights were tortured until they confessed to these trumped-up crimes and sometimes burned at the stake for heresy.

Over the following years, the king pressured the pope, Clement V, residing on French soil in these years and under the French king's protection, to officially disband the order. The pope convened the Council of Vienne from 1311 to 1312 in large part to examine the claims against the Templars and determine their fate. Only when the king arrived in March of 1312, with his army to emphasize his wishes, did the pope concede and dissolve the order. And although the king did have his debts voided, his request that all Templar holdings in monies and land be transferred to the Crown was disregarded. The pope instead designated their rival organization as their heirs, the Order of Knights of the Hospital of Saint John of Jerusalem, known as the Hospitallers. Although the Hospitaller order was also a military order of warrior monks, they were sworn to protect the Holy Land and provide care for pilgrims who fell ill. Consorors were the Hospitallers' lay sisters, who helped as nurses in the hospitals. Around the time of the Templars' downfall and the absorption of all their holdings, the Hospitallers made a new headquarters on the island of Rhodes.

The Grand Master of the Templar Order, Jacques de Molay, who had been imprisoned since 1307, recanted his confession in March of 1314, and was immediately condemned to death by burning at the stake. As the fire lapped his body, he was said to have uttered a curse against both the king and the pope for sealing the fate of the Templars for their own gain. Whether as a result of the curse or by chance, the pope and the king both died within a year, and the king's death without legal male issue resulted in a succession crisis that precipitated the Hundred Years War. Rumors spread that the majority of the Templars' vast treasure had been evacuated from France before the events of March, 1314, but no trace has ever been found.

Because this book was deeply intertwined with the real historical events mentioned above, one of the challenges Boyd and I faced was the fact that whatever Fox and Willa found in 1351 in the various cities would be different from what the clues indicated in 1314. We realized that our struggles to determine what had changed in that forty-year period was a parallel for what Fox and Willa would also encounter, and we decided to make that a key factor in designing the clues. Each of the artworks or architectural spaces our characters needed to see in order to work out part of the riddle would have been altered over time, and we used that to our advantage to make the race even more challenging. When Boyd, his wife Randi, and I planned our research trip to Italy in October of 2021, we took the same route that Fox and Willa would have, keeping a keen eye open for possibilities to add drama and interest to the plot along the way. Of course, as a medieval art historian, I was more than happy to suggest which artworks or buildings might best suit our purposes.

Siena, the first stop on the quest for the Templar treasure in our novel, experienced its golden age in the century before our book takes place. Originally the banking center of Italy, several important bank failures in the years around 1300 combined with the loss of a third of Siena's population during the Black Death contributed to its rapid decline by the mid-fourteenth century. It is estimated that Siena did not reach its pre-plague population again until 1900. Siena today almost seems as if the city was frozen in time in 1350, with the town center remaining very similar to its appearance in the mid-fourteenth century.

The most visible reminder of the city's changing fortunes at that time is the shell of the ambitious new cathedral that had been planned and never completed, which still stands today partially erected. It is difficult to imagine why they felt the need for a more grandiose cathedral, given the stunning edifice there already, although at the time of our book, the mosaics for which the existing cathedral is famed were not yet installed. Only two of these mosaics date to the fourteenth century, including the one of the She-Wolf that features in the novel and was first mentioned in the historical record in 1373.

The famed Siena Palio, in which Fox participates, took its modern form in 1633, but it was based on races that had been run in the city since the fourteenth century. The Palio now takes place as a circular race around the Piazza del Campo in front of the curved façade of the Palazzo Pubblico, a space that was paved in its current design in 1349. Formerly, the course was run across the entire city. We don't know the fourteenth-century rules of the Palio, but still today, the colorfully dressed riders don't use saddles, and the first horse across the finish line—rider or no rider—is the winner.

When Boyd and I visited the Piazza del Campo, we climbed the Torre del Mangia, which really is so narrow that you can almost reach across the stairwell to touch the other side. Back down in the square, as we tried to get a shot of the top of the tower, we kept almost backing into people. Boyd, who was learning Italian at the time, wondered how to say "look out" or "attention." Jokingly, I quipped "Alerto," in the common manner of simply adding an "o" to an English word to make it Italian. We laughed so hard that it became a running joke, and whenever we saw a gelato stand for the rest of the trip, we would both call "Alerto" to each other. You've probably already realized that this became an Easter egg in the novel itself, and when Boyd sent me the first draft of the chapter involving the Palio, I almost choked with laughter.

Florence was next on Fox and Willa's itinerary, as it was on ours. Unlike Siena, Florence's greatest period of prosperity began in the time of our book. Its famed Duomo (which simply means "cathedral") was begun in 1294, and construction of the nave was well along by 1350, although the celebrated dome wouldn't be finished until 1436. The octagonal baptistery directly across from the cathedral was built in the years around 1100 on the site of a Roman temple dedicated to Mars. The intricate glowing mosaics decorating the ceiling and interior surfaces were installed in the thirteenth century, and all the details we mention in the novel are still visible today. The baptistery is perhaps best known today for the famous bronze doors that stand at three of its doorways. Two sets of those doors, the ones by Lorenzo Ghiberti, date from the fifteenth century. The earliest doors, those by Andrea Pisano, were commissioned in 1329, and stood at the east side facing the cathedral at the time of our novel.

Just a few minutes' walk away is the civic heart of the city, the Piazza della Signoria. It was paved in 1338, and little is known about what the square looked like before that, although reusing Roman sarcophagus fragments for fountains was a common practice throughout the Middle Ages and Renaissance. Almost none of the interior of the Palazzo Vecchio (called the Palazzo della Signoria in the time of our book) dates from the fourteenth century, having been completely remodeled during the rule of the Medici family in the Renaissance.

Fox and Willa visit other parts of Florence during their stay there, including the Ponte Vecchio, which bridges the narrowest part of the Arno River. The bridge was swept away by floods multiple times during the Middle Ages, but was rebuilt in 1345 in its current form with shops lining both sides and a square at the middle. To either side of the bridge, the city spreads out, dotted by the most characteristic aspect of Florence, the tower houses. Built by the wealthy and noble, they served both as signs of prosperity and as family strongholds within the city. In the thirteenth century, there were over one hundred and fifty examples, some of them over two hundred feet high. The warring factions within the city eventually necessitated the Signoria limiting the height to one hundred feet to reduce in-fighting.

Our next stop was Venice, one of my favorite cities in the world. I've been to this magical city multiple times, but visiting in October of 2021, in a short lull between two outbreaks of COVID-19, meant that it was less crowded than I had ever experienced it before. It made me think that perhaps Luciana and Corosi felt the same way, visiting in 1351 after the worst depredations of the Black Death. Almost everywhere you turn in Venice is a reference to the city's patron, the Gospel writer Saint Mark, whose symbol is a winged lion. One of the most famous examples is the ancient bronze sculpture of the winged lion sitting atop a tall column overlooking the basin of San Marco.

According to legend, Saint Mark had been buried in Alexandria, Egypt, but by the ninth century, Venetian traders who had found his relics smuggled them past Muslim customs officials in barrels of pork. The incomparable basilica of San Marco was designed to house the relics in an astonishing reliquary called the Pala d'Oro (Golden Pall). Its golden framework encloses a series of exquisite Byzantine enamels and stands almost ten feet wide and over six feet tall. In 1345, a painted wooden cover by Paolo Veneziano was added to enhance a sense of drama by only revealing the face of the reliquary on selected feast days.

Other spoils from Constantinople, the capital of Byzantium, were also used in the basilica's decorations. The structure had originally been built in the eleventh century in the Byzantine style, including the breathtaking mosaics covering 85,000 square feet of the interior. At the end of the Fourth Crusade in 1204, Western armies sacked the wealthy city of Constantinople. The Venetians brought back booty to enhance the basilica, ranging from marble columns and bronze doors, to artworks including the sculpture of the Four Tetrarchs in purple porphyry marble, and perhaps, most famously, the four gilded horses known as the Triumphal Quadriga. They were placed atop the porch of the cathedral, gazing out across Piazza San Marco, where they stayed until the 1980s when they were conserved and moved inside to the cathedral museum. When we visited the museum, we spent a great deal of time marveling at the lifelike details of these magnificent creatures.

We also tried to capture some of the romance of Venice in the novel. No story set in the city would be complete without mention of the hundreds of canals. At their height, there were ten thousand gondolas plying the waterways, but now there are just four hundred. In order to plan our gondola chase, we of course had to take a gondola ride ourselves. Gliding along the narrow canals, watching the sunset turn the city golden, was one of our favorite memories of the trip.

Finally, we arrived in Rhodes, home to the Knights Hospitaller, where our quest for inspiration and Fox and Willa's quest for the treasure would end. We started at the port, and although we now know that the famed Colossus never bestrode the harbor entrance, it was difficult not to envision it rising up to beckon in sailors to safety as those in the Middle Ages thought it did. The impressive fortified walls that enclose the old city seem impregnable, and the narrow cobblestone streets leading up past the inns of the Hospitaller *langues* retain much of the charm that those in the Middle Ages would have experienced. Sadly, much of the massive Palace of the Grand Master was destroyed in 1856 due to an explosion from a nearby gunpowder warehouse, and the current structure is an imagined rebuilding from the 1930s, when it was converted into a retreat for the king of Italy. Although we don't know that a sundial ever graced its courtyard, the palace stands in the same place it did in 1351, and the walls extending from it are original. We spent a great deal of time exploring the old city and climbing the city's walls to absorb the medieval ambiance.

The finale of the book is, of course, the discovery of the Templar treasure. Thinking of all the wonderful objects that might have been hidden away was the best part of the writing process for me. I just imagined what might be in the greatest exhibition of medieval artifacts ever held, and that's what we described. Boyd had the idea of adding all sorts of weaponry, from the bows and swords you might expect to find, to more unusual armaments, like the barrels of gunpowder. First invented in China in the ninth century, gunpowder spread to Europe via Chinese mercenaries fighting during the Mongol incursions on Europe. By the thirteenth century, gunpowder was known in the Middle East, and thereafter traders and Crusaders, including the Knights Templar, would have encountered it.

We had already identified the abandoned castle of Feraklos as the resting place for the Templar treasure, but we still hadn't figured out where exactly it could have been hidden for decades before being found by our heroes. We arrived at the site and parked nearby, intending to hike up the rocky slope to the castle itself. There, dug out beneath the base of the castle, was a completely unexpected tunnel. The date and origin of this tunnel are unknown, but speculation runs from it being created as a stable for horses for the castle, to being a leftover from World War II. It seems that it is man-made, but otherwise remains mysterious. Whatever the case, it was perfect for our story. Boyd and I knew just as surely as Fox and Willa that we had finally found the final burial site of the Templar treasure. It was delightful to roam its dark corridors imagining the glint of gold and the gleam of gems lit by the flicker of torches (or in our case, the flashlights on our cell phones).

Our marvelous journey through Siena, Florence, Venice, and Rhodes helped us capture many site-specific elements that evoke the setting of our novel in 1351. Although medieval experts will no doubt find aspects that I did not get right, and I assume full responsibility for those mistakes, I hope the overall story nonetheless carries you along breathless with suspense to the conclusion. Imagining the medieval versions of these places was almost as much fun for me as visiting them in real life, and I hope you find that true as well. Enjoy the adventure!

Acknowledgments

For *The Last True Templar*, we were thrilled to work with the ongoing Tales of the Lawless Land team, including our fantastic agent John Talbot and our superb foreign rights agent, Danny Baror. Nicolas Cheetham and Greg Rees at our publisher Head of Zeus have been incredibly supportive, with creative ideas for Fox and Willa's future. Our content editor Richenda Todd was indispensable in spotting myriad ways to strengthen the plot and characters, while our copyeditor Helena Newton did a great job making sure the final draft was free of errors. Ben Prior provided the bold and compelling graphics for the cover, which will be the model for the look of the Tales of the Lawless Land going forward. Maxim Obsidianbone created the striking animal illustration on the cover, and Jeff Edwards provided the excellent maps for Fox and Willa's journey.

We relied on help from a number of friends and colleagues who generously contributed knowledge based on their specialties. Erik Van Eaton is a trauma surgeon who suggested plausible injuries and medical treatments. Doug Cavileer was eager to share information about medieval warfare, and Chet van Duzer provided help with nautical charts. Anne D. Hedeman was ready to suggest helpful illuminations for period accuracy, and Margaret Scott was an endless resource for the right clothing. Inspiration for Sofia's character came from Saundra Weddle, a Renaissance architectural historian who studies Venetian sex workers. Jens Daehner kindly consulted on Classical iconography and sculpture. In Italy, Mara Hofmann hospitably opened her home to us, as well as provided tips on fourteenth-century Florentine art and architecture. Davide Gasparotto and Julian Brooks were always willing to help us with questions about Italian language, names, and customs.

Our family continue to be our first readers, informal promoters, and biggest cheerleaders. Frank Moretti provides invaluable feedback during the drafting process. Our numerous siblings, nieces, and nephews are always eager to hear about our progress (and provide encouragement during our setbacks). We were heartbroken that our sister Nancy, who was so excited at our collaboration, passed away before she could see the fruits of our labor. Beth's partner John Espinoza never complains about her long hours on the phone and the computer, and makes sure that our two Labradors Hope and Willa are well taken care of when she's busy and are ready to play when she's not. Randi Morrison took every step of Fox and Willa's journey through Italy and Greece with us, and often was called on as a sounding board for plot problems as well as being our first reader. As a brother-sister team, the two of us continue to laugh our way through this novel-writing adventure, relying on each other for ideas, support, and friendship along the way.

About the Authors

BOYD MORRISON is the #1 *New York Times* bestselling author of fourteen thrillers, including six collaborations with Clive Cussler. His first novel, *The Ark*, was an Indie Next Notable pick and has been translated into over a dozen languages. He has a PhD in industrial engineering from Virginia Tech.

Twitter: @BoydMorrison
Facebook: BoydMorrisonWriter
Instagram: @BoydMorrisonWriter

BETH MORRISON is Senior Curator of Manuscripts at the J. Paul Getty Museum. She has curated several major exhibitions, including 'Imagining the Past in France, 1250-1500,' & 'Book of Beasts: The Bestiary in the Medieval World.' She has a PhD in the History of Art from Cornell University.

Twitter: @BethMorrisonPhD
Facebook: BethMorrisonWriter
Instagram: @BethMorrisonWriter